SOMAN CHAINANI

The SCHOOL for GOOD AND EVIL

THE LAST EVER AFTER

Illustrations by

IACOPO BRUNO

HARPER

An Imprint of HarperCollinsPublishers

Library of Congress Control Number: 2015938987
ISBN 978-0-06-210495-3 (trade bdg.) — ISBN 978-0-06-239625-9 (int.)
ISBN 978-0-06-241756-5 (special edition) — ISBN 978-0-06-243573-6 (special edition)
ISBN 978-0-06-243572-9 (special edition)

Typography by Amy Ryan
15 16 17 18 19 CG/RRDH 10 9 8 7 6 5 4 3 2 1
❖
First Edition

Now, in their love, which was stronger, there were the seeds of hatred and fear and confusion growing at the same time: for love can exist with hatred, each preying on the other, and this is what gives it its greatest fury.

T. H. White, *The Once and Future King*

IN THE FOREST PRIMEVAL

A SCHOOL FOR GOOD AND EVIL

TWO TOWERS LIKE TWIN HEADS

ONE FOR THE PURE

ONE FOR THE WICKED

TRY TO ESCAPE YOU'LL ALWAYS FAIL

THE ONLY WAY OUT IS

THROUGH A FAIRY TALE

PART I

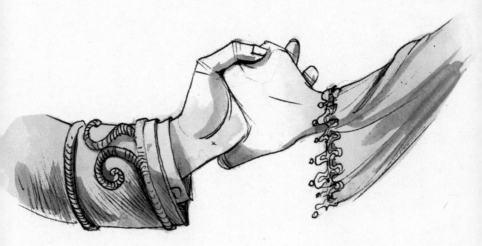

The Master and the Queen

It is natural to doubt your true love when you do not know if he is young or old.

He certainly looks young, Sophie thought, peering at the lean, shirtless boy as he gazed out the tower window, bathed in faded sunlight. Sophie studied his hairless white skin and snug black breeches, his thick spiked hair the color of snow, his tight-veined arms, his glacier-blue eyes. . . . He didn't look a day more than sixteen. And yet somewhere within this beautiful stranger was a soul older than sixteen—much, *much* older than sixteen. For the last three weeks, then, Sophie had refused his ring. How could she bond herself to a boy with the School Master inside of him?

And yet the more Sophie looked at him, the more she couldn't see the School Master. All Sophie could see was a fresh, ethereal youth asking for her hand, with sharp cheekbones and full lips—more handsome than a prince, more powerful than a prince, and unlike Prince You-Know-Who, this boy was *hers*.

Sophie reddened, remembering she was all alone in this world. Everyone else had abandoned her. Every desperate effort to be Good had been punished with betrayal. She had no family, no friends, no future. And now, this ravishing boy in front of her was her last hope for love. Panic burned through her muscles and dried out her throat. There was no choice anymore. Sophie swallowed and slowly stepped towards him.

Look at him. He's no older than you, she soothed herself. *The boy of your dreams.* She reached shaking fingers for his bare shoulder . . . until she suddenly froze in her tracks. *It was only magic that had brought this boy to life,* she thought, pulling her hand back into her sleeve. *But how long does magic last?*

"You're asking yourself the wrong questions," came the smooth voice. "Magic thinks nothing of time."

Sophie lifted her eyes. The boy didn't look at her, his focus on the sallow sun, barely a force through the morning fog.

"Since when can you hear my thoughts?" Sophie said, unnerved.

"I don't need to hear thoughts to know how a Reader's mind thinks," he replied.

Sophie took her place beside him in her black cloak, feeling the chill off his marble-colored skin. She thought of Tedros' skin, always sweaty and tan, with the warmth of a bear's. A hot flash bolted through her body—rage or regret or something in between. She forced herself closer to the boy, her arm brushing his pale chest.

He still didn't look at her.

"What is it?" Sophie asked.

"The sun," he said, watching it flicker through the mist. "Every day it rises weaker than the one before."

"If only you had power to make the sun shine too," Sophie murmured. "Every day could be a tea party."

The boy shot her a sour glare. Sophie stiffened, reminded that unlike her once Good best friend, her new suitor was neither Good nor friendly. She quickly looked back out the window, shivering at an icy breeze. "Oh for heaven's sake, suns weaken in the winter. Don't need a sorcerer to know that."

"Perhaps it takes a Reader to explain this too," he replied, sweeping to the white stone table in the corner, where a long, knife-sharp pen, shaped like a knitting needle, hovered over an open storybook. Sophie turned to the book, glimpsing the colors of the last page: her painted self kissing the School Master back to youth as her best friend vanished home with a prince.

The End

"Three *weeks* since the Storian wrote our Never After," said the boy. "Within days, it should have begun a new story with love on Evil's side now. Love that will destroy Good, one fairy tale at a time. Love that turns the pen into Evil's weapon instead of its curse." His eyes narrowed to slits. "Instead it reopens the book it just closed and *stays* there, hanging over The End like a play whose curtain won't *shut*."

Sophie couldn't look away from Agatha and Tedros on the page, embracing lovingly as they disappeared. Sophie's gut twisted, her face searing hot— "Here," she croaked, slamming the cover down on them, and shoving the cherry-red storybook next to *The Frog Prince, Cinderella, Rapunzel,* and the rest of the Storian's finished tales. Her heartbeat calmed. "Curtain shut."

Instantly the book ricocheted off the shelf and smashed into her face, knocking her against the wall, before it flew onto the stone table, swinging open to the last page once more. The Storian glimmered defiantly above it.

"This is no accident," spoke the boy, stalking towards Sophie as she rubbed her stinging cheek. "The Storian keeps our world alive by writing new stories, and at the moment, it has no intention of moving on from *your* story. And as long as the pen does not move on to a *new* story, the sun dies, day by day, until the Woods go dark and it is The End for us *all*."

Sophie looked up at him, silhouetted by the weak light. "But—but what is it waiting for?"

He leaned in and touched her neck, his fingers frigid on her peach-cream skin. Sophie recoiled, jamming into the bookshelf. The boy smiled and drew closer, blocking out the sun. "I'm afraid it has doubts whether I'm your true love," he cooed. "It has doubts whether you've committed to Evil. It has doubts whether your friend and her prince should be gone forever."

Sophie slowly gazed up at the black shadow.

"It meaning *you*," said the School Master, holding out his hand.

Sophie looked down to see the ring of gold in his cold, young palm and her terrified face in its reflection.

Three weeks before, Sophie had kissed the School Master into a boy and banished her best friend home. For a moment, she'd felt the relief of victory as Agatha silently disappeared with Tedros. Her best friend may have chosen a prince over her, but there was no such thing as a prince in Gavaldon. Agatha would die an ordinary girl, with an ordinary boy, while she basked in Ever After, far, far away. Wrapped in the arms of her true love, soaring towards his silver tower in the sky, Sophie waited to feel happy. She'd won her fairy tale and winning was supposed to mean happiness.

But as they landed in his murky, stone chamber, Sophie started to shake. Agatha was gone. Her best friend. Her soulmate. And with her, she'd taken a boy who Sophie had grown close to in so many forms: when she was a girl, when she was a boy, when he was her true love, when he was just her friend. Agatha had won Tedros, the only boy Sophie ever truly knew; Tedros had won Agatha, the one person Sophie never thought she'd live without. And Sophie had won a beautiful boy of whom she knew nothing, except the dark depths of his evil. As the School Master moved towards her, young as a prince, with a cocky smile, Sophie knew she'd made a mistake.

Only it'd been too late to turn back. Through the window, Sophie glimpsed Agatha's vanishing embers, the castles rotting vulturous black, boys and girls smashing into vicious war, teachers firing spells at students, at each other. . . . Stunned, she'd twirled to the School Master—only to see the frost-haired boy on one knee before her, ring in hand. Take it, he'd said, and two years of war would cease. No more Good versus Evil. No more Boys versus Girls. Instead, only indisputable Evil: a School Master and his queen. Take the ring, the beautiful boy said, and she would have her happy ending at last.

Sophie didn't.

The School Master left her alone in the tower, sealing the window so she couldn't escape. Every morning when the clock struck ten, he came and asked again, his young, sinewy body inexplicably clad in different clothes—one day a lace-up shirt, the next day a draping tunic or tight vest or ruffled collar—and his cloud-white hair just as fickle, whether sleeked or tousled or curled. He brought gifts too: exquisite jeweled gowns, luscious bouquets, lavender perfumes, vials of creams and soaps and herbs, always anticipating her next wish. Still Sophie shook her head each time and then he'd be gone without a word, scowling with teenage sulk. She'd stay there, trapped in his chamber alone, with the company of his fairy-tale library and his old blue robes and silver mask abandoned like relics to hooks on a wall. Food would appear magically three times a day at the moment she felt hungry, and precisely what she was craving, in perfect portions on plates made of bone—steamed vegetables, steamed fruit, steamed fish, and the occasional bowl of bacon and beans (she couldn't shake the cravings from her time as a boy). When night fell, a giant bed would materialize in the chamber, with velvet sheets the color of blood and a white lace canopy. At first, Sophie couldn't sleep, petrified he would come in the dark. But he never returned until the next morning for their silent ritual of ring and refusal.

By the second week, Sophie began to wonder what had happened to the schools. Had her rejections prolonged the war between boys and girls? Had she cost any lives? She tried to ask what had become of her friends—of Hester, Dot, Anadil, Hort—but he answered no questions, as if the ring was the price of moving forward.

Today was the first day he'd even spoken since he brought her here. Now, standing beside him in the glow of a dying sun, Sophie saw she could no longer delay without consequence. The time had come for her to seal her ending with him or slowly fade into death too. The gold ring sparkled brighter in the School Master's hand, promising new life. Sophie looked up at the bare-chested boy, praying to see a reason to take it . . . and saw nothing but a stranger. "I can't," she breathed, shrinking against a shelf. "I don't know the first thing about you."

The School Master stared at her, square jaw flexing, and put the ring back into his breeches. "What is it you would like to know?"

"For one thing, your name," Sophie said. "If I'm going to stay here with you, I need something to call you."

"The teachers call me 'Master.'"

"I'm not calling you 'Master,'" Sophie snapped.

He gritted his teeth about to fire back, but Sophie wasn't cowed. "Without me, your Never After doesn't exist," she preempted, voice rising. "You're nothing but a boy—a well-built, virile, obscenely handsome boy—but still, a *boy*. You can't lord over me. You can't scare me into true love. I don't care if you're gorgeous or rich or powerful. Tedros had all of those things and la-di-da, didn't *that* turn out well. I deserve someone who makes me happy. At *least* as happy as Agatha and Agatha doesn't have to call Tedros 'Prince' for the rest of her life, does she? Because Tedros has a name, like every boy in the world, and so do you and I will call you by it if you expect me to actually give you a chance."

The School Master swelled crimson, but Sophie was breathing flames now. "That's right. *I'm* in charge now. You might be the Master of this infernal school, but you are not my Master and you never will be. You said it yourself: the Storian won't write because it is waiting for *my* choice, not yours. I choose whether I take your ring. I choose whether this is The End. I choose whether this world lives or dies. And I'm happy to watch it burn to dust if you expect a slave instead of a queen."

The School Master glowered at her, veins pulsing beneath his ghost-white neck. He bit his lip so hard Sophie thought he was about to eat her and she stepped back in horror, only to see him slacken with an angry pant and look away. Then he was quiet for a very long time, his fists clenched.

"Rafal," he mumbled. "My name is Rafal."

Rafal, Sophie thought, astonished. In an instant, she saw him anew: the callow milk of his skin, the adolescent sparkle in his eyes, the erect puff to his chest, matching the storm and youth of a name. *Rafal*. What is it about a name that gives us a story to believe in?

She suddenly felt the blush of desire, craving to touch him . . . until she remembered what choosing him would mean. This was a boy who'd butchered his own blood in the name of Evil and he believed her capable of the same. Sophie held herself back.

"What was your brother's name?" she asked.

He spun, eyes aflame. "I don't see how that will help you get to know me any better."

Sophie didn't press the point. Then behind him, she noticed the fog abating, revealing a greenish haze over two black castles in the distance. It was the first time in three weeks he'd unsealed the window long enough for her to see through. But both schools seemed dead quiet, no sign of life on any of the roofs or balconies. "W-w-where is everyone?" she sputtered, squinting at the healed Bridge between the castles. "What happened to the girls? The boys were going to kill them—"

"A queen would have the right to ask me questions about the school she rules," he said. "You are not a queen yet."

Sophie cleared her throat, noticing the bulge of the ring in his tight pocket. "Um, why do you keep changing clothes? It's . . . strange."

For the first time, the boy seemed uncomfortable. "Given your refusals, I assumed dressing like the princes you chase would move things along." He scratched his rippled stomach. "Then I remembered the son of Arthur wasn't fond of shirts."

Sophie snorted, trying to ignore his perfect torso. "Didn't think the all-powerful were capable of self-doubt."

"If I was all-powerful, I could make you love me," he growled.

Sophie heard the petulance in his voice and for a moment saw an ordinary boy, lovesick and striving for a girl he couldn't have. Then she remembered this was no ordinary boy. "No one can make anyone love them," she hit back. "I learned that lesson harder than anyone. Besides, even if you *could* make me love you, you could never love me. You can't love anything. Not if you embrace Evil as a choice. It's why your brother is dead."

"And yet, I'm alive because of true love's kiss," he said.

"You tricked me into it—"

"You never broke your grip."

Sophie blanched. "I'd *never* kiss you and mean it!"

"Oh? For me to return to life, to return to youth . . . the kiss had to go *both* ways, didn't it?" He looked into Sophie's stunned face and grinned. "Surely your best friend taught you that."

Sophie said nothing, the truth extinguishing her fight. Just as Agatha once could have taken Tedros' hand before she chose Sophie instead, Sophie too could have sent the School Master back to the grave. But here they were, both beautiful and young, victims of a kiss she was trying to deny. Why had she held on to him that night? Sophie asked herself. Even once she knew it was *him* she was kissing? Looking up at the porcelain boy, she thought of everything he'd done to win her, across death and time . . . his unyielding faith that he could make her happy, beyond any family, friend, or prince. He had come for her when no one else wanted her. He had believed in her when no one else did. Sophie's voice clumped in her throat. "Why do you want me so much?" she rasped.

He stared at her, the clamp of his jaw easing, his lips falling open slightly. For a moment, Sophie thought he looked the way Tedros did when he let down his guard—a lost boy playing at a grown-up. "Because once upon a time, I was just like you," he said softly. He blinked fast, falling into memory. "I tried to love my brother. I tried to escape my fate. I even thought I'd found—" He caught himself. "But it only led to more pain . . . more Evil. Just as every time you seek love, it leads you to the same. Your mother, your father, your best friend, your prince . . . The more you chase the light, the more darkness you find. And yet still you doubt your place in Evil."

Sophie tensed as he gently lifted her chin. "For thousands of years, Good has told us what love is. Both you and I have tried to love in their way, only to suffer pain," he said. "But what if there's a different kind of love? A darker love that turns pain into power. A love that can only be understood by the two who share it. That's why you held our kiss, Sophie. Because I see you for who you really are and love you for it when no one else can. Because what we've sacrificed for each other is beyond what Good can even fathom. It doesn't matter if they don't call it love. We know it is, just as we know the thorns are as much a part of the rose as the petals." He leaned in, lips caressing her ear. "I am the mirror of your soul, Sophie. To love me is to love yourself," he whispered. Then he raised her hand to his mouth and kissed it like a prince, before he gently let it go.

Sophie's heart wrenched so sharply she thought he'd torn

it out of her. She'd never felt so naked in her life and huddled tighter into her black cloak. Then little by little, staring into the harsh symmetry of his face, Sophie felt her breath come back, a strange safe warmth flooding her core. He understood her, this dark-souled boy, and in the sapphire facets of his eyes, she suddenly saw how deep they went. She shook her head, rattled. "I don't even know if you're really a boy."

He smiled at her. "If your fairy tale has taught you one lesson, Sophie, it is that things are only as you see."

Sophie frowned. "I don't understand—" she started . . . but somewhere in her soul she did.

The boy looked out at the sun, frail and hazy over his school, and Sophie knew that the time for questions was over. As he slid his hand into his pocket, Sophie could feel her whole body trembling, as if pulled towards a waterfall she wouldn't escape.

"Will we be as happy as Tedros and Agatha?" she pressed, voice cracking.

"You must trust your story, Sophie. It has come to The End for a reason." He turned to her. "But now it's time for you to believe it."

Sophie looked down at the gold circle in his hand, breaths growing faster, faster. . . . With a shudder, she pushed him away. He reached for her and Sophie shoved him against the wall, pinning her own palm flat against his frigid chest. He didn't resist as Sophie moved her hand over his sternum, eyes wild, panting hard. She didn't know what she was looking for until she found it beneath her fingers and froze. Her hand rose and fell on his chest, rose and fell, his heart throbbing between them. Slowly Sophie looked up at him, drinking in his strong, hopeful beat, no different than her own.

"Rafal," she whispered, wishing a boy to life.

His fingertips caressed her face and for the first time, Sophie didn't flinch from the cold. As he drew her in, Sophie felt the doubts melt out of her, fear giving way to faith. Black cloak pressed to his white body, like two swans in balance, Sophie raised her left hand into the sunlight, steady and sure. Then Rafal slipped his ring onto her finger, the warm gold sliding up her skin inch by inch, until it fit tight. Sophie let out a gasp and the snow-white boy smiled, never breaking his gaze.

In each other's arms, Master and Queen turned to the enchanted pen over their fairy tale, ready for it to bless their love . . . ready for it to close their book at last . . .

The pen didn't move.

The book stayed open.

Sophie's heart stalled. "What happened?"

She followed Rafal's eyes to the red-amber sun, which had darkened another shade. His face steeled to a deadly mask. "It seems our happy ending isn't the one the pen doubts."

2

After Ever After

"You don't know the first thing about me," Tedros spat, and clubbed his princess in the face with a musty pillow. Agatha coughed and bashed him with a pillow right back, knocking him against her black bed frame, as feathers burst all over him. Reaper leapt onto Tedros' face, trying to eat them. "I know too much about you is the problem," Agatha snarled and grabbed at the poorly set bandage under her prince's blue collar. Tedros shoved her away— Agatha tackled him back, before Tedros snatched Reaper and threw the cat at her head. Agatha ducked and Reaper sailed into the bathroom, flailing bald, wrinkled paws,

before landing headfirst in the toilet. "If you knew me, you'd know I do things *myself*," Tedros huffed, tightening his shirt laces.

"You threw my *cat* at me?" Agatha yelled, launching to her feet. "Because I'm trying to save you from *gangrene*?"

"That cat is Satan," Tedros hissed, watching Reaper try to climb out of the toilet bowl and slide back down. "And if you knew me, you'd know I *hate* cats."

"No doubt you like dogs—wet-mouthed, simple, and now that I think about it, a lot like you."

Tedros glowered at her. "Getting personal over a bandage, are we?"

"Three weeks and the wound isn't healing, Tedros," Agatha pressed, scooping Reaper up and toweling him off with her sleeve. "It'll fester if I don't treat it—"

"Maybe they do it differently in *graveyards*, but where I come from, a bandage does the trick."

"A bandage that looks like it was made by a two-year-old?" Agatha mocked.

"You try getting stabbed with your own sword as you're vanishing," said Tedros. "You're lucky I'm even alive—one more second and he'd have run me through—"

"One more second and I'd have remembered what an ape you are and left you behind."

"As if you could find a boy in this rat trap town better than me."

"At this point, I'd trade you for a little space and quiet—"

"I'd trade you for a decent meal and a warm bath!" Tedros boomed.

Agatha glared at him, Reaper shivering in her arms. Finally Tedros exhaled, looking ashamed. He stripped off his shirt, spread out his arms, and sat on the bed. "Have at it, princess."

For the next ten minutes, neither spoke as Agatha rinsed the four-inch gash across her prince's chest with rose oil, witch hazel, and a dash of white peony from her mother's cart of herbal potions. Thinking about how Tedros earned the wound, a hairbreadth from his heart, made Agatha's stomach chill, and she forced her focus back to her task. She didn't need to think about it—not when the screaming nightmares did the job of reminding her well enough. The School Master turning young . . . grinning at Tedros, bound to a tree . . . eyes flashing red as he stabbed . . . How Tedros didn't have nightmares about their last moments at school, Agatha couldn't grasp, but maybe that was the difference between a prince and a Reader. To a boy from the Woods, every day that didn't end in death was a good one.

Agatha sprinkled boiled turmeric on his wound and Tedros clenched with low moans. "Told you it wasn't healing," she murmured.

Tedros gave her a lion's growl and turned away. "Your mother hates me. That's why she's never home."

"She's busy looking for patients," said Agatha, rubbing the yellow powder in. "Have to eat, don't we?"

"Then why does she leave her medicine cart here?"

Agatha's hand paused on Tedros' chest. She'd been asking herself the same question about her mother's long disappearances. Agatha rubbed harder and her prince winced. "Look, for the last time, she doesn't hate you."

"We've been trapped in this house for three weeks, Agatha. I eat all her food, am crap at cleaning, tend to clog the toilet, and she keeps seeing us fighting. If she doesn't hate me, she will soon."

"She just thinks you're a complication to an already complicated situation."

"Agatha, there is an entire town out there that will kill us on sight. There's nothing complicated about it," Tedros argued, sitting up on his knees. "Listen, I'll be sixteen in a month. That means I take over Camelot as king from my father's council. Sure, the kingdom's broke, half the people are gone, and the place is in shambles, but we'll change all that! That's where we belong, Agatha. Why can't we go back—"

"You know why, Tedros."

"Right. Because you don't want to leave your mother forever. Because I don't have a family anymore and you do," he said, looking away.

Agatha's neck rashed red. "Tedros—"

"You don't need to explain," her prince said quietly. "If my father was still alive, I'd never leave him either."

Agatha moved closer to him. He still didn't look at her. "Tedros, if your kingdom needs you . . . you should go back," she forced herself to say.

Her prince sighed. "I'd never leave you, Agatha." He pulled at a thread in his dirty socks. "Couldn't even if I wanted to. Only way back into the Woods is to make the wish together."

Agatha went rigid. He'd thought about leaving her behind? She swallowed hard and grasped his arm. "I can't go back, Tedros. Terrible things happen to us in the Woods," she rasped anxiously. "We were lucky to escape—"

"You call this 'lucky'?" He finally looked at her. "How long can we stay trapped in this house, Agatha? How long can we be prisoners?"

Agatha tensed. She knew he deserved answers, but she still didn't have them. "It doesn't matter where your Ever After is, does it? It just matters who you're with," she said, trying to sound hopeful. "Surely a teacher said that once."

Tedros didn't smile. Agatha lurched up and ripped a strip from a clean towel hanging on the bedpost. Tedros flopped back onto the bed, arms splayed cactus-style, and lapsed into silence, as Agatha bound his wound tight with the cloth.

"Sometimes I miss Filip," he said softly.

Agatha looked at him, startled. Tedros turned pink and picked at his nails. "It's stupid, given all he did to us—or she . . . or whatever. I should hate him—her, I mean. But boys get each other in a way girls can't. Even if he wasn't really a boy." Tedros saw Agatha's face. "Forget it."

"You really think I don't know you?" Agatha asked, hurt.

Tedros held his breath a moment, as if contemplating whether to be honest or to lie. "It's just . . . those first two years, we were chasing the idea of being together, rather than *actually* being together. I got to know Filip better than I ever got to know you: staying up past curfew together, stealing lamb chops from the Supper Hall, or even just sitting on a rooftop and talking—you know, about our families or what we're afraid of or what kind of pie we like. Doesn't matter how it all turned out, really. . . . He was my first real friend." Tedros couldn't look at Agatha. "You and I never even got to *be* friends. Don't even have nicknames for each other. With you, it was always stolen moments and faith that love would somehow be enough. And now, here we are, three weeks cooped up in a house, no time alone or room to go for a walk or a hunt or a swim, and then sleeping, eating, *breathing* with the other person hovering around like a keeper, and still we feel like strangers. I've never felt so *old*." He glimpsed Agatha's face. "Oh come on, surely you feel it too. We're like fusty married saps. Every tiny thing that bothers you about me must be magnified a thousand times."

Agatha tried to look understanding. "What bothers you about me?"

"Oh let's not play this game," Tedros puffed, rolling onto his stomach.

"I want to know. What bothers you about me?"

Her prince didn't answer. Agatha flicked hot turmeric onto his back.

Tedros flipped over angrily. "First off, you treat me like I'm an idiot."

"That's not true—"

Tedros frowned at her. "Do you want to know or not?"

Agatha folded her arms.

"You treat me like I'm an idiot," Tedros repeated. "You pretend to be busy every time I attempt conversation. You act like it's easy for me to give up *my* home, even though a princess is supposed to follow her prince. You clump around the house in those horrible shoes like an elephant, you leave the floor wet after your baths, you never even *try* to smile these days, and if I question anything you say or do, you give me this attitude that I shouldn't dare challenge you because you're just so . . . so . . ."

"So what?" Agatha glared.

"Good," said Tedros.

"My turn," said Agatha. "First off, you act like you're my captive, as if I kidnapped you away from your best friend, who doesn't even *exist*—"

"Now you're just being spiteful—"

"You make me feel guilty for bringing you here, as if I shouldn't have *saved your life*. You act like you're all sensitive and chivalrous and then declare things like a princess should 'follow' her prince. You're impulsive, you sweat too much, you make sweeping generalizations about things you know nothing about, and whenever you knock things over, which is *often*, you blame my *house* instead of yourself—"

"There's barely any room to walk—"

"You're used to living in a *castle*! With west wings and throne rooms and pretty little maids," Agatha snapped. "Well, we're not in a castle, oh princely one—we're in *real* life. Have you thought that maybe I'm spending all my time worrying about keeping us alive? Have you thought that maybe I'm trying to figure out how to make our happy ending *happy* and that's why I'm not spending all my time smiling like a clown and having deep conversations over cappuccino? Of course not, because you're Tedros of Camelot, handsomest boy in the Woods and god forbid he feel *old*!"

Tedros cocked a grin. "That handsome, am I?"

"Even Sophie was more tolerable than you!" Agatha yelled into a pillow. "And she tried to kill me! *Twice!*"

"So go into the Woods and get your Sophie back!" Tedros retorted.

"Why don't you go and get your Filip back!" Agatha barked—

Then slowly, they both blushed to silence, realizing they were talking about the same person.

Tedros slid next to his princess and put his arms around her waist. Agatha gave in to his tight, warm hug, trying not to cry.

"What happened to us?" she whispered.

When Agatha rescued Tedros from the School Master, she thought she'd found the way out of her fairy tale. She'd escaped death, saved her prince, and left the Woods behind, with her lying, betraying best friend still in it. As she clutched her true love, haloed by the white light between worlds, Agatha breathed in the relief of Ever After. She had Tedros at last— Tedros who loved her as much as she loved him . . . Tedros whose kiss she could still taste . . . Tedros who would make her happy forever . . .

Agatha smashed face-first into a wall of dirt.

Dazed, she'd opened her eyes to pitch darkness, her body on top of her prince's in Gavaldon's snowy cemetery. In an instant, she remembered all she'd once left behind in this tiny village: a broken promise to Stefan to bring his daughter home, the Elders' threat to kill her, the stories of witches once burned in a square. . . . *Relax. This is our happy ending*, she'd soothed herself, her breath settling. *Nothing bad can happen anymore.*

Agatha squinted and saw the slope of a roof atop the snow-capped hill, shaped like a witch's hat. Her heart had swelled at the thought of being home once and for all, of seeing her mother's euphoric face. . . . She looked down at her prince with an impish grin. *If she doesn't have a stroke first.*

"Tedros, wake up," she'd whispered. He'd stayed limp in her arms in his black Trial cloak, the only sounds coming from a few crows pecking at grave worms and a weak torch crackling over the gate. She grabbed her prince by the shirt strings to shake him, but her hands were flecked with something warm and sticky. Slowly Agatha raised them into the torchlight.

Blood.

She'd dashed frantically between jagged graves and sharp-edged weeds, clumps crunching through powdery snow, before she saw the house ahead, none of its usual candles lit over the porch. Agatha turned the doorknob slowly, but the hinges squeaked and a body bolted out of bed, tangled in sheets like a bumbling ghost. Finally Callis' head poked through, her big bug eyes blinking wide. For a split second, she colored with happiness, reunited with her daughter who'd been gone for so long. Then she saw the panic in Agatha's face and went pale. "D-d-did anyone see you?" Callis stammered. Agatha shook her head. Her mother smiled with relief and rushed to embrace her, before she saw her daughter's face hadn't changed. Callis froze, her smile gone. "What have you done?" she gasped.

Together, they'd fumbled down Graves Hill, Callis in her saggy black nightgown, Agatha leading her back to Tedros. Plowing through snow, they lugged him home, each grappling one of his arms. Agatha peeked up at her mother, just an older version of herself with helmet-black hair and pasty skin, waiting for her to balk at the sight of a real-life prince—but Callis' pupils stayed locked on the darkened town below. Agatha couldn't worry to ask why. Right now, saving her prince was the only thing that mattered.

As soon as they pulled him through the door, her mother lay Tedros on the rug and slit open his wet shirt, the prince unconscious and covered with cockleburs, while Agatha lit the fireplace. When Agatha turned back, she nearly fainted. The sword wound in Tedros' chest was so deep she could almost see the pulsing of his heart.

Agatha's eyes filled with tears. "H-h-he'll be okay, won't he? He has to be—"

"Too late to numb him," said Callis, rifling through drawers for thread.

"I had to bring him, Mother—I couldn't lose him—"

"We'll talk later," Callis said so sharply Agatha shrank to the wall. Crouched over the prince, her mother made it five stitches in, barely closing the wound, before Tedros roused suddenly with a cry of pain, saw the needle in a stranger's hand, and grabbed the nearest broomstick, threatening to bash her head in if she got an inch closer.

He and Callis had never quite seen eye to eye after that.

Somehow Agatha sweet-talked Tedros into sleeping, and that next morning, while he snuffled shallow breaths, his stitches half-done, Callis took her daughter into the kitchen, hanging a black sheet to close off the bedroom. Agatha had sensed the tension immediately.

"Look, first time we met, he threatened to kill me too," she'd cracked, pulling two iron plates from the cupboard. "He'll grow on you, I promise."

Callis ladled foggy stew from the cauldron into a bowl. "I'll sew him a new shirt before he leaves."

"Uh, Mother, there's a real-life prince from magical fairy land sleeping on our floor and you're worrying about his shirt?" Agatha said, perching on a creaky stool. "Forget that the sight of me within a hundred feet of a boy should be cause for a town parade or that you've been telling me fairy tales are real from the day I was born. Don't you want to know who he is—" Agatha's eyes widened. "Wait. Before he *leaves*? Tedros is staying in Gavaldon . . . forever."

Callis put the bowl in front of Agatha. "No one likes toad soup cold."

Agatha bucked up. "Look, I know it's crowded with him here. But Tedros and I can get work in the village. Think about it, if we save up enough, maybe we can all move to a bigger house, maybe even something in the cottage lanes." Agatha grinned. "Imagine, Mother, we could actually have *living* neighbors—"

Callis fixed her with a cold, brown stare and Agatha stopped talking. She followed her mother's eyes to the small, slime-crusted window over the sink. Agatha pushed out of her chair, bowl untouched, and grabbed a wet dishtowel from the rack. Pressing against the glass, she scraped at the gray smear of dust, grease, and mildew, until a stream of sunlight pierced through. Agatha backed away in surprise.

Down the snow-coated hill, bright red flags billowed from every lamppost in the square:

WANTED: WITCHES

GOLD REWARD

By Order of

ELDERS

"Witch?" Agatha choked, gaping at a hundred reflections of her own face. Beyond the square, the colorful storybook houses, decimated by attacks from the Woods, had been rebuilt as monotonous stone bunkers. A phalanx of guards in long black cloaks and black-iron masks carried spears, patrolling the cottage lanes and forest perimeter. Dread rising, Agatha's eyes slowly fell on the spot where her and Sophie's statues once glistened near the crooked clock tower. Now there was only a raised wooden stage, with a giant pyre made of birches, two flaming torches fixed to the scaffolding, and a banner of her and Sophie's faces hanging between them.

Agatha's stomach dropped. She'd escaped a public execution at school only to find one at home.

"I warned you, Agatha," her mother said behind her. "The Elders believed Sophie a witch who brought the attacks from the Woods. They ordered you not to go after her the night they surrendered her to the attackers. The moment you disobeyed them, you became a witch too."

Agatha turned, her legs jellying. "So they want to *burn* me?"

"If you'd come back alone, the Elders might have spared you." Callis was sitting at the table, head in hands. "You could have taken punishment, like I did for letting you escape."

A chill went up Agatha's spine. She looked at her mother, but there were no wounds or marks on her hooked-nose face or gangly arms; all her fingers and toes were intact. "What did they do to you?" Agatha asked, terrified.

"Nothing that compares to what they'll do to you both when they find him." Callis looked up, eyelids raw. "The Elders always despised us, Agatha. How could you be so stupid to bring someone back from the Woods?"

"The s-s-storybook said 'The End,'" Agatha stuttered. "You said it yourself—if our book says 'The End,' this *has* to be our happy ending—"

"Happy ending? With *him*?" Callis blurted, jolting to her feet. "There is a *reason* the worlds are separate, Agatha. There is a reason the worlds *must* be separate. He will never be happy here! You are a Reader and he is a—"

Callis stopped and Agatha stared at her. Callis quickly turned to the sink and pumped water into a kettle.

"Mother . . . ," Agatha said, suddenly feeling cold. "How do you know what a Reader is?"

"Mmm, can't hear you, dear."

"A *Reader*," Agatha stressed over the strident cranks. "How do you know that word—"

Callis pumped louder. "Must have seen it in a book, I'm sure . . ."

"Book? What book—"

"One of the storybooks, dear."

Of course, Agatha sighed, trying to relax. Her mother had always seemed to know things about the fairy-tale world—like all parents in Gavaldon who had feverishly bought storybooks from Mr. Deauville's Storybook Shop, hunting for clues about the children kidnapped by the School Master. *One of the books must have mentioned it,* Agatha told herself. That's why she called me a Reader. That's why she wasn't surprised by a prince.

But as Agatha glanced up at Callis, back to her, pumping water into the kettle, Agatha noticed that the pot was already full and overflowing into the sink. She watched her mother staring off into space, hands clenched, pumping water faster, faster, as if pumping memories away with it. Slowly Agatha's heart started to constrict in her chest, until she felt that cold sensation deepening . . . whispering that the reason her mother wasn't fazed by Tedros' appearance wasn't because she'd read storybooks . . . but because she knew what it was like to live through one . . .

"He returns to the Woods as soon as he wakes," Callis said, releasing the pump.

Agatha wrenched out of her thoughts. "The *Woods?* Tedros and I barely escaped alive—and you want us to go *back?*"

"Not you," said Callis, still turned. "Him."

Agatha flared in shock. "Only someone who's never experienced true love could say such a thing."

Callis froze. The skeleton clock ticked through the loaded silence.

"You really believe this is your happy ending, Agatha?" Callis said, not looking at her.

"It has to be, Mother. Because I won't leave him again. And I won't leave you," Agatha begged. "I thought maybe I could be happy in the Woods, that I could run away from real life . . . but I can't. I never wanted a fairy tale. All I ever wanted was to wake up every day right here, knowing I had my mother and my best friend. How could I know that friend would end up being a prince?" Agatha dabbed at her eyes. "You don't know what we've been through to find each other. You don't know the Evil that we left behind. I don't care if Tedros and I have to stay trapped in this house for a hundred years. At least we're together. At least we'll be happy. You just have to give us the chance."

Quiet fell in the sooty kitchen.

Callis turned to her daughter. "And Sophie?"

Agatha's voice went cold. "Gone."

Her mother gazed at her. The town clock tolled faintly from the square, before the wind drowned it out. Callis picked up the kettle and moved to the wooden stove. Agatha held her breath, watching her spark a flame beneath the pot and stew a few wormroot leaves in, circling her ladle again and again, long after the leaves had dissolved.

"I suppose we'll need eggs," said her mother at last. "Princes don't eat toads."

Agatha almost collapsed in relief. "Oh thank you thank you thank you—"

"I'll lock you both in when I go to town each morning. The guards won't come here as long as we're careful."

"You'll love him like a son, Mother, you'll see—" Agatha grimaced. "Into town? You said you had no patients."

"Don't light the fireplace or open the windows," ordered Callis, pouring two cups of tea.

"Why won't the guards come here?" Agatha pushed. "Wouldn't it be the first place they'd check?"

"And don't answer the door for a soul."

"Wait—what about Stefan?" Agatha asked, brightening. "Surely he can talk to the Elders for us—"

Callis whirled. "*Especially* not Stefan."

Mother and daughter locked stares across the kitchen.

"Your prince will never belong here, Agatha," said Callis softly. "No one can hide from their fate without a price."

There was a fear in her mother's big owl eyes that Agatha had never seen before, as if she was no longer talking about a prince.

Agatha crossed the kitchen and wrapped her mother in a deep, comforting hug. "I promise you. Tedros will be as happy here as I am," she whispered. "And you'll wonder how you ever could have doubted two people so in love."

A clang and clatter echoed from the bedroom. The curtain drew back behind them before collapsing entirely, and Tedros lumbered through, groggy, red-eyed, and half-naked with a torn, bloodied piece of bedsheet stuck haplessly over his wound. He sat down at the counter, smelled the soup and gagged, shoving it aside. "We'll need a sturdy horse, steel-edged sword, and enough bread and meat for a three-day journey." He looked up at Agatha with a sleepy smile. "Hope you said your goodbyes, princess. Time to ride to my castle."

That first week, Agatha believed this was just another test in their story. It was only a matter of time before the pyre came down, the death sentence lifted, and Tedros felt at ease with ordinary life. Looking at her handsome, teddy-bear prince who she loved so much, she knew that no matter how long they stayed in this house, they would still find a way to be happy.

By the second week, however, the house had started to feel smaller. There was never enough food or cups or towels; Reaper and Tedros fought like demented siblings; Agatha began to notice her prince's irritating habits (using all the soap, drinking milk out of the jug, exercising every second of the day, breathing through his mouth); and Callis had the burden of supporting two teenagers who didn't like to be supported at all. ("*School* was better than this," Tedros carped, bored to tears. "Let's go back and you can finish getting stabbed," Agatha replied.) By the third week, Tedros had taken to playing rugby against himself, dodging invisible opponents, whispering play-by-play, and flinging about like a caged animal, while Agatha lay in bed, a pillow over her head, clinging to the hope that happiness would fall like a fairy godmother from a star. Instead, it was Tedros who fell on her head one day while catching a ball, reopening his stitches in the process. Agatha belted him hard with her pillow, Tedros clocked her with his, and soon the cat was in the toilet. As they lay on the bed, covered in feathers, Reaper dripping in the corner, Agatha's question hung in the air unanswered.

"What happened to us?"

As the fourth week went on, Tedros and Agatha stopped spending time together. Tedros ceased his manic workouts and sat hunched at the kitchen window, unshaven and dirty, silently looking out at the Endless Woods. He was homesick, Agatha told herself, just as she'd once been in his world. But each day, a darker anguish settled into his face, and she knew it was deeper than homesickness—it was the guilt of knowing that somewhere out there, in a land far away, there would soon be no new king to take the crown from the old. But Agatha had nothing to say to make him feel better, nothing that didn't sound self-serving or trite, and hid beneath her bedcovers, reading her old storybooks again and again.

Gazing at beautiful princesses kissing dashing princes, she wondered how her Ever After had gone rancid. All these fairy tales had tied up so neatly and satisfyingly . . . while the more she thought about her own, the more loose ends seemed to appear. What had happened to her friends: to Dot, Hester, Anadil, who had risked their lives for her during the Trial? What had happened to the Girls, charging into war against Aric and the Boys? Or to Lady Lesso and Professor Dovey, now faced with the School Master's return? Agatha's chest clamped. What if the School Master started kidnapping children from Gavaldon again? She thought about the parents who would lose more daughters and sons . . . about Tristan and how his parents would learn about his death . . . about the balance in the Woods, tilting to death and Evil . . . about her once Evil best friend, left to fend for herself . . .

Sophie.

This time no anger came at the name. Only an echo, like the password to her heart's cave.

Sophie.

Sophie, who she'd loved through Good and Evil. Sophie, who she'd loved through Boys and Girls. Sophie, who she vowed to protect forever, young or old, until death did them part.

How do you turn your back on your best friend? How do you leave them behind?

For a boy.

Shame colored her cheeks.

For a boy who can barely stand the sight of me anymore.

Agatha's heart shrank as small and hard as a pebble. All this time, she thought she had to choose between Sophie and Tedros to find a happy ending. And yet, each time she picked one over the other, the story twisted back upon itself and the world fell out of balance more than before. Every thought of Sophie, alone in a tower with a deadly villain, brought on more guilt, more pregnant fear, as if she was trapped in a purgatory of her own making, as if she hadn't failed by choosing a prince over her best friend . . . but in making that choice at all.

"I think about her too."

She turned and saw Tedros at the window, watching her, his mouth trembling. "About how we just left her," he rasped, eyes welling. "I know she's a bad friend, I know she's Evil, I know Filip was a lie . . . but we just left her . . . with that *monster.* We left all of them. The whole school . . . just to save ourselves. What kind of prince is that, Agatha? What would my father think of me?" Tears spilled down his stubbled cheeks. "I don't want you to leave your mother. I really don't. But we're not happy, Agatha. Because the villain's still alive. Because we're not heroes at all. We're . . . cowards."

Agatha looked into her prince's messy, earnest face, and remembered why she loved him. "This isn't our happy ending, is it?" she breathed.

Tedros smiled, his old glow returning.

And for the first time since they came home, Agatha smiled too.

3

The New or the Old

"**M**aybe we have to close our eyes," said Tedros.

"Or do a rain dance in pajamas while singing 'Ring Around the Rosie,'" Agatha grumped, Reaper fast asleep in her lap. "It's past dinnertime and I'm starving. How many times can we try this?"

"Oh I'm sorry. Do you have somewhere better to be at the moment?"

Agatha watched a roach mosey by, cram under the double-locked front door, and disappear. "You have a point," she said, and shut her eyes.

"All right," Tedros sucked in, closing his eyes. "One . . . two . . . three!"

Agatha scrunched up her face, Tedros did too, and both of them thrust their index fingers at the other. They exhaled at the same time and opened their eyes.

Neither of their fingertips was glowing.

Tedros peered closely at Agatha's. "You bite your nails too much."

"Oh for crying out loud. We can't get into the Woods unless our magic comes back," she barked, shoving her hand in her pocket. "Magic follows emotion. That's what we learned at school. You said it yourself! If we both make the wish at the same time, the gates should open—"

"Unless one of us is having doubts," said Tedros.

"Then I suggest you get over them," Agatha huffed, standing up. "Let's try in the morning. Mother's never this late. She'll be here any second—"

"Agatha."

She saw Tedros giving her that lopsided grin . . . the one that said he knew exactly what she was thinking, even if she was doing everything she could to keep it from him.

"You're smarter than you look," she groused, sitting back down.

"And you're the one famous for not judging books by their covers." He scooted next to her. "Look, if you want to say good-bye to your mother first—"

"That'll just make the doubts worse," mumbled Agatha. "How do you tell your mother you're leaving her forever?"

"Wouldn't know. My mother left me without saying good-bye," Tedros replied.

Agatha looked at him, suddenly feeling very stupid. Tedros slid closer. "What is it, my love?" he asked. "What are you really afraid of?"

Agatha felt panic rising, something coming up she couldn't keep down—

"What if I'm the problem?" she blurted. "Every time I try to be happy, it goes wrong. First with Sophie, then with you, and all I can think of is that it's not us who's broken . . . it's *me*. The girl who ruins everyone's story. The girl who's meant to be alone. That's why I'm afraid to leave my mother. Because what if I'm not supposed to be with you, Tedros? What if I'm supposed to end here, just like her, never finding love at all?"

Tedros froze, taken aback.

Slowly Agatha felt the air return to her lungs, as if a boulder had lifted off her chest.

Her prince traced his finger between bricks in the floor. "We only see the finished storybooks, Agatha. How do we know every Ever After doesn't take a few tries? Think about it. Each time you left the Woods, you tried to come back to your old life. But this time is different, isn't it? When we get to our true ending, you'll have a new life with me. We'll have my kingdom to protect, until we're old ourselves and it's time to pass it on. Just like my father did and his father and all who came before."

Looking at him, Agatha realized how selfish and small-hearted she'd been by keeping her prince here.

"I promise," he said, squeezing her hand. "This time, we *will* be happy."

"All right, say we do get back to the School for Good and Evil," Agatha allowed. "What's our plan?"

"Make things right, of course," Tedros puffed. "Rescue Sophie, kill the School Master, take back Excalibur, free the other students, and you and I go to Camelot in time for my sixteenth birthday, and coronation as king. The End." He paused. "The real End."

Agatha made a sound halfway between a cough and a sneeze.

"All right, Sophie can come too, if you're going to be difficult about it," he sighed.

"Tedros, my love," said Agatha cuttingly. "You think we can just waltz through the school gates and kill the School Master like we're buying bonbons from the bakery?"

"I think buying anything from the bakery would pose far more obstacles at the moment," said Tedros, eyeing the triple-locked door.

Agatha let go of him and braced for a fight. "First off, the School Master is an all-powerful sorcerer who last we saw came back from death, turned young again, and stabbed you with your own sword. Second, for all we know, he's killed the Evers and has everyone on his side. And third, you don't think he'll have guards and traps and—"

"Merlin had a saying: 'Worrying doesn't solve problems. Just gives you gas,'" Tedros yawned.

"I take back the smarter than you look thing," Agatha groaned. Her cat stirred and staggered out of her arms, but not before spitting in Tedros' lap. The prince backhanded it and

Reaper fled, throwing Agatha a horrible scowl at her choice of mate.

"He used to love me," Agatha said, watching her cat gnaw the head off a dead canary.

"Agatha, look at me."

"Tedros, you don't even have your sword, let alone a plan. We're going to die."

"Agatha, please look at me."

She did, with folded arms.

"You can't plan your story any more than you can plan who you're going to fall in love with. That's the point of a story," said Tedros. "And even if you could, what's the fun of living through it if you know what's going to happen? All we know is that Good always wins, right? So if Good hasn't beaten Evil yet, our fairy tale *can't* be over. As soon as we make our wish, we'll be back where we belong, chasing our happy ending. Trust our story, Agatha. We'll know what to do when the time comes."

"And what about Sophie?" Agatha asked. "What if she hasn't forgiven us?"

Tedros thought for a moment. "Everything Sophie did, she did to get closer to you or me. We've all made mistakes, that's for sure. But Good or Evil, Boy or Girl, the three of us are in this tale together." He leveled eyes with her. "So how can Sophie be happy until we are?"

Agatha fell quiet, aware of the dark room hemming her in with her prince and yet keeping them apart.

Long before she ever met her best friend, she'd secretly read storybooks from Mr. Deauville's, buying them right after the shop opened, when no one else was inside, and paying for them with the coins her mother had given her for sweets. She drank in the lesson of those fairy-tale books more than any hot cream or fudge, that same lesson told and retold: you didn't need a hundred true loves to find Ever After . . . you just needed *one*. It didn't matter if an entire town called her a freak or a witch or a vampire. If she could just find that one person who loved her—one measly soul—then she'd have everything a princess did, minus the horrific pink dress, obnoxious blond hair, and moony-eyed face.

From the moment she met Sophie, Sophie *was* that soul: the friend who made her feel normal, who made her feel needed, who so clearly cared about her, despite all her efforts to disguise it. Back then, Agatha had done everything she could to ensure they'd end up together forever, rather than let her best friend be stolen away by a boy . . . until Agatha somehow fell in love with that boy herself. And so the story had turned on its head, this time Sophie doing everything she could to keep a boy and her best friend apart. It was a wicked love triangle, with Sophie the point that had to be removed, until finally Agatha and Tedros had rid themselves of her, turning that triangle into a straight line between them—prince and princess united at last, just like in the storybooks buried under her bed. But now, as Agatha sat in darkness, feeling more and more like the grave-yard girl of old, she wondered if the reason she missed her best friend was the simplest of all. What if Sophie wasn't the force that kept her and Tedros apart? What if Sophie was the force that brought them together?

Without Sophie, she never could have opened up her heart.

Without Sophie, she never could have learned to love.

Without Sophie, there never could have been a Tedros and Agatha.

"Princess? What is it?"

Agatha slowly looked up at her prince, new life in her eyes. "Let's go find our best friend."

Tedros blinked at her, stunned. His cheeked pinked and his Adam's apple bobbed, words swallowed by emotion. He placed his hand behind his back. "Wish to reopen our story, then?"

Agatha smiled and hid her hand. "Wish to reopen our story."

Tedros closed his eyes. "One . . ."

"Two . . . ," said Agatha, closing hers.

They took a joint breath and thrust out their fingers. *"Three—"*

The door slammed open to a sharp heel-crack of boots. Agatha lurched to her feet.

There was an Elderguard in the doorway, the outlines of a black cloak and slatted iron mask blending into the night.

Tedros instantly clasped Agatha and yanked her to the kitchen wall. He grabbed a meat knife from the sink and brandished it at the guard, blocking his princess's body with his. "Move another inch and I'll cut your throat!" Tedros spat.

The guard threw the door shut and hissed back at them. *"Hide!* Both of you!"

Agatha squinted at the big brown eyes glinting through the guard's mask. *"Mother?"*

"Hide *now!*" Callis shrieked, shoring her body against the door.

Agatha couldn't move, trying to process what was happening, gaping at her mother in the same uniform as the town guards ordered to execute her. "I d-d-don't under—"

But then Agatha heard them coming . . . footsteps . . . voices . . .

She tackled Tedros to the ground. Stunned, the prince lost his grip on the knife and flailed to reach it as Agatha yanked him by the belt buckle under the bed. Tedros lunged over her and snatched the knife—

The door flung open and Agatha spun to see Callis seized from behind and shoved to the wall by two guards.

"No!" Agatha gasped, leaping out, but Tedros pulled her down under the bed, fumbling his knife at the same time. He stabbed his hand for it, only to see Agatha's hip knock it away. In horror, they both watched the blade skid across the floor and halt beneath the heel of a muddy leather boot. Slowly their eyes traced up.

A tall guard prowled into the house, teeth bared through his mask. From his pocket, he pulled a fistful of eggs, rolling them around in his big hand like marbles.

"First time I saw her stealing them, I thought maybe she can't afford to pay. Second time, I thought maybe she's gone hungry. But the third time . . ." He let the eggs drop and splatter at Callis' feet. "I wonder who's she stealing 'em *for*."

He spun and kicked aside the bed, revealing Tedros, unarmed and fists up. The guard's brutal blue eyes honed in on the prince.

"You and I can duel like men," Tedros threatened. "But leave my princess *alone*."

The guard stared at him strangely . . . then lifted his gaze. His pupils froze, reflecting Agatha behind Tedros, prostrate on the floor.

In a flash, he threw Tedros aside, knocking the prince to the floorboards. But the guard's eyes stayed on Agatha.

She trembled as his boots crackled through the bleeding eggs, step by step, until he placed his sharp, filthy shoe tip upon her neck.

He took off his mask.

"So much for promises," Stefan snarled.

The cage was meant for only one prisoner, not three, so Agatha had to stand with her mother, Reaper curled in Callis' arms, while Tedros crouched in a daze, clutching his black eye. Back at the house, Agatha told him not to resist, but Tedros assured her Camelot's future king could flatten six armed guards with his bare hands.

He'd been wrong.

Agatha held on to the rusty bars, tottering for balance, as the horse dragged the cage through the darkened cemetery, Stefan at the reins. She could see a crowd forming in front of the torchlit pyre, watching the guards march down the hill ahead of the prisoners.

"That was your punishment for letting me escape, wasn't it? The Elders made you a guard," Agatha said, turning to her mother. "That's why they never searched the house. Because you were with them, protecting the town from your own daughter."

Callis paled as she saw the distant pyre, two fiery torches hanging from its scaffolding. "When the people blamed you and Sophie for the attacks, the Elders named me and Stefan leaders of a new patrol, responsible for catching you two if you ever dared return. It was a test of our loyalty, of course. Either we saw our own children as traitors and vowed to make them burn or we'd be burned as traitors ourselves." She looked at Agatha. "The difference between Stefan and me is that he took the vow seriously."

"How could Stefan betray his own daughter? It was the Elders who gave Sophie to the attackers. *They're* the Evil ones! Why would he obey them—"

But as the cage creaked into the moonlit square, Agatha saw the answer to her question. The widow Honora and her two young boys, Jacob and Adam, huddled near the back of the growing crowd, watching Stefan lead in the prisoners. Agatha knew how much the two boys meant to Sophie's father, who seemed to love them far more than his own daughter. But it wasn't the boys that Agatha fixed on. It was the gold band, gleaming on the ring finger of Honora's left hand.

"He had to obey them," Callis said quietly. "Because the Elders made Stefan choose between his old and new family."

Agatha looked at her, stunned.

"Leave it to me," a voice groused under them.

Tedros careened to his feet between Agatha and her mother, knocking both of them against the bars. "They've woken the beast," he boiled, struggling to blink his swollen eye. "No one's laying a *hand* on us."

The cage door swung open behind him and two guards gagged Tedros with a mucky cloth and hoisted him out by his armpits, before roughly nabbing Callis too. Before Agatha could react, Stefan leapt into the cage and took her for himself.

"Stefan, listen to me—Sophie needs our help—" Agatha appealed as he pulled her through the crowd, who was abusing her with cries of "witch" and "traitor" along with chunks of spoiled food. "I know you have a new family, but you can't give up on her—"

"Give up? You think I gave *up*? On my own *child*?" he seethed, pulling her up the stairs to the pyre behind Tedros, who kicked at his guards with muffled yells. "You promised me, Agatha. You *promised* you'd save her. And instead you left her there to die. Now you'll see how it feels."

"Stefan, we can still save her!" sputtered Agatha. "Tedros and me!"

"I always thought one day my daughter would abandon you for a boy," said Stefan. "Turns out I had the story all *wrong.*"

He bound her to the pyre with a long rope around her belly, as two guards shoved Tedros in next to her. Agatha could feel the heat of the flaming torches above her.

"Stefan, you have to believe me! We're Sophie's only hope—"

He gagged her with a black cloth, but just as he cinched it, Agatha managed one last breath—

"The School Master has her!"

Stefan's hands froze and his blue eyes met hers, big and wide. Then a hush swept over the crowd and Agatha knew her time was up.

The Elders had come.

4

Death at an Execution

"I'm afraid we only have room for two on the pyre," said the gray-cloaked Elder with the longest beard, grinning at Agatha and Tedros as he paced the stage, top hat in hand. He leered down at Callis at the front of the massive crowd, her hands tied, standing between the two younger Elders, both in gray cloaks and tall black hats. "We'll let mother *watch* before her turn," he mused, as the two Elders dragged Callis into the mob.

Agatha spotted Reaper's shadow sprinting away from her mother and towards Graves Hill, a scrap of what looked like parchment

between his teeth. Trapped on the pyre, she wrestled hopelessly against her binds, sweating from the heat of the torches above her. If her mother had entered the house one second later, she and Tedros would have had their magic back—they'd be far into the Woods by now, her mother no longer in danger. Stifling tears, Agatha searched for her again, but darkness rendered the crowd a sea of shadows. They'd called her a witch from the day she was born, destined to burn on a stake, and now they'd made their tales come true. In the front row, a few rosy-faced children gawked at Tedros, clinging storybooks to their chests, like talismans against the boy from inside of them.

"But we are not savages, of course," said the Elder, turning to the captives. "Justice is only delivered when there is a crime."

The crowd buzzed impatiently, eager to see the show and get to bed.

"Let us meet our guest from the Woods," the Elder proclaimed. His shiny eyes flicked to Tedros. "What is your name, boy?"

A guard ripped out Tedros' gag. "Touch her and I kill you," the prince lashed.

The Elder raised his brows. "Ah, I see," he said, peering between Tedros and Agatha. "For two hundred years, those from the Woods have kidnapped our young, ripped apart our families, and attacked our homes. For two hundred years, those from the Woods have brought our children nothing but terror, pain, and suffering. And here you are, the first to ever stand before us, claiming to *protect* one? An improbable twist . . ." He studied the way Tedros looked at Agatha, his tone easing.

"But if it's true, perhaps mercy is in the cards after all. Only the hardest of hearts can resist young love."

The crowd rumbled, as if they'd cast their own hearts in stone to see vengeance for all the curses of the Woods. But as Agatha searched the Elder's face, the old man's smile was almost friendly now.

"You'll let us live?" Tedros insisted.

Agatha's heart hammered, praying her prince had just saved them.

The Elder touched Tedros' chest with a shriveled hand. Tedros winced, his wound still tender. "You're young and handsome, with your whole life ahead of you," the Elder cooed. "Tell us what you know about those that attacked us and I promise we won't hurt you."

Agatha's stomach sank. That tone. She'd heard it before. It was the same way he'd told Sophie she'd be sheltered from her assassins . . .

Before he left her to die.

Agatha pressed her fist into Tedros' ribs. Whatever he did, he couldn't play this game—

"Tedros," the prince proclaimed to the Elder. "Tedros is my name."

Agatha bristled, shoving him harder.

"And how do you know our beloved Agatha, Tedros?" coaxed the Elder, leaning closer.

"She's my princess," Tedros declared, gently clasping Agatha's fist. "Soon to be *Queen* of Camelot and bloodline to King Arthur, so I suggest you unhand us at once."

The mob quieted in disbelief, children clutching their storybooks tighter. (Red-haired Radley gaped goonishly at Agatha. "Must be slim pickings in the Woods," he murmured.)

"A real-life prince!" The Elder stepped back. For the first time, he looked unsettled by Tedros, as if forced to acknowledge the possibility of a world bigger than his own. "And to what do we owe this honor?"

Agatha squirmed against her binds, trying to get Tedros to look at her.

"I'm taking her to my castle in the Woods," Tedros testified, eyes fixed on the Elder. "We pose absolutely no threat to you."

"And yet we were attacked only months ago by assassins from the Woods," the Elder said, masses clamoring behind him. "Attacks from which we are still rebuilding."

"Well, the attacks are over," retorted Tedros. "Your town is safe."

Agatha dug her heel into his foot. Tedros shook her off.

"Oh really? Do your princely powers come with foresight?" the Elder scoffed, the audience echoing his laughter. "How would you know anything about the fate of our town, let alone the attacks?"

Agatha shouted into her gag to stop him—

"Because I ordered them," Tedros fired.

The crowd went still. Agatha slumped against the rope.

The Elder stared at Tedros . . . then broke into a slow grin, color growing in his cheeks. "Well. We've learned all we need to know about our dear guest, haven't we?" He smiled wolfishly at the prince and walked off the stage, passing Stefan with a glare. "Do the witch first."

Roars detonated from the mob, flocking closer to the pyre.

Tedros spun to Agatha and saw her face. "But he promised us!" he cried.

The Elder glanced back as he descended the steps. "Every story has a lesson doesn't it, young prince? Perhaps yours is that you're too old to believe in fairy tales."

Agatha felt Tedros gush into a sweat as the guards regagged him. Frantic, the prince thrashed at the rope, trying to free his princess, but his flailing only made the rope cut tighter. Choking for breath, Agatha hunted wildly for her mother, but still couldn't find her. She whirled to Stefan, knowing she was about to die—

But Stefan hadn't moved from the side of the stage, his gaze fixed on her.

"Is there a problem, Stefan?" the Elder said, now at the front of the mass.

Stefan kept staring at Agatha.

"Or should we replace our prisoners with your new family?" the Elder said.

Stefan turned sharply. Guards held Honora, Jacob, and Adam in the crowd.

Stefan's teeth bit the inside of his cheeks. Then his expression darkened. He moved towards Agatha, no longer able to look at her. Body close to hers, he reached up and took a flaming torch from the scaffolding. Agatha cowered from the wrath of the flame as he drew it down, blinding her with smoke. She could hear Tedros' muffled yells, the echoes of the shouting hordes, but they were drowned out by the raging torch fire, hissing like a demon snake. Eyes watering, she caught flashes of Stefan's heaving chest, his quivering grasp on the torch, the red splotches across his cheeks . . .

"Please—" Agatha gasped into her gag.

Stefan still couldn't look at her, the torch shaking so much that embers scattered onto Agatha's dress, burning tiny holes.

"Stefan . . . ," the Elder warned in a menacing voice.

Stefan nodded, tears and sweat mixing. The crowd went dead quiet, seeing him bend towards the stake. He raised the torch to the sticks over Agatha's head, the flames about to lick onto the wood—

"Take me!" Callis' anguished voice pierced the silence. "Please, Stefan! Let me die with her!"

Stefan froze, his flame so close to Agatha it scorched the gag in her mouth. Heart stopped, Agatha watched him deliberate a moment, his face calcifying into a mask . . .

Then he backed away and turned to the Elder.

"It *is* a mother's last request," said Stefan, adding a snort. "Shove her in with her traitor daughter and watch the flesh melt off 'em. They deserve to writhe together, don't they?"

Even the most bloodthirsty spectators looked flummoxed, deferring to the Elder.

The Elder's pupils raked Stefan over, before his lips pursed in a flat line.

"Quickly then."

"No!" Agatha shrieked, her gag breaking away.

Guards wrenched Callis from the crowd onto the stage and shoved her next to Agatha, binding her waist to the pyre. Helpless, Tedros ripped at the rope, his bicep veins about to burst.

"This is my fault . . . ," Agatha sobbed. "This is all my fault—"

"Close your eyes, dear," said Callis, trying not to cry. "It will all go fast from here."

Agatha looked up and saw Stefan's hand wasn't shaking on the torch anymore. With an eerie calm, he advanced towards her and her mother, the dancing flame reaching for the wood sticks between them. He finally met Agatha's eyes, a strange sadness in his face.

"If you ever see my daughter again, beyond this world . . . tell her I love her."

"*Now*, Stefan," the Elder commanded.

Petrified, Agatha seized Tedros' hand as she leaned into her mother's shoulder. She saw Stefan looking at Callis, his lips trembling.

"I'm s-s-sorry," he whispered.

"You saved me once upon a time, Stefan." Callis smiled mournfully at him. "I owe you a debt."

"I c-c-can't," Stefan faltered.

"You must," said Callis, hard as steel.

"NOW!" the Elder thundered.

With a pained cry, Stefan plunged the torch at Callis. Agatha screamed—

Callis thrust out her finger from beneath the binds and shot a blast of green light at the torch. The fire turned green and ricocheted off the pyre like a comet, blasting Stefan off the platform, before circling the stage in a wall of green flames, sealing the captives in.

Before Agatha could suck in a breath, her mother cut her and Tedros loose from the rope with her glowing fingertip. She grabbed Agatha and spoke over the villagers' cries beyond the firewall—

"The spell won't last, so listen carefully. Stefan knew what I was, Agatha. From the night you went after Sophie, we had a plan to save you girls from the Elders if you ever returned. Stefan would do anything to keep his daughter safe. But when you came back without Sophie, Stefan had no reason to keep to the plan and endanger his new family . . . unless he believes his daughter still needs you. You must repay my old debt to him, Agatha. You must save Sophie as Stefan saved you. You hear me? *Do not fail*. Now run for Graves Hill as fast as you can—"

"You're a w-w-witch—" Agatha spluttered, trying to find air. "You were a witch all along—"

"The grave between the two swans. Help will be there, waiting for you," her mother cut in. "You must find the grave before it's too late."

Dazed, Tedros turned to Agatha, expecting her to know what her mother was talking about. But Agatha was paralyzed, staring ahead. Tedros spun back to Callis. "Who? Who will be waiting for u—"

Only now Tedros saw what his princess was looking at . . . the circle of fire falling around the stage, Callis' spell about to end. In the green firelight, Agatha glimpsed Stefan, stunned on the ground but unharmed, before a fleet of shadows jumped over him, throttling towards the stage. Tedros and Agatha raised their eyes at the same time to see the guards charging through the crowd with spears, dashing right for them.

Callis took Agatha's face in her hands. "Don't look back, Agatha." She kissed her daughter's forehead hard. "Whatever you do, promise me you won't look back."

With a scared cry, Agatha grabbed her mother's hand, but her prince was already dragging her towards the edge of the stage away from the sprinting guards. Tedros hooked his arm over Agatha and flung the both of them off the platform in a flying leap. Spinning around, Agatha pulled her mother with them, holding on to her hand with every ounce of strength—

Callis smiled at Agatha in the fading firelight and let her daughter go.

Agatha crashed in dirt, twisting her ankle, before Tedros lifted her up in darkness, towing her towards the town gates. "No—I can't leave her—" she croaked, resisting him.

"'Don't look back.' That's what she said," Tedros fought, goading her ahead. "Trust your mother, Agatha. She's a witch. A powerful witch. We're the ones who need saving now."

Hearing the guards' shouts, Agatha let Tedros shove her forward. She pinned her eyes on Graves Hill ahead, hobbling beside him. *Don't look back*, she begged herself, Tedros clenching her like a vise. *Don't look back* . . .

Agatha looked back to see three guards hurdle the sinking firewall towards Callis, spears about to impale her. Her mother held her ground.

"What is she doing?" Agatha choked, freezing in horror.

"Agatha, *don't!*" cried Tedros—

Agatha broke free of him and started running back. "WHAT ARE YOU DOING—"

"Kill her!" the Elder's voice shouted faraway.

Callis raised her arms, welcoming the guards.

They charged and Agatha's mother fell.

"NO!" Agatha screamed, voice tearing out of her throat. She sank to her knees at the foot of Graves Hill. Her eyes fogged. Her heart deadened. All she saw was a blur of shadows swarming her mother as the shallow fires extinguished, an army of darkness overwhelming the last ashes of light.

"She let them . . . ," Agatha whispered. "She let them kill her."

Little by little, she felt the dirt wet on her knees, the numbness wearing off to an onslaught of pain—the dagger-edged thoughts that she had no family anymore . . . that her only parent had deserted her . . . that her mother had given her nothing to come home to ever again. She curled into herself, sobbing with fury. Men were no match for a witch. She could have done another spell! She could have ripped them all to shreds! Agatha cried and cried until she heard a strange echo between shuddering breaths . . . the whispered sound of her name . . .

Agatha lifted her eyes to a swollen-eyed boy standing over her, beautiful and scared, and for a moment, she saw nothing but a stranger. It was only when Agatha saw his legs unsteady, that she knew her prince was trying to tell her something. Slowly Tedros pointed a shaky finger over her head. Agatha turned.

Six guards raced towards them from the square, armed with torches and spears.

"We have to run, Agatha," Tedros rasped. "We have to run right now."

Agatha didn't move, still nauseous. "How could she let them . . ."

"To save you, Agatha," her prince implored, watching the guards gain ground. "And everything she did, everything your mother and Sophie's father did to keep us alive will be in vain if we don't go *now*."

Agatha gazed into the wet pools of his eyes and suddenly she understood. Her mother didn't want her to stay with her. Her mother didn't want her to come back to Gavaldon. She wanted Agatha to save her best friend . . . to find happiness with her prince . . . to abandon this world for a better one, far far away . . .

Because her happy ending wasn't here. It was never here.

Her mother had died to set her free.

Do not fail.

She had to find her real ending.

She had to run.

Agatha looked up at the guards bolting towards them, spears gleaming in torchlight. Rage blasted through her blood and scorched through her muscles, nothing holding her back anymore. Lunging to her feet, she hurtled up the slope of Graves Hill.

"Come on! We'll lose them in the graves!"

Together, they ripped through the rusted graveyard gates

into the dark expanse of graves. Even in pitch black, Agatha knew every step, navigating the headstones like a wily squirrel, while Tedros collided with them, cursing so barbarically even the grave worms fled.

Panting fire, his princess led him into the thick of the cemetery. The Elders had taken her family from her. They wouldn't take her prince too.

"The grave between the swans," Tedros called out behind her. "She said help would be waiting there—"

"Swans?" Agatha blurted. "There are no swans in Gavaldon!"

Tedros looked back down the hill and saw the guards barreling up, carrying torches. "Thirty seconds, Agatha! We have thirty seconds!"

Agatha scoured stones and plaques and obelisks for evidence of a swan. "I don't even know what I'm looking for!"

"Twenty seconds!" Tedros voice rang out.

She couldn't see her prince anymore. Agatha whirled desperately, trying to steady her mind. The only birds she'd ever seen in Gavaldon were smog-colored ducks and obese pigeons. She'd never even seen a real swan, especially not on Graves Hill—

Agatha's heart pattered faster.

But she had seen swans before, hadn't she? Swans were the symbols of the School for Good and Evil: one black, one white . . . representing two School Masters in balance . . . one brother Good, one brother Evil . . .

If Callis was a witch, she'd have known the Good and Evil

swans. That's how she knew so much about the school, Agatha thought. Her mother must have seen it for herself . . .

"Ten seconds!" Tedros shouted—

Agatha closed her eyes and tried to focus, her temples throbbing.

Swans . . . school . . . Stefan . . .

"You saved me," Callis had whispered to him.

What had she meant? If Callis and Stefan had a history, maybe the swans involved something that connected her mother and Sophie's father . . . something that both of them had in common . . . or some*one* . . .

Agatha's heart stopped. Her eyes shot open.

She was already running.

"What is it?" Tedros yelled, seeing her shadow dart deeper into the cemetery, towards the house on Graves Hill.

"Here! It's over here!"

Tedros chased her, squinting at her outline fading into the dark. He looked back and saw the army of shadows smash through the graveyard gates, spears glinting. Tedros dove to the ground behind a domed stone. He peeked over it and saw the guards sweeping torches over the rows of graves. Tedros ducked down. "This is worse than the Woods," he wheezed, crawling through stones to follow Agatha. "Soooo much worse—"

Then he saw her, crouched in the final row of headstones, only a short distance from her house. Tedros skidded into dirt beside her. "They're coming, Agatha!"

"Sophie's mother. That's what connected them," Agatha said, gripping a tablet gravestone knifing out of the ground, engraved with the words "*Loving Wife and Mother.*" Two smaller dirt-caked graves, one lighter, one darker, flanked it on either side like wings. "Before Sophie, she couldn't have a child. Two boys, both born dead."

She ran her hand over the lighter of the two boys' graves, pulling away the grime. Tedros' eyes bulged as Agatha's fingers cleared the headstone, revealing a small black swan carved into the unmarked grave. Tedros tore away the moss from the darker grave, revealing a white swan set in the stone. He and Agatha both turned to the larger grave in the middle, towering between the two swans.

"When she couldn't have a child, Sophie's mother went to see mine as a patient. That's what Sophie told me," Agatha pressed. "Somehow it's all connected. Sophie's mother . . . my mother being a witch . . . the debt she owed Stefan . . . I don't know how it's connected, but it has to be—"

Firelight swept over the both of them.

Agatha and Tedros flattened to the ground and swiveled to see the guards five rows back.

"We found the swans—we found the grave—" Tedros panicked, gaping at the bigger headstone. "Where's the *help?*"

Agatha shook her head. "We can't fight the guards without magic, Tedros! We need to make our wish!"

The prince swallowed. "Wish to reopen our story on three, okay? Hands behind our back—" He stopped.

His right fingertip was already glowing gold.

Agatha looked down at hers, glowing almost an identical shade.

"Did you make the wish?" Tedros asked.

Agatha shook her head.

"Neither did I," Tedros said, confused. "How could our fingers be glowing, then?"

Torchlight shined in their faces.

"They're here!" a guard cried. *"They're over here!"*

Agatha spun to see shadows vaulting over the last rows of graves. "Unless my mother didn't interrupt our wish in the house. Unless our wish worked when we made it the first time. Unless our fairy tale was open all along."

Agatha looked at her prince, deathly white. "We're already back in our story, Tedros. We've been in our story from the moment the guards found us . . ."

Tedros looked up at the spears slashing towards their hearts. "Which means we die at The End, Agatha!"

Terrified, she and Tedros clasped hands, each backing away from the spears into one of the swans—

Just in time to see a pale hand reach out of the grave between them and pull them both in.

5

A Princess Returns

Graves are meant for dead people, who have no reason to see, breathe, or use the toilet. Unfortunately for Agatha, she needed to do all three. Trapped underground in darkness, she and Tedros inhaled mouthfuls of soil while tangled in each other's sweaty limbs. Agatha couldn't make out her prince's face, but heard him hyperventilating with panic.

"You're using up all our air!" Agatha hissed.

"Graves have b-b-bodies—d-d-dead bodies—"

Agatha blanched with understanding and gripped on to any of Tedros' flesh she could find. "Sophie's mother . . . *she* p-p-pulled us in?"

"C-c-can't see a thing. For all we know she's right next to us!"

"Magic," Agatha wheezed. "Use magic!"

Tedros gulped a breath and focused on his fear, until his finger flickered gold like a candle, lighting up a wide, shallow grave the size of a large bed. Shivering on top of each other, Tedros and Agatha slowly turned to their right.

Dirt.

No body. No bones.

Just dirt.

"Where is she?" Agatha choked, rolling off Tedros, who groaned and rubbed his chest. She snatched her prince's wrist and swept his fingerglow over the right half of the grave, spotting only a pair of dung beetles fighting over a dirt ball in the corner. She shook her head, baffled, and swung Tedros' hand to the left—

Both of them froze.

Two sparkling brown eyes glared at them through a black ninja mask.

Agatha and Tedros opened their mouths to scream, but the figure gagged them with slender hands.

"Shhhh! They'll hear you!" the stranger whispered in a low, breathy voice.

Tedros gaped at the ninja in the grave with them, wrapped in draping black robes. "Are you . . . are you Sophie's mother . . ."

The ninja let out a giggly squeak. "Oh how absurd. Now *shhhh*!"

Agatha tensed. That squeak. Where had she heard it before? She tried to catch Tedros' eye, hoping he'd heard it too, but her prince was smothering the stranger in a hug.

"Oh thank God! We've been trapped for a month in the smallest, foulest house you can imagine, almost burned at the stake, almost skewered by an army, and then you pulled us in, whoever you are, which means you have to get us *out*! We need to get to the School for Good and Evil and rescue our best friend. Surely you know it. It's halfway between the Murmuring Mountains and—"

The ninja gagged him with a fist. "I know cats that listen better than you."

"You have no idea," Agatha murmured, punchy from the lack of air.

A sharp crackle ripped above their heads, like a sword splitting earth, and the grave tremored, caving clumps of dirt into their faces.

"Check 'em all," someone growled gruffly, followed by more sharp tremors. "Intercepted a message from the League of Thirteen. Said they'd be comin' through a grave."

Agatha's stomach plunged. The voice didn't sound like an Elder's.

"Coulda been more specific. Thousands of 'em and I'm starvin'," a thick, oafish voice added. "Besides, should be out fixin' our stories like the others, not diggin' around in graves. What's so important about these two anyway?"

"School Master wants 'em. Reason enough for you," said the gruff one, punctuated by another violent crackle. "He'll give us a turn at our stories soon enough."

Agatha and Tedros swiveled to each other. The School Master's men in *Gavaldon*? How had they gotten past the guards? The ceiling shook harder, showering clumps of earth.

"Think he'll let us eat an Everboy as a reward?" asked the oafish one.

"Might even let us eat two," the gruff voice chortled—

A black furry claw smashed through the ceiling into the grave, with five knife-edged talons snatching right and left. Agatha and Tedros choked back screams as the ninja flattened them against the dirt wall, the hooked talons swiping at air, missing the inseam of Tedros' breeches by a whisker. It slashed in vain a few more times and then curled into a fist.

"Nothin' here," the gruff voice growled. "Come on, let's eat. Maybe we'll find a juicy little boy in the Oakwood."

The claw withdrew empty-handed and vanished, followed by loud, thudding stomps.

A terrorized silence passed . . . then Tedros and Agatha shoved mouths to a hole in the ceiling and sucked down air. Agatha glanced at Tedros to make sure he was okay, expecting he'd be doing the same for her. Instead, her prince was pulling at his breeches, looking down his own pants. Tedros smiled, relieved . . . then saw Agatha frowning.

"What?" Tedros said.

Agatha was about to question his priorities, then noticed the footsteps had stopped. The voices too. Agatha's eyes shot wide open and she dove for her prince—"Tedros, watch out!"

The black claw crashed through the ceiling and grabbed

Agatha off her prince, dragging her out of the grave. Tedros leapt to clasp her leg too late. He craned up in horror to see the claw pull his princess into the night sky, dangling her like a caught mouse.

Agatha stared into the bloodshot yellow eyes of a tall, bony brown wolf on two legs, fur and flesh flaking off his face, leaving gaping holes over pieces of his skull.

"Lookie here. A princess returns," the wolf snarled gruffly, cheekbones poking through one of these holes.

Agatha paled. Was *he* the one talking about the School Master before? How could an Evil wolf have crossed into Gavaldon? And where was the Elderguard? Her eyes darted around, but all she could see in the darkness was a smattering of crooked headstones. She tried to make her finger glow, but the wolf was gripping her hand too tightly.

"Storian ain't writing, world dying, armies rising—all 'cause of *you*?" he purred, tracing her pallid skin and charcoal hair. "Less princess, I'd say, and more . . . skunk. How Good's fallen in my time away. Even runty Red Riding Hood was a more tempting treat."

Agatha had no idea what he was talking about, but after all she'd been through tonight, the last thing she needed was to be insulted for her looks by a puny wolf with a skin condition.

"And yet, Red Riding Hood's wolf learned his lesson, didn't he?" she warned, knowing her prince must be nearby. "Messed with Good and a hunter tore out his stomach."

"Tore out his *stomach*?" said the wolf, appalled.

"With his bare hands," Agatha lied loudly, signaling Tedros.

"And is this wolf . . . dead?"

"Very dead, so beat it before MY hunter comes," Agatha yelled, cuing Tedros again.

"Dead as in doornail dead?" the wolf fretted.

"Dead, dead, dead," Agatha snapped, squinting angrily for her prince.

"Dead, dead, dead, dead, dead," mumbled the wolf, mulling this gruesome fate. "Well, if that's true . . ." He lifted big, shiny eyes. "How am I still *here?*"

Agatha's eyes lowered to his other claw, tapping at a hideous scar crisscrossing his belly. Her face lost all of its blood. "I-i-impossible—"

"Can I eat this one?" an oafish voice said behind her. Agatha spun to see a 10-foot, bald, humpbacked giant, swinging Tedros upside down by his bootstrap. The giant's flesh peeled off his skull, covered in zigzagged stitches, as he probed and pinched Tedros' muscles. "Ain't seen such firm meat since young Jack came up my beanstalk."

Agatha's heart rose into her throat. Red Riding Hood's dead wolf . . . Jack's dead giant . . . *alive?* Tedros met her eyes, ashen and upside down, clearly petrified by the same question.

"I told you. School Master wants 'em conscious," the wolf groused.

The giant sighed miserably . . . then saw the wolf smirking.

"But that don't mean we can't break off a piece or two," the wolf said, gripping Agatha harder.

She and Tedros let out twin cries as the giant and wolf

raised them high in the air and slowly lowered their legs into their mouths like pork ribs—

"That would be a very poor decision," said an airy voice.

The wolf and giant both froze jaws over their prey, eyes flicking to the ninja on the ground. The wolf pulled Agatha out of his mouth and smiled at the masked stranger, prepared to delay a snack if it might result in a larger meal. "And why's that, oh Faceless One?"

"Because if you release them, I'll let you go on your way," said the ninja.

"And if we don't?" snorted the giant, mouth full of Tedros, shivering between the giant's teeth.

"Then you'll be woefully outnumbered," said the ninja.

"Strange...," the wolf replied, prowling towards the stranger, Agatha in hand. "Given your prince and princess are a bit *held up,* I see one of you and two of us." He loomed over the ninja in the moonlight. "Which means it's you that's outnumbered."

Slowly the ninja looked up. The black mask came off, revealing almond-shaped eyes, olive skin, and black hair flowing in the wind.

Princess Uma smiled. "Then you're not looking very closely."

She let out a piercing squeak through her teeth and a roar echoed from every side of the darkness, a thunder beneath their feet. For a moment, the wolf and giant spun dumbly, the roar crashing towards them north and south, east and west ... until they dropped their two prisoners like hot potatoes. From the ground, Agatha raised her glowing finger just in time to see a stampede of bulls leap over her body and ram into the wolf and giant like balls to bowling pins. Horses and bears sprang over Tedros, tearing into the monsters with their hooves and claws. By the time Agatha and Tedros wobbled to their feet, their gold glows illuminating the scene, the wolf and giant were howling for mercy atop the beastly tide bucking them into the darkness. Princess Uma whistled a cheery thank-you and her animal army echoed with singsong growls. Soon their shadows faded and the wolf and giant were gone.

Agatha whirled to Princess Uma, a teacher at the School for Good who she'd once mocked as helpless and passive and weak, but who had just saved her and Tedros' lives. "I thought the princes killed you!" Agatha cried. "Hester said Dean Sader left you to die in the Woods. We all thought you were dead—"

"A professor of Animal Communication unable to survive in the Woods?" Princess Uma swished her finger and turned her black robes to pink, a silver swan crest stitched over the heart. "Even your mother had more faith in me and we've never met."

"You . . . you know my mother?" Agatha asked. *Knew*, a voice corrected. Agatha battled a fresh wave of nausea. She couldn't bring herself to say it.

"Only through her messages to the League," Uma replied.

"League? What League?" Tedros broke in.

"The League of Thirteen, of course," said Uma, unhelpfully. "Her last message to us made three things very clear:

That we protect your lives. That we get you to Sophie. And that we'd find you right *here*."

Tedros and Agatha followed their teacher's eyes down to the empty grave that once held Sophie's mother. . . . Only the headstone was different now. Instead of a tall rectangle, it was a murky oval, with a long crack down the middle, carved with thick black letters.

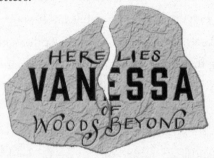

"Vanessa was Sophie's mother. 'Butterfly,' I think the name means," remembered Tedros, studying the stone. "Sophie told me one night when she was Filip."

"Sophie never told me her mother's name," Agatha said, hurt.

"Perhaps because you never asked," said Tedros. His face changed. "Wait a second. Her name wasn't *on* the grave before. And look, it doesn't say *'Loving Wife and Mother'* like it used to." He squinted at the shadows of crooked slabs around them. "We're in the same graveyard, in the exact same spot. Doesn't make any sense. A gravestone can't just change—"

"Unless you're not in the same graveyard at all," Princess Uma said behind them.

Agatha and Tedros spun to see their teacher shoot a bolt

of white glow into the sky. From every direction, thousands of fireflies whizzed to it like a signal, swarming over the Evers' heads and detonating neon-green wings into a giant light cloud, illuminating a sprawling landscape in every direction. Prince and princess gazed out at a vast cemetery, with thousands and thousands of gravestones sloping over steep, barren hills. For a moment, Agatha thought Graves Hill had magically grown bigger. But it was what lay beyond the cemetery that made Agatha feel faint—a dark, endless gnarl of black trees, rearing high into the night like a primeval monster.

They weren't on Graves Hill.

They weren't in Gavaldon at all.

"We're in the Woods," Agatha rasped.

She was suddenly aware of the sea of dead bodies under her feet. In an instant, the images she'd been damming up broke through with a vengeance—guards, spears, her mother falling . . . Agatha buckled, about to retch—

Tedros' hand touched her arm. "I'm right here."

His voice brought her back to the moment. Agatha swallowed the acid taste in her mouth and uncurled to stand, clutching her prince by the shirt laces. She steadied her legs, trying to see a graveyard in front of her, just a graveyard and nothing more . . .

"Hold on. I've been here before," said Tedros, searching the landscape.

"Each Forest Group makes a trip first year to scavenge meerworms. No doubt Yuba accompanied you," Princess Uma replied.

"The Garden of Good and Evil," said Tedros. "That's what he called it. Every Ever or Never whose name makes it into a storybook is buried here."

Under the firefly cloud, he scanned thousands of coffins down one side of the hills, teeming with glittering gem-crusted memorials for pairs of Evers, united in life and now in death. "That's Ever Embankment, where the greatest heroes are," he said. "Except Dad, of course."

Agatha looked at her prince, waiting for him to go on, but he turned back to her. "We must have come out the other side of Vanessa's grave. One end is Gavaldon, the other end the Woods. It's the only explanation. But how would your mother have known the grave was a portal?"

Agatha thought of the black and white swans on the two graves flanking Sophie's mother's. "Even if she did know somehow, why would Sophie's mother's grave connect the two worlds?"

"You're asking the wrong questions, students."

Agatha and Tedros looked up at Princess Uma, studying them intently.

"You should be asking why her grave is *empty*."

Uma circled her finger at the sky and the firefly cloud swept over their heads, illuminating the slope Agatha and Tedros were standing on. A bank of cracked and moldy head-stones glowed in the alien green light, jutting from ragged black mounds.

"Necro Ridge," said Tedros. "It's where the worst villains are buried."

"Sophie's mother was a *Never?*" Agatha asked, disoriented.

"Not according to our findings. The League of Thirteen has no evidence of a Vanessa of Woods Beyond attending the School for Good and Evil, being mentioned in a fairy tale, or having her body buried here at all," said Uma, pocketing gooey gray meerworms off a tomb. "And yet, she has a grave amongst our most famous Nevers."

"You keep talking about this League," Tedros rankled. "I've never heard of them—"

"As you shouldn't," said Uma, even more unhelpfully than before. "Listen to me, Agatha. There are no words to ease the pain you're in right now. But your mother died before she could give the League the answers we needed. Think back. Do you have any idea why Vanessa's name is carved into a headstone on Necro Ridge? And where her body might be?"

"I don't see why we should help a League we know nothing about," Tedros grouched.

But Agatha's head was still swimming. Her own mother, Callis, had moved between the two worlds as a witch without anyone in Gavaldon knowing, including her own daughter. And yet, her mother fit all the traits of a Never—unmarried, mysterious, reclusive. . . . If anything, Agatha should have seen the clues. But *Sophie's* mother? Sophie had spoken only rapturously of her mother, doting on her wicked, unfaithful husband until her dying day. There was no hint of her being anything other than a radiant, loving caretaker and wife. So how could her name be on a villain's tomb? Agatha shook her head, at a dead end . . . until her eyes suddenly flared wide.

"The Crypt Keeper will know!"

Quickly she scoured the horizon for the blue-skinned, dreadlocked giant she'd learned about at school, responsible for digging and filling graves. "Hort said he buries everybody himself. Never lets anyone interfere. That's why Hort's dad's been waiting for a coffin all these years. So the Crypt Keeper has to know why Sophie's mother has a headstone here . . ." But the hills were deserted, except for a few hovering vultures nearby. She turned to Uma. "Where is h—"

Agatha stopped cold, seeing Uma's expression.

Slowly Agatha turned back to the vultures.

Lying on the ground beneath them was a massive, blue-skinned body crumpled in a spray of dirt. His bones were broken and his throat split open, the blood staining his neck long dried out. Agatha could see the whites of his wide-open eyes, as if the shock of dying paled to the shock of what killed him.

Agatha felt Tedros squeeze her hand with his sweaty palm, telling her she hadn't seen the worst of it. Dread growing, she tracked his gaze past the dead Crypt Keeper and across the 200 graves on Necro Ridge, marking the resting place of famous fairy-tale villains. But now Agatha saw why there were so many mounds of dirt, blacking out the grass. Every single one of the famous villains' tombs had been dug up, the insides of all of them . . .

"Empty," said Agatha. "The villains' graves are empty."

Legs shaky, Tedros gaped at the bodiless graves. "Red Riding Hood's wolf . . . Jack's giant . . . and a whole lot worse . . ."

Agatha whitened, remembering who the wolf said they worked for. "And they're all under the School Master's control."

Princess Uma came up behind them. "For hundreds of years, Evil lost every story because Good had love on its side. Love gave Good a power and purpose Evil couldn't match. But those happy endings held only as long as Evil wasn't able to love. Things have changed, students. The School Master has found someone who loves him and who he loves in return. He's proved Evil deserves a chance to rewrite its fairy tales. Now every old villain gets a new turn at their story. Every dead villain is reborn."

True love? The School Master? Agatha shook her head, trying to understand. How could anyone love *him*?

Suddenly Agatha noticed Vanessa's empty grave again and her heart seized. "Wait—Sophie's mother . . . body missing . . . means she's . . . she's—"

"She wasn't buried here, remember?" Uma said, cutting her off. "We don't even know if her body was buried at all. And yet, the Crypt Keeper saved this grave for Sophie's mother amongst the famous Nevers—the Crypt Keeper, who answers to no one but the Storian itself. *Why* he saved a villain's grave for her could be our greatest clue to understanding how the School Master came to choose his new queen."

Agatha felt a cold darkness rip through her stomach. She had a thousand questions: about her mother and her best friend's mother, about letters and Leagues, about empty graves and undead villains . . . but only one mattered.

"Queen?" she whispered, slowly looking up. "Who?"

Uma met her eyes. "Sophie took the School Master's ring. She is his true love."

Agatha couldn't speak.

"But . . . but we came to rescue her from him," Tedros said, stunned.

"And you *must*. But it will not be an easy task," said Uma. "Sophie's kiss may have brought him back to life—but it is his ring on her finger that makes the power of that kiss last. As long as Sophie wears his ring, the School Master remains immortal. And yet, there is a way to undo the kiss, children. A way to destroy the School Master once and for all. And it is our one and only hope." Her voice was fiery, urgent. "You must convince Sophie to *destroy* the School Master's ring by her own hand. Convince Sophie to destroy his ring and the School Master will be destroyed with it forever."

Agatha was still lost in a fog.

"But beware," Uma added. "While you seek your true ending to *The Tale of Sophie and Agatha*, the School Master seeks his too."

Tedros could see Agatha staring into space, no longer listening. "And what ending is that?" he asked.

Uma leaned in, her soft features hardening. "The wolf and giant were no accident. War is coming, Son of Arthur. As long as Sophie wears the School Master's ring, all of Good is in terrible danger, past and present, young and old. Either you and your princess bring Sophie back to Good . . . or Good as we know it will be wiped out forever. That is the ending he seeks."

Agatha's heartbeat swirled in her ears.

Once upon a time, she and Sophie had slain a deadly villain who'd torn them apart.

Now her best friend had given her heart to that villain.

"But he's Evil. She *knows* he's Evil . . . and Sophie isn't Evil anymore," Agatha breathed, looking up. "Why would she want to be with him?"

"For the same reason you and your prince want to be with each other." Uma gave her a wistful smile. "To be *happy*."

Agatha and Tedros watched the Princess circle her finger, extinguishing the fireflies, and hasten towards the dark Woods beyond the hills. "Quickly, Evers," she said, snatching a few more meerworms off a grave. "It's a two-day journey to school and we must get to Sophie before they find you."

Tedros frowned, lagging behind. "Before who finds us?"

"*Who?*" Uma glared back, incredulous. "Whoever else was in those *graves*."

6

A Forest No Longer Blue

Rafal never slept in his chamber, so when the pen finally began to write, in the first hours of dawn, it was Sophie who was there to see it.

She'd been ill for six nights, ever since she took his ring— so ill, with a scorching fever and bone-numbing chills that she'd yet to leave her bed. Curled up in blankets, she imagined Tedros and Agatha gallivanting about town, snacking on Battersby's cupcakes (*maybe he'll get fat*, she hoped) and watching the sunset by the lake (*maybe he'll drown*), while here she was cooped in a sooty tower, sniffling and shivering like a snotty Rapunzel, and no one liked Rapunzel because she was boring.

"You said—I

could—see the—school," she'd babbled to Rafal in a sweaty fit this morning. "I want to see—Hester—Anadil—"

"And infect them with whatever plague you're carrying?" he teased, wrapping her in a fresh blanket.

She'd have pressed her case, if only he hadn't been taking such good care of her. He barely left her side during the day: sponging her forehead, feeding her bone-marrow soup, bringing her baggy, black nightdresses that she could hibernate inside, and enduring her inane blathering about Tedros and Agatha and how little or much fun they must be having, depending on whether her jealousy was at a peak or a valley in any given moment. Soon Sophie began to dread the nights, when Rafal would go away, just as she once dreaded those first mornings when she was afraid he'd come. In her delirious haze, she began to crave the marble cradle of his arms . . . his fresh, teenage scent . . . his cold touch on her burning skin . . . his silvery voice pulling her out of nightmares . . .

"I bet you . . . made me sick . . . so I'd need you . . . ," Sophie slurred as he'd left.

The young School Master looked back and smiled.

As her fever deepened, Sophie's nightmares grew clearer. Tonight she'd been dreaming of a pitch-black tunnel with a halo of light at its end. Floating in the dark tunnel was a giant gold ring, lined with razor-sharp teeth, spinning in midair and blocking her path. As she moved towards it, the ring spun faster, until she could see her reflection in the mirrored blur of teeth. Only, as she drew towards the ring, Sophie realized the reflection wasn't hers at all. It was a face she'd never seen before—a strange man's, with wild brown hair, dark, leathery skin, and a fat, hooked nose. Confused, Sophie leaned in to see him . . . closer . . . closer . . . until the man lifted black, bloodshot eyes, with a dangerous grin—

Then he stabbed out his hands and slammed Sophie into the guillotine of teeth.

Sophie gasped awake, scared out of her wits—

She froze dead still. Someone was in the chamber. Scratching and rustling, like a black cat sharpening its nails.

Chest hammering, she squinted into the early morning. No one there. Slowly she turned her head and to her relief, saw it wasn't a person making the sounds, but a whirring gleam of steel. Still half-asleep, she first thought it a spindle, before she remembered spindles were for Sleeping Beauty, the lamest princess of all time and surely dead by now since she was old and old people die and Sophie wasn't old or dead . . . and well, that finally got her out of bed.

She had to blink a few times to make sure what she was seeing was indeed there: the Storian itself doing all that scratching and rustling—the pen that had dimmed the Endless Woods by refusing to write, now . . . *writing*.

But how? she thought. The Storian had been stalled over the last page of her and Agatha's storybook for weeks. It hadn't moved an inch when she took the School Master's ring. Which meant it wasn't *her* ending the pen had been doubting, but rather—

Sophie's heart skittered. *Impossible* . . .

Pulling her blankets around her, she tiptoed forward in her

saggy black nightdress, afraid the slightest sound might disrupt it. But as Sophie grew closer, she saw the pen wasn't writing at all, but chipping at her storybook like a bricklayer removing bricks, scraping off the last line, letter by letter, until *"THE END"* was fully gone. With a red-hot glow, the Storian twirled into the air, like a butterfly freed from its cocoon, and dove back down to the book, continuing the story right where it left off. The steel nib spilled ink onto brand-new pages, filled by dozens of flurried paintings Sophie could hardly follow: walls of emerald flames . . . guards in black masks . . . swan-marked tombs . . . a cadaverous wolf and giant . . . until swirls of forest green streaked across a blank sheet.

Two lean bodies came into view, framed by the high, twisting trees of the Woods. Sophie watched the pen fill in the blankness of their faces . . . a boy's slate-blue eyes and juicy lips . . . a girl's flat brows and sunken cheeks. . . . *It can't be*, she thought, waiting for the Storian to slash an errant line. But every stroke made the scene more and more real, as if birthed from her own memory, until Sophie was sure this was all still a dream, for the pen was drawing two people in the Woods— two people who *couldn't* be in the Woods, because they'd found a happy ending somewhere else. She pinched her arm hard, expecting to wake up in bed, but they only grew clearer: Agatha and Tedros, alive on the page, gazing at her with wide eyes, inviting her in.

They're . . . back? Sophie gasped, heart swelling. Jealousy and betrayal and pain broke away like a soft eggshell and a warm wave of hope flooded through her before she could keep it down. She caressed her two best friends, looking out of her storybook, and let herself feel what she'd been ashamed of all this time.

I miss you, Aggie.

I miss you, Teddy.

Tears rising, she imagined herself in the empty space on the page between them—

Until the Storian drew Agatha and Tedros' hands intertwined across the gap, the two Evers following a shadow into the darkness of the Woods.

Sophie studied their clasped fingers, no longer any room for her.

"They're coming for you," said a voice behind her.

Sophie turned to Rafal, gorgeously posed against the window like a teen rebel, clad in a lace-up black shirt and black leather pants. His ice-blue stare lingered on the storybook, but carried no surprise, as if he'd been waiting for the prince and princess to return.

"I told you it wasn't our ending the Storian questioned," he said. "Turns out your friends aren't happy without you. They think you need to be rescued from me. That your ending is with them."

Sophie looked back at the Storian, writing beneath the painting of Agatha and Tedros in fresh ink:

"Love wasn't enough for them anymore. They needed their best friend."

Sophie gaped at the storybook. Here she'd been, berating herself for thinking of Aggie and Tedros every spare second . . . when they'd been thinking of her too? She smiled at the thought, touched. Then her smile evaporated.

"How can three people have a happy ending?" Sophie asked.

Rafal watched her carefully. "If one person is happy alone, of course."

"While two get each other?" Sophie asked, frowning.

"Oh you'd get used to it. Watching them kiss by the fireplace . . . sitting alone during supper while they nuzzle each other . . . trailing behind them on garden strolls like a puppy on a leash . . . settling year by year into your role as the third wheel . . ." Rafal glided towards her, half of his face still in shadow. "Then again, you could always meet a boy in Camelot. Not much of a kingdom anymore, but plenty of peasant boys to choose from. Sunburnt cheeks, yellow teeth, chubby backsides, not a coin in their pockets. But a nice, normal boy and isn't that what matters?" He drew her into his arms. "A boy who lives with his old, wrinkled mother in her ramshackle house, raising goats and pigs. A boy who will give you an ordinary life, where you fry his meat and bathe old Mummy and raise sunburnt, chubby little sons . . ."

Sophie was tensing so much she couldn't breathe. "That will never happen," she whispered and her muscles relaxed in his grip.

"Didn't think so," Rafal whispered back. He touched her shoulder, his long, milky fingers tracing up her neck. Sophie's skin quivered. She'd never had a boy hold her that she hadn't manipulated. She'd never had a boy touch her that didn't mind the storms and rages of her heart. She'd never had a boy love her for everything she was, warts and all.

Sophie looked up and saw him in the light—pearly, angelic skin, powder-blue eyes, luscious pink mouth, like a young Jack Frost—so white-hot and handsome that she suddenly felt the uglier of the two. "You might like me now, but what happens when I get old?" she asked. "Will you still want me then?"

Rafal smiled. "My brother and I stayed young as long as we loved each other. When I broke our bond, I was destined to age and die like every other villain who proved they couldn't love. But your kiss restored my youth, Sophie. Your love will let me live forever, just like my brother's love once did. Just like my love once kept him alive too. Which means as long as you wear my ring, neither you nor I will ever grow old."

Sophie turned to him. "I'll live forever?"

Rafal pulled her in once more. "*We* will. Together."

Live forever? Sophie thought in a fog. Old but young . . . young but old . . . just like the beautiful boy holding her. What would it be like to love someone forever? Could love even last that long? She thought of Agatha on the lakeshore, vowing to be her friend forever . . . Tedros on a moonlit bridge, promising to be her prince forever . . . Agatha and Tedros kissing, swearing to each other . . . *"Forever . . ."*

Only Forever never seemed to last.

Sophie lay against Rafal's firm chest, studying the gold ring on his finger, matching the one on hers. All this time she'd been so hurt by her two best friends who deserted her, so sure they'd forgotten her and gone on to perfect happiness. Instead they'd come back to redo their Ever After, wanting *her*, needing *her* to be happy. Sophie waited to feel the same feeling, to choose her best friends even it meant she ended up alone . . .

But all Sophie could feel were the arms of a boy who'd stayed loyal to her from the beginning, a Forever that finally sounded like the truth.

She spun and kissed Rafal, his mouth cold against hers, holding it long and slow, waiting for something in her heart to stop her. Nothing did. As their lips parted, she saw the Storian conjure a new page, capturing their kiss in brilliant colors, before adding a closing line:

"But friendship wasn't enough for Sophie anymore. She needed love."

Sophie looked up at Rafal, her forehead beaded with sweat. He put his hand to it.

"Look at that. Fever's broken."

Together, they watched the sun slide out from behind a cloud, Sophie expecting its return to brilliant life . . . only to see the sun still yolky and anemic against a cold blue morning, even weaker than before. Only it wasn't just weaker, it was leaking small gobs of yellow light into the sky, *drip, drip, drip,* like an icicle in summer. Sophie stepped closer to the window ledge, eyes wide. There was no question about it.

The sun was melting.

She whirled to the School Master. "But you said if the Storian wrote—"

"A *new* story. And ours still needs an end," said Rafal soberly. "Our storybook can't close now that your friends have come back. Not as long as they have a new ending in mind. An ending where Good wins and Evil dies . . ."

He paused, locking into her emerald eyes.

"They're coming to kill me, Sophie."

Sophie held his stare, stunned, and looked down at Agatha and Tedros, on their way through the Woods to rescue her. In their version of the story, they would save her from an Evil School Master. But to Sophie, her Good friends were about to slay the only boy who'd ever loved her, so she could be a sidekick to someone else's Ever After.

Sidekick. That's the ending they thought she deserved.

Sophie burned, glaring at her gold ring. She was a *queen*.

"I won't let them hurt you," she seethed.

"You'd do that for me?" The School Master's boyish face contorted with emotion. "You'd fight your own friends?"

Sophie tensed. "F-f-fight Agatha and Ted—? But I thought—"

"That they'll leave us in peace and go on their way if you tell them to?" Rafal asked sweetly.

"But I can't fight *her*. Surely there's another way—" Sophie pressed.

His eyes hardened. "*War* is the only way."

Sophie bristled at the change in his tone. But she knew he was right. After the young School Master nearly killed Tedros with Tedros' own sword, the prince was coming for his blood, and Agatha would be behind him. War was on the horizon and Sophie had to take a side.

Sophie thought of all the times Agatha had allied with Tedros against her: during the Circus of Talents and Evil Ball, then in her secret plan to kiss Tedros and banish her home during the Boy-Girl War. Sophie's blood simmered to a boil. Agatha had even believed she was turning into a witch in the Blue Forest, believing *Tedros* over her, when it was Dean Sader's magic all along. *"I'm not this!"* she'd cried, begging her friend to see the truth. But Agatha had stayed firmly by her prince's side.

Sophie too had a side to take—even if it meant fighting her best friend. Just like Agatha would protect her prince, she would protect her one true love.

"This is it, isn't it?" she whispered, watching the melting sun. "Either they die . . . or we do. Good versus Evil. That's the way all fairy tales end."

She saw Rafal's chest rise on a breath, as if at last they were on the same page. "Your friends think they can stop our book from closing, my love," he said, sweet once again. "They think they can stop the future. But they're too late."

He watched the fading sun, as if studying an hourglass. "The war against Good has already begun."

Sophie saw him look back at her with a snakelike grin and she began to sense there was more to his return than kisses and rings. "But Good always wins in the end—" she started, only to see the School Master grinning wider.

"You've forgotten the one thing I have on my side that they no longer do." Rafal moved towards her, slowly, smoothly . . . "*You*."

Sophie met his gaze, breathless.

"Come my queen," he said, fingers slipping into hers. "Your kingdom awaits."

Sophie's heart pumped faster. *Kingdom*. . . . Once upon a time, there was a beautiful little girl in a pink princess dress, waiting by her window to be kidnapped, convinced that one day she'd be the ruler of a faraway land . . .

She looked up at Rafal, the old glint back in her eye. "So much for Camelot."

Sophie smiled, her ring brushing his, and she followed her love hand in hand to fight for their happy ending—just like a prince and princess on the page she'd left behind.

"Shouldn't I change first? I can't go gadding about in *this*," Sophie huffed, trying to pin down her nightdress, battered by the wind.

Her glass slippers wobbled on the window ledge, sending silver pebbles cascading into the abyss of green fog. She wrenched back against the tower wall, clutching Rafal's bicep. They were so high in the sky she couldn't see the ground. "Surely there are stairs we can take. Only a half-wit would build a tower without stairs or a rope or a suitable fire escape—"

"Do you trust me?"

Sophie looked into Rafal's eyes, hot with adrenaline, not a trace of fear in them.

"Yes," Sophie whispered.

"Then don't let go." He seized her by the waist and dove off the tower.

Green mist gobbled them as they plunged at bullet speed into arctic cold. Any instinct for Sophie to scream vanished because of how tightly Rafal held her, muscles sealing her to his chest. Safe in his arms, she let herself go, gasping as Rafal slip-turned like a hawk with dangerous speed, their entwined limbs spinning towards earth. With a full somersault, he rocketed back up and Sophie howled with abandon, closing her eyes and holding out her arms against him like wings. They soared in and out of shadows, amber sunrays flickering on her eyelids, the taste of clouds in her mouth. If only Agatha could see her now, she thought—happy, in love, and recklessly alive, like a princess riding a dragon instead of fighting it. Rafal shot across the bay like a fireball and she pressed her cheek into his neck, electrified by his skin on hers, his steaming breaths faster and faster, his hands tighter and tighter . . . until his feet gently touched down without a sound and Sophie felt herself suspended in space like the Storian over her book.

She nestled into him, scarlet and hot.

"Do it again," she whispered.

Rafal chuckled, touching her face, and slowly Sophie opened her eyes to the world.

The first thing she noticed is that the Blue Forest was no longer blue.

She pulled away from Rafal, windswept and dizzy, and

staggered forward from the tower, anchored in the middle of the forest.

The Blue Willows had rotted to black husks. The once-weatherproof blue grass was now urine yellow, cracking and breaking under her feet. Bracing from the wintry breeze, Sophie crawled through diseased, fallen trunks in the Turquoise Thicket, her nightgown catching on cancerous fungus and mold. Worst of all was the stench: an acrid, acid reek that made her eyes water and grew stronger the deeper she went into the Forest. By the time she reached the Tulip Garden, a stinking ashpit of amber and brown, she'd covered her face with both hands, barely able to stand straight. She looked back for Rafal, but couldn't see him.

Sophie gasped a shallow breath and plowed forward. She had to get out of here.

She shambled into the Fernfield, desperate to find the North Gates and stopped short. The ferns, once thigh-high with lush, cobalt fronds, was a wasteland of dead animals, swarming with roaches and flies. Under the jaundiced sun, carcasses of emaciated rabbits, storks, squirrels, and deer littered the dirt in front of the sealed gates, as if they'd all tried to flee and failed.

Then she heard a familiar hissing.

She raised her eyes to dozens of black spiricks, coiled around the gates, flicking red tongues. Sophie shrank from the flat-headed snakes with deadly barbs through every scale, that once prevented anything from getting into the School for Boys, and now prevented all the animals from getting out. Sophie slowly looked up at the School Master's tower in the distance, looming over the Blue Forest like a landmark in a demented park.

Sophie's heart sagged. The Blue Forest had once been the school's kitschy backyard, a safeguarded replica of the deadly Woods. She smiled, reliving her liveliest moments here: running circles around a rabid stymph in the Blueberry Fields while Agatha berated her; seducing Tedros in the Thicket with couture Evil uniforms; her heart pattering as the prince leaned in to kiss her over the Blue Brook. . . . Then her smile slowly dissipated as other moments from the Forest came back too. Tedros rejecting her in the Shrubs when she didn't save him in a Trial; Tedros in the Blue Willows, looking so betrayed as she reverted from Filip's body; Agatha and Tedros recoiling from her in the Pine Glen, before they'd tried to send her home. . . . Soon the bad memories overwhelmed the good and as Sophie looked up at the Forest, it turned a shade blacker and bleaker before her eyes.

"It likes you," Rafal drolled, coming up behind her.

Sophie spun. "What? *I* did that?"

"You did all of this," he said, scanning the whole dead Forest. "You and me together."

"I-I-I don't understand," Sophie stammered. "I don't want the Forest like this—"

"It doesn't matter what you *think* you want. It only matters what's truly inside you," said Rafal. "The Schools mirror back their Masters' souls, as does the Storian they both protect. When my brother ruled with me, the castles reflected the balance between us: one light for Good, one dark for Evil. Last year, with Evelyn Sader and Tedros at war, the castles reflected the balance between Boys and Girls." He caressed Sophie's ring. "But now with you by my side, there's a *new* balance . . . beyond Good and Evil . . . beyond Boys and Girls . . ."

Sophie tracked his gaze up to the two black castles lording over the Forest, tipped with alien-green fog. At first glance, both castles appeared indistinguishable . . . but then Sophie peered closer. The old Evil castle had turned to jagged stone, resembling the jaws of a monster, while the once bloodred creepers coiling its three towers were the same eerie green as the fog. The old Good castle was black too, circled with the same green mist, but its four towers had sharpened turrets and smooth, shiny walls that looked wet, as if the entire school was made out of polished obsidian. Linked by the foggy bridge in the distance, the two schools seemed like a Before and After: one castle a fiendish, saw-toothed crumble; one castle a cold, sleek fortress.

Confused, Sophie inched closer towards the Forest gates, trying to get a better view of the schools . . . when the spiricks' eyes all darted to her. Sophie stumbled back, expecting them to spit their noxious poison—instead, they all bowed their heads like slaves and the golden gates parted, offering a clear path into the Clearing.

Spooked, Sophie scampered out of the Forest. Thankfully there were no surprises in the Clearing. Just as before, there were two Tunnels of Trees diverging out of the field, one into each castle. During the war between Boys and Girls, the tunnels had been sealed with giant rocks, but now they were wide open like they were first year. Only as Sophie drew closer, she saw that both tunnels were labeled with wooden boards, nailed over the entrances. Crooked black letters slashed across each one.

The tunnel leading into the jagged, pockmarked castle said:

OLD

The tunnel leading into the smooth, shiny castle said:

NEW

A hand took hers and Sophie jumped. She looked up at Rafal, grinning sharp teeth.

"A time-tested Master. A fresh, young queen," he said. "And a School for Evil *reborn*."

Sophie smiled weakly, shoving down the sinking feeling in her stomach.

He led her into the tunnel marked NEW and Sophie hurried to catch up, reminding herself that she'd finally found love, *real* love, and it was worth anything she had to do to keep it.

7

Evil Is the New Good

The Tunnel of Trees led straight to the Good castle doors, lit by candles usually visible by now through the branches. But the deeper Sophie went, the darker the tunnel became, a sharp clacking sound amplifying ahead, like an aggressive clock. Uneasy, she took Rafal's hand.

"I didn't expect Dean Sader to make a holy mess of things," he sighed. "I thought that by putting a piece of my soul into Evelyn, I'd have some control over her in the event of my death—"

Sophie could hear the sounds growing louder. *Click clack. Click clack. Click clack.*

"From within Evelyn's body, I had enough control to ensure she brought you back to school . . . and, one day, to me," he continued. "And yet, I couldn't control *all* of her. That crude business of slaveboys and worlds without princes, and girls good, boys bad . . . She was always resentful of her brother's gifts and I'm afraid my students had to suffer for it."

Sophie could hardly hear him over the clacking, as she glimpsed frosted doors ahead, black instead of the old white, the once blue torch flames above it now green.

"She left behind an ugly war, with Boys and Girls hell-bent on destroying each other," he was saying, "but in the end, it wasn't hard to make them lay down their arms. After all, no matter how divided they'd become, now they have something even stronger uniting them . . ."

He stopped at the doors with a dashing grin. *"Me."*

Sophie stared at him. Confused, she flung open the doors—

A crush of bodies nearly flattened her and she hugged a wall for dear life.

"Welcome to the School for *New* Evil," said Rafal.

In a black-marble foyer, boys and girls in crisp black uniforms and black berets marched by in perfect lines. Chins up, chests out, they stomped with steely stares, *right-left, right-left*, past the four glass staircases, now hued green. The boys were in belted leather breeches, half-sleeved black shirts with starched collars, narrow green ties, and thick-heeled boots, while the girls wore skin-hugging black pinafores over plunging green blouses, knee-high socks, and flat black slippers. Two of the girls marched in front of Sophie: green-skinned Mona and one-eyed, bald Arachne, tight lipped and eyes fixed ahead. Ravan was right behind them, his oily face scrubbed clean, his once long, matted hair clipped short and neat. Impish Vex tramped next to him, head shaved, spine straight, subtly picking at breeches wedged up his bottom.

Sophie stiffened in shock. Nevers chic . . . clean . . . in straight lines? She'd once despised the villains for their poor appearance, but now it was Sophie who felt embarrassed by her own unwashed cheeks and dumpy black nightgown. She tried to catch more Nevers' faces beneath their berets, but the foyer was dark, holding them in shadow. The only lights seemed to come from fleeting flashes of green glow, dispersed over the army in sync with the march, as if there was an invisible swarm of fireflies keeping time.

Then Sophie noticed another haze of green light over the Legends Obelisk, centered between the four staircases, crammed with student portraits. Looking for the source, she scanned up the high stained glass windows (once haloed visions of a white swan, now replaced with a glaring black swan) to the domed sunroof, sealed over with deadly stalactites, glowing snake-green like a malevolent chandelier. As Sophie's gaze roamed to the buffed staircases, shiny onyx arches, and ruthless marchers, she saw that Good's home and all that came with it—elegance, discipline, style—had been usurped entirely by Evil.

And yet, watching this parade, Sophie felt her stomach relax, for there wasn't anything the least bit sinister about Evil wanting to be "New" or adding a dash of color or showing off a bit of thigh. Indeed, she'd held lunchtime rallies her first year, pleading for all three—

Suddenly, beneath the stalactites, she caught sight of another face in the Never army: a scared-looking boy with a big chest and hairy arms. Chaddick's gray eyes met Sophie's, just as shocked to see her as she was to see him. Out of the corner of his lips he mouthed the word "Help"—before a burst of green firefly lights detonated near him, and he whipped his gaze forward, wincing with pain.

Flummoxed, Sophie slid along the wall, trying to catch a last look as he vanished into the wings. Chaddick? Good's most loyal sidekick? Why was he with *Nevers*?

But from her new vantage point, Sophie saw more Evers in black uniforms spliced into the march: luscious, caramel-skinned Reena . . . tall, willowy Giselle . . . sleek dark-skinned Nicholas . . . redheaded, freckled Millicent . . . baby-faced Hiro . . . all trembly and tense as fireflies popped off around them like warning shots.

Dread rising, Sophie turned back to the Legends Obelisk. The Evers' portraits, once smiling and kind, were painted with baleful scowls and sneers, matching the Nevers' frames, now jammed onto the same column.

"Evers learning . . . *Evil*?" Sophie breathed, looking up at Rafal.

"Evers and Nevers both," the young School Master corrected. "After two years of war, a unified school, protecting the future of Evil." He surveyed his troops. "The students had to adjust to all being in the same castle, of course. More of them per room, more competition in classes . . . but if anyone has any complaints, *I* haven't heard them."

Sophie squinted out the window, remembering the other tree tunnel. "But what's in the 'Old' school?"

Rafal eyed the rotted towers across Halfway Bridge. "If the School for New will write Evil's future, then the School for Old rewrites its past . . ." His pupils shot to Sophie lizard quick. "But you are not to step foot in the School for Old. It is *forbidden* to all students and to you. Understand?" He stared her down, looking like a headmaster despite his youth.

Sophie nodded, startled.

"Your responsibilities are here and only here," he commanded, "ensuring your young colleagues adjust to their new school. With the volatility of the past two years, all students will be held to—how should I put it—a *higher* standard than before."

"But you told us all souls are born Good *or* Evil," Sophie prodded, "that they can't be changed—"

"And yet, a wise girl taught me it isn't who you are that matters, it's what you *do*. And now all of them will *do* Evil." His gaze slid past her. "Just like their new queen."

Sophie followed his sightline to the foyer's wall murals, all featuring her and the young School Master kissing against celestial night skies. They were both in black leather, wearing jagged metal crowns, as fiery stars cast halos over their heads. In each mural, a single green letter was superimposed on their embracing bodies. Once spelling out G-O-O-D, the wall paintings now spelled . . . E-V-I-L.

As students kept filing past, Sophie turned full circle,

soaking in her painted image on every wall: her golden hair fanned beneath a spiked queen's crown; her lips pressed against her true love's, a boy so smoldering, so intense, so *unnerving* that he'd have made Snow White, Cinderella, and Sleeping Beauty dump their princes at first sight. All her life, she'd devoured storybooks, desperate to have her own face big enough someday for the world to worship . . . to have an Ever After that would make girls writhe with jealousy. . . . And now Sophie realized she'd won. She was the face of a school. The face of a generation. The face of the *future*. Sophie couldn't stop an imperious grin, feeling more and more like her old self.

"For hundreds of years, Readers like you wanted to be Good because Good always wins. But our story will change all that," said Rafal, pulling her into him. "Evil is the new Good."

Sophie felt so safe in his arms that his words washed over her. "Evil is the new Good," she burbled, cuddling into him . . . until she saw sweet, cherubic Kiko in line, sniffling back tears, an elaborate black veil over her face, as if on her way to a funeral. "But suppose they can't be Evil?" Sophie said guiltily, pulling away.

"Every student has a choice: join Evil or *die*," he snarled, simmering with hot-blooded youth. "And it is not enough to join Evil. They must excel at it."

He was looking at the green glass staircases at the corners of the room, the banisters no longer carved with the four values of Good. Instead each staircase had a new inscription:

LEADERS
HENCHMEN
ANIMALS
PLANTS

"Third year is tracking year," Rafal said. "We'll house students by rankings, as they prepare to enter their new lives beyond graduation. And if that isn't enough incentive to perform . . . let's just say I do better than *butterflies*."

With a swish of his finger, he brightened the glow of the chandelier and now Sophie saw the fireflies weren't fireflies at all. Floating over the students was a cloud of black-winged fairies, armed with whippy green stingers and jaws of black shark teeth. If any Ever or Never lagged in line or glanced in Sophie's direction, the fairies stung them with a blast of angry light, jabbing and biting them on until the last of the terrified students disappeared into the wings. As the fairies whizzed after them, Sophie caught a glimpse of their faces—hideously peeling skin, serrated stitches, and eyes cloud-white like zombies. Sophie recoiled in surprise, only to see one fairy in the group stop and peer straight at her: a boy fairy she knew with sunken cheeks and short, wispy wings.

Bane. The Good fairy she'd killed first year.

Except now Bane was right here in front of her, zombified and Evil, glowering back at his killer.

Sophie plastered against the wall, looking for somewhere to hide, but it was too late. Bane ripped towards her with a violent hiss, his knife-edged teeth gleaming—

The School Master shot him with white sparks, sending

Bane sputtering out of the foyer like a popped balloon.

Cowering with relief, Sophie looked up at Rafal. "Dead f-f-fairies . . . *undead?*"

"Once upon a time, Nevers who failed at being Evil were turned into slaves for Good. Now they have a second chance to prove their love of Evil and their loyalty to me." His eyes seared into hers. "Just like you." He walked away, humming a soft tune. "Come, my love. There's more to see."

Sophie didn't follow, her breath stoppered.

Don't go, whispered a soft voice inside her.

Agatha's voice.

This isn't you, Sophie.

This isn't real love.

Sophie felt her back sweating, the gold ring on her finger suddenly scalding hot.

He's using you.

Light flooded through her and Sophie couldn't breathe. She closed her eyes, the ring boiling on her skin as if about to eat through her—as if she had to destroy it right *now*—

"Sophie."

Her lids opened.

"No one loves you but me," said Rafal, his voice like a dagger. "No one will *ever* love you but me."

Sophie stared into his pupils and saw her own reflection. The ring went cold on her finger. Agatha's voice quieted inside of her.

Rafal took her by the waist and this time, Sophie didn't resist. As he guided her ahead towards the Leaders staircase, she heard his voice echoing inside her . . . *No one but me* . . . echoing deeper, echoing deeper, like a pebble down a well until it settled at the bottom, an undeniable truth. Looking up at Rafal, she nestled tighter into his side, afraid to let him go—

She stopped cold.

A raven-haired boy was standing ahead, at the edge of the foyer. Tight chest and stomach muscles pressed against his black uniform shirt, and his breeches revealed smooth, chiseled calves. His dark bangs draped over his forehead and his long nose was the only feature out of proportion on his small, heart-shaped face. Sophie drew a breath, taken by his cool, erect stance, and for a moment she thought him the strange man from her dream. But he was too young, clearly a student. Only she didn't recognize him from either school—

But then Sophie saw his eyes.

Scorching her with hate.

His beady, weaselly eyes.

"Shouldn't you be somewhere, Hort?" the School Master said, glowering at him.

Hort's glare slashed deeper into Sophie, honing in on her hand in Rafal's, before he finally glanced up. "I was throwing hammers in the gym, Master," he said, flat and hard. "Earned extra time."

"Right. You've been racking up the first ranks, I hear," said the School Master, pulling Sophie tighter and making sure Hort saw it. "Keep up the good work, Captain."

Hort gave Sophie a last deadly look before he walked into the wings.

Sophie didn't move, her heart thundering. First ranks? . . . gym? . . . Captain? *Hort?*

"Shall we?"

She looked up at Rafal, who was staring blackly at where Hort had just been.

"I don't want you to miss your first class," he said, slipping a small scroll of paper into her hand, before he glided up the stairs in front of her.

Sophie lagged behind, still dazed by Hort's reappearance and the weird looks between him and Rafal—

Then her eyes bulged wide.

"My first *what?*"

"Class?" Sophie fluttered after the School Master, frantically scanning the parchment. "Advanced Uglification . . . Advanced Henchmen Training—this is a *schedule*! You said I was a queen! A queen doesn't go to *class*—"

"A queen has responsibilities," said Rafal, calmly stepping off the first-floor landing.

"Oh I'm sorry, did Cinderella go to class for her happy ending? Did Snow White find true love and then go do homework?" Sophie squawked. "A queen's life should be a cornucopia of servant briefings, bodice fittings, court meetings, caviar tastings, attaché dinners, ball planning, and sea-salt massages by scantily clad boys. Not a return to plebeian students and insipid class—"

Sophie stopped short, noticing her surroundings. The entrance hallway to sea-themed Honor Tower, whose walls and ceiling once mimicked a princely blue tidal wave, now had its surging waters painted the same slime green as the fog tipping the two castles. For a moment, she was confused by the change, until she looked out a porthole window and saw Halfway Bay in the melted sunlight. For the first time in two years, there was no dividing line between the waters, no halves to the bay at all. Its entire body was the same slime green as the painted tides on the walls around her.

"One dip and it'll rip the flesh right off your bones," said Rafal, posed against a column. "Good deterrent against anyone who might try to swim into the school or swim . . . *out.*"

Sophie heard the warning in his voice, for she'd tried to escape through the bay each of the past two years. Clearly Rafal was still testing her new allegiance to him. *Where had the crogs gone?* she distracted herself, searching for the stymph-eating white crocodiles that once protected the moat. Then she glimpsed a flesh-eaten, disembodied snout floating along the bright green surface. The crogs had lasted about as long as the stymphs.

Sophie followed Rafal across the seashell floor, now artistically smattered with bloody splashes, while an old statue of a smiling, barechested merman, trident on his lap, had been rechiseled with a gnashed scowl, curled fists, and a trident poised to kill. Turning the corner, Sophie took in epic murals along the walls, once visions of Good's most honorable victories, now flaunting different endings: a wolf biting into Red Riding Hood's neck . . . a giant atop a beanstalk snapping Jack like a twig . . . Snow White and her dwarves facedown in blood . . . Captain Hook plunging his hook into Peter Pan's heart . . .

Sophie knew she should be sickened by what she was

seeing, but instead felt a mutinous thrill at the sight of Evil winning so defiantly, so matter-of-factly, as if Good was never supposed to win at all. How could she not take secret pleasure in the thought? Her whole life she'd tried to be Good. She'd tried to join their school where she thought she belonged. Only Good had rejected her, again and again until here she was, Queen of Evil . . . queen of the same school she once thought a mistake. Soaking in the last mural—Sleeping Beauty and her prince, lashed to a spinning wheel, set aflame by a black-caped witch—Sophie started to feel disoriented, as if she couldn't remember the *real* endings anymore.

What if I'd learned these stories as a child? Would I have ever wanted to be Good?

Doesn't matter, Sophie thought, breaking from her trance. "An inspired bit of redecorating, Rafal. But it still doesn't make any of it true."

"Says who?" he called back.

Sophie frowned at the murals. "Says the storybooks, obviously. I can paint an ending where I bask on a tropical island, serviced by well-muscled slaves. But it's just a fantasy. All of these are fantasies. They don't mean anything. The real endings already happened."

Rafal turned. "And what about your kiss with Agatha? Or Agatha's kiss with Tedros? Weren't those *real* endings too? And yet here we are, back in your story, as if those endings never happened. Endings can change, my queen."

He gazed out a window at the School for Old. "And change they *must*."

Sophie could have sworn she heard a roar from deep within the Old castle, like a monster breaking out of its cage.

"The Deans are eager to meet you," he said, heading towards the rear staircase. "They'll take you to your class."

Sophie didn't move, hands on hips. "You said it yourself. Agatha and Tedros are on their way to kill you. I can't be in *class*! I have to protect you . . . I'll fight with you—"

"And who do you think will be your army against Agatha and Tedros, if not your class?" he said, not looking back.

"What? No one at this school even likes me—they'll never listen to me—"

"On the contrary, they have to listen to you," Rafal said, fading up the stairs.

Standing alone in the hallway, Sophie watched his shadow spiral up the banister. She groaned, glancing quickly at her schedule.

Session	*Faculty*
1: ADVANCED UGLIFICATION	Prof. Bilious Manley
2: ADVANCED HENCHMAN TRAINING	Castor
3: ADVANCED CURSES & DEATH TRAPS	Queen Sophie
4: ADVANCED HISTORY OF VILLAINY	School Master
5: LUNCH	
6: ADVANCED SPECIAL TALENTS	Prof. Sheeba Sheeks
7: WOODS TRAINING	Lord Aric

Sophie snorted, confused. "There's a mistake on here—has my name for—"

"*Your class.*"

Your class.

No.

Not possible.

Sophie dropped the schedule like a stone.

"I'm a *teacher*?"

8

When Good Rescues Go Bad

The path through webbed trees was so narrow and dark that the three Evers had to travel one behind the other, like ducks out of a pond. While Tedros fixed his gold fingerglow on Princess Uma ahead, he kept peeking back at Agatha, whose gold fingerglow was pinned on him.

"Stop checking on me," Agatha finally snapped.

"Oh, no, it's just . . . I didn't remember our glows matching so much," Tedros fumbled and quickly turned around.

Agatha didn't answer. For one thing, she was sick of his worried glances and sugar-sweet conversation, as if she was about to have a nervous breakdown or drown herself in the nearest pond. For another, she didn't feel like talking to anyone (least of all about inane color symmetries), anxious the conversation might drift back to her mother. But most of all, she was preoccupied with wresting Sophie away from the School Master, rehearsing again and again what she'd say to her best friend when they finally made it to school.

Tell her how much you miss her . . . or should I apologize first? . . . How do you apologize for ruining someone's life? "Sorry I tried to banish you forever" . . . "Sorry I thought you were a witch" . . . "Sorry I never asked your mother's name and I'm a crap friend . . ."

Agatha gulped. *Oh, why drudge up the past? Just get her to destroy the ring and then focus on the future. The three of us at Camelot—a clean slate—*

Agatha smiled, trying to be confident . . . and slowly deflated.

Apologize first.

Agatha tensed again. *But suppose she won't destroy the ring?* she thought, remembering how handsome the young School Master was. *She thinks he's her true love,* Uma had said, and Agatha knew from experience that Sophie wasn't one to give up on love once she thought she'd found it. *What if she's happy without me? What if she doesn't want me anymore?*

"I'll rescue Sophie when we find her," Tedros broke in, as if he'd decoded her silence. "Not sure she'll want you there, to be honest. Let me talk to her alone."

Agatha looked up, aghast.

"For one thing, you've been through enough already, my love," her prince added, hopping over a log. "Second, you tend to faint at crucial moments. And third, Sophie and I have our own special bond."

Agatha followed him, stumbling over the log. "First of all, I'm *fine*. Second, I fainted once—"

"Twice: waltz class and by the lake—"

"And third, she's *my* best friend—I'll rescue her—"

"Look, it's best if I do it," Tedros said, walking faster. "You two seem to have serious communication issues."

"And you two *don't*?" Agatha said, chasing him.

"All you and Sophie ever do is fight—"

"Because it always involves *you*!"

"Well, without you, she and I get along just swell," puffed Tedros.

"When have you two even had a conversation?" said Agatha.

"We were roommates last year—"

"When she was a *boy*!"

"What does that have to do with anything—"

"A boy you tried to *kiss*!"

Tedros whirled, beet red. "*So?* You're allowed to kiss her and I'm not?"

"Not when she's a boy!" Agatha barked.

"You kissed her when she was a *girl*!" roared Tedros—

"I like you two better when you're quiet," Princess Uma hissed, glaring from the path.

Tedros mumbled something about "females" and "hypocrites" and stamped ahead, no longer checking back on his princess.

For the next three hours, Uma, Tedros, and Agatha slogged and shivered single file through the Endless Woods, stopping only when Agatha collided with a tree (often) or Tedros needed to pee (even more often). ("What's wrong with you?!" Agatha growled. "It's cold!" Tedros yelled.) Agatha tried to ask her teacher about her mother's past—had Callis been in a storybook? How did she end up in Gavaldon?—but Uma said there'd be time for questions once they made it to League Headquarters.

"League Headquarters?" frowned Tedros. "I thought we were going to school—"

"And who do you think will get you *into* school?" said Uma. "The School Master has turned the castles into a fortress of Evil. Try and enter alone and you will be dead before you breach the gates. Your mother knew the League of Thirteen is your *only* hope to get to Sophie alive." Uma glanced worriedly at the sun. "Besides, you'll be safe at Headquarters tonight. Won't last a minute in the Woods after dark on your own."

"Have you seen any other undead villains? Besides the wolf and giant?" Agatha said, trying to keep their teacher talking.

"Not yet." Uma looked back at her. "Another reason to be *quiet.*"

Dawn blossomed to a crisp, windy morning, and the students no longer needed their fingerglows to see. As Agatha and Tedros moved deeper into the Woods, huddled in their cloaks, Agatha noticed an eerie green haze thicken the air, sour smelling and cold. It reminded her of the jellied mildew on her front porch, where Reaper collected his headless birds. Her stomach turned, thinking of her bald little cat, all alone in her house. She wrenched her focus back to the present, to the tree branches passing over her head, spindly and jointed . . . like a skeleton's hands . . . ticking on her mother's clock . . .

Agatha's gut twisted deeper.

"When will it w-w-warm up?" Tedros asked, teeth chattering. "Sun's acting like it's half asleep."

Indeed, Agatha had been waiting for the sun to brighten too, but with each hour, it stayed sickly pale, even as it rose higher in the sky. She began to notice cankered tree trunks and fragile ferns, a skeletal chipmunk quailed in mulch, and the corpses of a few malnourished crows. Agatha fingered a single flowering plum, quivering on a bare tree; it withered under her fingers and rotted to black.

"Agatha, look," Tedros said.

She followed his eyes to a titanic wreckage of vines, trees, and glass thirty yards off the path, glittering in sun mist like an imploded greenhouse. Tedros deviated off the trail to get a closer look, Agatha tailing behind him. As she neared the colossal ruins, at least fifteen feet high, she glimpsed petals and leaves flaking off the tree trunks, catching the light like new blossoms in spring. But drawing closer, Agatha saw all these petals and leaves were dead, sprinkling the dirt between decaying blue frogs. Agatha ran her hands along one of the fallen trunks, her fingers tracing letters etched into the wood: HIBISCUS LINE.

"It's a Flowerground train," said Tedros, inspecting a dead vine. "Whole Forest seems to be dying. Maybe the sun's too weak to keep any of the plants alive?"

Agatha didn't answer, still riled up from their earlier spat.

"But why would the sun be any weaker than before?" Tedros prodded.

Silence hung awkwardly.

They both mumbled about getting on and spun from each other, as if to follow Princess Uma, but she was far ahead on the path, a miniature shadow, and they had to run after her when they realized she wasn't going to stop.

They followed her through Willow Walk, Thicket Tumble, and Pumpkin Point, as rickety wooden signs named these parts, which all mirrored portions of the Blue Forest back at school, only bigger and drearier. Occasionally Uma stopped to let them eat a few sludgy meerworms from her pockets (Uma herself abstained, saying it'd be rude to eat her "friends") or to ask a sparrow or chipmunk to guide them to the nearest pond, where they'd inhale palmfuls of brackish water. Still, for all the menace of the Woods, they didn't come across anything that resembled a human being, let alone a zombie villain, and Agatha started to wonder if she'd imagined everything that had happened on Necro Ridge.

As if reflecting her easing mind, the tangled forest opened up the farther they went, with more air between trees and the thorny brush turning into a green carpet of grass, though Agatha could see slivers of yellow starting to creep in. When they passed a gilded plaque that said Foxwood, Uma's shoulders noticeably relaxed, and soon the dirt path widened so that they could all walk together, breathing in clearer air and a tangibly safe feeling, as if they'd entered a protected realm.

"The oldest Ever kingdom," Uma said, finally at ease.

Over the trees to the west, Agatha could see the thin spires of a golden castle shimmering like organ pipes, but her teacher was already steering them to the east, down denser paths.

"We'll avoid the thoroughfares and go through the glens. Best to avoid you meeting any Evers for the time being."

"Why's that?" Agatha asked, but Uma was too busy gibbering to a passing bee.

By the late afternoon, they came upon a large stone well, its wooden roof draped in browning white roses, while a dove pecked at the dry bucket. Agatha brushed away the roses to read white words painted on the roof:

Snow White's
COTTAGE
• 1 MILE •
Museum Tours Daily
NO NEVERS ALLOWED

"League Headquarters is only an hour's walk from here, so we'll easily make it by sunset," said Princess Uma, slipping a meerworm in front of the dove. The dove perked up at the sight of Uma and chirped back brightly. "He says that with the School Master's return, Evers have been keeping out of the Woods. But he knew I'd still come to check on my friends."

The dove peered at Agatha and Tedros and let out a few inquisitive tweets.

"Yes, sweetie, they're the ones," nodded Uma, stroking the dove, and the bird gave the young couple nervous glances, adding a few whispered peeps. "He hears you're the Evers destined to vanquish the School Master." Uma held in a grin. "And he thinks your children will look very . . . interesting."

Tedros laughed. Agatha didn't.

"Might as well show you Snow's house along the way," Uma said, forging up the trail. "Princes occupied it after the Boy Eviction, until the School Master returned and the girls begged all the boys to come back and help protect the kingdoms. Turns out all it takes to bring enemies to peace is a bigger enemy. Probably hasn't been anyone here in weeks, then. I used to have sooo many friends at Cottage White, you know—sheep, pigs, even horses! Always wanted to bring my classes here to talk to them, but Clarissa said the animals in the Blue Forest were perfectly adequate for lessons. She's never liked field trips. Thinks the students spend all their time kissing behind trees." Uma fluttered ahead. "A bit true, I suppose."

As Agatha watched her go, Tedros slid next to his princess.

"Just hear me out. I don't mean to say you're not as good friends with Sophie as I am—"

"You barely *know* her," Agatha fired.

"Can you listen for two seconds without trying to eat me?" Tedros shot back.

Agatha fumed quietly.

"Look, both of us know you're her best friend. That you're the one who's spent the most time with her," said Tedros. "But you don't understand why Sophie took his ring in the first place. Sophie just wants to be *loved*, okay? She's willing to embrace the darkest Evil, all so that she doesn't end up alone. I know how much pain is inside her, because she told me. Pain she would never confess to you, because she doesn't want you to see it."

"You think Sophie's more honest with you than with me?" asked Agatha.

"It's more complicated than that. Sophie thought I loved *her* once, Agatha. She thought I was her prince. You told me yourself: all Sophie ever wanted was a happy ending that looked just like ours. If you talk to her, she'll never destroy that ring. She'll compare herself to you and all those feelings will come up. She'll feel like a third wheel to you and me. She'll feel *alone*."

"And let me guess: only you can make her destroy his ring," Agatha needled.

"Yes," Tedros said fervently. "Because I can make her see that if she comes with us, she'll still have a chance at true love one day, even if it isn't with him. I can make her see how beautiful and vibrant and alive she is . . . how soft and clever and fun and . . ." He smiled, lost in his memory of her. "I can make her feel loved in a way you can't."

Agatha took in her prince's glazed smile as he stared off in space. He used to look at her the same way once. Now he was talking about another girl with that very same look.

Tedros blinked out of his trance and saw Agatha burning pink.

"*I* rescue her alone. Got it?" she said, shoving past him and trundling up the path, before she stopped and glowered back. "And if you ever dare faint anywhere near me, I'm not catching you!"

Tedros snorted. "Princes don't faint!"

Agatha gritted her teeth and stormed ahead, until she caught up with her teacher.

Princess Uma gave her a look and glanced at Tedros, muttering to himself a ways behind. "Ever Afters always look so easy in storybooks, don't they?"

"Sometimes I feel like he needs a *real* princess," murmured Agatha.

"Have you been a ghost all this time and I haven't known it?"

"You know what I mean. I feel like deep down, he wants someone pretty and bubbly and who treats him like a prince." Agatha peeked up at her teacher. "Someone whose kids won't look so interesting."

"I had a prince with shiny hair and a small nose like me and who I always put first," Uma replied. "Ever After wasn't any easier."

"You had a prince?"

"Kaveen, Prince of Shazabah. Aladdin's great-grandson. Saved me from a hive of bloodsucking bees during the Trial by Tale my first year. The bees nearly killed him and Kaveen lost his chance to win Captain . . . but in the end, he'd won me. Clarissa used to catch us hiding in the library after curfew. That tortoise was always asleep and there's this cushy little nook behind the Love Spells shelf. Our initials are still carved into the wood." She smiled, reminiscing. "After we were married, I was kidnapped by a warlock from Netherwood, intent on ransoming me back to my prince. Part of me knew I should wait for Kaveen to come and rescue me. But I couldn't risk my prince's life! Suppose Kaveen got hurt? Suppose the warlock killed him?" Uma's caramel eyes glistened. "A white stag from the Woods answered my call for help. He ripped the warlock through his heart with his horns and battled his henchmen while I escaped. By the time Kaveen arrived, I was already free."

"I remember seeing it in a painting," Agatha said, for Uma had presented her storybook the first day of school. "It was your happy ending."

"Looks like it on a page, doesn't it?" her teacher said softly. "The Storian wrote the triumph of Princess Uma for all to hear—only my prince wasn't a part of it. I became legendary for my deep friendship with the animals, while Kaveen was endlessly taunted for arriving to save his princess too late. A princess famous for all time and her prince, a failure. No one sees that in a storybook, do they?" She paused. "He never said he blamed me, of course. But the stress slowly takes its toll, day after day, until one day you realize you're always fighting or ignoring each other and you can't go back to the way it was before. Your happy ending no longer feels happy at all."

A hot rash rose on Agatha's neck. "What happens then?"

"Then you're both better off with someone else, aren't you? Or even alone . . ." Uma's voice cracked. "Like me." A tear slipped down her cheek. "Once happiness is gone between two people, I don't think it ever comes back."

"But . . . but it has to come back!" Agatha fought. "That's why Tedros and I came back—to be happy together—"

Uma smiled sadly. "Then you'll have to prove me wrong, won't you?"

Agatha shook her head. "But you're a *real* princess! If you couldn't keep your prince, then how can—"

"Does Snow White still live in the cottage?" Tedros piped, busting in between them.

Agatha cleared her throat. Uma dabbed at her eyes with her pink sleeve. "A queen in a cottage? Don't be silly," she pooh-poohed, walking quicker. "Snow lives in the king's castle, the one you saw before. She's on her own now, since the king died of a snakebite five years back and her dwarf friends are scattered in other kingdoms, rich and well taken care of. When the School Master returned, the League offered to shelter Snow at Headquarters, but she said she was quite happy in her new life and had no intention of revisiting the old."

"What does the League have to do with Snow White's old life?" asked Agatha.

"And why would the League protect someone whose story is *over*?" Tedros scoffed—

A chilling, high-pitched scream tore through the Woods.

The three Evers stopped dead, looking up at a long, eight-foot-high wall of wilting lilacs, stretching out at the end of the path.

The scream came from behind it.

"We'll take another route!" Uma panicked. "Let's use the— *Tedros!* What are you doing?!"

Tedros hustled towards the hedge. "Sounded like a girl's cry for help."

Speechless, Uma whirled to Agatha. "Come, follow m— *Agatha!*"

"If he's going to rescue a random girl, I should keep my eye on him, don't you think?" said Agatha.

Uma was about to level them both with a stun spell, but it was too late; they were already clawing through the lilacs. "'*Rescue them from a grave*'—those were my orders," Uma puffed as she smushed through the flower wall after them. "Not 'chase grandstanding princes' or 'manage jealous girlfrien—'"

She came through and froze. Agatha and Tedros stood rigid next to her.

Nestled into the back of a clearing, Cottage White lay ahead, half in shadow, two stories of lumpy wood, with a coned, pink roof shaped like a princess's cap. An explosion of colorful shrubs and flowers had grown untended on the roof and first-story eaves, and rain had bled the colors into the wood, so that the house had the tint of a rainbow on all its sides. In the front garden, amidst the unkempt blooms and a meeting post for tours, there were seven pairs of brass shoes laid out in a row, tarnished and dented, a tribute to seven old dwarves who'd gone on to new lives. Only now, as the three Evers stared out at fourteen shoes that were supposed to be empty, they saw they weren't empty at all.

Before each brass pair lay a dwarf's body, facedown in a puddle of blood. Each was dressed in a tunic of a solid color from head to toe, with matching velvet nightcaps, their tiny feet perfectly fitted into the sculpted shoes.

From the pallor of their hands and the stiffness of their legs, it was clear at once they were all dead.

"No . . . not . . . not possible—" Uma gasped, stumbling back.

"You said they were g-g-gone from here!" Agatha stuttered, recoiling against the hedge.

"For *decades*!" Uma choked out. "Someone must have—someone must have brought them back—"

"What monster would bring dwarves back just to kill them?" said Agatha.

Uma looked at her, blank.

"Well, whoever did it is gone," rasped Tedros, scanning the Woods around them. He bucked up, struggling to act the prince. "I'll, um, check if any of them are still alive."

Uma rushed after him. "If so, we must bring them back to the League!"

Agatha stayed behind, gaping at the bodies and bright red puddles. Death everywhere: dwarves . . . Crypt Keeper . . . her mother . . . She spun away, bursting into chills, trying not to connect them. Heaving tight breaths, she focused on the grass under her feet, on her chapped, tingling fingers, until her mind slowed enough for her to think. Who would take all the trouble to bring seven dwarves from different places back to their old home? Who would kill them in cold blood and organize their bodies so precisely? Agatha shook her head, thinking of that horrible scream for help. Who could be so grotesque . . . so *Evil*—

Agatha's heart stopped.

That scream.

High-pitched. Female.

It hadn't been a dwarf's.

Slowly Agatha lifted her eyes to Snow White's cottage, like a moth finding a flame.

Neither her prince nor her teacher noticed her move from the hedges, nor the door creaking in the wind, as they went on from dwarf to dwarf, listening to each small heart.

By the time Tedros heard the silence of the last, Agatha was already inside.

9

The Worst Evers Ever

The first thing Agatha noticed about Snow White's house is that it smelled like Sophie. Standing in the shadowed doorway, she closed her eyes and inhaled the scent . . . *lavender cotton candy . . . vanilla-coated fog . . .*

The pink front door shivered and groaned behind her. She'd left it open and she could hear Tedros and Uma in the garden, debating what to do with the bodies. She didn't know why she hadn't made Tedros check the house with her; perhaps after their argument in the Woods, she wanted to do something without him . . . or perhaps she wanted to test if he'd even notice her gone . . . or perhaps she'd spent so much of the journey acting touchy and weak that she wanted to make up for it. . . . Whatever the reason, here she was, all alone, looking for whoever made that scream.

Agatha opened her eyes. On a breath, she forged deeper into the house.

The living room had a snuggly feel to it, with a sooty fireplace facing big-armed calico chairs, a fluffy red-brown rug made out of hawk feathers, a shelf of gemstones, seashells, and animal eggs beneath a shut, slatted window, and a steep, stumpy wooden staircase in the back corner, barricaded with red velvet rope. Agatha peered at a brass plaque on the wall:

hile living in the cottage, Snow White decorated it herself using knickknacks the dwarves collected on their travels. Here the cottage den is preserved precisely as she left it when she moved to Foxwood Castle to marry her prince. The only addition to the room is a hand-sewn chair made of lambskin and cat hair—a wedding gift from the wicked queen, who snuck into the banquet disguised as an old peddler. But the sight of Snow White with her prince, fair as ever, made the queen scream with rage, giving her away. As punishment, Snow White ordered her to dance before the guests in red-hot shoes until she fell down dead. The queen's gift is kept at Cottage White as a permanent reminder that Good always triumphs over Evil.

Cottage White Museum is sponsored by the Everwood Society for Cultural Preservation. No babies, animals, or giants allowed inside.

Behind the den, the kitchen was roped off, just like the staircase, but Agatha peeked in to see a dusty, deserted nook, no footprints on the floor or signs of life, except for a few flies milling around a leaky faucet.

"Agatha?" Tedros called outside. "Where are you?"

Agatha sighed, stomach relaxing. The scream must have been one of the dwarves' after all. She shuddered at such a morbid thought and hustled towards the front door, determined to get to League Headquarters. Whoever this League was, her mother had trusted them to help her. *"You must save Sophie as Stefan saved you,"* Callis' voice echoed—

Agatha stopped cold in the foyer.

A creak echoed somewhere upstairs . . .

Then it went quiet.

Slowly she raised her eyes to the ceiling.

She knew a sensible princess would have called her prince, but instead, she was moving into the den again, slipping off her clumps one by one before she left them on the lambskin chair. She felt her bare toes rake through the feathers of the rug, her eyes pinned on the ceiling until she squeezed under the rope at the rear of the room. She slid up the stairs on her hands and knees like a cat, taking time between steps, so the cricks and cracks of the stairs were camouflaged by the swinging squeaks of the front door.

At the top of the stairs was a narrow hallway with two rooms. Agatha rose up carefully and peeked into the first. Seven small beds lay in a cramped row, as if in an orphanage hall, each neatly made with different colored sheets, matching the tunics of the seven dead bodies outside.

Agatha felt a rush of sadness. Death had been rare to her before last night and now it followed her like a shroud. What was it like to be alive one moment—like her mother, like the

Crypt Keeper, like these seven helpers of Good—and then be gone the next? What happens to all your thoughts, your fears, your dreams? What happens to all the love you've yet to give? Her body quivered, as if she'd gone too deep, and she was suddenly aware of the stillness around her. *Why am I still here?* she berated herself, turning around. Tedros would be worried sick by now. Quickly she stepped out of the dwarves' quarters and leaned over to check the next room—

Agatha grabbed the wall in shock.

In a frost-white bedroom, a frail female's body lay facedown on the wood floor, her head hidden under the canopied bed. A crystal crown gleamed on its side nearby, as if it'd tumbled off her when she fell. But the dead woman wasn't what made Agatha gape in horror.

An old crone in black was kneeling next to the body. She had red eyes and a pig nose, a patchwork of stitches, and brown, shriveled flesh flaking off her, just like Red Riding Hood's wolf and Jack's giant in the Woods. In her clawlike hand, she clutched a musty storybook, pulled open to its last page: a painting of a prince kissing Snow White back to life, while seven dwarves smiled on blissfully, a dead witch on the ground behind them.

A dead witch that looked just like the old crone holding the storybook.

"That was the old," the witch purred, leering at the book's last page . . .

Before Agatha's eyes, the painting magically redrew, until the old witch now crouched over Snow White's dead body instead, the dwarves behind her all slain.

"And this is the *new*," the witch grinned.

Agatha's focus swung back to the corpse half-hidden under the bed . . . to the royal crown askew . . . and a deep dread snaked up her spine, remembering something Jack's giant had said on Necro Ridge . . .

"Should be out fixin' our stories like the others."

"He'll give us a turn at our stories soon enough," Red Riding Hood's wolf had answered.

The witch snapped the storybook shut with a triumphant cackle, jolting Agatha out of her thoughts. She glanced up to see the hag rearing to her feet, her back angled to the door—

"Agatha!" Tedros' voice yelled outside.

The witch dropped the book to the floor. Before Agatha could move, she spun and met her eyes with a lethal stare.

Agatha shrank into the hall's corner, flattening against the wall.

The witch drew a thin, jewel-handled dagger from her cloak, caked with dried blood.

Agatha whirled towards the staircase. Too far to run. She spun back to see the witch prowl towards her, trapping her in the corner. Agatha's finger glowed gold with terror, the witch ten feet away, but she couldn't remember a single spell from class. Agatha opened her mouth to scream for her prince. The witch was too fast. She hurled the knife for Agatha's throat like a bullet—

With a cry, Agatha shot a ray of gold light from her finger and the knife turned into a peach-petaled daisy, floating to the floor.

Gulping breaths, Agatha stared at the flower, thankful Sophie had used the hex against her first year. It was the only spell she'd never forget.

"Agatha!" Tedros shouted again.

Agatha looked up urgently, but it was too late. The witch slammed her against the wall, appallingly powerful, reeking of decay, and held her up by the throat with her liver-spotted hand. Breath choked, Agatha glimpsed the charred scars across the witch's ankles and legs. *"Ordered to dance . . . until she fell dead . . . ,"* Agatha remembered, struggling to stay conscious as the witch squeezed her neck harder. She and Sophie once danced in red-hot shoes too . . . a first-year punishment from Yuba . . . *Or was it second year?* . . . Agatha could feel her mind fading, the witch's thumb crushing her windpipe. She tried to think of Sophie's face as they danced . . . her helpless face, those suffering eyes . . . Darkness strangled her, pulling her under. *No . . . please . . . not yet . . . Sophie—I'll save—you—*

A bolt of will flashed through her and she sank her teeth into the witch's bony arm and bit as hard as she could. The old crone shrieked and let go. Agatha doubled over, gagging and wheezing, the witch still gaping at her, as if biting wasn't part of a Good girl's playbook, as if this greasy-haired, bug-eyed punk might be one of Evil's after all—

Agatha kneed her in the gut and dove for the stairs, about to reach the first step, only to feel the witch's boot crush the back of her leg. Agatha buckled to the floor, slamming her nose into the wood. She felt the hot blood seeping out of it and staunched it with her hand as she twirled around to defend against the witch—

But the hallway was empty, the witch gone.

Agatha hobbled to the edge of the stairs. The den was as quiet as when she came in, the slatted window over the book-shelf wide open and blowing in the breeze.

Tedros burst through the front door, his face cherry red. *"Agatha, where are—"* He saw her on the staircase and flushed two shades redder. "DO YOU WANT ME TO HAVE A HEART ATTACK! I'M SCREAMING LIKE A FOOL, NOT KNOWING IF YOU'RE ALIVE OR DEAD, AND HERE YOU ARE PLAYING HIDE-AND-SEEK LIKE A CHILD ON A PLAYGROUND, LOOKING A HOLY BLOODY MESS AND—"

Tedros' face changed.

"Agatha," he whispered, looking very scared. "Why are you bleeding?"

Agatha shook her head, tears welling, hyperventilating too fast to talk—

A cry came from outside.

Agatha and Tedros went rigid with twin gasps. *"Uma."*

Instantly, the prince dashed out the door, Agatha racing behind him—

Princess Uma sat against a tree, near the dwarves' corpses, her eyes spooked wide and legs out straight like a porcelain doll's.

Tedros skidded to his knees in front of her, jostling her by the shoulders. Uma didn't move. "What's wrong with her!" he cried.

Agatha landed next to him and touched Uma's face. Her

fingers made a hollow sound on her teacher's ashen skin. "Petrification," she said, remembering the curse once used against the teachers.

"What's the counterspell?" her prince pushed.

Agatha paled. "Only the one who casts the spell can reverse it." She looked at Tedros. "That witch . . . that witch did it—"

"What witch?" Tedros pressed, but Agatha was frantically scouring the deserted glen . . . She slumped. They'd never find that old hag. Princess Uma was as good as dead.

Not her too. Not our only hope. Agatha tuned out a bird's loud chirps and sank her face in her hands. *How do we get to Sophie now?*

"Agatha . . ."

"Not now," she whispered, head throbbing with fear, grief, and strident birdcalls.

"Agatha, look . . ."

Agatha spun. "I said not *no*—"

She frowned.

The dove from the well was in the prince's lap tweeting angrily at both of them.

"What's it saying?" Tedros asked her.

"How should I know?"

"You're the one who took Animal Communication!"

"And burned down the school in the process—"

Agatha stopped because the dove was drawing in the dirt with its wing. "Why is he drawing an elephant?"

The dove let out a torrent of chirps, furiously modifying his picture.

"It's a weasel," Tedros guessed. "Look at the ears."

"No, it's a moose—"

"Or a raccoon."

The dove was apoplectic now, slashing more lines.

"Oh. A rabbit," said Agatha.

"Definitely a rabbit," Tedros agreed.

He looked at Agatha. "Why's he drawing a rabbit?"

The dove rolled his eyes and stabbed his wing ahead.

Tedros and Agatha turned and saw a fat, balding white rabbit glaring at them from behind a tree, wearing a dirty blue waistcoat with a silver swan crest over the heart, a hideous white cravat, and crooked spectacles low on his nose. The rabbit yanked a pocketwatch out of his coat, pointed crabbily at it, and scampered down a dirt path out of the glen.

"Um. I think he wants us to follow him," said Agatha.

"Well, what are we waiting for?" said Tedros, slinging Uma over his shoulder and lumbering ahead. "Stay any longer and we might end up as dead as those dwarves."

"But shouldn't we know where he's taking us?" Agatha called out. "We can't just follow a strange animal in a scarf—"

"Sooner we follow him, sooner we find someone who knows how to unpetrify a teacher," her prince called back.

They followed the rabbit through inky trees as blackness swept over the Woods like a plague, the sun offering no resistance against the night. Soon they could barely see at all, and if it wasn't for the rabbit's corpulent pace, they'd have lost him in the dark. Ominous howls and low screams crackled ahead of them and Agatha tried to ignore the skitters and slithers in the underbrush lining the path. Yellow and red eyes peeped over-head like malevolent stars, warning her that danger was coming and coming fast. *If only we knew where League Headquarters was*, Agatha thought miserably. Her mother had sacrificed her life to make sure they reached the League . . . *and I didn't bother to ask Uma where it was? Why didn't I have a backup plan in case something happened? Why can't I think straight?* Now instead of finding the one place where they'd be safe tonight, they were on some wild-goose chase, carrying a petrified teacher and chasing a time-obsessed bunny to who knows where. With Tedros lagging under Uma's weight, Agatha kept pace with the rabbit for more than an hour, silently punishing herself for their predicament, until she finally glimpsed a wisp of white smoke emanating through pine trees ahead.

Drawing closer, Agatha began to smell a faint tinge of sandalwood mixed with a familiar scent she couldn't quite place, and as they moved into a tiny clearing, she saw that the smoke plumes were coming from a hole in the dirt, half-covered with dead fern fronds. The rabbit kicked the ferns aside and disappeared down the burrow, before peeking his face through the gap impatiently.

Agatha paused, reluctant to follow a stranger into a hole—

Tedros barreled right by her. "Nothin' to lose," he mumbled.

Before Agatha could argue, her prince lowered Uma into the hole and slid in behind her. Irritated, Agatha lowered herself down after him, landing awkwardly in darkness before Tedros caught her into his chest, soaking her with sweat. *He smells good*, Agatha noticed, inhaling his minty fresh scent. How could a boy possibly smell like spring fields after everything they'd just been through? She suddenly thought of Sophie, who'd smelled of honeycream even after traipsing up Graves Hill in the worst heat. Maybe that's why Tedros missed Sophie, Agatha thought bitterly . . . they could lie around all day sniffing each other, flawless gold-haired idols, while here she was, a "holy bloody mess," reeking of stress, dirt, and undead witch—

"Anyone here?" Tedros called.

Agatha snapped to attention, embarrassed by her thoughts. It was pitch-black in the hole, the rabbit nowhere to be seen.

"Hello?" Tedros echoed.

Nothing answered him.

The prince held out his hand and felt a wall of solid earth in front of him. "Why do we always end up in *dirt*?"

Agatha's stomach rumbled. "Maybe the dove was telling us to eat the rabbit instead of follow him."

"Or maybe the rabbit was telling us to leave Uma here, while we go look for League Headquarters."

"You want us to dump a petrified teacher in a hole and *leave*?" said Agatha, flabbergasted.

"It's not like she's going anywhere."

"Suppose you'll dump me in a hole the moment I'm inconvenient too," Agatha murmured, strangely confessional in the dark.

"Huh?"

"Then you can go get your sweet-smelling, beautiful, vibrant

Sophie all alone," Agatha vented, unable to stop herself.

"You didn't happen to eat any strange mushrooms on the way, did you?"

"Go ahead, laugh. You can name your children Blond and Blonder."

"Never pegged you as a jealous type," Tedros marveled.

"Jealous? Why? Because you almost kissed her as a boy *and* a girl? Because you can make her feel loved in a way that I can't? Me? *Jealous?*" Agatha ranted, thoroughly ashamed of herself now.

"Isn't Sophie supposed to be the crazy one?"

"Bet you wouldn't leave *her* in a dark pit—"

"And we thought Tweedledee and Tweedledum were hopeless," said a hoary voice.

Agatha and Tedros choked, recognizing it at once, and twirled to see a torch spark to flame in the grip of a white-bearded gnome wearing a belted green coat with a silver swan over the heart and a pointy orange hat. A gnome Agatha thought had been killed in a fire, but now here he was, alive in a secret den. She burst into a smile, glowing with relief—

Yuba didn't smile back. "First you lose a teacher because you fail to protect each other in the face of mortal danger. Then you fight so often and *loudly* that you've alerted the entire Woods as to your whereabouts. Now you're so busy insulting each other that you forget to use a simple glow spell to illuminate your surroundings in the time that a Cave Troll could have bashed both your heads to smithereens. If it wasn't for a rabbit rescuing you from yourselves, you two nincompoops would be dead before dawn," he lashed, fingers twitching on his white staff as if he wanted to beat them with it. "A Bad Group is one thing. But you two Evers might just be the Worst Evers . . . *Ever.*"

Agatha and Tedros looked down, humiliated.

Yuba sighed. "Lucky for you, the League needs you as much as you need it."

Torches roared to flame, lighting up a squad of strangers behind him in a giant cave headquarters the size of a small house.

"Presenting the honorable League of Thirteen, legendary legion of Good and Enlightenment," Yuba proclaimed with an imperious smile, clearly expecting the Evers to look impressed, awed, or at least grateful for the glorious platoon that they had come all this way to see.

Agatha and Tedros blanched in horror instead.

Because the League of Thirteen that was their only hope to save Sophie, the League of Thirteen that was their only hope to stay alive . . . were all very, very *old*.

10

The Missing Thirteenth

"You've got to be kidding," Tedros cracked, as he and Agatha goggled at the saggy, ancient crew.

Agatha counted four men and four women—a geriatric gang of liver spots, turkey necks, hairy ears, foggy eyes, yellowed teeth, beady grins, bony limbs, and heads of sparse, colorless, or poorly dyed hair. Two of the eight were in rickety wheelchairs, three had walking canes, two were hunched and bandy-legged, and one was a morbidly obese woman in a muumuu, slathering on makeup at a mirror.

All of them had silver swan crests over their hearts, like Uma, Yuba, and the White Rabbit, badges of membership to a League her mother had trusted with her daughter's life.

She sent us here for a reason,

thought Agatha desperately. Would they rip off masks, revealing invincible warriors? Would they magically turn young like the School Master? Agatha held her breath, waiting and praying for something to happen . . .

The League blinked back, like fish in an aquarium, waiting for something to happen too.

"Told ya they wouldn't recognize us," grumped the fat woman at the mirror.

"Recognize you?" In the reflection, Agatha glimpsed the woman's pink, hoggish pallor, squinty green eyes, wide jowls, hideously rouged cheeks, and nest of flat curls that she'd tried to dye brown and had turned blue instead. She looked like a doll salvaged from the bottom of a swimming pool. "I'm quite sure I've never seen you—or any of you—in my life," Agatha said, scanning the group. She turned to Tedros, hoping he'd seen something in them she hadn't, but her prince was red as a fire ant, about to explode.

"*This* is who's supposed to get us to Sophie?" he barked, blue eyes raking the puke-colored carpet, flower-patterned sofas, moth-eaten curtains, and thirteen hard, thin mattresses split into two rows. "A *retirement home* for the about-to-be dead?"

Yuba yanked him to the corner. "How dare you speak that way to the League!" he hissed, peeking to make sure the others couldn't hear. "You know the lengths I've gone to find them? To bring them here? And here you act as if they have to introduce themselves to you like common folk—you, a boy who has no accomplishments to his name—"

"Tell that to a *king* in a few weeks!" Tedros bellowed.

"You arrogant prat! The way you've bungled things, you won't make it a few days, let alone to a coronation!" Yuba shot back.

"First thing I'll do is outlaw old gnomes!"

"Listen, my mother knew the League would help us," Agatha broke in, giving Tedros a "calm-down" look. "That's why she wrote them. So clearly we're missing something—"

"Yeah, like people who aren't a thousand years old!" Tedros lashed, earning another miffed look from his princess. *"What,"* he said, turning his fury on her. "We barely escape our own execution, then we learn our best friend loves an Evil sorcerer, then we travel night and day, surviving zombies and witches and graves, all to find a League your mother promised would get us to Sophie and *this is it?* Bollocks. Let's go. Better chance of breaking into the school ourselves—"

"She was my *mother*, Tedros," Agatha said. "And I trust her more than anyone in this world to know what's best for us. Even you."

Tedros fell quiet.

Agatha glanced back and saw the old, swan-crested strangers completely ignoring them now, knitting, reading, napping, card playing, and pulling out false teeth to eat their gruel. Her faith in her mother suddenly wavered.

"Listen to me, both of you," said Yuba. "When our thirteenth member returns, your questions will be answered. Until then, you both need some strong turnip tea and a bowl of oat porridge. Having survived in the Woods these last few months after 115 years of sanctuary at school, I know firsthand how intense your journey must have been—"

"Thirteenth member?" Agatha skimmed the room. "I only count eight." Then she noticed the White Rabbit in the corner, slicing a carrot into fifths on a plate, the silver swan over his heart glimmering in torchlight. "Um, nine."

"Ten, actually," said Tedros, and Agatha followed his eyes to the silver swan on Yuba's green coat.

"A founding member of the League," the gnome puffed proudly. "And Uma makes eleven, of course, and—" Yuba flushed. "*Uma!* Goodness me!" He whirled to the Princess petrified in the corner. "Leaving her there like a house cat! Tink! Tink, where are you!"

Something snored loudly behind Agatha and she turned to see a pear-shaped fairy the size of a fist bolt awake and fall off a dirty ottoman. The fairy craned up groggily, with poufy gray hair, a green dress eight sizes too small, ragged gold wings, and garish red lipstick. Eyes darting right and left as if she knew she was supposed to be awake but had no idea why, she spotted Uma frozen in the corner and yelped, flapping and sputtering towards her like a dying bee. Then she slipped her hand into her dress, snatched a handful of what looked like moldy soot, and dumped it goonishly over Uma's head.

Nothing happened.

"Dad took me to Ali Baba's harem for my birthday once. This is so much more embarrassing," Tedros mumbled, stomping towards the entrance hole to leave—

Uma coughed behind him. Tedros swiveled to see the

princess levitating three feet off the ground, her skin filling out from pasty white to its usual rich olive color. Uma stretched her smooth, lithe arms into the air with a yawn, smiled at the fairy glassily . . . and collapsed to the ground, asleep once more.

"Here you were worried about your fairy dust being too old, Tink," Yuba chuckled, patting the fairy's head.

The fairy still looked gloomy and spurted squeaky gibberish.

"Don't be ridiculous, Tink. You can't expect to have the same stamina as when you were sixteen. Besides, we didn't need Uma to fly from here to Shazabah; we just needed your dust to unpetrify her. A few sound hours of sleep and she'll be good as new. Now where were we," the gnome mulled, turning back to the Evers. "Oh yes, rabbit makes nine, Uma makes ten, I make eleven, and Tinkerbell makes twelve, so that just leaves—"

"Tinkerbell?" Agatha blurted.

"The *real* Tinkerbell?" asked Tedros, staring at the fairy's mottled face, potbelly, and ash-colored hair. "But she's so . . . so . . ."

Agatha gave him a lethal look, but it was too late. Tinkerbell burst into sobs and hid under an ottoman.

"He didn't mean it, Tink," Yuba huffed and smacked Tedros in the backside with his staff.

"I don't understand," Agatha said, bewildered. "What is Tinkerbell doing here?"

"Really found yourselves some smarties, didn't you, Yuba," said a bald, skinny man in a green vest with elfish ears and delicate features, knitting a lime-green sock. "Still can't see who we are."

"Maybe we need to count your rings like a tree," Tedros muttered, rubbing his behind.

"Go ahead, make all the old jokes you want, pretty boy," the bald man fired. "As if you won't get to our age yourself someday."

"Well, it seems our two amateurs need introductions after all," Yuba scolded, giving Tedros and Agatha furious scowls before shoving them into two of the rocking chairs. He turned back to his League. "Who wants to go first?"

"Don't see why we should introduce ourselves," the sock-knitting man crabbed. "Don't see why we should let these two stay here at all."

Yuba exhaled impatiently. "Because these two Evers are our only hope to—"

"What's the point? You heard the boy. We're on death's door anyway," the bald man pouted.

"Oh come now," Yuba said, softening. "What'd you say when I came to fetch you from Neverland? Holed up in your tree house all alone, refusing to join the League, even when I told you your life was in terrible danger. But then I told you about these two young Evers and you lit up like a little boy. Told me you'd do anything to be around young people again . . . that they were the only ones who ever truly understood you, Peter . . ."

Peter looked up at Yuba, blue eyes glistening. Then he looked back down. "Tink *made* me come," he muttered. The fairy squealed in protest and pelted him with a lump of gruel.

Agatha and Tedros gawped at each other. Peter? Peter *Pan?*

"I'm with Peter," boomed the huge, blue-haired woman, spinning from the mirror. "Not even out of school, these little brats. Should be lickin' our feet and beggin' for autographs! Instead they somehow get their own fairy tale—students! a fairy tale!—and now that tale's got its panties in a knot, wakin' our old villains from the dead and draggin' us straight out of our Ever Afters—"

"Ever Afters! Ha!" chimed a gangly, high-voiced man in suspenders and beige breeches, with big, twinkly eyes, a long nose, and a full head of white hair. Tiny round scars marked all the joints of his long, tanned limbs, as if he'd once been screwed together. "First of all, Peter can barely leave his house he's so depressed at growing up. Second, I'd never have wished to be a real boy if the Blue Fairy told me real boys end up with arthritis and bad eyes and permanent constipation. And third, Ella told me herself she preferred sweeping cinders to being a queen."

"When did I ever say *that?*" the fat woman squawked.

"Last night," the long-nosed man replied, looking surprised by her question. "You drank a barrel of wine and told me you miss cleaning for your stepsisters, because at least you felt useful and stayed fit and now you're old and bored and big as a house—"

"WHO ASKED YOU?" thundered the woman. "YOU SPENT HALF YOUR LIFE AS A *PUPPET*!"

"First they get mad at me for lying. Now they get mad at

me for telling the truth," moped the long-nosed man, curling into a sofa.

Agatha's and Tedros' eyes bulged even wider. *"Pinocchio?"* said Tedros.

"Cinderella?" said Agatha.

"Don't give me that face," Cinderella sneered back at her. "For bein' Camelot's supposed future queen, you ain't much to look at yourself." Her hawkish green eyes shot down to Agatha's clumps. "Bet no one wants to see *those* feet in glass slippers."

"Hey now! She's my princess!" Tedros jumped in.

"I don't blame you, handsome," Cinderella smirked, voice smooth as an eel. "Your daddy didn't have good taste in girls either."

Tedros looked like he'd been kicked in the pants.

Yuba sighed. "Professor Dovey had just as much faith in Agatha as she did in you, Ella. So I suggest you treat our guests with respect—"

"We have the respect when these two *studenten* fix the mess!" croaked a wild-haired, hunchbacked man in a wheelchair with owlish gray eyes and a harsh foreign accent. "Think they're special because Storian writes their story? Well, at least our stories have *end*, yes? But these two change ending again and again—*'Are we heppy yet?' 'Are we heppy yet?'* Bah. Fools! Now see! School Master young, Evil redoing stories, and dead witch hunting me I have to kill all over again—"

"I killed her, Hansel and I am not killing smelly witch again," said a wild-haired woman in a wheelchair next to

him with the same accent, her big gray eyes flaying Agatha and Tedros. "*Your* story bringing villains out of graves, *your* responsibility put them back." She smiled phonily. "And I'm Gretel, since the bossy little gnome said we must introduce ourselves."

"Which leaves me and Briar Rose (or Sleeping Beauty for the uneducated Reader), who were planning our fairy-tale wedding until *you* came along," said a freckle-faced man with salt-and-pepper hair, wearing a brown tunic and white lederhosen. He was holding hands with an elegant, white-haired woman in a revealing puce gown. "Now we're hiding from my man-eating giant and Rose's curse-obsessed fairy—"

"When Jack and I should be picking out a *cake*," Briar Rose glared.

"That makes seven of us who think these young twerps should sleep in the Woods," trumped Cinderella.

Tink squeaked.

"Eight," said Cinderella.

Tedros and Agatha gawked at the gang of famous old fairy-tale heroes who just voted them out of their cave.

"It's why I tried to avoid you meeting Evers on the trails . . ." Uma yawned in the corner. "Everyone blames *you* for messing up the Woods." She fell back asleep.

"Well, I don't know about the rest of you, but I think they're adorable," chirped a short, big-bottomed old woman with a dyed brown bob and a red-hooded cape. "Isn't that what being old is for? Mentoring younger folk to get through their stories?"

"Oh go back to granny's, you blithering ass," growled Cinderella.

Red Riding Hood shut up.

"You all act as if we don't *need* our young guests," Yuba's voice slashed through the cave.

Everyone twirled to see the old gnome standing in front of the moth-holed curtain hanging across the cave wall, the White Rabbit standing at his side like a magician's assistant. "Let me remind you that one week ago, the School Master placed his ring on his queen's finger, earning her vow of true love. That same night, the villains rose from their graves on Necro Ridge and the Crypt Keeper was killed."

On Yuba's cue, the rabbit drew the curtain back, revealing dozens of storybooks spread open to their last pages, tacked to the wall with sharpened sticks.

"Two days later, Rapunzel and her prince were kidnapped by Mother Gothel and hurled from her tower to their deaths," the gnome declared, illuminating one of the storybooks with his staff and its gruesome new ending to Rapunzel's story. "Then yesterday Tom Thumb was eaten alive by a giant, while Rumpelstiltskin killed the miller's daughter who'd once guessed his name," Yuba went on, lighting up two more storybooks with revised endings. "And today, Snow White and her seven dwarves have been murdered at Cottage White, where they once lived happily." He snapped his staff like a whip, lighting up a last storybook with a loud crack. "All of these victims refused to leave their homes and join our League in hiding, as did many others who may soon suffer the same fate."

A tense silence filled the cave as Agatha took in the painting of a dead maiden and her seven dwarves—the same scene the witch had presided over as it transformed. Agatha rubbed unconsciously at the deep bruises on her forearm and wrist.

"S-S-Snow is dead?" Pinocchio whispered.

"Pretty, sweet Snow?" echoed Peter Pan.

("Wasn't *that* pretty," Cinderella mumbled.)

The League members all gazed at Snow White's terrible new ending, their eyes wet and scared, as if her death suddenly made the others real.

"I saw who killed her."

Agatha's voice came out before she even knew it.

The whole League slowly looked up at her.

Agatha slid her focus to the floor, palms clammy as she relived the scene in the glen. "It was the wicked queen in an old woman's disguise, her ankles and legs burnt up, just like the fairy tale said. Her skin was peeling off like a corpse and she smelled like decaying flesh. And her eyes . . . they were bloodshot and dead, like there was no soul inside of her." Agatha shook her head, trying to understand. "She could have killed me or Uma or Tedros, but she didn't. As if she'd already done what she came to do." She looked up at the League. "The wolf and Jack's giant talked about it on Necro Ridge too . . . getting a turn at changing their stories . . . we didn't know what they meant—"

"Wolf on Necro Ridge?" Red Riding Hood cut in. "*My* wolf?"

"And *my* giant?" echoed Jack, clutching Briar Rose.

"They're all out there, then," Agatha said anxiously. "Dead villains. Waiting for their turn to rewrite their fairy tales. That's what's happening, isn't it?"

"Doesn't make a shred of sense," said Tedros, turning to Yuba. "Why would the School Master's army waste time rewriting a bunch of old stories? Why kill old heroes who aren't a threat to anyone? Why not attack the Ever kingdoms instead?"

Even Yuba was tight-lipped, fingers fidgeting on his staff, as if he'd pondered the question and had no answer.

The old heroes blinked at the gnome, fear filling their faces.

"We are heroes, yes?" Hansel challenged. "We must fight back!"

"Against two hundred dead witches, monsters, and who-knows-what running around the Woods? Don't be an imbecile," Gretel snapped. "Why do you think we're here in stinky cave hiding?"

"Can't hide for long. They'll find us all eventually, no matter how often we move Headquarters," soured Cinderella. "School Master's got love on his side now. He's invincible. What do we got except age spots and cricked necks?"

"Ella's right," Jack sighed. "As long as the School Master's got a queen who loves him, all of us are gonna end up dead as Snow."

"Then what do we do?" mewled Red Riding Hood.

"The only thing we can do," said Yuba, eyes shifting to Agatha and Tedros. "Convince his queen to destroy that love."

The League went quiet.

"The crackpot plan again," Cinderella murmured.

"You really think you can do it? You really think you can make your friend destroy the School Master's ring?" Peter Pan asked, peering at the two young Evers.

"Why would she give up true love for you?" Pinocchio prodded.

Agatha felt emotion rising into her throat. "I wish there was a way to explain me and Sophie. We're different—*very* different—and still the same. Sure, we fought and pushed each other's buttons and we're terrible at listening to each other, but we shared the same heart. Saw life through each other's eyes. I never thought I could live without her." She paused, tangled in memories. "Somehow things changed. Maybe that's growing up, I don't know. Every time we tried to hold on to each other, we hurt each other instead. It was both our faults, but mine most of all. I stopped telling her the truth. I stopped trusting the one person who taught me how to trust in the first place. I thought I'd lost her forever, that it was too late to ever make things the way they were before . . . but deep down I still feel like there's a way. There *has* to be a way." Agatha managed a sad smile. "Because if anyone can make Sophie see what love really is . . . it's her best friend, isn't it?"

The League's old faces melted to childlike stares, as if finally seeing the young girl with hope instead of disdain.

Tedros stepped next his princess, chest proud. "Exactly. Leave Sophie to me."

Agatha's smile vanished.

The League looked between them, thoroughly confused

who Sophie's best friend was.

"All that matters now is that we *get* to Sophie—" Tedros started.

"Right," Agatha interjected. "And we know she's somewhere in the School for Good and Evi—"

"Which means getting in and finding her without being caught," Tedros spoke over her.

"Wait, wait, wait," Gretel shot back. "School Master is young and strong, School Master has both castles, School Master has army of dead . . . and you think you can get into his *school*?"

Agatha frowned. "Um, that's the whole reason we came to you, obviously. Because we need your help breaking into—"

"*Help?* Your mother's message said 'hide you,'" Hansel jeered from his wheelchair. "Does it look like we can *help*?"

"We can barely can get to the toilet these days, let alone lead a raid on a castle," cracked Cinderella, expelling a loud fart.

The League members burst into laughter. Even the White Rabbit.

"Some sneak attack! With my joints, they'll hear us five miles away!" Pinocchio quipped.

"Don't worry, P! We can beat them with our canes!" said Peter.

"Or my basket of goodies! Hard and crusty by now!" giggled Red Riding Hood.

Gretel shrieked a snort and the others howled so loudly, doubled over with tears, that even Uma jolted awake at the noise.

Agatha glanced at Tedros, who scowled at her venomously for trying to make him believe in these useless old fogies. She swiveled back to the heroes. "But t-t-that's why we came all this way! That's why we trusted in you! My mother wrote the League to protect us—my mother told us you'd help—"

"Because your mother knew that the League of Thirteen had a thirteenth member," said a deep voice.

Agatha and Tedros turned to see a tall shadow standing at the cave entrance.

"She knew these twelve would keep you safe. But help?" the voice said, as the shadow slid into the light. "I'm afraid that's only *me*."

"Ah, just in time . . . ," smiled Yuba.

Agatha stared at a long, gangly nut-brown old man with a thick white beard and twisty white moustache. He wore a sweeping violet cape lined with fur tippets and stitched with the signs of the zodiac, a droopy, dented cone hat patterned with stars, large horn-rimmed spectacles, and a pair of plushy violet slippers.

I've seen him before, Agatha thought, too tired to think clearly. *In the Woods?* No . . . it was a storybook, wasn't it? . . . a storybook that Dean Sader had taken her whole class inside. This old man was there, inside a dusty cave, filled with burbling laboratory vessels and shelves of grubby vials and jars . . . arguing with a king about a spell . . . a king that looked a lot like . . .

Agatha's heart seized, her eyes shooting open, and she spun to Tedros behind her—

But her prince was already pale as a ghost.

"Merlin," he gasped.

His legs crumpled and he fell all at once like a tree in a forest, his princess right there to catch him.

11

Appointment with the Deans

As midnight came and went, Sophie sat calmly in the School Master's window, her hair wet, her ebony dress bunched at the knees as she pressed bare toes against the wall. She looked out at the fluorescent green bay, reflecting the shadows of two black castles, both dark and quiet.

Just this morning, she'd been reeling with doubts: from a school that turned Evers into Nevers . . . from Agatha's voice, impelling her to destroy Rafal's ring . . . from a schedule that called her a teacher of Evil when she still didn't *feel* Evil at all.

She turned to the Storian over her story-book, painting a scene of Agatha and Tedros following a white rabbit through the Woods. With every minute, her friends were getting closer to school,

closer to seeing her again, closer to convincing her to leave Evil behind forever . . .

Sophie smiled, feeling the gold ring lock tight on her finger.

Or so they think.

How quickly things changed in a fairy tale.

Twelve hours earlier, Sophie had been chasing after the School Master, as he crossed a green breezeway tunnel into the old Valor tower.

"*Teach* Evil? Teach Curses and *Death Traps?*" Sophie yelped, gripping her schedule as she floundered after him in her black nightgown and glass heels. "Have you lost your mind!"

"It was the Dean's suggestion. Wish I'd come up with it myself, if only to prevent her the satisfaction of a good idea," Rafal groused, ascending the staircase carved HENCHMEN. "Now that I'm young, she's been treating me like I'm incapable of running my own school. Even had the gall to tell me that my flights over the bay are disruptive since students keep peeking out the window during challenges. I *am* the School Master, thank you. If I want to go for a spin, I'm perfectly welcome to—"

"*Rafal.*"

Sophie's voice was so sharp that he stopped and stared down at her through the gap in the black staircase.

"I wish we had time for adolescent rants, but whoever this Dean is, she expects me to be a teacher at this school, when a) all the students are my age, b) none of them like me, and c) I don't know the first thing about teaching!"

"Really?" He resumed his ascent. "I distinctly remember you hosting Lunchtime Lectures for the entire school."

"Teaching kids how to cure dandruff is different than teaching them how to be Evil!" Sophie said, chasing him towards the top floor. "Let me get this straight. Agatha and Tedros are coming to kill you and here I am in a nightgown, expected to give homework and grade papers—"

But Rafal was already at the lone black-marble door atop the staircase.

"Professor Dovey's office?" Sophie asked, accosting him. "*She's* who wanted me to be a teacher? *She's* Dean of Evil?"

But then Sophie saw that the door once inlaid with a glittering green beetle was now inlaid with two violet, intertwined snakes. Beneath the snakes, letters cut from amethysts spelled out a single word:

DEANS

"*Deans?*" Sophie wrinkled her nose. "There's more than one? But who are—"

The door swung open magically, revealing a thin, tight-jawed woman with a long black braid and a sharp-shouldered purple gown, studying a scrap of parchment at Professor Dovey's old desk.

"Lady Lesso?" Sophie rasped. "But where's Professor Dovey?"

Then Sophie saw the second desk near the window,

identical to the first, which had never been in the office before. No one was sitting at it.

"Let me guess, Rafal. Took her for a joyride over the bay?" said Lady Lesso, not looking up from the parchment. "Supposed to have her here twenty minutes ago. Would be nice to prepare our new teacher before she assumes my old class, don't you think? Never mind. I'll take it from here."

Rafal scowled. "I believe I give the orders at this school, Lady Lesso. And I believe you forgot a 'Master,' along with your respect. Something your fellow Dean seems to have in spades."

Lady Lesso's slitted violet eyes slowly raised to the teenage boy in front of her, dressed like a dark prince. "Apologies, Master," she said, her tone snide and cold. "Shall I take it from here?"

Rafal gave her a filthy look and pulled Sophie into his flank. "See you at lunch, my love," he whispered, kissing her tenderly on the cheek. He shot Lady Lesso a last glare and slammed the door behind him, rattling the two desks.

"Lady Lesso, how can I teach your old class!" Sophie blurted. "None of this makes any sense—"

"Sit down," said the Dean, eyeing the gold ring on Sophie's finger.

Sophie dropped into the chair facing her. Lady Lesso stared at her carefully, framed by the usual plum basket and crystal pumpkin paperweights on Professor Dovey's desk. *Why wasn't Lady Lesso sitting at her own desk?* Sophie thought, glancing at the desk across the room.

"Our first year, we got off to a rather poor start. But with time, I've grown fond of you, Sophie." Lady Lesso leaned back in her chair. "You and I share quite a bit in common."

"Other than our love of high heels and good bone structure, I have to disagree," Sophie replied.

"Look closer. Both of us are naturally gifted at Evil, both of us have a vanity that is uncharacteristic of Nevers, and both of us make sensational witches when provoked," the Dean explained. "And yet, each of us is afraid of being alone. Each of us has tried to hold on to love at some point in our lives . . . only to see that same love turn against us one day. You with your best friend and me with my own child."

"You have a *child*?" Sophie said, stunned.

"Nevers have children, just like Evers. But as I've said in class, the difference is that our families cannot last, for there is no real love at their core. Villain families are like dandelions—fleeting and toxic. Try to hold on to them and you are battling against the wind." Lady Lesso fingered a pumpkin paperweight. "I should have abandoned my child forever when I came to the School for Evil as its Dean fifteen years ago. Just like you should have abandoned your friend when she was placed in the School for Good. Thankfully both of us learned our lesson before we could make any more mistakes."

Her clenched jaw eased. "But what's remarkable is that for all our errors, we're both still alive. And not just alive—we're finally on the winning team! Once upon a time, Evil had majestic victories too: Finola the Fairy Eater, Children Noodle Soup, Rabid Bear Rex, and others, long forgotten. All anyone remembers now is two hundred years of Good victories, over and over, robbing balance from our world, until Evil became a death sentence, pitied and maligned, until Good became nothing but Balls, kisses, and arrogance. But you've changed all that, Sophie. For the first time, Evil has love on its side because of how hard you and Rafal have fought for each other. Don't you see? Your fairy tale can reverse the slaughter I've fought against my whole life. All you have to do is prove you love Rafal as much as Agatha loves Tedros . . . that you'll sacrifice for your love as much as Agatha would for her prince . . ."

Lady Lesso glowered darkly at her. "Which means *you* must kill Agatha and Tedros when they come for you."

"K-k-kill— *Me?*" Sophie squeaked like a squirrel, bursting into shivers. "My b-b-best friends? No, no, no, no, no—I said I'd fight with Rafal—that I'd defend him if they came—"

"Defend? No, no, my dear. Evil attacks and Good defends. And when Evil attacks, it *kills*. I warned you our very first day of class, Sophie. When you are Evil, there is no escaping your Nemesis. The moment you began having Nemesis dreams of Agatha's face your first year, your fate as enemies was sealed forever . . . much as I tried to believe both of you an exception."

Sophie was still shaking her head, emitting yips and croaks instead of words.

"Listen to me, Sophie." Lady Lesso's tone cut sharper. "I told you the story of my child for a reason. As long as Agatha is alive, you will never have a happy ending. Either you kill Agatha and her true love . . . or they will kill yours. Those are the only two ways your fairy tale ends."

"I c-c-can't—I just want to be happy! Why do I have to kill anyone—"

"Because this is *your* storybook. You and Agatha's," said Lady Lesso. "That is why the Storian has yet to close it. It is waiting for you to make your choice between who lives at The End: your best friend or your true love. Good or Evil."

Sophie clutched her ring with shaking fingers. "But what if Agatha doesn't feel like my Nemesis anymore? What if I don't even feel Evil at all!"

Lady Lesso gripped Sophie's hand across the desk. "Sophie. You wear the ring of Evil's darkest soul. You brought Evil back from the dead and unleashed hell on Good, just so that you can have a boy to love. Can you think of anything *more* Evil?"

Sophie rankled. "That isn't fair! I didn't know any of this would happen!"

"Ask yourself, then. If you could save Good, would you sacrifice Rafal? After finally finding someone who loves you for your true self, would you choose to be alone? Just so Agatha and Tedros can be happy?"

Sophie followed her eyes out the window to Rafal soaring over the Blue Forest, back to his tower in the sky. Everyone else in the world had betrayed her when she needed them most— family, friends, princes. But not him. She could still feel herself flying in his arms, safe and protected. She could still feel his passionate warning, cold at her core . . . *"No one will ever love you but me"* . . .

"Could you give him up, Sophie?" Lady Lesso pressed.

A single, scared tear fell down Sophie's cheek. "No," she whispered.

"Then you aren't just Evil," said Lady Lesso, letting go of her. "You are its deserved queen."

Sophie shook her head. "But you know who I really am! Last year you and I fought for Good with Agatha and Professor Dovey. All of us were a team!"

"And you and I have paid our *price* for that disloyalty. Your price is that you must now destroy the friends you should have disowned long ago. And my price is . . ." Lady Lesso's lips quivered, her gaze drifting to the empty desk across the room. She swallowed subtly and straightened in her chair. "Look, I'm here to help you, Sophie. Because like you, I too have a second chance to prove my loyalty to Evil. And this time, we can't fail. Even if our leader now has the maturity of a pubescent boy." She grimaced sourly. "Now pay attention to what I'm about to say."

Lady Lesso flattened both hands on the desk and crouched forward like a panther. "Agatha and Tedros will soon try to break into this school to see you. The fate of Good rests on them earning back your loyalty and killing Rafal before the sun extinguishes completely. Do not doubt their resolve or wiles. They do not care about your happy ending, only theirs. And if they take away Rafal, what will you have left?"

Sophie looked away, an old darkness rearing into her heart. "Just like my mother."

Lady Lesso arched her brows, intrigued.

"My mother was the third wheel, watching my father and her best friend fall in love," Sophie said, eyes pinned to the floor. "And my father and Honora didn't care."

"Because they knew your mother didn't have the courage to fight them."

Sophie nodded. "It's why she died so young. She couldn't face the rest of her life alone. She just . . . gave up."

"Then it looks like your best friends are betting an old story can be made *new*," said the Dean.

Sophie slowly lifted red eyes.

"Like mother, like daughter," said Lady Lesso. "Is that what you want?"

Sophie's body hardened to steel.

"My job as Dean is to ensure *you* do not end up alone, Sophie," Lady Lesso soothed. "My job is to ensure you and Rafal win your Happy Never After. But I made you a teacher because I need you to find out how Agatha and Tedros plan to break in."

Sophie frowned. "How would I know how they plan to—"

"Because there is a spy working for your friends *inside* this school," said Lady Lesso harshly. She shoved forward the crumpled scrap she'd been studying. "The fairies snatched this from a white mouse near the school gates, before it escaped."

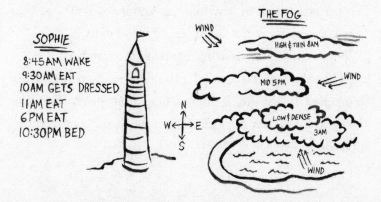

SOPHIE

8:45 AM WAKE
9:30 AM EAT
10 AM GETS DRESSED
11 AM EAT
6 PM EAT
10:30 PM BED

THE FOG

WIND

HIGH & THIN 8AM

MID 5PM

WIND

LOW & DENSE

3AM

N
W —|— E
S

WIND

"It's a map of your movements," said the Dean. "Why the notes about the fog, I haven't the faintest clue. But someone in this school is telling Good how to find you."

Sophie looked up, the last of her fear draining away. Good was *spying* on her? That's how desperate they were to destroy her happy ending? Suddenly, any remaining desire to see her best friends scorched to wrath.

"I haven't told Rafal, of course. He's so drugged up on teenage testosterone that he'd exterminate every last student in this school," griped Lady Lesso. "I need *you* to find out who the spy is, Sophie. A white mouse messenger suggests it's an Ever, but you know Agatha and Tedros' friends better than I. As a teacher, you can keep your eye on any suspects and help us uncover how exactly your friends plan to invade our castle."

Sophie bridled. "But I don't have the foggiest idea how to teach a class!"

"Pollux has been teaching your class the past few weeks and will stay on to help you settle in, especially with double the number of students to manage. That said, I'm quite sure they'll prefer you to that twit even if you pick your nose the whole time. Focus on finding the spy, Sophie. We don't have much time. Agatha and her prince will be here in days. And if you don't end your fairy tale now, the sun will soon end it for *all* of us."

Sophie nodded, adrenaline coursing through her . . .

Then she saw the empty Dean's desk in the corner. Guilt dampened the storm inside of her. "But surely Professor Dovey knows a way to close our storybook without me hurting anyone—"

"Professor Dovey is no longer a Dean," Lady Lesso said stiffly.

"Where is she?" Sophie asked, startled.

"She and the other Good teachers have been imprisoned in a secure location, where they will remain until the School Master deems otherwise."

Sophie gawked at her. "But she was your friend! You two always helped each other!"

"Like you once helped Agatha." Lady Lesso's purple eyes cast down as she caressed the basket of plums. "But a witch can't be friends with a princess no matter how hard she tries, Sophie. Haven't we learned that lesson well enough?"

Sophie's mouth dried out, her voice trapped in her throat. "But then . . . then who is the other Dean?"

The door flung opened behind her and a tall, menacingly handsome boy in a sleeveless black leather shirt swaggered through with spiked black hair, deathly pale cheeks, and lethal, violet eyes.

"Morning, Mother. Brought you fresh coffee," he said in a deep, strapping voice.

He put a mug of blackish liquid on Lady Lesso's desk, then leered at Sophie. "Well, well, I see you're getting our new teacher settled in." He leaned against the sunlit window, a coiled black whip gleaming on his belt. "Funny, we've never quite met have we, Sophie of Woods Beyond? You've seen me, of course, in your invisible cape and in your elfish boy's body, sneaking through the School for Boys . . . Filip of Mount Honora, was it? Threw me against a wall one night to stop me from torturing your precious Tedros. Oh yes, now I see Filip in there . . . those same pretty eyes and succulent lips. But of course you aren't Filip anymore, are you? So perhaps I should forgive your impertinence . . ." His purple eyes slashed into her. "I wouldn't want to hurt that delicious little face." The boy licked his lips and slid his hands into tight pockets, blue veins flexing through his biceps. "Wish I could stay, ladies, but I have to administer punishment to a few Everboys in the Doom Room. Caught them writing letters to their parents, asking to be rescued. As if anyone could get in or out now that the School Master's returned." He headed for the doors, then looked at Sophie. "You do remember my name, I hope?"

Sophie cowered into her nightgown, unable to speak.

"Aric. Best remember it this time, since I *am* your Dean," he purred, backing through the door. "See you at lunch, impertinent little Sophie. Faculty gets its own private spot on the balcony. Now that we're friends, I look forward to getting to know you more . . . *intimately.*"

He winked at her like a devil and then he was gone.

Sophie slowly turned to Lady Lesso, eyes big as marbles.

Lady Lesso sniffed the coffee and poured it into the plum basket. The plums liquefied with a smoking, poisonous reek.

"School Master forbade him to kill me but he still tries," she said grimly, pitching the mug out the window. "Yesterday, he put an asp in my toilet."

"Aric is your . . . your son?" Sophie gasped. "He's a monster—a murderer—he killed Tristan!"

"Nearly managed to kill me too in the brief chaos after the

Trial, before the School Master took control," the Dean said much softer now. "I don't blame him, of course. When I accepted the position of Dean of Evil fifteen years ago, it was my duty to sever all attachments—children included. But instead, I hid Aric in a cave near school, stealing in to see him at night, year after year, pretending like he had a mother who would always love and protect him." Her voice quavered and she fiddled with the plum basket. "The School Master found out and sealed me inside the gates. Never even had the chance to say goodbye to my son. Aric will never forgive me for it . . . leaving him there, six years old in the Woods, all alone. And he shouldn't." She looked at Sophie. "Like I said, you and I must both pay the price of our mistakes—and mine is having my own son vengefully plot my death, while he shares my power as Dean."

She glanced out the window with a wistful grin. "Suppose it's just like the School Master wants. Mother and son as Deans . . . a former student teaching my class . . . a timeless Master and his young queen . . . Old and New working together for Evil."

Sophie followed her eyes to what used to be the School for Evil across the bay, now the crumbling, pockmarked School for Old. There were shadowy figures on the roofs now: hulking, misshapen, and clearly not human, with bows and arrows slung on their backs, like a monstrous castle guard. Then beneath them, through a tower window, Sophie noticed another shadow—this one human. Stepping closer, she glimpsed a man's silhouette with a boat-shaped hat, like a pirate's . . . and where his hand should be, a sharp flash of metal instead . . .

A tuft of fog floated in front of him and when it cleared, the man was no longer there.

Sophie bit her lip. Rafal had refused to tell her anything about the Old castle. But she *was* queen, wasn't she? She had a right to know what he was hiding in the other school.

"Lady Lesso, please tell me what's in the School for Old," she said firmly.

"Students of the old fairy tales, of course, just like we teach a new fairy tale here. But the School for Old is the School Master's domain—not yours," the Dean snipped, before a cacophonous crackle broke through the castle, like an army of demented crickets. "That's the fairies signaling end of session." She stood up and clacked towards the door in her steel stilettos. "Shall we? Students won't respect a Curses teacher who's late. Especially a teacher who's supposed to be the new *me*."

Sophie rooted deeper in her chair, arms crossed over her nightgown. "First of all, if I'm going to stand in front of a class full of teenage boys, I at least need something to wear. Besides, even if you do get me into that classroom, I don't know any of the new fairy tales!"

"I said a new tale. Not tales."

"Well, whatever fairy tale this is, I can't possibly teach it—"

"Of course you can, since it's the only fairy tale we teach at the School for New." Lady Lesso glowered at her, holding open the door.

"*Yours.*"

12

Find the Spy

The old lollipop room in Hansel's Haven was still made of lollipops, but they'd been blown up into thousands of rainbow-colored shards and pieced into new murals across the walls.

As students flurried in from the crowded hall, Sophie sat on Professor Sheeks' old lollipop desk that had been slashed, scarred, beaten into lumps, and riddled with holes. Wearing black-suede stiletto boots and a formfitting, lacy black dress, she studied the murals of herself at her most Evil in *The Tale of Sophie and Agatha*—riding a rat to slay Agatha during the Good-Evil War . . . invisibly attacking Tedros during the Boy-Girl War . . . throwing

Agatha into a sewer . . . pushing Tedros off a cliff . . .

You fought them before, the voice inside her said. *You can do it again.*

Her hands started to shake.

I can't, Sophie panicked, looking away. *I'm different now.*

She waited for the voice inside her to agree, to speak reason and protect her friends . . .

Instead a different voice came this time. Darker. Angrier. Spewing bile.

Like mother, like daughter.

Like mother, like daughter.

Like mother, like daughter.

Like mother, like daughter.

Slowly Sophie lifted her eyes back to Agatha and Tedros, painted on the walls . . . and for a moment she saw Honora and Stefan instead.

Sophie's hands stopped shaking.

Find the spy, the witch inside whispered.

Find the spy, she obeyed, locking to the task.

A throat cleared loudly.

Sophie looked down at a class of almost forty Evers and Nevers in black-and-green uniforms crammed into seats— Beatrix, Reena, Chaddick, Nicholas, Mona, Arachne, Ravan, Vex, Millicent, Brone among them—all wearing the same putrid scowls.

"Oh hello there, um . . . c-c-class," Sophie sputtered, startled by both their expressions and the sheer number of students. "It's been a w-w-while, hasn't it?"

The student's scowls intensified.

"But we're a family now, aren't we?" Sophie fawned, trying a new tactic. "And look at you, so smart in black! Never used to like black (such a nihilistic color), but Lady Lesso said this dress belonged to Rumpelstiltskin's niece, who used to teach this very same class. Small-boned woman—not surprising since her uncle was a dwarf—so no one's been able to fit into it until me."

The students looked positively hateful now.

"Um, Lady Lesso said Pollux has been teaching in my absence," she puttered, "so perhaps we should wait for him to—"

Vex let out an angry fart.

Sophie held her breath, appalled.

Find the spy, she refocused. Someone in this room was on Good's side, trying to help kill the boy she loved . . .

And yet, with their matching scowls, all the students in the room looked equally capable of betraying Evil, Evers and Nevers alike. That is, except for Kiko in a black babushka and veil, sniffling at the back of the room. Sophie glimpsed the small pink ribbon pinned to her uniform:

Kiko saw Sophie looking at her and gave her the same horrible glare as everyone else.

"Did someone put frownies in the school gruel this morning?" Sophie simpered, trying to keep her cool.

A spitball hit her in the eye.

Sophie exploded red, not even bothering to look for who shot it. "Look, it's obvious why you're all upset, okay? When I first came to this place, you were vile to me, even though I was nothing but nice to each of you, whether greeting you in hallways, enduring your odious hygiene, or educating you about the evils of white flour. And now you're mad because the most handsome boy in the world gave me his ring, which makes me queen of the school, sitting up here with all the power, while you're down there, with no power at all. But you know what? Tough *tooties*. I've been alone my whole life, trying to find someone who loves me who won't leave me, someone who actually likes me for who I am, warts and all. And now I found him! I don't care if he's a sorcerer. I don't care if he's the most Evil boy in the world! He's *mine* and he loves me, even if I'm emotional and complicated and brutally misunderstood. So pout and be mad all you like, but after all I've endured in my life, I deserve to have true love, whether you like it or not, and the least you could do is be happy for me!"

Silence.

"That's not why we're mad," snapped Beatrix.

"No one gives a hog's behind if you have a boyfriend," Mona stabbed.

Sophie pursed her lips. "Oh. Then what's the problem?"

All the kids turned towards the window. Sophie followed their eyes to the colossal scoreboard over the Blue Forest, listing the students in order of their scores. Glowing red lines divided the board into three sections: a top group, a middle group, and a bottom group. She couldn't read any of the names through the hazy green air, except for Hort's, firmly atop the rankings.

"Third year is tracking year," growled Ravan, picking miserably at his shorn black hair. "Starting next week, we're split into dorms as Leaders, Henchmen, or Mogrifs, based on our rankings."

"Which means Evers like me have to excel at Evil or we'll end up poisonous toads!" Millicent carped to Sophie. "This is entirely your fault!"

"And it's no better for Nevers either," Mona added. "We have twice as many people to compete against now that the whole school is Evil!"

"And even if you do end up a Leader, they get double the homework as everyone else," said Vex.

"And Henchmen have to follow their Leaders and do everything they say," fretted Reena.

"And Mogrifs have to go to class as animals!" said Beatrix. "And god forbid you fail three challenges in a row. Then you end up a plant!"

"What are you upset about? You're on track to be a Leader!" Kiko said, whirling to her. "I'm third to last in the whole school! Suppose I get turned into a tulip? I can't even concentrate ever since . . . ever since . . ." She burst into tears. "Tristan *adored* tulips! Used to put them in his hair." Kiko blew her nose into her veil. "That boy loved me so much."

"Oh for Pete's sake, that boy wouldn't have loved you if you were the last girl on earth," Beatrix hissed. "Besides, I don't want to be a leader of Evil, you dimwit! Once upon a time, I was almost Class Captain in the School for Good. And now I have to uglify and curse people and have *henchmen?*"

"Sounds like a typical day for you, actually," Sophie murmured.

Beatrix gasped.

"Even the School for Boys was better than this," Chaddick contended. "Sure our castle was a little rank but at least we didn't have fairies stinging us like bees if we're a second late and Aric sending us to the Doom Room to be tortured for rules he's completely made up. He's punished every boy in school like ten times already."

"He got me for an untucked shirt yesterday," Nicholas said. "That kid is Evil."

"And not in a Good way," muttered Vex quietly.

Sophie waited for them to elaborate, but all the boys glanced at each other in tortured brotherhood, before swiveling back to her.

"Everything was fine for the last two hundred years, until you came along and messed up Good and Evil," barked Ravan.

"Boys and Girls too!" Brone boomed.

"I hope Agatha and Tedros break in and kill the School Master!" seethed Arachne. "I hope they bring Good back!"

"*Bring Good Back!*" Beatrix shouted, and all the students stomped their feet in solidarity, cheering along: "*Bring Good*

Back! Bring Good Back!"

Sophie gaped, speechless. How could she find the spy for Good if all of them were on Good's side?

"That's your job, you ninny—" a sharp nasty voice echoed outside.

The door flew open and three students pattered in, tittering loudly.

"—to follow me around and do whatever I say," grouched a pasty girl with dirty hair streaked black and red and a fearsome buck-horned demon tattooed around her neck.

"Hope I get tracked as a Leader and you as my Henchman," retorted an albino girl with a throaty rasp and three black rats sticking out of her pockets. "I'll make sure you spend the rest of your life kissing my—"

"Daddy said he'd buy me a new horse if *I* made Leader," chirped a girl behind them, round as a balloon, snacking on a bundle of chocolate daisies. "Killed my last one by accident."

"Sat on it?" scoffed the albino.

"Fed it too much fudge," said the round girl.

Suddenly all three girls stopped in their tracks and craned their heads to Sophie. They broke into toothy smiles and dropped into their seats in unison, hands folded over their bags.

"Sorry we're late," said tattooed Hester.

"Castor made us clean up after a dragon in Henchmen," said albino Anadil.

"Dragons poo a lot," said paunchy Dot, mouth full.

Sophie nearly leapt off the desk to hug her old roommates. "Oh praise heavens! My *real* friends," she beamed, so relieved to see the three smiley witches against the sea of snarls. "At least someone's happy to see me!"

"I wouldn't go that far," Hester mumbled. She started opening her book bag—then noticed the furious faces around her.

"Oh here we go," she moaned. "For the last time, you're all in the School for Evil now and that means you're fighting *for* Evil. Look at me: Aric stabbed a blade in my stomach during the Trial and now I obey his every word. You want to stay alive? You want the sun to stop melting? Then do what the teachers say and help Sophie kill Agatha and Tedros."

"I thought Agatha was your friend," Ravan sniped.

"Excuse me? *These* are my friends," Hester said, pointing to Anadil and Dot with a glowing red fingertip. "The coven everyone fears and yet wants to be in. The clique that doesn't give a damn what you think. The sinful, sinistral, all-around-original Three Witches of Room 66."

"Dot's even fat again," Anadil quipped.

Dot frowned.

"Sure, Agatha was likable in a handicapped-dog kind of way," Hester went on, "but I learned my lesson when I almost died at Aric's hands defending her. All I ever wanted was for Evil to have a normal school again, where we learn Evil things and learn to be better villains than my incompetent mother was. And now because of Sophie, we don't just have one Evil school, we have *two*."

"Plus for the first time, villains can have a Never After!" Dot reveled. "You know what that means, don't you?" She gave Ravan a wink. "Evil Valentine's Day!"

Ravan gagged.

"And if we don't want love, that's fine too," said Anadil, with a repulsed look. "Once Sophie's storybook closes, Evil will prove it can win, with villains no longer cursed to die."

"Here's to free Evil!" hollered Hester.

"Here's to free will!" hooted Dot.

"Here's to Queen Sophie!" Anadil proclaimed, banging fists loudly on her desk, as Hester and Dot chanted and three black rats squeaked: *"Here's to Queen Sophie! Here's to Queen Sophie!"*

No one else joined them.

"Did the 'Bring Good Back' cheer already, didn't they?" Dot sighed.

Sophie smiled at her three witch champions. At least she knew who *wasn't* the spy.

The door flew open behind her and an obese pink flamingo stumbled in—or rather most of an obese pink flamingo, since a dog head was attached to its body, trying and failing to navigate it. "Apologies for the late arrival," he smarmed, resting awkwardly against a wall. "Castor was feeling ill, so I took over his Henchmen class and led the students in a rousing anthem I've composed for Lord Aric, our illustrious Dean. Would you like to hear it? It's best performed by a 52-piece symphony and soprano choir, but I'm sure I can replicate the effect—"

He saw Sophie at the teacher's desk. "Oh. Hello . . . former *student*," the dog sniffed.

Sophie glowered at Pollux, one half of a two-headed Cerberus who routinely lost the battle to use their body to his rabid brother Castor. She could have gone the rest of her life without seeing this oily, spineless, brown-noser again, who'd clearly buttered up Aric in order to avoid being imprisoned with the rest of the Good teachers, just like he'd buttered up Evelyn Sader last year to avoid being evicted with the Boys. Even worse, Pollux was clearly lying about why he was late, since her three witch friends said they were just helping Castor clean up dragon poo.

"Would you like to take a seat amongst your kind?" Pollux jabbed, as if reading her thoughts. "I assumed you'd leave the class to me since it has been *mine* the past few weeks."

"I'm quite fine where I am," Sophie retorted, suddenly happy to be a teacher if it meant riling up this boob. She turned back to the class. "Might you tell me what you've been learning, students?"

"*The Tale of Sophie and Agatha*, inside and out," said Hort, rolling into the room without books or a bag, his hand slid up his shirt, showing off his rippled stomach. "You know, trying to spot Agatha's and Tedros' weaknesses, so we can kill 'em and finally stop being losers." He dropped into a seat, blew his dark bangs out of his glittering black eyes, and stretched his chest with a yawn.

Sophie goggled at Hort's broad shoulders, casual stubble, and laid-back slouch. In a month, he'd gone from wimpy, earnest pipsqueak to teenage heartthrob. She noticed all the other girls slyly checking him out, Evers and Nevers both. *It must be a makeover spell*, she thought, watching him toss his hair. *Or a twin brother or a deal with the devil or something . . .* Hort caught her looking and scowled at her murderously like he had in the foyer. Sophie stiffened and pretended to listen to Pollux.

"As Hort points out, the first week we did a unit on Tedros' shortcomings as a prince," the dog said, plopping on the teacher's desk and shoving Sophie over. He waved a wing and the lollipop colors on the walls rearranged to scenes of Tedros' worst moments from *The Tale of Sophie and Agatha*. "And what did we learn class? Yes, Hester!"

"He has serious daddy issues," Hester said, leering at a painting of Tedros killing a gargoyle in Merlin's menagerie.

"Excellent! Yes, Anadil?"

"He doesn't trust girls since his mother left him," said the albino, pointing at a painting of Tedros shooting an arrow at Agatha in Evil's Grand Hall.

"Spot on! Yes, Dot?"

"He's obsessed with swords," chimed Dot, nodding at a scene of Tedros almost kissing Filip in a forest.

Pollux blinked at her. "Moving on to our challenge . . ."

Thoughts of Hort fell away as Sophie studied the painting of her and Tedros together when she was Filip. He'd been so vulnerable with her when she was a boy, so nurturing and soft, and she'd seen the real Tedros underneath his macho facade. They'd become so close in that short time, blood and soul mates, like she and Agatha once upon a time. Sophie blushed, reliving the moment when he finally touched her in the Blue Forest. It was all based on a lie, of course. Tedros would have never opened up to her if he'd known who she was. She'd lost that Tedros forever . . . that perfect, beautiful boy who'd tried to kiss his best friend . . .

Sophie scorched red. Tedros wanted to kill Rafal and she was *blushing* over him?

You have a new love, she gritted, pinching her thigh hard. *Stop thinking about old ones.*

"So with all this in mind," Pollux prattled, his bird bottom shunting Sophie to the edge of the desk, "today's class challenge is to delve even deeper into Tedros' mind. In a moment, all of you will be concealed under magical Tedros masks. Since Sophie insists on playing '*teacher*,' she'll be responsible for judging who most acts like the real prince. Whoever she deems the most Tedros-like wins first rank." He rammed Sophie off the desk, knocking her to the floor.

"Shall we?" he snipped down at her.

A few minutes later, Sophie stood, blindfolded with a smelly black rag, as she listened to students rearrange seats.

The spy must be Tedros' friend if they're going to help him break in, she thought. *And the spy is the only one who's been in touch with him since he vanished.* Which meant that whoever won this challenge, whoever knew Tedros well enough to mimic him, would surely be the prime suspect.

"Everyone find a new place? We don't want Sophie remembering where you were," Pollux's voice called, before she heard the last backside plunk down. "All right. The cloaking spell will cover your face in a phantom mask. Don't touch or it might glue to your face permanently. You hear me? *Don't touch.*"

"This school is so unsafe," Reena's voice crabbed.

"Ready?" Pollux said. "One . . . two . . . three—"

Sophie heard a loud, windy crack, and then dead quiet.

"The masks are hot," Ravan's voice grumped.

"And *blond*," Hester's voice groaned.

"Shhhhh!" hissed Pollux. "Sophie, on your mark . . . get set . . . go!"

Sophie flung off the blindfold.

If she'd blushed pink before looking at Tedros' face on the walls, now she was as pink as Pollux's feathers.

There were forty Tedroses seated in front of her, reflecting back his crystal-blue eyes, fluffy gold locks, and tan, flawless skin. Yet, there was a strange haziness to the faces, rubbery thick and oddly luminous at the edges, so she couldn't discern the necks and clothes beneath the masks. Some of the Tedroses were smiling, some sneering, some frosty and blank eyed, but as she scanned the sum of these gorgeous princes, Sophie felt her cheeks burning even hotter.

Stop blushing, you idiot! Tedros isn't your friend anymore! No, he was the boy who'd rejected her for her best friend; the boy who wanted to kill her true love; the poster boy for Good who had a spy working against her in this very room . . .

"Well?" Pollux huffed.

Sophie braced herself and waded into the sea of princes. One by one, she analyzed them, but it only took seconds to see the fraudulence each time. The smile was too snarky or dopey, his posture too rigid or slouched or there was a flicker of self-doubt—a hang of the head, a bob of the throat—that the real Tedros never had. One Tedros nearly fooled her in the second row, but he flinched as she made eye contact, and the real Tedros would have held his stare, strong and unyielding, until your heart turned to putty and you were his. None of the others around him even came close and soon she was in the final row, no closer to finding Good's spy . . . until the last Tedros stopped her cold.

She locked into his steady blue eyes, sparkling with mischief. He bit his juicy lower lip and cocked a brow, almost more Tedros than Tedros himself, and Sophie felt a flash of fire rip through her body.

This one, she thought, girding her loins. *This is the one that knows him best. This is the spy.*

She leaned in teasingly, daring the spy at his or her own game. But the closer she drew, the more she felt the warmth off the prince's dewy skin and smelled that stirring mix of mint and wood, until Sophie's heart began to hammer and she knew this wasn't a spy—this was him, the *real* him, and he'd ditched Agatha to be with her! Stunned, panicked, exhilarated, she hugged him with a gasp: "Teddy, it's *you*!"

Rubber instantly melted to skin and Hort glared back at her.

"*Don't touch.*"

Sophie recoiled in shock—

A "1" rank exploded over Hort's head in a crown of green smoke, as rankings popped up over everyone else, their masks melting away over their usual faces.

"Well done, Hort!" Pollux said. "You'll no doubt help our queen kill the *real* Tedros."

"No doubt," said Hort, still staring daggers at Sophie.

"I'm so going to end up a pea shoot," Kiko mewled behind him, a black-cloud "20" raining on her head.

Sophie was in such a fog that by the time she'd gathered her wits, the fairies had clamored and the students were all rushing out the door into the crowded hall. Punch-drunk, she lumbered after them still trying to grasp how Hort had become Tedros and Tedros back to Hort and why she'd tried to hug Tedros at all—

Three witches suddenly scooted past her doorway.

"Almost caught us on dragon poo!" Dot whispered.

"I told you we should have a different excuse," Hester growled.

"No one noticed a thing," shushed Anadil.

Sophie shook off her daze and hurried after her former roommates, eager to debrief like they always did. "Hey! Wait up!" she called excitedly—

But instead of waiting, the three witches stopped dead at the sound of her voice and scurried ahead even faster than before.

Alone in the doorway, Sophie watched them blend into the black-robed mob, her smile slowly flattening, at a loss to explain why her only three friends at this school had just acted like they weren't her friends at all.

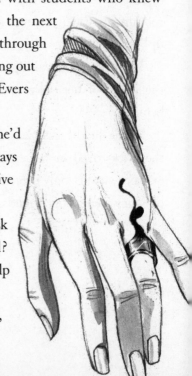

13

Too Many Boys

Normally teachers at the School for Good and Evil taught multiple sessions, but Lady Lesso had given Sophie only one, which the Dean had filled with students who knew Agatha and Tedros best. But as the next class began, Sophie wandered through Hansel's Haven, no closer to finding out who the spy was or how the two Evers planned to get in.

It can't be Hort, even though he'd won the challenge, for he'd always hated Tedros and had no incentive to help him.

But who then? Who would risk their lives to help Good slay Rafal? Who would risk their lives to help Good win *her* back?

She roamed past classrooms,

peeking through doors at teachers preparing students to ambush Agatha and Tedros. In Uglification, Professor Manley led students in a Camouflage Challenge that magically blended them into school furnishings in order to surprise the enemy; in History, Rafal lectured the students on ways intruders had once tried to break into the School for Good and Evil; in Special Talents, Professor Sheeks hosted an open-sparring tournament where students deployed their special talents against each other; and out in the Blue Forest, Aric forced students through a boot-camp obstacle course, while fairies stung anyone who lagged behind.

Standing on the third-floor balcony, Sophie marveled at Aric, hulking and sweat-soaked in his sleeveless shirt, barking orders at his students. For a murderous, cretinous thug, he was sickly good-looking.

Her face reddened. *Did I just have that thought?*

Aric suddenly looked up at her, as if he was inside her head, and gave her a knife-edged smile.

A hand touched her and Sophie screamed.

"Glad to know I'm still scary," Rafal smirked.

Sophie stared at her handsome young beau, his shirt strings untied. "Sorry . . . was just . . ."

Rafal glanced down and saw Aric in her sightline. The young School Master stopped smiling. "How did class go?"

Sophie noticed Hort over his shoulder, as Beatrix flirted with him in a corner.

"Sophie?"

"Mmm?"

Rafal caught her glancing at Hort. Sophie instantly looked back at Rafal. "Oh! Lovely! Class was just lovely," she blithered.

The School Master frowned. "Look, I have to go in, but I'll see you at lunch. We have a private spot on the balcony—"

But now Sophie was staring at Reena and Ravan as they walked by, both wearing white swan pins that said *"Bring Good Back!"* with Tedros' handsome face painted on them. The prince was painted so heroically, so dashingly, that Sophie's heart ignited—

Rafal spun and the two kids' pins instantly reverted to black swans with Rafal's young face and the words *"Evil Rules!"* He narrowed his eyes and turned to Sophie.

"You seem distracted," he said icily.

"Me? No, no—" Sophie forced a cough. "Just tired. You know, still recovering from being sick . . ."

Rafal's gem-blue eyes sliced into hers, as if shaking down her soul, and Sophie's stomach twisted. She kissed him on the cheek, squeezing his arm. "I'll see you at lunch, okay?"

Rafal searched her face a long moment . . . then softened. "Don't be late. I'll be waiting for you." He touched his cold fingers to her lips.

Sophie watched him head into his classroom, making sure to give him a bright smile and wave as he went inside . . .

The moment his door closed, she took off like a hare, scampering straight out of Hansel's Haven, desperately in need of a place to think.

Rafal was right. She *was* distracted, suddenly unable to pay attention to her one true love, the true love whose ring she was wearing, the true love she'd fought her whole story to find. And she was distracted by the same thing that had distracted her from the day she was born—

Boys.

Too many boys.

Sophie shut the frosted door behind her and stood in cold, gray sunshine on the roof of the old Honor Tower. Slouching against black glass, she looked out at the Endless Woods beyond the slimy green bay, hidden beneath weakly lit skies that made morning look like dusk. With a deep breath, she pulled herself up and headed towards Merlin's Menagerie, the topiary tribute to King Arthur that had always been her and Agatha's favorite spot to think—

Her eyes widened.

The hedges of the menagerie no longer reflected King Arthur's story—but his son's instead. Sophie moved through the garden, taking in scenes of barechested Tedros meeting Agatha for the first time, Tedros asking Agatha to the Evers Snow Ball, Tedros rescuing thorn-gashed Agatha from the Endless Woods . . .

Why would the School for Evil celebrate a Good love story? she thought, studying Agatha in Tedros' arms. Old pangs of jealousy stirred and she tried to hold them down, reminding herself that Tedros wasn't her true love anymore. He was Agatha's. *Like Rafal is mine.*

And yet, ten minutes later, she was still drifting through

hedges and poring over every inch of Tedros and Agatha's romantic memorial, unable to tear herself away, before she arrived at the final sculpture of the prince and princess, wrapped in their first kiss beneath a willow.

Strange, wasn't it, Sophie thought, moving closer. She'd kissed Agatha . . . Agatha had kissed Tedros . . . and yet, *she'd* never kissed Tedros. And she never would. Because he was the enemy now, he was the villain . . . and besides, she had her own boy to kiss . . . a boy so much fairer and smarter and better than the one Agatha was kissing right in front of her . . . So why was she on tiptoes, then, inhaling the smell of their minty kiss, touching a gold-ringed finger to her friends' locked lips—

Her fingertip burst into a violent, blistering rash.

Sophie choked in surprise.

The bloodred pox chased up her hand, her arm, her shoulder like a carnivorous animal, sizzling so hot she couldn't breathe . . .

Seconds later, Sophie barreled through the old Valor breezeway like a rhinoceros, crashing through students leaving fourth session, who plastered against walls at the sight of her. Hurtling up the spiral stairs, she threw open the door to the Dean's office, her entire body covered in raging blisters, the rash surging up her neck towards her face—

Professor Manley and Lady Lesso calmly looked back at her, both teachers silhouetted at the window.

"Told you someone would get hurt, Bilious," sighed Lady Lesso.

"Only if they were stupid enough to touch an Evers' love

story," Manley growled at Sophie. "Get to the Groom Room at once and soak in the steam bath."

"But Dean Sader incinerated the Groom Room!" Sophie breathed in pain.

"Only the Girls'," said Lady Lesso. "Use the Boys'."

Sophie hightailed for the stairs, Rafal's ring knifing into her swollen finger—

"Sophie?" Manley called out.

She turned.

"Your love for Rafal has inspired all of Evil," he said, softening. "Teachers included."

Sophie smiled tightly and ran away.

By the time Sophie made it to the Boys' Groom Room, four flights down, the rash had devoured her entire face, with her skin and eyelids so inflamed she could barely see. Thankfully the boys' spa looked deserted. Peering through tearing slits, she scanned the Midas Gold sweat lodge, peasant-themed tanning room, gymnasium with Norse hammers, saltwater lap pool, and steaming Turkish baths, smelling of sulfur and sweat. Her left eye suddenly ballooned thicker, sealing up tight, and she stumbled like a cyclops towards the steamiest bath before she slipped on its rim and careened headfirst into scalding water, her dress inflating like a parachute—

Instantly the red pustules began to recede.

Bubbles flowed over her numb, swollen face, restoring her skin little by little until she felt water jets blast her clear cheeks and Rafal's ring loosen on her finger. With a relieved breath,

Sophie flung to the surface, whipping her hair like a mermaid out of the sea and opened her eyes with a smile.

Hort glowered at her through steam.

"If it isn't Little Miss Liar."

Sophie blanched and scrambled back like a crab to escape.

"Scared, are you?" Hort taunted.

"No, I'm just not in the habit of taking steam baths with random boys," snapped Sophie, pulling out of the tub.

"Random boy?" Hort smirked. "I was your *best friend* last year, remember? The best friend who helped you survive boys' classes, who helped you beat Tedros, who you promised to take into the Trial, only to take Tedros instead—"

"Nice chat," Sophie babbled, hurrying away—

Only then did she notice the red cluster of pox on her arms, still healing.

"Couple more minutes and they'll clear up," Hort said behind her. "Leave now and they might scar *forever*."

Sophie glared at him through the mist, shirtless in his black shorts, his pale, toned chest flushed pink from the heat.

"Couple more minutes," she muttered, sliding into the tub as far away from him as she could.

"Perks of being top-ranked. Can work out whenever I want and the teachers don't say much," said Hort, picking at a small pimple on his arm. "Now I see why Tedros was obsessed with this place. Narcissists must love it here. Lucky they had that woodpecker keeping track of time or Prince Pretty Face would never have left. Bird's probably locked up with the other Good teachers by now, of course. Nymphs too. You should see who's stuck working the Laundry."

"I don't get it. Why is there still a Groom Room in an Evil castle?"

"Ask your new boyfriend," Hort spat. "Uses it more than anyone. Clearly trying to look good for you."

"*Rafal* uses the Groom Room?"

"Oh, that's his name now? Suppose he needs a new name to go with the new face so you're not reminded of the old one. Nice try, but I'll stick with 'School Master.'"

"He's no older than you or me," Sophie defended.

"Keep telling yourself that. Can't speak too poorly about the man though. Gave my father a proper tomb when I begged him to. I mean, it wasn't Necro Ridge with the best villains, where Dad shoulda been buried, but Vulture Vale was good enough. Especially considering the School Master don't like me much. You know, since I was in love with you and all. But at least he had the decency to let my dad rest in peace."

"See, he's not so bad, is he?" Sophie soothed. "And now your father finally got the grave he deserved. Because he had a noble, persistent son who made sure of it."

Hort nodded, hiding a sniffle.

"Meanwhile, seems like you've been spending a fair amount of time in the Groom Room yourself," Sophie ribbed. "Almost as Tedros-like as your imitation of him."

"Well, I should know him better than anyone, shouldn't I?" Hort retorted, hardening.

"Huh? Why would you know anything about Tedros?"

Hort snarled. "Either you're lying again or you're as stupid as you look. You ditch me first year for him when you were a girl. You ditch me second year for him when you were a boy. You lie and cheat and steal for him while he treats you like crap, and I help you and care for you and worship you like a queen while you treat *me* like crap! What does that guy have that I don't? What makes him so lovable and me so unworthy? Know how many times I've asked myself that question, Sophie? How many times I've studied him like a book or sat in the dark picturing every last shred of him, trying to understand why he's more of a person than me? Or why the moment he's gone, you take a ring from the School Master—or Raphael or Michelangelo or Donatello or whatever you want to call him to make yourself feel better—just because he looks like you want him to look and says what you want to hear? When you could have had someone who's honest and kind and real?" His black, beady eyes lanced right through her.

Sophie checked her arm, desperate to get out of this tub, but her blisters were still raw. "First of all, don't call me stupid, Hort. Second of all, please believe me when I say I'm sorry for last year, okay? I still don't know why Tedros' name came out of my mouth instead of yours. I'm done with him . . . I really am. I don't know what else to say—"

"As if I'd believe anything you said anyway," Hort snorted. "I've already killed you and kissed you more times in my head than you deserve."

Sophie stared at him.

Hort sighed, flicking the water. "But I learned my lesson.

No one wants Old Hort. So meet New Hort instead. Modeled right after your cool, manly prince. The Hort chicks dig."

"But that Hort isn't real at all," said Sophie, frowning. "That Hort isn't you."

"Well, whoever it is . . ." Hort raised his gaze. "Finally got your attention, didn't he?"

Sophie fell silent.

"Yikes, getting pruney," Hort deflected, assessing his wrinkled fingers. He started to push out of the tub. "Besides, your new boyfriend's probably waiting for you."

Sophie watched him get out, water sliding down the curves of his back.

"Hort?"

He stopped, still facing away from her. The only sound in the room was the drip of his shorts onto the carpet.

"Do you still love me?" she whispered.

Slowly Hort turned to Sophie with a sad smile, looking like the raw, openhearted boy she once knew.

"No."

Sophie averted her eyes. "Oh good. Yes. Glad to hear it," she chimed, fussing with her dress before looking up. "You know, with my new boyfriend and all—"

But Hort was gone.

For a long time, Sophie stayed in the steaming pool, sweating and gazing at the spot where he'd been, even after her arm was well healed, even after her skin had shriveled dry. And only when she heard the shriek of fairies rip through the castle did Sophie realize then that she hadn't just missed the start of lunch.

She'd missed it completely.

As midnight came and went, Sophie sat calmly in the School Master's window, her hair still wet, her ebony dress bunched at the knees as she pressed bare toes against the wall. She looked out at the fluorescent green bay, reflecting the shadows of two black castles, both dark and quiet.

How quickly things changed in a fairy tale.

Rafal hadn't been too upset, thank goodness—she claimed she'd gotten lost in the throng on the way to lunch *("It's like an overcrowded zoo, Rafal.")* and trapped herself in a broom closet *("So much black in this place—hard to tell the closets from the students!")*. Rafal interrupted her, looking stressed: he'd barely been at lunch himself, he said, and told her he had important business in the School for Old that would keep him there until the morning. With a kiss, he left her on her own and off the hook (except for a stern visit from Lady Lesso, who'd chastised her for being no closer to finding the spy).

Sophie curled her knees to her chest and glanced at the Storian, paused over a blank page. It hadn't drawn a new scene since early in the evening, when it painted Agatha and Tedros disappearing into a rabbit hole and Tedros fainting at the sight of a bearded old man. She'd tried to flip back in the storybook to see who this old man was and where Agatha and her prince were in the Woods, but the Storian had stabbed her when she'd tried to turn pages, nearly impaling her hand. Once a story was unfolding, it seemed you couldn't go back.

Sophie did a few half-hearted yoga poses, trying to take her mind off the two Evers, then gave up and slumped onto the edge of the bed, looking out the window again.

Somewhere out there her best friends were writing their own side of the story. Somewhere out there they were coming to rescue her from a school she would have once done anything to be rescued from . . . coming to convince her to leave Evil and its Master behind forever . . .

Or so they think.

Because now she felt at home here in Evil. Sure, there were a few pitfalls her first day, but she was still a teacher and queen, superior to all the other students. More importantly, she was about to win Evil's first fairy tale in two hundred years! She was about to be a legend for all time, more famous than Snow White, Cinderella, and every other old, blank-eyed, pink princess who never had a mind of her own . . .

And to think, I used to be like those fools.

But now she was ready to fight for Evil.

Kill, even.

Because unlike all Evil that came before her, she had someone to fight for.

Rafal, she thought, admiring her ring, imagining his gorgeous, snow-cold face in its reflection . . .

Only now she was seeing Hort instead, pink and warm in steaming blue mist . . .

Then violet-eyed Aric, primal and perspiring in the Forest . . .

Sophie shrank against the wall, nauseous.

After finally finding her true love, now she was fantasizing about Hort? About Aric? After everything she'd done to find love?

Rafal *had* to be the one, after all.

No one else loved her anymore.

Not even Hort.

I need proof, she thought. *That's all.*

I need proof Rafal is the one.

Then I'll stop doubting.

Then I'll stop thinking of other boys.

She lifted her eyes to the dark, empty room.

Prove it, she begged her heart.

Prove he's my true love.

The School Master's chamber was dead silent.

All of a sudden, the ring on her finger started to move.

Slowly it slid down her finger by its own power, settling below the knuckle.

It was still for a moment, cold against her left hand. Then the ring magically melted before her eyes, the gold turning darker and darker, softer and softer, deconstructing into a circle of gleaming black liquid.

Sophie held her breath, staring at the ring of ink, warm and wet on her finger, gripping her skin like a leech—

But now she saw what the ring was doing.

It was writing a first letter into her finger.

It was writing the name of her true love.

Just like she'd asked.

Sophie smiled and closed her eyes, letting her inner fairy godmother do her work.

Inky and wet, the ring calmly slashed into her skin, controlled by something deep within her. With every new letter, Sophie's soul breathed freer, lighter, as if a crushing weight had been lifted, as if the force moving the ring was her true self, her purest self . . . until at last, the ring finished the last letter and hardened back to solid gold, leaving the name "Rafal" upon her without a doubt . . . Rafal who she'd be with forever . . .

Slowly Sophie opened her eyes and saw the name in squid-black ink.

It wasn't Rafal's.

She fell off the bed in shock.

Petrified, she grabbed the hem of her dress and scrubbed at the name, trying to erase it.

Still there.

She scraped with her nails, buffed it on the floor, chafed it against the wall—but the name was even darker than before. Thunderstruck, she cowered against the bed, hiding her hand in her dress, trying to calm her screaming heart.

It didn't matter what name was there!

There was no way that name was her true love.

There was no way that name was her happy ending.

Because the name the ring had tattooed on Sophie's skin, the name it had promised was her one true love, was the name of the prince she was supposed to kill.

14

Where Wizards Go to Think

"I suppose the entrance was a bit dramatic," Merlin mulled in his musical baritone as he reclined Tedros onto the sofa, his purple cape accidentally smothering the prince's face. "But a good wizard can't very well loaf in like a delivery boy, can he?"

"Don't *talk* to me!" Tedros mumbled, his voice cracking as he shoved Merlin and his robes away. "You think you can mosey in and tell jokes and pretend everything's *okay*?" He smeared angry tears, turning his ire on Agatha. "And just so you know, I didn't faint, so don't even think about it!"

"Put your legs up here," Agatha said calmly, stripping off the prince's socks and lifting his clammy feet onto the ottoman.

"Tell all the old farts that

I didn't faint. *Tell* them."

"They're busy eating supper, not even paying the slightest attention to you," Agatha replied, peeking up to see Yuba and the other League members instantly duck their heads to their plates of mashed carrots and gruel at the dining table, pretending to have a conversation.

"And even if I did faint, you fainted *twice*," Tedros snapped, wiping his runny nose with his sleeve.

"Nice to see the future of Camelot is in mature hands," said Agatha, jamming another pillow under his head.

"He was even more emotional as a child. Imagine that!" Merlin piped, smacking the dust out of his robes before he plunked down in a rocking chair, doffed his hat, and pulled a cherry lollipop out of it like a carnival magician. "Of his future princess, his father would say, 'Look for the girl who is truly Good.'" Merlin sucked loudly on the lollipop. "I, on the other hand, said, 'Look for the girl who will give you a good kick in the rump.'"

Tedros glowered, red-eyed. "You think this is funny?"

Merlin burped and tugged at his moustache. "Tedros, I know I have a lot to explain—"

"No. *No* explaining. There's nothing to explain!" Tedros waved him off. "Mother runs off with Father's best friend when I'm nine. Runs off with Lancelot, of all people—Lancelot, the knight I idolized, who carried me on his back and gave me my first sword and acted like he was my friend too. She didn't even say goodbye, Merlin! As if Dad and I were strangers, as if we were *nothing*. But no matter how much I cried or cursed her, no matter how many times I watched Dad lock himself in his chamber, at least we still had you. You kept our family together when it was falling apart." Tedros welled up again. "And then a week later, you disappear in the middle of the night, just like she did. Not a word to my father after guiding him his whole *life*. Not a word to me, who you took questing in the Woods like I was your own. Father said you left because your life was in danger—said you'd created a spell that messed with boys and girls and could bring down whole kingdoms; that word of the spell had spread and armies were coming for you. . . . But the Merlin I knew was stronger than any army, bigger than any danger. The Merlin I knew would have put my dad before his own life."

Tedros heaved a breath. "I was ten years old and had to watch my father die, as weak as he was once strong. I kept telling myself you'd come back. Merlin couldn't abandon me like this: an orphan in a giant castle, with no mother, no father, no one to care about me. But years went by and I told myself you were dead. You had to be. So I mourned you like I did Father, promising to make you proud for the rest of my life, wherever in heaven you were." Tedros let out a sob, burying his face in a pillow. "And now you show up . . . *alive?*"

Agatha gazed at Tedros, her own eyes misting. She wanted to touch him, but he was too raw. Slowly, she looked up at Merlin, seeing a selfish old villain now instead of a hero.

The brightness in Merlin's face drained away. He flicked his finger and the lollipop evaporated as he leaned into his chair. "I should have left the castle long before that night, Tedros. Your father had stopped viewing me as his friend and more as an old fool, there only to nag and point fingers and hold him back. Indeed, he'd come to my cave only days before demanding a spell to spy on Guinevere, but I'd held firm that matters of the heart were too delicate for magic. The young Arthur would have trusted my advice and confronted her, even if it wounded his pride or led to a truth he wasn't ready to accept. But the old Arthur, green-eyed and arrogant, stole a spell recipe from my cave like a vengeful child, changing himself from a boy to a girl in order to trap his own *wife*. I had to leave Camelot. Not just to protect myself, but to protect your father most of all. Had the spell not been there for him to take, perhaps Arthur and I may have found a different ending. Though that in itself may be wishful thinking. As he told me many times before that day in anger, 'I don't need you anymore.'"

Tedros rubbed his eyes, scarlet fading from his cheeks. "And what about me? What if I needed you?"

"I couldn't make the same mistakes with you as I'd made with your father," said Merlin. "I'd sheltered him from his own weaknesses, and because of it, those weaknesses won. I had to let you write your own story, Tedros . . . to let you grow up on your own, until the day when you truly needed me to survive. If I'd tried to say goodbye, you would have followed me into the Woods. Still, you'll never know how hard it was to leave you. As much as you may have needed me, I needed you far more." The wizard's voice wavered slightly. "I took solace in the fact that I was never truly gone, watching you as an eagle watches from the sky, following every twist and turn of your story. Cringing perhaps, at some of your mistakes, fatheaded as they were. And yet knowing that all these mistakes were yours, beautifully yours, and you came out the better for it . . . the boy I left behind well on his way to becoming an extraordinary man and an extraordinary king." Merlin smiled. "If only from your choice of princess alone."

Tedros and Agatha looked at each other and turned away, blushing, as if unsure whether they were still in a fight.

"Though you will certainly have interesting children," Merlin murmured, studying them.

Agatha's buttocks clenched.

Tedros yawned and balled his knees to his chest. "Well, after everything you've put me through, the least you can do is make me one, M," he grumbled, peeking at Merlin. "Double marshmallow and candy cream as usual, please."

Merlin cracked a smile. "What'd I tell you? The second I show up they turn back into little boys," he sighed. Out of his starry cone hat he pulled a tall stone mug of steaming chocolate with two giant fluffy marshmallows and a mountain of rainbow-sprinkled whipped cream and slid it into the prince's hand.

Tedros was about to take a sip . . . then looked up at Agatha. "Want to try?"

Agatha blinked at him. Her prince was the poster boy for chivalry, except when it came to food; he'd practically eaten her out of the house in Gavaldon, stolen last bites from under her too many times to count, and never offered her a single morsel of his own meals. So as he held out his mug, looking

so handsome and earnest, Agatha teared up like an idiot—
because after all the fights and tension and resentment, it
meant that Tedros still loved her.

Taking the warm mug from him, she slurped at the bub-
bling, rich chocolate and candy-studded cream and a riot of
sweetness exploded on her tongue, as if she'd inhaled all of
Hansel's Haven in one bite. "Whoa," she shivered, going
for another sip, but Tedros snatched it back so violently that
Agatha burst into cackles.

"Where were you all these years, Merlin?" Tedros finally
asked, with a whipped-cream moustache that looked remark-
ably like his mentor's.

"Exploring the Woods, my dear boy!" Merlin declared,
digging deep in his hat for a round yellow balloon. It magically
flitted out of his hands with a mousy squeak and inflated over
his head. "They really are Endless, you know. The man-eating
hills of Mahadeva, the upside-down kingdom of Borna Coric,
the haunted fog of Akgul, the black seas of Ooty, led by an
eight-armed queen—" The balloon frantically contorted into
the images he was describing, trying to keep up. "I even spent
Christmas one year in Altazarra, a kingdom where everything
is made entirely out of milk or honey, with rivers of fresh but-
ter cream, castles of Swiss cheese and honeycomb, and roads
paved with thick yogurt. Everyone is quite obese, of course,
but brilliantly happy, though not as happy as the villagers of
Nupur Lala, who have a rare birth condition that leaves them
all born without tongues. You'd be surprised how deliriously
happy people are when they can't speak. And yet, no matter

where I went, they recognized me from King Arthur's story-book and treated me as an honored guest, though it meant I often had to do a bit of musty magic to earn supper and a bed (or in the case of Kingdom Kyrgios, a giant peapod). Amazing how tales travel, really, and it never ceased, no matter how far I went, each kingdom just as familiar with the legend of Arthur as the next, inspiring me to journey farther and farther, intoxicated with novelty, celebrity, and most of all inexhaustible beauty . . ."

The balloon popped with a gunshot crack, sputtering back into the hat. Merlin plopped it on his head with a sigh. "Yet as anything else, beauty grows tiring. For all my adoring fans, I began to feel a rot inside, as if finally turning as old on the inside as I was on the outside, as if there was no point to seeking adventures if I had no one to share these adventures *with*. . . . And yet, just as I told myself that it might indeed be time to die after all, Yuba managed to track me down on a glacier in the middle of the Piranha Lakes. The League of Thirteen had reconvened, he said. And a lad named Tedros was bringing his princess to meet it."

Agatha and Tedros gaped at him, as if still stuck on the honey and cheese.

"Reconvened?" asked Agatha, her brain catching up. "The League of Thirteen existed before?"

"Why did it convene in the first place?" Tedros asked.

"Here come the questions," Merlin moaned, yanking his hat down over his eyes. "I wish I was a seer. Then I would have an excuse not to answer them. No questions until after dinner.

Both of you must be ravenous."

"Not for old-people food," Tedros grouched, eyeing the others finishing up their carrots, gruel, and prune stew.

"Well, then I'm afraid you can't have any of this," Merlin said and began pulling a sumptuous spread out of his hat, with pork ribs, sweet potato mash, creamed corn and bacon cubes, pickled cucumbers, and coconut-curried rice heaped on silver platters which he lay across a white silk picnic blanket which had magically appeared on the cave floor. "After all, given that I, an old person, just made it, I believe it would fall squarely under the term 'old-people food.' Come, Agatha." He drew a plate out of his hat for her and lavished it with pork, cucumbers, and corn.

Mouth salivating, Agatha was about to start shoveling food, when she saw Tedros' face, like a beaten puppy's. She cocked a grin and held out a rib. "Want to try?"

Tedros beamed and the two of them assaulted the spread in rapturous silence, while Merlin rocked pleasantly in his chair and licked a new lollipop.

"What I miss most about being young," Cinderella crabbed, slurping liquefied prunes as she watched them.

"Fun?" said Peter Pan wistfully.

"Feasting," Cinderella grumped.

"Looks like you've done enough feasting for a lifetime," snorted Pinocchio. He saw the whole table staring at him. "Did I say that out loud?"

The young prince and princess ate and ate until they were stuffed, topping it off with a hunk of cappuccino mousse cake, before they collapsed against the wall, groaning against each other, letting their puffed bellies rest. Afterward Yuba brought them a pot of hot water and a scrub cloth and Agatha and Tedros took turns behind the curtain washing themselves, once Merlin conjured cottony white pajamas for each of them. As the other League members tucked into their mattresses for an early bedtime, Agatha looked up at Merlin nervously.

"We have to convince Sophie her happy ending is with Tedros and me. You can help us get into school to see her?"

"What if she won't destroy the ring? What if the School Master catches us?" Tedros pushed worriedly. "Merlin, he still has my sword. *Father's* sword! I can't be crowned king without Excalibur—"

Merlin huddled into the pair of pajama-clad Evers. "Let's go someplace where we can think."

Agatha frowned. "We can't go into the Woods after dark. Suppose one of those old villains finds us—"

"Who said anything about the Woods?" said Merlin. He flung open the lining of his cape, revealing a swathe of dark purple silk embroidered with five-pointed stars, like a child's crude rendition of a night sky. "*This*, my dear, is where wizards go to think."

Agatha had no idea what he was talking about, but then she saw Tedros smiling. "Come on, silly," he said, and grabbing her by the hand, he pulled her right into the starry sky stitched on Merlin's cape. Agatha felt herself smothered by silk and then falling through darkness, comets of light zooming past and blinding her, until she closed her eyes and landed on something so soft and fluffy and warm that she knew she wasn't in the Woods anymore.

"Your mother is the reason the League of Thirteen even exists," Merlin said to Agatha, his bony legs poking out of his purple robes and dangling over the edge of a puffy white cloud.

Agatha still wasn't paying attention. Seated cross-legged with Tedros on the same cloud, both of them in angelic white, she scanned a purple night sky lit up by thousands of silvery five-pointed stars, as if the childish pattern on Merlin's cape had come to life in brilliant, wondrous dimension. "The Celestium," Tedros had called it once she'd opened her eyes—Merlin's favorite thought spot, where he'd brought Arthur's father, then Arthur himself, and eventually Arthur's son. Dazed, Agatha had peered up into the dark, starlit infinity, feeling her heartbeat slow to a crawl. Unlike the icy chill of the Woods, the air here was toasty and humid, inviting her muscles to relax. The fuzzy cloud beneath her stretched out like a cotton field, sinking her in all the way to the navel. But most marvelous of all was the silence, a big, wide emptiness as endless as the sky around them. Suddenly every rustle of her body was a disturbance, every thought in her mind a nuisance, until she, like Merlin and Tedros, had found a perfect stillness, as if they'd become the silence and the silence had become them.

Only then had Merlin spoken.

"Indeed, without Callis the members of the League may never have met each other at all," he continued now. "During the Great War, when the School Master brothers battled for supremacy, Good against Evil, only one emerged victorious—though no one was sure who, given he wore a mask to conceal his identity. Still, he managed to win the allegiance of both sides by vowing to rise above Good and Evil and protect the balance as long as he was alive."

Agatha stifled a yawn and saw Tedros' lids drooping. Not only were they both exhausted, they knew all of this from Professor Sader's history classes.

"I'm sure this is familiar territory," Merlin said sharply, "but it's quite crucial for the rest of the story I'm about to tell. After the Great Truce, Good would go on a 200-year streak of victories, obliterating Evil ruthlessly in every new story, which naturally raised the hackles of Nevers around the Woods, who believed the Good brother had won and tilted the Storian to reflect his own soul. I was a young Ever myself during this period, notorious for my unkempt hair, magical talents, and disregard for school assignments in favor of my own research. While the other Evers believed Good had become invincible and thus grew shallower and lazier as a result, I, on the other hand, became deeply suspicious of our winning streak. The Storian, after all, sustains our world through *balance*. It is the first lesson taught at every Welcoming. The sun rises on the Woods only as long as the pen preserves that balance, correcting any inequity through each new story. Which meant, of course, that for the Storian to make Good win in every new tale . . . it must be correcting for something terribly Evil indeed."

He exhaled, looking out at the purple night. "Perhaps everything that followed could have been avoided if the teachers at the School for Good had taken my inquiries seriously, but they too were drunk on victory and we didn't have a Dean nearly as sharp as Clarissa Dovey at the helm. At the end of third year, I was tracked as a Helper to Arthur's father and moved to Camelot upon graduation, where I became Grand Vizier and eventually resident tutor to his son. Still, I made it my mission to keep watch over the goings-on at school, in case my suspicions proved correct. For years, I'd give guest lectures in History of Heroism or come for tea and crumpets with old professors or write Arthur for news once he was old enough to be a student himself. But Good's winning streak continued and there was no sign of any resistance from Evil or untoward behavior by the School Master. Soon, my worries dulled and instead I began to devote my energy to a spell that had become my life's work—a potion that could briefly turn boys into girls and girls into boys in the hopes to foster experimentation, sensitivity, and peace. A potion I believe both of you know well."

Agatha and Tedros murmured sleepily, thinking of the bright purple potion that had caused so much chaos at the School for Boys and Girls.

"Given the spell was based in gnome biology, Yuba generously offered to test each new version of the potion as I developed it," said Merlin, his pupils honing in on Agatha. "It was during one of these visits to him that he mentioned the School Master had taken an interest in a new teacher at the school named Callis."

"What! My mother was a *teacher*?" Agatha blurted, jolting from her daze.

"Professor Callis of Netherwood," Merlin affirmed.

"N-N-Netherwood?" Agatha stammered, shell-shocked. "That means she wasn't from Gavaldon? My mother was from . . . the *Woods*?"

"And quite the popular professor of Uglification," Merlin replied.

Agatha gawped at him incredulously. Her mother taught Evil kids how to uglify and disguise themselves? The same mother who used to beg her daughter to tell her about the school as if trying to imagine it for herself? Agatha tried to picture her mother trundling through the Evil castle halls in a pointy-shouldered teacher's gown, leading challenges in Manley's rancid classroom, uglifying and shape-shifting with her repellent students. . . . Her stomach hollowed. Either this was all a terrible mistake, or she'd lived with a stranger her whole life.

"When positions open up at school, the Deans are responsible for scouring the Woods and finding qualified professors whose tales are long over or who've accepted that the Storian will never choose them for a tale once they sign up for the seclusion of faculty life," said Merlin. "Imagine the School Master's surprise, then, when the Storian begins to tell the story of this new Evil teacher: Callis of Netherwood, heart and soul committed to Evil . . . and yet still dreaming of finding her one true love."

"Oh, you've clearly got it wrong," Agatha said with relief. "That couldn't have been my mother. She didn't care about love in the slightest—"

Her voice trailed away. Agatha was thinking about the way her mother fumbled the kettle that morning when Agatha had accused her of never having found true love. She suddenly felt that cold feeling again, the one she'd had watching Callis pumping water at the sink . . . that feeling that told her that her mother hadn't learned about fairy tales from reading storybooks . . .

But from living through one herself.

Slowly Agatha looked up at Merlin. "Keep going," she rasped.

"Now as Yuba rightly pointed out at the time, the School Master should have thrown Callis out of school immediately," the wizard resumed. "Teachers are here to shepherd students during their education, not endanger them. And fairy tales often end in so much violence and bloodshed that to have the Storian telling a *teacher's* tale within the school's walls is to invite chaos and death into students' lives. And yet the School Master didn't throw Professor Callis out. Not only did she stay at the School for Evil, but Yuba swears he saw Callis' shadow in the School Master's window on a number of nights, long after the other teachers had gone to sleep. Yuba tried to press her as to why she was in the School Master's tower, but Callis denied she'd ever been there. Meanwhile, the teachers were abuzz with theories as to why the School Master would let her remain within school gates, especially given Callis was quite pretty—"

"*Pretty?* Teachers have low standards, apparently," Tedros yawned.

Agatha fired him a glare and he bit his tongue.

"But in the end, the teachers reached the same conclusion. With Evil losing miserably in every new story, the School Master must have believed a villain like Callis posed little threat to anyone but herself. After all, the faculty, like the students, were convinced the School Master was Good and would relish the chance to see an Evil teacher perish within school walls," said Merlin. "And yet, now my own suspicions were reawakened. Why would a School Master take interest in an Evil teacher dreaming of her one true love? If the School Master was indeed Evil and *not* Good, could Evil's true love somehow be a weapon against Good? Could Evil's true love finally help Evil win? And if so, did the School Master believe that Callis was *his*?"

Merlin paused. "On one of my visits, I accosted your mother in the Blue Forest but she refused to answer any of my questions about her relationship with the School Master, even though I could sense her anxiousness about it. I tried to return and press her again, but the School Master had enchanted the gates to repel me, no matter what spell I tried. Clearly he did not want me speaking to Callis and banished me from the school. Now fully convinced the School Master was Evil and using Callis as part of his plot—a plot to fight Good's love with Evil's—I recruited Yuba to help me gather some of the most famous heroes in the Woods, including Peter Pan, Cinderella, and others comfortably in retirement, into a League of Twelve, prepared to foil the School Master's attack once it came. . . . Only that attack *never* came. Instead, Callis of Netherwood simply vanished one night from the School for Good and Evil without a trace and the Storian abandoned her fairy tale, as if it had lost track of her entirely. Soon the pen began a trifling new story about a girl named Thumbelina, Good's winning streak continued unabated, and the League of Twelve was disbanded and forgotten, as no one but me still questioned the School Master's Goodness. . . ." Merlin stared Agatha down. "Until almost forty years later, when the School Master found his Evil Queen after all. Only it wasn't Callis who wore his ring now . . . but the best friend of Callis' own *daughter.*"

Agatha's eyes were as big as saucers, her heart rattling against her rib cage. She glanced at Tedros, expecting him to be just as shaken, but he was curled up, asleep on the cloud, a trail of drool on his cheek.

Merlin pulled a wisp of cloud over the prince like a blanket and turned back to Agatha. "Why your mother fled to the world of Readers or how she got there we do not know. All we know is that just before her death, Callis sent a note with her cat, instructing the League of Twelve to protect you and help you rescue your best friend from the School Master. How Callis knew of the League's existence remains a mystery to me. I would let you keep the note she sent us, but I myself never saw it, for it was intercepted by the wolf and giant who almost took your lives." Merlin smiled wryly at Agatha. "But as I'm sure you know, Reaper is smart enough to read the contents of a note before he carries it."

"Reaper?" Agatha breathed. "Reaper was . . . here?"

"He managed to locate Yuba in the Woods, who unfortunately didn't speak a word of Cat. Luckily, Yuba had been hiding out with Princess Uma, who found the gnome after he'd barely escaped being burnt alive by Evelyn Sader. Once Uma translated Reaper's message, Yuba urgently reconvened the League, with Uma added to the ranks, despite the others' prejudice against youth and superstitions against thirteen as our final number."

"Where's Reaper now?" Agatha pressed. "Can I see him?"

"He's away on League business, I'm afraid, which you'll learn about in time," said Merlin. "But that is where the story ends for now, Agatha, as it's time for you to sleep."

Agatha tightened. "But—"

"Any more questions will have to wait until the morning, my dear . . . except for two that I invite you to ponder in your dreams."

Agatha looked up as Merlin leaned in, his dark eyes reflecting the stars.

"If your mother is the Never the Storian wrote about . . . if your mother is the Never who made it into a storybook . . . then why is it *Sophie's* mother who has a villain's grave in our world?" Merlin leaned closer, his face no longer friendly. "And if it's your mother the School Master wanted, then why, after all these years, is it Sophie who's the School Master's queen . . . and not *you*?"

Agatha locked eyes with him as the cloud caved in beneath her and she plunged like an angel sent back to earth. Gasping, flailing, she looked up for Merlin, for Tedros, but her eyes were already closing, and soon she was lost to the dark, falling, falling, and never hitting ground.

15

The Magician's Plan

Agatha dreamt of Reaper in the toilet, trapped in the bowl, unable to be pulled out. Her only choice was to flush him down and swim into the toilet after him, which seemed a perfectly logical choice at the time, so follow him she did, into swirling, funneling water, then a dim, snaky passage, and finally into open sea.

The water was ice-cold and a squalid, slimy green, obscuring any sign of her cat, until she saw Reaper's bright yellow eyes floating far below like signal flares. Down she swam, into pitch-dark deep, holding her breath, until her feet touched the sand. Unable to see anything but his two disembodied eyes, blinking and darting in blackness, she focused on her finger until it glowed gold, lighting up the sea floor. Reaper was digging frantically at a grave with his bald, wrinkly paws, an oval-shaped headstone looming over him.

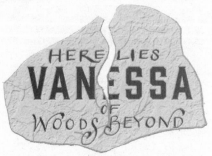

Breath running low, Agatha tried to pull Reaper away, since she knew Vanessa's grave was empty, but he dodged her grip and kept clawing and digging into sand. She snatched him again, only this time Reaper bit her wrist hard and Agatha screamed, losing the rest of her air as droplets of blood blurred into the water. Incensed, she grabbed her cat by the neck to tug him to the surface, when she glanced down through the hole he'd been digging into Sophie's mother's grave . . . and saw two green eyes glaring back at her.

Agatha woke, soggy with sweat, to a sea of empty mattresses around her. Her whole body ached from the previous day's journey and her forehead pounded so hard she had to squint, pulsing with the remnants of her dream and everything Merlin had told her last night. With a groan, she slid her feet onto the sandy cave floor and sat up on the edge of the bed.

The cave was fully lit, the League members eating porridge and stewed peaches at the dining table. They were watching Tedros doing shirtless push-ups, while old, paunchy Tinkerbell reclined on his back like a sunbather at the beach, enjoying the ride up and down.

"Should've seen *my* muscles when I was his age," Peter Pan scoffed.

Tink made a low chinkling sound that sounded like a snort.

"Never fall for a handsome man. Think they're entitled to the whole world, even once they're bloated and balding," pecked Cinderella, picking at Peter's peaches once she'd lapped up her own. She caught Agatha watching and smirked back nastily. "Besides, if Pretty Boy chose *that* as his true love, means all the other girls said no. Probably doesn't measure up, if you know what I mean."

Tedros heard this and collapsed mid-push-up, sending Tinkerbell flying into the wall.

"Don't be rude, Ella," puffed Red Riding Hood. "You're just jealous they're young and happy."

"Happy? Not what Uma says," Pinocchio chuckled.

Everyone turned to Uma, Agatha included. Uma froze with a teapot in hand and turned straight back to Pinocchio.

"What? You told me all they ever do is fight and the girl thinks the boy should find a princess who's cute and stupid and kisses his bum," said the long-nosed old man.

Tedros looked at Agatha, stunned, before his blue eyes narrowed coldly. "Sounds pretty great right about now." He stalked past her and vanished behind the curtain to wash up.

Agatha sagged at the edge of her bed, the cave dead silent around her.

"I'm never talking again," sulked Pinocchio.

"Doesn't matter, does it? Not like the whole Woods and all our lives depend on those two working together!" Jack cracked, clasping Briar Rose.

"Too bad it isn't *their* ring that has to be destroyed," sighed his bride-to-be. "It'd be done by tonight."

"Ha!" Hansel pipped.

Agatha threw Uma an irritated look, then felt guilty, for her teacher had done nothing but try to help her. Tired, grimy, battling a migraine and now a resentful prince too, Agatha crawled out of bed in her pajamas—

A burlap satchel shoved into her chest, filled with toasted crackers, a laundered tunic, and a tin of lemon tea.

"And here I thought your prince would wake you. He's been up for hours," said Merlin, flouncing towards the cave entrance, a second satchel on his arm. "Come, come, off we go."

"Huh?" Agatha croaked. "Go where?"

"To rescue your best friend, of course. Would you like ham croissants for breakfast later or masala pancakes? My hat is asking and he can be rather unpleasant if he doesn't know the menu ahead of time."

"But we can't go back into the Woods yet! We haven't even discussed the plan!" Agatha said, tailing him. "How are we supposed to get into school to see Sophie? How are we supposed to make her destroy the ring—"

"All that on the way. Need to get to the School for Good and Evil by lunchtime and we can't be wasting time with plans. Take cover, dear." Merlin twirled and flung the second satchel at her head. Agatha ducked and Tedros caught it on his shoulder as he elbowed past her, smelling fresh in a clean tunic, his hair still wet from a bath.

"Didn't wake you on purpose," Tedros said brusquely, not looking back. "Easier for me to rescue Sophie if you stay here."

Barefoot in dirty pajamas, Agatha frowned, watching him climb after Merlin through the cave hole. "Shouldn't we at least say goodbye?" she called at them, glancing back at the League members, obliviously playing cribbage at the dining table.

Merlin poked his head upside down through the hole. "Oh, it's certainly not the last you'll be seeing them, my dear. Besides, it's too early in the morning for goodbyes."

Outside the cave, the early morning was dark and grim, but there were no clouds to be seen. The sun was simply too weak to do anything but cast a pearlescent glow, leaving the sky ashy blue and the air bitterly cold. As Agatha lagged behind two men, one young, one old, she noticed the Woods looked deader than it did the day before, with bird corpses and slow-moving worms and bugs sowed throughout the mulchy path. Merlin left a trail of sunflower seeds, hoping struggling animals would sneak out to eat, but none appeared and soon the wizard had to magic the seeds away in case any dead villains came following.

"Dripping like an icicle now," said Merlin, studying the sky. "We must seal your fairy tale quickly. Sun won't last more than a few more weeks."

"The sun is dying because of *us*?" said Agatha, surprised.

"And faster by the day—a sign your story is bringing our

world further and further out of balance," said the wizard. "Your fairy tale has been open too long, children. The pen must move on to a new story to keep the Woods alive . . . along with all of us in it." Merlin twirled his beard around his finger. "Suppose this is what happens when the Storian tells a tale of amateur students instead of the properly trained."

"Don't blame it on me. It's called *The Tale of Sophie and Agatha* for a reason," growled Tedros. "Father never agreed with Readers being brought to school. Told me to stay away from 'em like the plague."

"Maybe you should have listened to your father's advice," said Agatha. "Besides, it's not like we asked for our fairy tale to be told."

Tedros ignored her and glowered at the sun. "No way is the world dying before my coronation. Need to rescue Sophie quickly, get Excalibur back, and move on to Camelot. I can't let my father's kingdom languish any more than it has. Not after everything my mother did to disappoint them. The people need a king."

"And queen," Merlin added.

"A stupid queen who kisses my bum, apparently," said Tedros.

"Look, I didn't mean it that way," Agatha argued.

"'Stupid' and 'bum' have alternate definitions I'm not aware of?"

Agatha didn't bother responding.

"And to think, last night you two were sharing hot chocolate," the wizard murmured.

The two young Evers didn't speak another word to each other as Merlin led them out of the damp thicket and into Knobble Hill, a bumpy maze of brown mounds covered with thousands of mushrooms of every size and shape. Agatha wished she hadn't said what she did to Uma . . . but it was true wasn't it? In storybooks, queens were majestic and elegant and inspiring. She couldn't possibly ever be one—

But if she stayed with Tedros, she *would* be one, wouldn't she? The one to take his mother's place.

Agatha watched him scaling the hill, looking so gorgeous and well built against the sky that she couldn't breathe. She'd been so focused on rescuing Sophie that she hadn't thought of what would happen after it. A coronation . . . a kingdom . . . *a queen? Her?*

Her face went hot and she tried to put it out of her mind. Sophie was the priority now. Besides, the way she and Tedros were going, he'd dump her long before they ever made it to Sophie. As he crested the mushroom hill, she could see his square jaw clenching, his muscled arms flexed, the prince still stewing at her, with his ire no doubt compounded by his utter hatred of mushrooms. (Her mother had served them once for supper and he'd turned green: "Mushrooms are fungus and fungus reminds me of feet and I don't eat feet.")

But as her anxiety over Tedros grew, Agatha was suddenly distracted by a view of a small Ever kingdom beyond the hills, made entirely of red sandstone. She could see the ant-like figures of men and women, building up a giant wall of brick around their domain.

"What are they keeping out?" Agatha asked, confused. "They're in the middle of nowhere."

"As soon as the School Master came back to life, the Ever kingdoms started fortressing for a second Great War," Merlin explained, as he led them down the slope into the misty valley. "They assume he will marshal his Dark Army and attack the Good realms any day now."

"So why don't the Ever kingdoms join forces and attack the School Master instead?" Tedros asked.

"For the last time, my boy, Evil attacks and Good *defends*. First bloody rule of the Woods. A rule you've had trouble with since birth," said Merlin, firing him a look.

Tedros grumbled and dropped behind the wizard.

"Then what's the School Master waiting for?" Agatha pushed, taking the prince's place beside Merlin. "You said it yourself: he has an army of the greatest villains ever written. He could wipe out whole kingdoms of Evers. So why is he wasting time killing old heroes and rewriting old storybooks—"

Merlin raised a brow at her. ". . . unless the Old gives him power over the *New*."

Before Agatha could press further, the wizard stopped cold. She and Tedros both followed his gaze to the mist clearing over a sprawling, half-frozen lake, spanned by an elaborate wooden bridge. Only the bridge had since been smashed to pieces and the lake's glaciers and shore completely blanketed in splintered shivers and shards. Lying in a heap amidst the wreckage were three corpses, flesh eaten to the point they were practically skeletons. As Agatha and Tedros inched closer behind Merlin, they saw that the little skin left on the bodies was old and haggard, with downy coatings of gray and white hair.

"Those aren't humans," Tedros winced, repulsed. "They're—"

"Goats?" Agatha kneeled for a closer look. "Who would do all of this for . . . goats?"

"Very *special* goats, my dear," said Merlin, kicking aside scraps of wood to reveal a bloodstained storybook. It was open to its last page: a painting of a giant horned troll feasting on three goat brothers. "The End" was written beneath the scene in bold, black letters. Merlin crouched down and touched the words. Fresh ink smeared onto his fingertips.

He snapped the book shut. "Hurry, children," he said, walking faster now. "Every second we delay, more of our old friends are at risk."

As Agatha followed, she looked back at the storybook on the shore and its mud-soaked cover . . .

The Three Billy Goats Gruff

Keeping ahead of the young Evers, Merlin guided them through a snow-dusted valley between mountains of cliff rock that took nearly two hours to cross. The temperature plummeted as hulking gray clouds moved in over the melting sun and soon it began to rain. With a glacial wind lashing at them and the grass slippery with frozen droplets, Agatha and Tedros clung their cloaks to their bodies and battled forward, dropping farther and farther behind the wizard, who was moving like a man half his age. Agatha saw Tedros' face chapped hot pink, his nose runny and red. She threw him a few darting looks, hoping he'd forgive her for what she'd said back at the cave, but Tedros looked away each time.

Agatha's heart sank. Ever since Merlin had mentioned Tedros needing a queen, she'd felt self-conscious around her prince. . . . Was Tedros having the same doubts?

"Here we are, bang on schedule," the wizard declared at last, looking fresh and bright as his charges caught up.

Hunched and haggard, Agatha eyed a dead end of rock fifty feet high. "Um, that isn't a s-s-school," she stammered, teeth chattering.

But Merlin was already climbing the rock wall, grinning down at Tedros. "Never beaten me, have you, dear boy?"

"You didn't say 'Go'!" the prince yelled, bounding after him.

"Always falling behind, then and now," Merlin tutted, as he glided up the wall, pebbles raining down on Tedros' head.

"That's 'cause you always cheat—*Hey!* No magic! You're not even touching the rock!"

"Something wrong with your eyes, boy. Must be getting old—"

Agatha watched Tedros straining after Merlin, the prince at once irate and puffing with laughter. She suddenly felt like a small girl again in Gavaldon, watching boys playing ball with their fathers, pelting each other with snow clumps, flicking and nudging each other for no reason at all. What would her father have been like? Would he have been mischievous and batty like Merlin? Would he have been quiet and gentle like August Sader? She'd tried to ask her mother about her father over the years, but she'd concede only that he'd died in a mill accident many years before and she hardly remembered him. . . . Her stomach knotted, thinking of all the lies her mother had told.

Was that story even true?

What if her father wasn't dead at all?

A pebble smacked her in the chest. Agatha craned to see Tedros almost catch up to Merlin, who shot the prince with a spell that glued his foot to the rock wall, slowing him down. "Age before beauty!" Merlin crowed.

"Go back to honey-cheese land!" Tedros barked.

Agatha waited for her prince to look down and check on her as he pulled over the ridge to the top, but he never did.

"Don't mind me," she sighed, and climbed up the wall, using her fingerglow to painstakingly burn crevices that she gripped with frozen fingers, so that by the time she belly flopped over the cliff top, wind-whipped and pooped, her irritation had grown tenfold. "What's next? Potato sack races and water balloon fights? While you two are chasing each other like frisky baboons, I'm worrying how we're possibly going to get past an Evil School Master and make his queen destroy his ring, when we don't even have a plan to get int—"

Agatha stopped.

She slowly rose to her feet and stepped beside Tedros. Together, they gazed silently at two black castles in the distance, towering against the horizon . . . one castle old and crumbling, one castle shiny and new, both ringed with slime-green fog over an eerie green bay.

Merlin smiled ominously at Agatha. "Now *that,* my dear, is a school."

On a pocky clifftop peppered with rocks and shrubs, Merlin pulled all the ingredients for a picnic out of his hat: a quilted purple blanket, a bundle of logs that he lit into a fire, and a morning feast of ham and Swiss cheese croissants, truffled egg salad, avocado and tomato bruschetta, and chunks of walnut fudge.

"Listen carefully," Merlin said, as the two Evers shoveled food into their mouths. "The School Master now divides his school into Old and New, but each is dedicated to the cause of Evil. Professor Dovey and the Good teachers have been imprisoned in a secret location. In their absence, the School for Good has been turned into the School for New Evil, where your fellow youth are being trained in the art of villainy—Evers *and* Nevers both. Which means all your young colleagues obey the School Master now, forced to prove their allegiance to Evil or suffer dire consequences at the hands of his teachers." Merlin paused. "Sophie being one of them."

Tedros and Agatha choked, mouths full. "Sophie is a *teacher?*" the prince blurted.

"Her first day of class was yesterday. The students gave her a rather chilly welcome, I hear," said Merlin.

"How do you know any of this?" asked Agatha. "You said the School Master barred you from ever getting through the gates—"

"Hold on. That's just the School for New," Tedros broke in, studying the other rotted castle. "What's in the original Evil castle . . . the School for Old?"

Merlin fiddled with his beard. "That I cannot say for sure. Only that the word 'Old' on its gates is surely no accident. The answer to why the School Master is rewriting old fairy tales may very well be within that castle and it is an answer we must find. The problem, however, is that there is no way *inside*. The School Master forbids both students and teachers from crossing to the School for Old and Halfway Bridge still carries an impassible barrier. Even if someone did miraculously manage to cross that Bridge, the Old towers are well guarded. Which all leads me to one conclusion . . ." Merlin squinted across the bay. "Clearly the School Master is protecting something in the School for Old he doesn't want found."

"Well, it doesn't matter. You said Sophie is teaching in the School for New," said Tedros, licking cheese off his fingers. "All we have to do is break in and convince her to destroy the ring."

Merlin looked amused. "Ah, the simple-mindedness of youth. There are three wrinkles in that plan, dear boy. First, remember that *only* Sophie can destroy the School Master's ring and no one else, if the School Master is to be killed forever. And yet, Sophie took his ring because she believed him her true love. Convincing her to destroy that ring will be no easy task."

Agatha bit her lip, knowing Merlin was right. Sophie hadn't just taken the School Master's ring, she was a teacher now—a teacher for *Evil*—as if willingly taking sides against Good. Was it too late to bring her back?

"The second problem," said Merlin, "is that the School Master's ring is surely crafted by the darkest magic, born of Evil. Therefore, it can only be destroyed by a weapon equally powerful, born of Good—a weapon that no Evil can withstand. I know of only one on earth that fulfills such a description . . ."

"What is it?" said Agatha expectantly.

But Merlin was looking at Tedros.

The prince's eyes bulged. "*Excalibur!* My sword! The Lady of the Lake made it for my father and he gave it to me before he died. The Lady of the Lake is Good's greatest witch . . . that means Excalibur can destroy anything—"

"Including the ring!" Agatha jumped in quickly. "Sophie just has to use Tedros' sword!"

"Indeed," nodded Merlin. "So if you can just *produce* this sword . . ."

Agatha's and Tedros' smiles dissipated at the same time.

"Oh no," Agatha breathed.

"He . . . he has it . . . ," Tedros sputtered. "The School Master—"

"And it's no accident that he does," said Merlin. "He knew full well to take it from you the night he came back to life. As long as *he* has Excalibur, Sophie cannot destroy his ring, even if she wanted to." The wizard's gaze hardened. "No doubt he's hidden your sword in an impenetrable fortress . . . somewhere neither Sophie nor any other student is allowed to go . . ."

Agatha and Tedros slumped deeper. "The School for Old," they groaned.

"And that is only your *second* problem," said Merlin, pulling a shaker from his hat and seasoning a scoop of eggs.

"How can there be a third?" Tedros rasped. "It can't get any worse."

"I'm afraid it can," snarfled Merlin as he chewed. "The School Master knows you're coming."

"What?" Agatha said.

"The Storian writes your story, after all," replied the wizard, reposing against a shrub. "As long as you remain Agatha and you remain Tedros, the Storian will tell him precisely when and where you break into his school."

"We're *doomed,*" said Agatha and stuffed a block of walnut fudge into her mouth, waiting for Tedros to chime in with his usual pep talk. Instead, her prince shoved an even bigger piece of fudge in his mouth and twiddled with his sock. Agatha knew they were really doomed now: Tedros never gave up, no matter how dire a situation, and he cared too much about his body to eat dessert two days in a row.

"Goodness, you're both a sight," chortled Merlin. "As if I'd have brought you all this way if I didn't have *something* up my sleeve. I am a Woods-famous wizard, after all."

Tedros dropped his fudge instantly and he and Agatha looked up at Merlin with new hope.

"You see, we have two secret weapons that the School Master hasn't quite anticipated. Two secret weapons that will break you into school, right under his nose, without him knowing," said Merlin, peering down his spectacles. "The first explains just how I know so much about what's happening within those castle walls . . ." The wizard huddled in with a catlike smile. "*Spies.*"

"You have spies *inside* the school?" asked Agatha, gobsmacked. "But who—"

Tedros waved her off. "Doesn't matter who. Even if you have spies to get us in, it still doesn't fix the problem of the School Master knowing we're coming—"

"Pay attention, boy. I said the Storian will tell him you're coming only as long as *you remain Agatha* and *you remain Tedros,*" the wizard said. "Which brings me to secret weapon number two."

Like a magician performing his final trick, Merlin carefully pulled a tear-shaped vial from his hat into the glow of the rising sun. At first they were blinded by a purple glare and Agatha and Tedros shielded their eyes from the vial. But as they slowly leaned closer, they saw a purple potion fluorescing hot against the stopper . . . until a shred of its smoke slid out of the vial and Agatha caught a familiar whiff of wood and roses . . .

She rocketed to her knees. "Oh no . . . noooooo way—"

Merlin grinned mischievously. "It is *my* recipe after all. Made just enough for two."

Agatha wheeled to Tedros, who looked utterly lost.

"What? I don't get it," he said, shaking his head. "I mean, that isn't . . . that can't be—no, of course not. Right?" He saw Merlin's face and launched to his feet. "*Right?*" He whirled to his princess, violent red. "He couldn't possibly make you into a . . . and me into . . . into a—"

But now he saw Agatha's face too.

Tedros stiffened like a corpse. "Oh my God!" He clutched his heart as if he'd been stabbed and crumpled for a second time into his princess's arms.

Merlin stared at the fainted prince a long while, before he pursed his lips and looked up at Agatha holding him. "Well, my dear. At least you can say you're even now."

16

Edgar and Essa

"Tedros?" said the honey-edged voice.

"Tedros," Sophie repeated sleepily, coddled in silky black blankets like a cocoon.

"What about him?"

"Who?" Sophie breathed, still deep in a dream.

"Tedros. You've been saying his name again and again."

Sophie launched awake. Rafal was sitting in the window, peering out at the dull morning, looking younger than ever in a black sleeveless shirt and short leather breeches that showed off his pale, sculpted legs.

"Seems strange you'd whisper the name of the boy you're supposed to kill," he said.

Suddenly remembering, Sophie looked down in a panic and saw *TEDROS* carved into the skin beneath her ring. She smushed her hand under her thigh and sat up on her elbows. "Oh, um, just thinking . . . no matter where I go, he seems to follow me like a rash . . ."

Rafal pushed onto his feet. "Then you'll have to erase him once and for all, won't you? Along with his fair princess."

Sophie gritted a smile, her wary eyes following him as he sauntered towards her storybook on the altar table. The Storian was paused abruptly over a painting of Agatha and Tedros, surveying the School for Evil from a clifftop. Sophie noticed the two Evers weren't holding hands anymore and that Tedros' body was leaning away from Agatha's. *Had something happened between them?* Her heart flipped at the thought—

She quashed it. *Are you insane?* a) Tedros already had a girl: her best *friend,* b) she already had a boy: Tedros' mortal *enemy,* and c) Tedros was on his way to kill that boy!

"Before you woke, the Storian drew Tedros and his princess only a few miles away and hasn't moved since," Rafal mulled, black boots clacking on stone as he circled the table. "It's like there's a glitch in the story, preventing the pen from telling us where they've gone."

"Maybe they gave up and went back to Gavaldon," gushed Sophie hopefully. "Maybe we've won this story after all! Maybe I'll never have to see them, and if I don't have to see them, then I don't have to kill them—"

"Then why is the book still open? Why hasn't the sun restored?" Rafal narrowed his eyes at the storybook, his mouth a tight line. "No, Tedros and his love are somewhere close. . . . The Storian just can't find them yet. . . ." He glanced back, unruffled. "But it doesn't matter, my love. As long as my name is the one written in your heart, their days are numbered."

Sophie hacked a cough. "Right . . . course . . . sorry, allergies," she wheezed, shunting her hand further beneath her leg.

She couldn't dare let him see Tedros' name under her ring! He'd know what it meant! And if Rafal knew he might not be her true love after all, he'd . . . he'd . . .

Kill me.

Sophie could feel her palm sticking to her thigh with sweat. *How is this happening?* All she'd ever wanted was love, and she'd finally found it in the snow-faced boy in front of her. But instead of reciprocating, instead of being faithful, now her heart was insisting her true love was *Tedros?* Tedros who'd rejected her twice for her best friend?

Rafal is my true love! she begged herself.

Please. Change it to Rafal.

Rafal.

Rafal.

Rafal.

She peeked down at her hand.

TEDROS.

Sophie gulped. Whatever happened from here, she couldn't be anywhere near the prince again, let alone in the same room with him.

Ever.

She peered out at the iron-spiked school gates . . . the monstrous shadows guarding the School for Old . . . the pestilent green bay . . . all barriers to Tedros and Agatha finding her.

And yet, there was still a spy amidst the students, planning to break them in somehow. She needed to catch the mole *before* her friends breached the castle.

But who is it? Sophie pictured her crowded classroom of Evers and Nevers, trying to recall if there were any clues . . .

"Sophie?"

She looked up at Rafal, who was staring at her. "Is there a reason you're hiding your hand?" he asked.

Sophie gaped like a toad. "Mmm?"

"You keep adjusting your position so that your hand stays covered."

Sophie cleared her throat and straightened against the bedpost. "Honestly darling, I know you come from the Bluebeard school of love, but I haven't the faintest clue what you're talking about. While I have your attention, though, perhaps now's a good time to discuss campus business? Last year I found the choice of school play deeply underwhelming, to say the least. Given my light teaching load, I'm happy to take up the burden myself: namely, a grand one-woman show, with performances each night at 7:30 in the Supper Hall and an additional matinee on Sundays, followed by coffee and canapés. *La Reine Sophie*, we'll call it, an appropriate name, don't you think, for a sumptuous, 3-hour pageant of—"

"Let me see your hand," Rafal said, glowering.

"W-w-what?" Sophie croaked.

The young School Master slunk towards the bed. "You heard me."

"Excuse me. You might be Master of this school, but you

are not Master of my limbs," Sophie puffed lamely, left hand sandwiched under her buttocks.

But Rafal was six feet away, suspicion glowing in his eyes.

Sophie's heart throttled against her sternum. "Really, darling, you're being utterly ridiculous—"

He was two feet away now.

"Rafal, please!"

He seized her arm, yanking it out from under her. In a flash, Sophie lanced her thumbnail hard into her ring finger, gashing the skin—

Rafal held up her hand and blood streamed down it, obscuring Tedros' name. His eyes flared. "You're hurt!"

"This is precisely why I hid it. Knew you'd overreact like you always do," Sophie pooh-poohed, shoving her bloodied hand in her pocket and rushing past him. "Just a lingering blister that keeps reopening . . . a stupid little accident in the menagerie. Now about that show, darling. It begins with a saucy little number called 'Thunder Down Tundra,' so I'll need glaciers, nubile *danseurs*, and a male lion, preferably tamed—"

"Wait. You touched Agatha and Tedros' kiss?" Rafal stalked towards her. "Manley made that scene poisonous, specifically to catch anyone still loyal to Good. No Never would get within ten feet of an Evers' kiss. Why would you *touch* it—"

"Oh heavens to Betsy, look at the time! Can you fly me down to my classroom, dear?" Sophie snatched her teacher's dress off a hook and bustled towards the window, back turned. "You know how Lady Lesso is about tardiness.

Wouldn't want her to think you're more irresponsible than she already does."

This time Sophie felt very different in Rafal's arms as he flew her over the bay.

Instead of safe, she felt scared; instead of loved, she felt caged. With her right hand glued inside her pocket and the left clinging to him for dear life, she ground her teeth and clamped every muscle, as if riding a wild beast she'd tried to tame and lost control over. And yet, despite the roller coaster in her stomach, she realized Rafal was flying glacially slow, zigzagging off path. She glanced back and saw his leery blue gaze locked on her instead of the sky, clearly thinking about her behavior in the tower.

"Eyes on the road, darling," Sophie chided, faking a smile.

The air was chillier than usual for a cloudless March day, the dappled sun streaking empty blue with copper and gold. She noticed a rawboned raven flapping and panting behind her; with the Woods decaying and its body weak, it was no doubt hunting in vain for a new home. Loud shouts echoed below and Sophie spotted a Woods Training class in the rotting Blue Forest, with Evers and Nevers, boys and girls, each spearing a stuffed effigy of Agatha, as Aric barked out a succession of swordplay moves.

Sophie took in this dying forest filled with Agathas, feeling like she'd wandered into a surreal dream.

All this time, she'd been obsessing about Tedros, Tedros,

Tedros and blocking out the one person that mattered more to her than Tedros ever could. Even thinking of Agatha's name kicked up a storm of opposites—*love hate friend foe lost found truth lies live die*—until words and labels slipped away and Sophie felt a hole at the center of herself, as if she was incomplete without Agatha and Agatha incomplete without her.

And suddenly, as she looked at forty stuffings of her bug-eyed, flat-browed, pasty-white best friend, Sophie found herself snickering, because she knew Agatha would snicker at them too. Sophie would needle Agatha about the time she'd tried to add "tweezers" and "suntan" to her vocabulary, only to see the poor girl erase an eyebrow and give herself second-degree burns, while Agatha would remind Sophie how she'd chased her down Graves Hill, one-browed, hair bleached orange, a turtle-egg-yolk mask dripping off her face as she walloped her with a broomstick . . . and before they knew it, they'd be rolling on the floor together, giggling at how terrible and wonderful they were to each other . . .

Sophie's smile shriveled. Just yesterday she'd felt like a witch again in Lady Lesso's office, ready to slay Agatha and her prince for Rafal, ready to do whatever it took to keep the young School Master as her true love and not be alone. And now today, she had Tedros' name tattooed on her skin, was reminiscing about makeovers with Agatha, and couldn't wait to get out of Rafal's cold arms.

What's happening to me?

Her feet skidded into stone and Sophie braced to see a black balcony off the old Honor Tower and students stampeding by to get to their next sessions on time. Quickly Sophie scrunched her hand deeper into her pocket and broke away from Rafal without looking back—

"Find me at lunch, darling!"

"Sophie."

Sophie slowly turned to Rafal, shadowed by the sun's glare against the railing.

"You will kill them. Tedros *and* Agatha." His voice was a hot, teenage snarl. "Or I'll know whose side you're really on."

His eyes flayed her for what seemed like an eternity, before he rocketed straight up into the sky and she lost him in ashes of sun.

Alone in the hallway, Sophie felt her hand sweating through her pocket.

Rafal was onto her.

If he saw Tedros' name carved into her . . . she was good as dead.

If she didn't kill Agatha and Tedros . . . she was even deader.

Which meant only one thing, Sophie thought.

It was her friends' lives or her own.

Sifting into the crowd of students, Sophie veered towards the lollipop room, determined to catch the spy for Good. If she caught the spy, then the spy couldn't break Agatha and Tedros into school. And if Agatha and Tedros couldn't break into school, then she'd never have to see them again, and if she never had to see them again, then she'd never have to kill them—

Sophie froze still.

A white mouse was motoring past her shoe tip, a wooden stick in its mouth.

It couldn't be the traitorous mouse Lady Lesso had warned her about, for it wasn't carrying a note or a key or anything useful to a spy. And yet, there was still something odd about the rodent, frantically weaving and skidding between boots, as if racing against a clock—and something even odder about the stick between its teeth, knobby, aged, and tapering to the top, as if it wasn't a stick at all, but some kind of *wand* . . . a wand Sophie was quite sure she'd seen in this very school . . . *But where?* Wands were never used in classes or challenges and most teachers mocked them as archaic training wheels or remnants of fusty godmothers. So who at the School for Evil could possibly have use for a—

Sophie yelped.

Like a runaway bull, she barreled headfirst into the crush of bodies, chasing after the mouse. Wherever this little vermin was headed, toting Professor Clarissa Dovey's wand, it was surely leading her right to the spy. Did Dovey's wand have special powers? Is that how the spy planned to help Agatha and Tedros in? Was Professor Dovey the spy herself? But *how*, given Dovey was locked up somewhere with the Good teachers? Sophie didn't have time to think—

Bucking and flinging kids aside, she tracked the mouse down dark spiral stairs, almost losing sight of it, before her clacking heels woke a few sleeping fairies on the banister, who glowed angry green and lit up the mouse as it skittered into the foyer. Hoisting her dress, Sophie sprinted after it through the Supper Hall kitchen, where enchanted pots stewed sardines and cold cabbage; past the Laundry, where Beezle, the red-skinned dwarf, was singlehandedly trying to wash 240 uniforms ("Mama!" he screeched, drowning in bubbles); and into the enormous Gallery of Good, refurbished black and green, which instead of reflecting all of Good's great victories, now depicted something else . . .

Sophie slowed her pace, taking in the museum cases around her. The glass boxes, once filled with hero's triumphant weapons and proof of dead villains flaunted new exhibits: Rapunzel's severed hair, Tom Thumb's clothes, Snow White's crown, and seven dwarf-sized pairs of shoes . . . all splattered with blood.

These weren't trophies of obscure Evil victories from hundreds of years ago.

These weren't Finola the Fairy Eater, Children Noodle Soup, and Rabid Bear Rex.

These were stories every Reader knew, only with the villains winning instead of the heroes.

Sophie rolled her eyes at these clearly faked relics. First the murals in the hall and now the Gallery too? Rafal obviously couldn't accept the *real* endings—

Then she remembered something he'd said.

"Endings can change, my queen. And change, they must."

Sophie shuddered, thinking of the way he'd grinned out at the School for Old . . . the strange roar from inside . . . the dark shadows on the rooftop . . .

Had Rafal found a way to change the old fairy-tale endings?

And was that way hidden in the other school?

Sophie's stomach dropped like a stone.

She'd lost the mouse.

Panicked, she ransacked every corner of the Gallery. No sign of it. She groaned, furious with herself. Her one chance to catch the spy and she'd botched it like a fool. She took a quick peek at her left hand, still tattooed with Tedros' name. Shoulders slumping, cursing under her breath, she tromped out of the museum, late to her own class, spy still unfound, fully convinced her true love was going to kill her—

Something caught her eye down the hall.

A flit of white scampering towards the castle doors.

Got you.

Hurtling after the rodent like a castaway after a boat, Sophie blasted out of the Gallery, through the black-marble foyer, into the mirrored entrance hall (every mirror now cracked), and out the swan-frosted doors onto the Great Lawn, quite sure she was the first pretty girl in history to run towards a mouse rather than away from it—

A wall of green smoke blinded her.

Sophie shielded her eyes, but wind was blowing more green mist towards her, off the surface of the steaming, corrosive bay. Determined not to lose the mouse again, she hobbled down the hill, her suede stiletto boots snagging in dead, muddy grass as she scanned the ground, hoping the mouse had snagged somewhere too. But every time she thought she found it, it turned out to be a stray crog bone, which she punted in anger, until she skirted the shore of the lethal moat, looking left, then right, at a loss which way to go—

A human shadow skulked towards her out of the fog.

Sophie stumbled back.

Aggie?

Only it wasn't one shadow.

It was two.

Aggie and . . . Teddy?

"S-s-stay where you are!" she called out.

The pair of shadows advanced faster.

Sophie's fingertip burned pink with terror. "Stop! Stop right there!"

But the shadows were coming even faster now and Sophie held out her glow like a dagger, ready to stun them both as they broke through the mist—

"Oh." Sophie dropped her right hand, glow evaporating. "It's you."

"Had to fetch the new students," Hester puffed, looking winded.

"School Master sent us to welcome them," said Dot, panting beside her.

"Since we're the only ones that seem to *like* this school," Anadil groused, coming out of the mist, trailed by two black rats, the third one flagging, looking wan and half-dead.

"You might need another rat," Sophie cracked, relieved her friends were acknowledging her again. She pressed her tattooed hand deeper into her pocket. "Listen, can we reconvene

Book Club after lunch? I really need to talk to—wait a second. Did you say *new* students?"

Over Hester's shoulder, Sophie saw two more shadows breaking through the fog: a teenage boy and girl she'd never seen before, both wearing Evil's black uniforms and equally black scowls.

The boy resembled a malevolent penguin, with sickly pale skin, dark bulging eyes, sunken cheeks, and a hideous dome of black hair. He had scrawny thighs and calves, no muscle tone in his sticklike arms, and walked stiffly as if afraid something might fall out of his pants.

The girl was broad-shouldered and golden tan, with glimmering blue eyes, a small button nose, and long black hair that was so harshly black it didn't look her natural hue—as if it'd been dyed in a hurry by someone who didn't understand the careful calculations of proper coloring, most certainly a man. Still Sophie found her pretty overall and for a moment felt threatened, until she noticed the girl's thuggish, swaggery walk, like a troll in search of something to club.

The new boy and new girl spotted Sophie and stopped short. Sophie saw their legs go shaky, their foreheads sweaty, and their mouths hold back huge smiles as if they wanted to hug her, touch her, or at least get an autograph.

"Uh . . . they're big fans of your storybook," Hester mumbled, glaring at the gaping strangers.

Good grief, that explains everything, Sophie sighed, suspicions melting away. She'd forgotten how famous her fairy tale was in the Woods. She must have adoring fans like these *everywhere.* For all she knew, thousands of obsessed admirers had tried to get into the school to be close to her and these were the first who succeeded.

"Well, the School Master said nothing of this to me," Sophie sniffed, at once flattered and in no mood to interact with common groupies when there was a spy to catch. "Surely he'd have at least mentioned their names—"

"I'm Essa of Bloodbrook, Coldhearted Ever Killer, Sworn to Protect Evil," the girl interjected, her voice high and thin, layered with the snootiest accent Sophie had ever heard. She clutched the boy's hand. "And this is Edgar."

"I can introduce myself thank you," the boy growled at her in a low tone and turned to Sophie. "I'm Edgar of Bloodbrook, Coldhearted Ever Killer, Also Sworn to Protect Evil."

Sophie peered at their joined hands. "Two Coldhearted Ever Killers . . . in love?"

The boy and girl looked at each other, as if prepared for every question but this one.

"Cousins. They're cousins," snapped Hester. "Part of Captain Hook's family tree."

Edgar instantly let go of Essa's hand. "We don't like to talk about it."

"Private people," Essa clipped.

"Doesn't make any sense," Sophie said. "Since when does the School for Evil take new students?"

"Weren't old enough to be picked as Nevers the first go-round," Anadil broke in.

"Must be quite the Ever Killers if the School Master's

willing to bring them in now," chimed Dot, snacking on a crog bone turned to fudge.

Sophie noticed the cousins studying Rafal's ring on her finger, seeming less like Ever Killers and more like jewel appraisers. She hid her hand. "Well, like I said, the School Master didn't mention anything to me about new students, so I really should check with—"

"Course he didn't mention it to you," scoffed Hester, marching past Sophie towards the castle. "Bringing in outside assassins . . . doesn't want you to think he's doubting *your* ability to kill Agatha and Tedros, does he?"

"Since he's *your* true love," said Anadil, following Hester.

"And it's *your* job to kill them," said Dot, following Anadil.

Sophie bristled nervously and looked at the two strangers.

"Death to Agatha!" Edgar blurted, raising a fist.

"Death to Tedros!" squeaked Essa, fist up too.

They hurried after the witches.

As the two Ever Killers ran up the hill, Sophie felt her heart curdle with dread. From the day he put his ring on her, Rafal had never trusted her loyalty to Evil. Now he'd brought in two trained murderers to force her hand. Would Rafal make them kill her best friends if she wouldn't? Would Rafal kill *her*? And how long could she possibly keep Tedros' name hidden from him?

Watching Edgar and Essa approach the castle, Sophie made a desperate wish to keep Agatha and Tedros away from this school . . . to stop them from trying to rescue her . . . to never see them again and save all of their lives . . .

But as with most of Sophie's wishes, this one had gone wrong, for without realizing it, she was watching Agatha and Tedros *right now*, darting into the castle.

She hadn't kept her friends out.

She'd let them in.

17

Missions Impossible

As soon as the three witches thrust Edgar and Essa into their smelly, burnt dorm room, Hester locked the door and scowled at Essa.

"Tedros, you brain-dead cow! Why'd you grab Agatha's hand! Almost gave yourselves away!"

Tedros and Agatha were both bent over, slurping breaths. "Sophie! She's . . . wearing . . . ring . . ." Agatha wheezed. "Almost hugged her—"

"Should have taken your chance. No way we're getting out of this place alive," Tedros panted, glowering down at his shapely girl's body. "Did you see the way those Everboys in the hall goggled at me?"

"We saw our best friend again and we're still in one piece. I'd call that success," said Agatha,

flopping boy limbs across a bed and knocking over a frame on the nightstand.

"I'd call it suicide," said Tedros, yanking at his shorts.

"Calm down, princess. So many kids crammed into this castle that no one knows who's who anymore," sneered Hester, fixing the picture of her mother in front of a gingerbread house.

"You'll both be safe in our room until tonight," Anadil added, watching two of her rats nuzzle the weak and exhausted third. "Though if 'Essa' talks any more in that horrible accent, I might slit her throat."

"It's the only way I can keep my voice high!" Tedros fought.

"Makes you sound like a milkmaid from Maidenvale," said Dot airily, rummaging in the closet. "Daddy likes milkmaids. Kept one in our basement."

Everyone in the room looked at her.

"Glad you find this funny," Tedros spat, still clawing at his shorts. "Can't even think in this stupid body! Whatever spell Merlin used to dye my hair is itching like mad, my backside won't fit in my pants, my feet are too small, my legs are *freezing*, and I keep having to pee—"

"At least one thing hasn't changed," mumbled Agatha.

Tedros gave her a toxic look. "And who came up with those idiotic names! Edgar and Essa, as if we're born with croquet mallets in our mouths, sipping tea in Malabar Hills."

"Names were my idea," Dot blushed, pulling out of the closet, looking hurt. "Hester let me pick them, on the condition that I got fat again. Said if I was fat like first year and the three of us pretended to love this place, no one would suspect us being spies for Good. We had to help you, of course—first, Agatha's our friend; second, Aric almost killed Hester and now he's *Dean*; and third, we can't just let the School Master turn the whole school Evil. No point being Evil if there's no Good to fight, is there? What would we do all day? Eat popcorn and give ourselves pedicures? Besides, I figured if I help you rescue Sophie, maybe I can't wear these now"—she held up her old skimpy blue bodice from the School for Girls—"but at least I'll do something with my life and Daddy won't call me a failure anymore," Dot said, sniffling. "Spent all our classes trying to think of nice names for you and that's why my ranks are low and I'm going to end up a plant, but Edgar sounds like Agatha if you say it with a lisp, and Essa rhymes with Tedros if you don't think too much about it, and I thought you'd be proud of me for doing such a good job." She blew her nose into the bodice.

Hester, Anadil, and Agatha all glared at Tedros.

"Put yourself in my shoes, Dot," he said guiltily, itching his hair. "I'm Prince of Camelot, soon to be King if I don't die first. I came back into the Woods with my princess to rescue our best friend and I didn't sign up to do it as the girl, all right?"

"As 'the girl'? Is that what I am?" Agatha rocketed up in her string-bean body. "'The *Girl*'?"

"Hey now, all I'm saying is that if any of my friends ever saw me like this—"

"Pretty sure they just saw you in the hall," Agatha snarled, boiling with boy hormones. "Think Chaddick even winked at you."

Tedros looked like he'd been slapped.

"There's the old Agatha," Hester smirked.

"Back in the coven at last," said Anadil.

"Not as an official member, of course," Dot snipped.

Agatha splayed onto the mattress, stirring up soot. "Are boys angry and starving all the *time*? I could eat this pillow."

The pillow turned to chocolate.

"And that is why I'm not an official member," Agatha said as she bit into it, throwing Dot a grin.

Tedros stared at his princess, now a ravenous, belligerent boy; at three Evil witches, still sniggering at his expense; at his long-tressed, soft-jawed, smooth-legged reflection in a glass picture frame . . .

The prince burst into a sweat. "I can't do this . . . I just can't . . ." His fingertip started glowing hot gold. "I'm doing the counterspell and reversing the potion—"

Agatha lurched up and grabbed him. "They'll catch you the second you walk out this door! They'll kill all of us!"

"We've come this far, all right?" begged Hester, coaxing his girl body down to the bed.

"It's the only way, Tedros," soothed Anadil, gripping his glowing finger.

"Might even make you a better person," Dot huffed, before adding under her breath: "Less dramatic, at least."

Tedros dumped his peachy cheeks into his hands and hunched over the bed. "We're never going to make it! We're never going to get Sophie out of here! I'll never get back to Camelot, I'll never get to be king, and I'm going to die as a *girl*!"

Hester's demon swelled red on her neck. "You sniveling, cock-brained, yellow-bellied imp! The four of us girls have spent our whole lives proving we're *more* than girls and here you are acting like being a girl is a death sentence! Your whole life you've relied on your dimpled chin and moony eyes and washboard stomach to substitute for a soul. Well, now you're one of us, *Essa*, and all of our lives are depending on you, so if you don't stop whining and *man up*, you sorry excuse for a prince, I'll send this demon right up your—"

She saw Agatha shaking her head and stealthily blowing smoke letters off her own glowing fingertip: "MOTHER ISSUES."

Hester bit her lip. "Tedros. My *friend*," she said, trying to sound sympathetic with mixed results. "I know this isn't easy, but you've made it into this hellish school. That was the hardest part. Now we just need you and Agatha to finish the missions Merlin gave you."

"You have the whole day to figure out how you're going to do it. In the meantime, Hester, Dot, and me better get back to class or Sophie's going to suspect something," said Anadil, shooting Hester a look.

Hester kneeled to Tedros' level and clasped his small, dainty fingers in hers. "We'll leave you here with Agatha and be back after dinner. That's when your missions start. Okay?"

Tedros didn't answer.

Hester held up the tail of her shirt, revealing an ugly pink scar on her belly. "I took Aric's knife to protect your princess. To protect *your* true love, Tedros. Now it's your turn to prove what you're made of." She glanced up at Agatha's gawky, penguinish boy. "Both of you. If we're going to rescue Sophie and save our world, we need you to be a team."

Agatha and Tedros didn't look at each other.

"One smile, Edgar and Essa," said Hester. "Please."

"Hester asking for a smile? World's dying after all," Dot chipped.

Slowly Edgar and Essa made eye contact. They turned to Hester and conjured identical smiles.

Hester slackened in relief. "Back soon, lovebirds. Use your time wisely," she said, as her two roommates followed her out. "And try not to break any school *rules* if you know what I mean."

Agatha and Tedros held their smiles as the door closed and locked from the outside.

Then they looked at each other and frowned.

Less than an hour earlier, Edgar and Essa were squashed side by side on a tree stump in the Woods, watching Merlin sprinkle glitterdust on a grove of carnivorous purple thorns, putting the thorns to sleep.

"When can I turn back?" Tedros demanded in a deep voice, creamy girl cheeks glowing pink.

"Once you return alive," the wizard said, poking testingly at a limp thorn.

"Which means never," Agatha murmured, squinting ahead at tall, spiked gates that blocked entry to the School for Good and Evil. The lethally sharp slats that once shimmered solid gold now glowed acid green, flashing a familiar sign:

TRESPASSERS WILL BE KILLED

Agatha gulped. They'd had a short nap on the clifftop and a hat-made snack of kale omelets and strawberry-vanilla smoothies before Merlin dressed them in Evil's black-and-green uniforms ("*Spies*, obviously," as to how he acquired them) and brought them to the threshold of the school without informing them how a girl and boy—now boy and girl—could get through gates vowing to kill them.

"Only a teacher can open those gates," Agatha argued. "If we touch them, we'll get blasted to pieces!"

"Gates are the least of my problems. Suppose the counterspell doesn't work? Suppose I'm stuck a girl forever?" said Tedros.

"Please don't use your boy voice in a girl's body, my child," said Merlin, picking his teeth with a thorn. "It's a bad habit and reeks of cheap burlesque. Now you won't get very far without being able to convince people you're a girl, so let's start with your name."

"My head itches," Tedros said, still in baritone. "Why can't I have my normal blond hair?"

"Because we need you to look like an Evil assassin, not Goldilocks' lovelier sister."

"You're a magician. You'd think you could dye hair without giving me lice—"

The lance of a thorn landed between Tedros' legs.

"The finer art of hair care is not a priority when our world is on the line," said Merlin, searing him with a stare. "Now let's hear that voice before I *really* make you itch."

Tedros crossed his arms. "My name is Essa," he squawked in a shrilly, ear-piercing snoot.

"Goodness, it's like a schoolmarm from Runyon Hills," Merlin said, then saw Agatha giggling, her high-pitched cackles mismatching her male frame. Merlin raised his brows. "Really, you two could make a killing in the circus."

"My name is *Essa*," Tedros repeated angrily, even more strident and prim.

Agatha was laughing so hard she couldn't speak. "You're using too much nose! Breathe from your stomach!"

Tedros whipped back his hair. "What, *you're* the expert on being a girl?"

Agatha stopped laughing. She stood up, looming over Tedros in her boy's body. "What's that supposed to mean?"

"It means you have the easy job, since you look and act like a boy most days anyway!" Tedros blared.

"Oh yeah?" Agatha shoved him with surprising force. "You think this is *easy*? My hips are so stiff I can barely walk, my Adam's apple is the size of a small animal, my jaw feels wired shut, and now I'll have to speak for the both of us, since you clearly can't handle it."

"Handle it? I'm the one rescuing Sophie, not you!"

"You can't even say your own *name*!"

"I'm the prince and you're the princess and rescuing our friend is *my* job. Just ask Merlin!" Tedros yelled, practically a shriek—

"Yes, now you've got it, boy," Merlin spouted, not looking as he trimmed his beard with a thorn. "Sound perfectly female now."

Tedros gaped at him.

Agatha burst into howls. "Hahahahahahahahahaha—"

Tedros tackled her.

"Boys can't hit girls!" Agatha yelled, grabbing Tedros in a headlock.

"Lucky for you I'm not a boy!" Tedros shouted, flinging dirt into Agatha's face—

A spell zapped them both, ricocheting them to opposite trees.

"This is the future King and Queen of Camelot? This is whom we've entrusted with our future?" Merlin lashed, no longer the friendly old guide. "My spies and I have risked everything so that you may rescue your best friend and find a happy ending that will save Good, old and new. Countless lives are in your childish, untrained hands, least of all yours, only you're too busy argle-bargling and fiddle-faddling like two monkeys fighting over a spot to poo. So from now until it's time to go through those gates, I don't want to hear another *word*."

Agatha and Tedros looked down sullenly, before Tedros' peeked up. "Then can I be a boy again?"

Merlin gave him a black scowl and Tedros looked back down.

"Listen, both of you. My spies will arrive in less than five minutes to break you into school," the wizard continued. "With guards on the roofs, fairies on the rounds, and who knows what else lurking about, you'll have mere seconds to cross these gates without being caught."

"But we still need a teacher to unlock them, Merlin," said Agatha.

"Agatha's right," said Tedros. "The gates only opened for us first year because Dovey gave me permission to be in the Woods."

"Trust me, my dears, I am smarter than the both of you," said Merlin. "Now once you safely arrive in the School for Evil, the two of you will split up on two missions. One of you will go to the School for Old and find Excalibur. The other will remain in the School for New and rescue Sophie. As to *which* one of you will rescue Sophie—"

"Me!" his charges shouted.

Merlin sighed. "Uma did warn me this would happen. Nevertheless, the one to rescue Sophie should be the one who knows her best." He cleared his throat and pulled what looked like a pack of purple playing cards from his star-covered hat. The wizard peered down his spectacles at the first. "What is Sophie's favorite food?"

"Cucumbers!" Agatha and Tedros yelled.

Merlin muttered and shuffled to the next card. "What does Sophie use to wash her face?"

"Beetroot!" the Evers overlapped.

"What color is Sophie's fingerglow?"

"Hot pink!"

"What position does Sophie sleep in?"

"On her back!"

"What scent is Sophie's perfume—"

"Lavender vanilla patchouli!"

Merlin tugged at his moustache. "It seems switching sexes has improved your brain capacities. Perhaps you should stay this way permanently." He shouted into his hat like a bullhorn: "*HARDER*, PLEASE."

The hat ejected a single card that Merlin fumbled and caught. "Dearest me," he said, squinting hard at it. "This seems rather unfair given Agatha practically grew up with the girl, but all right. Which of you knew Sophie's mother's name when you were on Necro Ridge?"

Agatha's stubbly cheeks grayed.

Tedros' girly face grinned.

"A twist in the tale, indeed! And so it seems *Essa* will rescue Sophie from the School for New," the wizard said to Tedros, before turning to Agatha, "which means Edgar will go to the School for Old and find Excalibur. Now listen to me closely. We'll have only one chance for you to escape the school upon completing your missions. We must meet here at midnight, *precisely* midnight, in this very spot—Tedros with Sophie; Agatha with Excalibur—and I'll whisk the three of you to safety. Understood?"

"What about Sophie destroying the ring?" Tedros asked.

"For the last time, *please* use your girl voice, Tedros—"

"What about Sophie destroying the ring?" Tedros squawked.

Merlin rubbed at his ears. "I'm afraid destroying the ring is too much to ask of both you and Sophie for one night, my child. Tonight, your duty is to convince Sophie to escape the young School Master and follow you to a place where he will not find her. I am well aware gaining Sophie's trust would be far easier in your princely form, but remember: as long as you are in the wrong bodies, the Storian ceases to write your whereabouts. Once you return to Tedros' body, however, the Storian will tell the School Master exactly where you are and his entire school will murder you on sight. So if you plan on staying alive beyond tonight, don't do anything *stupid*."

Tedros blanched as Merlin turned to Agatha. "As for you, my girl (or my boy, since we may as well be accurate) you must find a way to break into the School for Old all on your own, as difficult as it might be. Tedros' sword is hidden somewhere in that castle and it is your duty to steal it back. Remember, we cannot destroy Sophie's ring nor kill the School Master without that sword—" Merlin's eyes thinned. "Agatha?"

She was still glaring sullenly at her girl-faced prince.

"Agatha, my spies will be here any second and we can't have you pouting over your assignment like a spoiled cat," said Merlin.

Agatha noticed Tedros' gloating grin. She shoved down her disappointment, determined not to give him the satisfaction. "Look, I'll find the sword, but you still haven't told us who these spies even ar—"

But now she and Tedros saw three ravens flapping out of green fog over the bay, one thin, one fat, and one albino-white.

All three were hopeless flyers, with the albino zagging off-track, the fat one snarfing chocolate worms, and the thin one screeching a signal to dive before all three birds crashed into each other and plummeted like failed parachutes into a bush behind the gates.

"I can't find the uniforms!" Anadil's voice croaked from inside the bush. "I left them right here—"

"Dot's sitting on 'em," Hester's voice grouched.

"Was wondering why the ground's so soft," Dot's voice wisped.

"Unmogrify on three," said Hester. "One . . . two—"

"With you watching?" Dot gasped.

"As if we *want* to see you naked, you idiot!" Hester yelled. "Three!"

A burst of red, green, and blue light exploded from the bush as it rocked side to side, with flashes of skin through leaves.

"I think this officially makes us a coven," Hester's voice grumped.

"Has someone got my underpants?" Dot clucked.

"Let no one question my allegiance to Evil because there is *nothing* more Evil than what I'm seeing right now," snarled Anadil.

All at once, the three witches stood up in the bush, covered in pine needles and fully dressed in Evil's uniforms. Through the spiked gates, they saw Edgar and Essa blinking at them.

"I take that back," said Anadil.

"*You're* the spies?" Tedros blurted in his deep voice (Merlin frowned). "But I thought you were Evil!"

"And I thought you were a boy. Things aren't so black and white are they?" Hester huffed. "Merlin, fairy patrol will be here in two minutes. We need to break them in *now*."

"Where's the wand then?" said the wizard, grimacing at Hester through the gate.

Hester stared at Anadil and the two black rats peeking out of her pockets. "The wand isn't here, yet?"

Anadil went a shade whiter (if that was possible). So did the rats. "H-h-he was s-s-supposed to arrive before us—"

"One minute until fairy patrol," Dot warned, listening to jangling chinks in the distance.

"And now we have an even worse problem," said Agatha, big boy eyes narrowed across the bay.

Everyone spun and glimpsed Sophie's small shadow through the mist, tottering down the Great Lawn, head bent to the ground, as if searching for something in the grass.

"She'll see us if the mist clears," Tedros fretted, voice somewhere between Essa's and his own.

"Thirty seconds until fairies," Dot said, the ugly jangling growing louder.

"Anadil, we need that wand," Merlin pressed.

For the first time, Agatha saw a crack in the wizard's poise. Hester, too, normally unsinkable, was blotched red, haranguing Anadil.

"You told Merlin it could find anything . . . that it'd find Dovey wherever she's imprisoned and get her my message . . . you promised it'd bring back her wand in time!"

"It's a talent, not a guarantee," Anadil said weakly, her two black rats looking just as uptight.

"Fifteen seconds!" said Dot.

But now there were green fairy flashes from the east, flitting along the bank . . . while green mist receded along the south shore, about to reveal three Evil witches and a famous Good wizard, breaking in two strangers at the gates . . .

"Five seconds!" Dot cried—

"There!" Anadil hissed, pointing behind her.

Everyone whirled to see a white mouse hurtling out of fog, Professor Dovey's wand in its mouth. Only as the mouse scuttled towards them, wheezing and sweating, Agatha saw its body engorging, its white fur blackening, its front teeth sharpening, its black eyes reddening, until the white mouse was no longer a mouse at all, but a rabid black rat charging straight for its master. With a last flail of effort, it flyingleapt towards Anadil, flinging the wand through the air in seeming slow motion. The albino witch caught it and whirled to the school gates, stabbing the wand tip at the glowing spikes . . .

The gates parted magically, opening a thin gap.

"Thanks, fairy godmother," Anadil sighed in relief. "Wherever you are."

She tossed Dovey's wand to Merlin and the wizard jammed Agatha and Tedros through before the bars slammed tight behind the intruders. Together, Agatha and Tedros swiveled to see Merlin on the other side of the deadly gates.

"Midnight," said the wizard. "Do not fail."

Then he pulled off his hat and jumped through its brim

like a genie into a lamp, before the hat vanished too with a thundering crack.

For Agatha and Tedros, being trapped in a witches' dorm room was a lot like being trapped in a house on Graves Hill.

The first few hours they simply didn't speak. Each claimed a bed—Agatha took Hester's, Tedros' took Dot's— with Anadil's between them like a castle moat. Neither even acknowledged the other, partly because they were embarrassed by their new bodies, but more because both had a lot of thinking to do. Hugging a moldy pillow, Agatha mulled every possible path into the School for Old—Halfway Bridge, sewers between castles, tree tunnels in the Clearing, or a long slog around the bay—while Tedros, charred pillow over his face, racked his brain for ways to get Sophie alone.

Soon Agatha heard neighbors returning after sessions, then complaining about dinner (stewed sardines and cabbage, she gathered, leaving her extra thankful for Merlin's magic hat), and before she knew it, the wintry light had dimmed through the window, melting into nighttime. Agatha lit Hester's claw-shaped candle on the nightstand and pored over some of the witch's books (*Advanced Spells for Suffering*, *Why Villains Fail*, *Frequent Witch Mistakes*) hoping she'd find something useful. Tedros, meanwhile, was scribbling at Dot's desk in the dark, balling up pages every ten seconds, breaking quills in frustration, and cursing loudly in his boy voice.

Agatha ignored him and focused on her task. Her best bet was Halfway Bridge, she thought. It's how she'd broken into both the School for Evil and the School for Boys. Surely she could find her way into the School for Old the same wa—

Tedros broke another quill.

"Oh for God's sake. What *are* you writing?"

Tedros slouched, like a maiden failing to spin straw into gold. "Figured I should write down all the things I want to say to Sophie, but there's so much I don't know where to start."

"You'll think of something," Agatha grumbled, nose still in her book.

"If you haven't noticed, I'm crap under pressure."

Agatha glanced up at him, her prince's earnest, puppy-dog eyes blinking through his girl's face. Strangely, he'd never looked more adorable.

"What happened to 'I'll know what to do when the times comes?'" she asked.

"I know what to do when I'm with *you*. Never really thought I'd be rescuing her on my own. No matter how much I acted like it."

Agatha blushed and went back to her book. "You've never been at a loss for words when it comes to Sophie. You flirted with her when she was a girl . . . when she was a boy . . . I'm sure you'll be charming her in no time."

"I was *me* both of those times. This is different." Tedros stretched his arms and climbed onto Anadil's middle bed. "Besides, I already have a princess. Even though she picks fights with me for no reason."

"And I have a prince who doesn't listen to me and always thinks he's right," Agatha snapped.

"Because you act like you don't need me half the time."

"Because you act like I'm supposed to do what you say!"

"Because you're always trying to be the *prince*!"

"Well, I don't have the faintest clue how to *be* a princess!" Agatha barked—

"OBVIOUSLY!" Tedros roared. "WHY DO YOU THINK I LIKE YOU SO MUCH!" He rolled onto his other side.

Agatha watched him in silence, all the stress she'd been festering slowly seeping away.

Tedros didn't flinch as she climbed onto the bed next to him, keeping a space between their bodies. Together, they lay side by side in the dark, staring at the burnt ceiling.

Girl and boy.

Boy and girl.

"Hester's right. All I've ever had going for me is a crown, a fortune, and a face," Tedros said quietly. "Dovey used to say we'd need more than looks and charm to find our happy ending. Chaddick and the boys made fun of the old bat, and I'd join in. But when I saw Sophie on the shore and I was no longer a prince, I knew she was right. I felt naked, powerless . . . like I was hollow inside. You all think I'm scared of being a girl? It's not being a girl I'm scared of. It's that I'll only be loved for what's on the outside, rather than the real me. That's been my biggest fear my whole life. That all anyone sees is a tall, blond prince, straight out of a storybook, and fills in the rest without seeing what's actually there. But now, for the first time, that outside is gone and I'm in a weird body that isn't mine . . . and all I have is the Tedros inside me. The Tedros that I don't know is good enough for anybody to love."

He blinked faster. "That's what happened to my father, isn't it? He made my mother see the king as long as he could, until she saw underneath the power and good looks and saw what was really inside of him . . . Arthur . . . just Arthur, who wasn't even worth a goodbye to her. What if I'm the same as my father, Agatha? What if you see what I am when you take away the prince and it isn't good enough? Maybe that's why you've been fighting with me so much the closer we get to Camelot. Because underneath the prince, you see I'm . . . I'm . . . *nothing.*" He smeared at his eyes. "I've always been the Prince. Without that Prince, I don't know how to do this. I don't know how to get Sophie alone. I don't know what to say to her, I don't know how to convince her to trust me, I don't know how to get her out of this castle without the School Master killing all of us."

Agatha looked into his tear-streaked face. "And I don't know how to get your sword," she said.

Tedros couldn't help but laugh through his sniffles.

Agatha cozied her head under his soft arm, her big, boyish palm wrapping his delicate hand.

"When I look at you, I don't see a prince," Agatha breathed. "Even when you're at your most handsome and macho and charming, I *can't* see a prince. Because if I see a prince, then I'll have to see the king, and if I see the king, then I'll have to see myself as a queen . . . a queen of the most famous kingdom ever known . . ." She could feel the panic rising and held it down. "That's why I struggle so much. That's why I said what I did to Princess Uma. Because to be with you, I have to pretend you're *not* a prince. I have to pretend it'll always be you and me like we were those first few days in Gavaldon, an ordinary girl with an ordinary boy, and no kingdom waiting for you. And I can only do that by looking closer, beyond what's in front of me, to the heart and soul that made me fall in love with you. A soul that's sensitive, honest, and deep feeling. A heart whose love is like a big golden sun that makes you feel so warm when you have it and so cold when it's gone and all anyone wants to do is find their way back to it." A tear slipped down Agatha's cheek. "It doesn't matter if you're a boy or a girl. It doesn't matter who your father is or where you come from or what you look like. Here you are worried that I'll leave when I see your real self . . . when that's the part of you that lets me stay."

Tedros propped up on his elbows and gazed at Agatha, his blue eyes wide and wet. Even though their bodies hadn't changed, Agatha didn't feel like a boy anymore and Tedros no longer felt like a girl. As he slowly leaned towards her, she smelled his minty breath and closed her eyes . . .

"This is where you tell me how to get your sword," Agatha whispered.

"No idea," Tedros whispered back.

She tasted his lips against hers—

"Well, well," a sharp voice stung.

Agatha twirled in Tedros' arms to see three shadows in the doorway, Hester's eyes gleaming through darkness.

"So much for using your time *wisely*."

18

Tedros in the Sky with Chocolate

It wasn't until after she and Tedros split up that Agatha wondered if she would ever see him again.

"Showtime, kids," said Hester, storming into the room and snatching Agatha off the bed. "Ani, Dot, you take Essa. Edgar's with me. We have two hours until midnight."

"Why do we get the twit?" Anadil moaned.

"Because you're the henchmen!" Hester snapped, sweeping Agatha out of the room. Agatha looked back frantically just in time to see her prince-turned-

princess lunge off the bed and catch her at the door.

"See you soon," he breathed.

"See you soon," Agatha said.

The door closed between

them and Tedros was gone.

Hester yanked Agatha's boy body down a dim hall. "Anadil and I tried for weeks to find a path into the School for Old with zero luck, so you better have a damn good plan."

"Barely said goodbye," Agatha mourned, looking back at the receding door.

"Didn't look like you two were *saying* much of anything," Hester snarked, pulling her past a few Evers and Nevers hightailing into rooms as if their lives depended on it. Kiko froze in her tracks, gawking at them.

"What are you looking at?" Hester growled.

Kiko shut her door, her voice echoing from inside: "Mona, Hester has a *boyfriend*!"

Hester dragged Agatha ahead. "Halfway Bridge is suicide, obviously; we'll be sitting ducks and no way can you get past the invisible barrier a third time. Sewers are still blocked off from last year, so that's a no-go. Best bet is to risk the fairy patrol around the bay—"

"Hold on. *We*?" Agatha asked excitedly. "Merlin said I'd be on my own—"

"Because Merlin thinks you're the only one who can get into the School for Old alive," said Hester. "What he doesn't understand is that a coven is a coven and we protect each other to the death. Besides, no chance I'm letting you see inside that school without me." She saw Agatha's expression, grateful and moved, and Hester glowered impatiently. "Well? Which way? Anything but the—"

"Bridge," Agatha smiled.

"I knew you'd say that," Hester sighed, towing her into a dark breezeway. "And don't tell Dot I said you're in the coven. She'll turn us both to mocha pudding."

Agatha followed her out the glass passage into a shadowy Honor dormitory, noticing more students ducking into rooms as if outrunning a monster. "How did you get to be Merlin's spies anyway?"

"We used Anadil's rat to ferry a message into the Woods, looking for help to fight the School Master. Turns out your cat Reaper was in the Woods at the same time, delivering your mother's message. Well, cat found rat and chased it halfway to Maidenvale, intent on eating it, before Yuba discovered both of them. Ever since then, Reaper—*so* cute, by the way—brings Merlin's messages to us while Ani's rat brings our messages back to Merlin."

Agatha slowed down. *"League business,"* she thought, remembering why Merlin said she couldn't see Reaper. Meanwhile, her bald, mashed-up cat who she thought had no other use than scaring away strangers and decapitating birds had been communicating with her three witch friends all this time. She suddenly missed that vile old coot even more and wondered if Reaper knew her mother was dead. Agatha's heart sank. She didn't have the strength to tell him.

Hester was far down the hall now and Agatha could barely see her, with the sky ink-black out the porthole windows and a brisk crosswind blowing through. As her eyes adjusted, she had to put her hands out to find a stuccoed wall and resisted calling out Hester's name—

Only then did she notice the mural splashed beneath her fingers . . .

Seven brightly dressed dwarves facedown in blood.

Slowly Agatha backed up, taking in more scenes: Tom Thumb devoured by a giant . . . Rapunzel and her prince thrown from a tower by a witch . . .

Good endings she'd seen tacked to a wall in Yuba's cave. Good endings already rewritten for Evil.

Agatha remembered what Merlin had warned her in the Woods. The School Master was behind all of this. Each fairy tale revised a piece of a bigger plan.

But what plan?

Why was he killing old heroes? Why did he need the old stories at all?

"Unless the Old gives him power over the New," Merlin's voice echoed.

Stomach squeezing, Agatha crept further along the muraled walls: Captain Hook plunging his hook into Peter Pan's heart . . . a wolf biting into Red Riding Hood's neck . . . a pockmarked old witch jamming Hansel and Gretel into an oven . . .

"Hurry up!" Hester hissed ahead.

Agatha bustled to catch up, terrified for the old League members she'd left behind, safe in a cave for the time being. Whatever the School Master's plan, they had to destroy his ring before any more of these scenes came true.

As the tower clock tolled ten o'clock, Agatha noticed the dormitories dead quiet now. "Where'd everyone go?"

"Aric declared mandatory study time, since tracking week

is next week," said Hester, tugging her up the rear staircase. "No club meetings, no common rooms, all bodies in assigned rooms. Anyone who saw us thinks we were trying to make curfew. Weird hearing your voice come out of that body, by the way. You look like a creepy page boy."

"What if teachers see me? Or fairies?" Agatha pushed.

"Doing room checks, starting with first floor. Relax, no one will stop you if you're with me. Teachers all love me, except—"

Hester froze, staring upwards. Agatha squinted through the dark gap in the staircase to see a tall, spike-haired shadow glaring down from the fifth floor. Glittering purple eyes flashed like warning flares.

"Hester, my sweet. Shouldn't you be in your room?" said Aric, slinking down the stairs.

"Edgar forgot his book bag in the library," said Hester, foisting Agatha past Aric. "You know how disorganized boys are—"

Aric barred them with his big arm. "You may be teacher's pet, but that doesn't mean you can break the rules, Hester. Even *I* can't break the rules, or I'd have cut my mother into pieces by now and served her as a midnight treat." His tongue traced his teeth, his eyes on Hester. "Strange, though. My mother insists you're one of Evil's Great Hopes, sure to become an illustrious witch. And yet, I can't imagine Evil's Great Hope cavorting about with a dodgy boy after curfew." His pupils flicked to Agatha. "Stranger indeed, given I've personally punished almost every boy in school but don't recognize this one in the slightest." He fingered the coiled whip on his belt hook, prowling towards the twiggy stranger. "The muscleless legs . . . flaccid wrists . . . weak jaw . . . almost feminine, don't you think?"

"Edgar keeps to himself," Hester replied calmly. "With all the Evers and Nevers mixed together and your being new here, no wonder you don't recognize—"

"Oh I'd remember a boy this . . . *soft*," Aric purred, backing Agatha against the banister. "You see, Edgar, I don't like boys who don't act like boys. I spent years trapped in a cave, abandoned by my own mother, and yet I taught myself not to shed a tear. Boys don't cry or snivel or bend over like passive little princesses. Boys fight. Boys *dominate*. It's what I told Tristan in the Trial, when he begged for his life like a dog. No matter how many times I'd taken that tart to the dungeon, teaching him what it meant to be a boy . . . still he didn't learn his lesson. And then to find him high up in that tree, unashamedly a *girl*!" Aric's cheeks raged red. "Never again. Every boy in this school belongs to me now. Especially ones like my new friend Edgar, who don't seem much like boys at all." He leaned in, his lips almost touching Agatha's, as he grinned into her eyes. "Best move along, Hester dear. I need some alone time with our young Edgar tonight. And when I send him back in the morning, he'll be a *real* boy."

Agatha couldn't breathe.

Hester didn't move.

"Go," Aric hissed at Hester, viper-quick. "Because this time, when I slit you open, you won't have a Trial flag to save you."

Hester swallowed and gave Edgar a helpless stare.

Legs shaking, Agatha watched her friend quail up the stairs and vanish. Agatha hastily focused on her fear, feeling her own fingertip start to burn gold. She had only one hope to escape—

Aric's whip lashed around her wrist. Agatha's glow extinguished in surprise.

"Magic? How feeble." He yanked her down the stairs by the whip like a leash. "Can't even fight like a boy."

Agatha's fear scorched to adrenaline. "How's this, then?"

Aric turned—

She punched him in the face.

Aric reeled backwards into the wall, nose gushing blood, before he recovered and charged her like a bear. Agatha dove under him, but he grappled her by the belly, ramming her headfirst into the banister. Bleary with pain, Agatha made out a hard stone floor four flights down—

Aric hoisted her over the deadly drop and smiled brutally, teeth speckled with blood. "Say hello to Tristan for me." He loosened his grip—

A red, horned demon smashed into his groin and Aric cried out in shock, throwing Agatha's boy body to the stairs. Shrieking like a banshee, the shoe-sized demon spread-eagled on Aric's face like a mask, blinding him as he writhed against the wall.

Agatha gaped at Hester, slithering down the staircase.

"Best move along, Edgar dear," Hester cooed, lurking towards Aric. "The Dean and I have some old business to settle."

"No! I can't leave you alone!" Agatha hissed in her ear. "Not like last time!"

"This isn't like last time at all." Hester swished her red-lit finger and her demon squeezed Aric by the throat, choking him until he gurgled.

"But he's dangerous!" Agatha sputtered. "What if—"

"You're forgetting something very important about me, my dear," said Hester. She turned to Agatha, eyeballs clouding with blood. "I'm a *villain*."

Agatha didn't ask any more questions. She sprinted up the last two flights, hearing Aric's muffled wails as she pushed through the frosted door and slammed it shut behind her.

Fingerglow lighting her path, Agatha dashed along the dark, chilly rooftop between the scenes of Merlin's Menagerie, guzzling in air—*Hester's fine, Hester's fine, Hester's fine*—

What wasn't fine was the fact that she was all alone in her mission now, just as Merlin predicted, and the fact that teachers were surely on the way, given the noise they'd made in the stairwell. She didn't risk the time to study the hedges or see how they'd changed. She had to find the scene with water . . . that was the secret portal from the roof to the Bridge . . .

Just find water.

Three minutes later, Agatha was still running in circles, hyper breaths fogging, spying nothing but landlocked hedges as she swerved deeper and deeper into the maze . . .

Agatha stalled, fingerglow pinned ahead.

Dead center in the garden was a leafy sculpture of herself as a girl, floating magically above a rippling pond in Tedros' arms. Beneath them Sophie raged on the pond's shore, fists gnarled, mouth wide open in a scream.

Agatha shivered, reliving the moment by the lake on the night of the Evers Snow Ball. That single moment when three friends had been torn apart.

Now it was up to her and her prince to bring them back together.

From the shore, Agatha lifted her gaze to the black towers of the School for New, menacing outlines in the night. *What happened to Tedros?* she thought. *What if he never makes it to Sophie? What if I never see him again?*

Shouts rang out from the stairwell inside. *"Check the roof!"* Lady Lesso cried. *"Find who did this to my son!"*

Agatha gasped. No time to worry, only to act.

On an inhale, she closed her eyes and leapt into water.

Meanwhile, in the School Master's tower, Sophie was still thinking about Edgar and Essa.

After the discomfiting morning—barely hiding Tedros' name from Rafal, botching her chance to find the spy, meeting those two strange fans on the shore—the rest of the day had taken a decided upturn. By the time she'd gotten to her class, Pollux had already begun the challenge, a repeat of yesterday's test to get inside the enemy's head, except with the students in phantom Agatha masks. (Hester won easily this time, despite arriving late herself.) After class, Sophie managed to catch up with the three witches in the hall, who seemed aloof as to the whereabouts of Edgar and Essa. ("Different schedules than us," Hester snipped.) With her friends rushing off to History, Sophie barely had time to ask them for a spell that might cover an "imperfection" of the skin.

Dot grabbed her cheeks. "You're not turning warty and psychotic again are you!"

"No, no, just an oddly placed pimple . . . you know, unbecoming of a queen . . . ," Sophie warbled.

"Well, if I you're 'queen' of anything, it's curing pimples," said Hester. "Come on, girls. Can't be late to the School Master's class."

Anadil followed, but Sophie overheard her whispering. "Don't know why we bother going. All he talks about is Sophie this and Sophie that and how she inspires Evil's future. Whatever that means."

"Means we got a love-sloshed teenager as School Master," Dot chirped, toddling after them.

Sophie lingered behind, stunned. Rafal was gushing moonily to the whole school about her and here she was, still terrified of him? All he'd asked of her was loyalty and love— the same things he'd given her. And so far she'd failed on both counts. She bit her lip guiltily, hand fidgeting in her pocket.

TEDROS had to be dealt with *now*.

The old Library of Virtue, once a gold, impeccable coliseum, was a musty, weed-grown mess, with books strewn out of order (not surprising considering Evelyn Sader had killed the old tortoise librarian, who'd yet to be replaced). Even so, Sophie managed to excavate an old copy of *The Recipe Book for Good Looks*, and spent the rest of the morning brewing a

"Flesh-Over" potion of beets, wildflower, and dwarf sweat (Beezle was filched of the last, before yipping "Grand Witch Ultimate!" and bolting away). According to the book, the spell would only last until the covered area grew wet—and yet, the moment Sophie slathered the potion on her finger and watched Tedros' name flesh over with fresh skin, she felt good as new, as if she'd earned a fresh start with Rafal too.

The young School Master also seemed to have turned the page, for he no longer acted angry when they met for lunch on the faculty balcony. Instead, while Sophie pecked at a fresh salmon salad he'd brought in a basket, Rafal nervously picked at the laces of his black shirt.

"Sophie, I was thinking . . . I've been asking your loyalty without truly earning it first. Maybe we haven't spent enough time getting to know each other like um, normal young people . . ." He glanced at the other teachers on the balcony and the students on the ground, all sneaking peeks at him and Sophie together. "So, uh, perhaps you and I could do that . . . I mean, spend time without other people around—like away from school, you know, like a . . . a . . ."

Sophie raised her brows. "Date?"

"Right. Yes. Exactly." Rafal tugged at his sticky shirt. "I could take you on a tour over the Woods, maybe? You know, after everyone goes to sleep? Lady Lesso won't get on our case about going too fast and we can stay out as late as we want because—well, *obviously*. Wait until you see the Netherwood from really high up. With the trees all dead, it looks brilliant, like a devil-made scarecrow, and the stars over the Murmuring

Mountains connect into a giant skull," he rambled, like a nerdy Neverboy. "Could even do it tonight, after supper . . . you know, get some time together without everyone watching us . . ."

Sophie looked into his milky face, which seemed to be getting younger and younger. For a moment, he sounded so open to love.

"I'd like that very much," she breathed.

Rafal smiled, relieved. The young Master and Queen spent the rest of lunch in bashful silence, like two normal teenagers who'd just arranged their first date.

That evening, after dinner, as Rafal flew her back to his tower, Sophie nestled into his arms, no longer doubting who her true love was. Tedros' name was fleshed-over and forgotten, the Storian had written nothing further of him or Agatha, and for the first time, even Rafal wondered whether the two Evers had left the Woods entirely.

"Perhaps they came to their senses," he said as they landed in the chamber. He gave the Storian a cursory glance, still paused over a blank page. "Let me change and then we can go on our . . . our, you know . . ." His larynx bobbed. "I'll go change."

Sophie looked out the window. After all this, she'd never see her best friends again, she thought, battling a wave of sadness. . . . She shook it off, remembering this is what she'd wished for: Agatha safe with her true love, and she safe with hers. Bucking up, she looked back at the handsome, loving boy in the corner, doffing his sweaty shirt. The boy about to take her on her first real date.

"Well, with no Agatha and no Tedros, we'll finally have time to focus on *us,* won't we?" she said. "And what better way to start than a proper date night?" She fixed her hair, gussying up for their evening. "Goodbye troubles! Goodbye ordinary life! I can picture it now: going to school together every morning, gossiping about our students, quiet dinners in the tower, planning the places we want to go and things we want to see, like a princess and prince, in the throes of Ever After—"

"I'm not your prince. This is not Ever After. And everything you described sounds like ordinary life to me," said Rafal, his back turned.

Sophie bristled. "Well, I'm sure a bit of routine will be good for us after everything that's happened," she said, straightening books on a shelf to fill the silence. "At the very least, we can send those Ever Killers back to Bloodbrook."

"Ever Killers?" Rafal said, sniffing at a pile of dirty shirts, looking for one clean enough to wear.

Sophie made a mental note to do his laundry in the morning. He was becoming more of a teenage boy by the minute. "You know, the new students you brought in," she yawned, noticing the new flesh on her ring finger starting to wear thin. She'd have to apply more potion tomorrow. "Edgar and Essa, I think it was. You didn't think I'd find out, did you?"

"I'm sorry. Who?"

"Those *cousins,* Rafal." Sophie plopped stomach-down on the bed. "Captain Hook's family . . . strange pair, really. Clearly obsessive fans of mine but couldn't bring themselves to ask for an autograph. Spent the whole time sizing up my ring. Don't blame them, of course. It is rather lovely. Said you'd brought them here to kill Agatha and—"

But now she saw Rafal staring at her.

"Hook murdered his whole family," he said. "By the age of ten."

Sophie bolted up, confused. "What? But then . . . then who . . ."

Slowly Rafal's gaze moved to the Storian, still frozen inexplicably over the storybook. A light dawned in his pupils, red patches growing on his cheeks and bare chest.

"You didn't bring any new students in, did you?" Sophie said quietly.

The School Master fixed his eyes on her and Sophie saw there would be no date tonight.

"If anyone—*anyone*—dares to enter this tower, *kill them*," he hissed.

Then he leapt out the window and was gone.

"You want us to *break into* the School Master's tower?" Tedros shouted through blustering green mist, as he stood on a window ledge high over the bay.

"Not us. *You*," Anadil said, flattening next to his girl body against a black stone wall. "And stop using your boy voice. You'll be alone with Sophie in a matter of seconds!"

"Seconds?! The tower's half a mile away!" Tedros barked in his boy's voice again, pointing at the School Master's spire, far into the Blue Forest. "How am I possibly supposed to get from here to there—"

"Stop waving your hands, you ninny! Someone might see you," Dot said, peering through binoculars from inside the window. "Ani, the School Master just left, so this is our chance. Sophie's in there alone until he comes back. Plus, fog's at its peak."

Indeed, Tedros could hardly see the School Master's tower now, cloaked in green mist blowing off the bay. "First of all, what does fog have to do with getting me into *that* tower? Second, there's no such thing as 'flying' spells. Third, I can't mogrify into a bird without reverting to a boy once I land. And fourth, I don't see either of you carrying fairy dust, so please tell me what I'm doing in a girl's body ten miles above ground in the middle of the night!"

Anadil and Dot looked amused. "You didn't think Merlin was going to leave the details to you, did you?" said Anadil.

"Fog patterns and mapping Sophie's movements were my job," said Dot. "And Ani's job was . . . well . . . show him, Ani."

Ani drew a black rat from her pocket, paws up and whimpering on its back, with a small black helmet fitted over its head. "This is how you're getting to Sophie," she said, plunking the rat in Tedros' palm.

"This?" Tedros goggled at the rodent. *"This* is how I'm supposed to fly halfway across the school?"

"Rat #1 got you through the gates, didn't it?" said Anadil, stroking the still-pooped pet in her pocket. "Rat #2 gets you to the tower."

"And Rat #3 negotiates world peace?" Tedros bellowed, glaring at the shaking, shivering rat in his palm. "Last time

I checked, villain talents have limits, Anadil. Maybe you have the talent to make a rat small or white or dance the rhumba, but rats don't fly, that's for sure, especially 'Rat #2,' who's acting as if I'm about to chuck it off this tower!"

"Smart rat," Anadil grinned.

"Huh?" said Tedros—

Dot stabbed out her glowing fingertip and a tuft of green fog floating over his head froze to ice, before turning a dark toast brown. Tedros looked up and a single drop of condensation dripped onto his lips.

Chocolate.

Like flames racing up dynamite, the green fog around him started to freeze and spread to cocoa brown, morphing into frozen fractals and swirls—some flat, some loopy, some blade-sharp, some spaghetti-thin—until the entire sky over the bay looked like a chocolate roller coaster, camouflaged by the night.

Running out of steam, Dot focused harder, her flickering fingerglow chasing a last thin trail of green fog as it surged towards Tedros' girl body, plastered against the castle wall.

"Dot, that's the important one . . . ," Anadil warned.

Dot gritted her teeth, trying to keep her glow steady, aiming right at the whip of fog lashing for Tedros' face . . .

"*Now*, Dot!" Anadil cried—

Dot screeched with effort and shot a blast of light. The fog froze into a knife-sharp icicle, an inch from Tedros' eye.

Tedros blinked in shock, eyelashes grazing the chocolate spear. . . . Then slowly he looked down at the shaking, helmeted rat in his hand.

The rat locked its paws onto the icicle, with Tedros still holding on to the rat's body.

"Oh no," Tedros peeped.

Anadil kicked him off the ledge and Tedros let out a howling scream, clinging to the rat like a handlebar as it zip-lined down the chocolate icicle. At the end of the icicle, the rat flew off, like a sled off a track, before hooking onto another piece of fog-turned-chocolate. The rat zip-lined so fast along the chocolate tracks—corkscrews, dive-drops, sidewinder spins—that Tedros saw nothing but a kaleidoscope of cocoa and stars, as if magically sucked into one of Merlin's hot toddies. He could hear the chocolate rails splintering as he zoomed past and the rat squealing with terror, knowing it was only a matter of time before the entire ride shattered under their weight. The rat flew into an upside-down loop and blood surged into Tedros' head, his mind blanking blissfully, his legs kicking through air, detached from gravity. Above him, the rat's claws shredded even faster along the chocolate tracks, sending creamy brown flakes scattering like snow. Delirious, Tedros closed his eyes and stuck out his tongue, tasting cottony sweetness, wondering if he'd died and gone to Prince Heaven, where he could ravish and pleasure without duty or responsibility forever and ever and ever . . .

He smelled a sharp, awful stench and the rat jammed to a stop, ejecting him off the chocolate roller coaster, over the rancid Blue Forest, through a wide-open window, and onto a hard stone floor, flat on his bottom.

Tedros didn't move, panting on the floor. "I . . . want . . . Agatha's . . . mission."

Then he remembered where he was, the body he was in, and what he was supposed to be doing.

His eyes jerked open.

Hobbled and hurting, he lumbered onto his legs, still unused to his girl's squishy form. He peered around the School Master's deserted chamber, licking the last chocolate off his lips.

"Sophie?" he squeaked in his girly snoot, moving deeper into the room. "Sophie, it's Essa! Essa from Bloodbrook. We met this morning? Sorry to barge in like this, but you're in terrible danger." He imagined Agatha at his side, her spirit egging him on. "We have to leave here *now*, Sophie," he said, confidence growing. "Before the School Master comes back. So if you'll just listen to me, girl to girl—"

A blast of pain exploded through his head, knocking him out, and he crashed face-first to the floor.

Far across the bay, inside the witch's room, Anadil and Dot gaped in horror through binoculars at Sophie, who was looming over Essa's fallen body, wielding a giant storybook like a club.

Anadil slowly turned to Dot.

"Never was much of a girl's girl, was she?" Dot quipped.

As soon as the fog started turning to chocolate, Agatha saw her chance.

She'd been hiding at one end of Halfway Bridge, trapped in her boy body, ogling ten hulking, armed shadows atop the School for Old.

None of them looked human.

Agatha's heart seized. She had no hope to get past one of

the School Master's guards, whoever they were, let alone a fleet of them—

That's when the fog over the bay started detonating into iced chocolate.

Flabbergasted, she swiveled and saw Dot's fingerglow pulsing from a dark window, high in the other school.

Shouts of shock and panic rang out from the shadowy guards over the Bridge, who flooded off the balconies into the castle, leaving the roof unattended.

Agatha smiled, hidden at the other end. Whatever Dot was doing in the School for New, it served as the perfect diversion in the School for Old.

Not a coincidence, Agatha thought.

Merlin and his spies had done everything they could to help her and Tedros finish their missions.

The rest was up to them.

As fast as she could, Agatha darted from her hiding place and sprinted across the dim, frigid Bridge, feeling the wind on her scrawny boy chest, hands held out in front of her, knowing the barrier was coming—

Bam! She slammed into it a quarter of the way down the span, leaving her palms stinging and her body fully exposed in the moonlight. The guards would spot her the second they returned.

"Let me through," she begged, hands flat on the barrier.

Her crystal-clear reflection magically appeared in the mirror, dressed in Evil's uniform—only it was her usual girl self, instead of a boy.

"Old with Old,
New with New,
Back to your tower
Before—"

Her reflection peered at her. "Wait a second, lad . . . you're not a student here at all." Her face darkened. *"Intruder."* Her reflection opened her mouth wide. *"INTRU—"*

"No! It's me!" Agatha yelped. "It's Agatha!"

"All I see is an underfed, googly-eyed boy," her reflection said, opening her mouth again to scream—

"I'll prove it!" cried Agatha, knowing she had no choice now. She closed her eyes, visualizing the counterspell. . . . Her hair began to thicken, her jaw to round, and all at once her body eased back into her girl's shape, filling out her uniform. "See. *Me*," she smiled, now matching the reflection in the barrier. "So let me pass—"

"Oh. *You*," her reflection growled, not smiling back. "You nearly got me destroyed for confusing the sides the past two years. First you convinced me you were Evil, when you were Good. Then you convinced me you were a Boy, when you were a Girl. No way are you getting past me a third time. So listen clear:

"Old with Old,
New with New,
Back to your tower
Before I call You-Know-Who."

Agatha tightened. Out of the corner of her eye, she could see the chocolate patterns in the sky starting to evaporate. The sound of guards storming to the rooftop amplified inside the castle.

"And how do you know I'm not supposed to be on the Old side instead of the New?" Agatha asked her reflection, trying to stay calm.

"Easy," her image huffed. "Because you're as young as me and I'm as young as you."

"So if I'm young, I can't be old?"

"Have you ever met an old person who's young?" her reflection fleered.

"Well. Would a newborn baby see me as young or old?" said Agatha.

"Old, but that's because it doesn't know any better—"

"So what about a child?"

"Depends on how old the child is," her reflection snapped.

"So how young or old you are 'depends' on things?" Agatha asked.

"No! It's obvious to anything that's full-grown!"

"What about a full-grown flower? Or a full-grown fish?"

"Don't be stupid. A flower or fish can't see age," said her reflection.

"But you said anything full-grown—"

"A full-grown person!"

"So *you're* a person, if it's obvious to you," reasoned Agatha. "Yet you've been on this Bridge for thousands of years. So what does that make you? Young or old?"

"Old, of course," her reflection puffed.

"And if you're me and I'm you, then what does that make me?" Agatha said, lips curling to a smile.

Her reflection gasped, realizing the answer. *"Definitely old."*

Agatha's mirror image could only gape in anguish, fading into night, as the real Agatha reached her fingers through the barrier and felt the cold, empty wind.

Seconds later, the monstrous shadows swarmed to their post and saw nothing on the Bridge but a glint of black and green sliding into the castle, which they thought an errant piece of mist blown from the bay.

If they'd looked closer, they may have seen a small rain puddle still rippling over stone . . . a single clump print gleaming under the moon . . . or the two specks of light across the Bridge, floating low like fallen stars . . .

The bold yellow eyes of a bald, wrinkled cat, watching Agatha vanish safely into a den of danger, before the cat pulled into darkness and pit-patted away.

19

Old School Reunions

Do girls have softer heads than boys?

All Tedros could feel was drool dripping off his lip, his scraped-up cheek, and his skull ripping with pain. He couldn't feel his eyes, let alone open them, and he wondered if this is how mangos felt when they fell off trees and smashed to bits, before he realized mangos don't have feelings and he was likely suffering from a violent concussion.

Between pangs of nausea, he tried to touch the back of his head and check for blood, but his hands wouldn't budge.

Slowly he slit open his eyes to see he was still in a girl's body, splayed on a white canopied bed, his mouth gagged and wrists lashed to bedposts with red velvet sheets.

Stomach sinking, he turned his head to see Sophie perched on a stone altar table in the corner, the Storian paused over a blank page.

"Well, *Essa*—if that is indeed your name—you've told me so many lies that listening to you, '*girl to girl*' seems rather pointless, don't you think? But let me tell you what I do know. You're not a new student. You're not a Never assassin. You're not a Never at all. You and your 'cousin' are spies for Good, here to destroy my happy ending. Only you're too late, Essa dear. Agatha and Tedros are long gone, as this blank page attests, and Rafal and I would be in the throes of a heavenly romantic evening if it wasn't for *you*."

Tedros garbled urgently into his gag.

"Still have something to say? Oh dear," Sophie drawled, standing up. "Well, since the School Master and you are such bosom buddies, why don't you just tell it to *him*." She raised her fingerglow towards the window, about to shoot a flare into the sky—

Sophie dropped her hand, eyes widening.

On the bed, Essa's long hair was lightening from black to gold.

It shrank into her scalp, as her chin dimpled and her cheeks hardened, amber stubble stippling her jaw. Faster now, her legs and arms sprouted with fuzz, her feet ballooned two sizes and her shoulders and chest broadened, shredding her shirt seams. As the girl stranger writhed in pain, her calves chiseled, her biceps rippled, her forearms swelled, bursting the knots of her binds, until at last she tore away the gag with a virile roar, no longer a girl or stranger at all, but a prince in his body like a lion uncaged.

Sophie backed into a corner. "Teddy?"

A familiar scratching sound filled the chamber and Sophie looked down to see the Storian spill a new scene on the blank page: a bow-legged, helmet-haired girl hurtling across Halfway Bridge into the School for Old.

"Aggie?" Sophie squeaked.

She looked up at Tedros, legs shaking, breath shallowing.

"Don't panic," the prince soothed, as he inched across the bed. "Just don't panic, sweet pea . . ." He reached for her, breaking into a winning smile. "A prince is here to rescue you, okay? Everything is just fi—"

Sophie panicked. She lurched for the window, finger glowing, and shot a hot pink flare into the night—

A blast of gold light obliterated it and Sophie spun to see Tedros' glowing finger pointed at her.

"Listen. I'm a boy now. So either we do this the easy way or the hard way," he warned, waiting for Sophie to stop hyperventilating and come to her senses.

Instead, she ran for the window, trying to fire off another flare.

"Hard way it is," sighed Tedros.

Two minutes later, Sophie was cuffed to the bedpost with red velvet sheets, shouting every possible curse word into her gag.

Tedros glared back from the altar table, shirt ripped and covered in scratch marks.

"Now, for once in our lives, Sophie, the two of us are going to have a *normal* conversation."

The Storian knows where I am, Agatha thought, as she stole through a dark corridor, back in her girl body. It was only a matter of time before the School Master came hunting her.

A clock clanged high in the castle. Eleven o'clock. One hour left.

Her clump steps quickened, muffled by loud drips from the moldy ceiling. She had to find Tedros' sword *now*. Excalibur was their only hope to destroy the School Master's ring—and thus the School Master himself.

But where was it?

Even with a head start, she had no idea what was inside the School for Old, let alone who was lurking within its castle or where to look for a single sword blade that could be hidden any-where: in a secret cabinet, behind a fireplace, under a doormat, through an invisible door, beneath the stones she was treading on. . . . Who was she kidding! This was a fool's mission!

Agatha buckled against a wall, trying not to throw up. *I can't do this. I'll never find it.*

An old voice answered inside of her.

"Do not fail."

Merlin's last words.

The same as her mother's.

The wizard had put Good's fate in her and Tedros' hands for a reason.

Maybe she doubted herself. But she didn't doubt Merlin.

Do not fail.

This time the voice was hers.

On a deep breath, Agatha turned into the foyer.

The entrance chamber was quiet, empty, and insufferably humid. Any trace of the military-themed, refurbished School for Boys had been rubbed out, with the black stone foyer back the way it was first year: leaky, lumpy and dimly lit by gargoyles wielding torches in their mouths. With no sign of guards, Agatha scampered into the sunken anteroom adjoining the foyer, where three twisting staircases ascended to the dormitories. The portraits of the new Nevers were gone, no doubt moved across the bay. But the rest of the walls were still jam-packed with old Evil students, each frame carrying a portrait next to a scene of what they became after graduation.

Only now, as Agatha inched closer, she saw that the frames of Evil's most famous villains had all been defaced.

Captain James Hook's old student portrait as a young, broodingly handsome boy was splotched in graffiti from multiple people:

DON'T BLOW IT THIS TIME!
Payback for Pan!
NO ONE BEATS HOOK TWICE!

Over a gluttonous boy who became Jack's giant, there were more scribbled exhortations:

SECOND CHANCE AT GLORY!
KILL HIM AND HIS LITTLE COW TOO!
JUST STEP ON THE LAD!

Agatha scanned more frames along the wall: a willowy girl who'd become a famous Evil fairy ("NO SPINNING WHEELS THIS TIME!"), a blond boy with a scanty blue moustache who'd become Bluebeard ("YOU GONNA LET A *GIRL* WIN AGAIN?"), and dozens more notorious villains, their portraits splashed with more motivational creeds . . . until her eyes stopped on a Nevergirl whose face looked eerily familiar. Then Agatha noticed the graduation scene next to it: a raven-haired witch standing in front of a gingerbread house with her daughter. It was the same picture as the one on Hester's night table, only here scrawled with a single taunt:

Hear your kid's a better witch than you!

Agatha inched closer. *Who did all this?*

Voices suddenly floated from the foyer—

She dove behind a staircase.

An undead ogre and an undead hobgoblin stalked into the stair room, both stitched up and shedding off skin like the zombie villains she'd seen in the Woods. The ogre, bald and potbellied, had a thick gray hide, a serrated spine, and wielded a wooden cudgel, while the slimy, green hobgoblin with stumpy white horns carried a twisted brass dagger.

"Turnin' fog to chocolate? Bloody good prank if you ask me," chortled the ogre in a gravelly voice. "Few'a those New whippersnappers might amount to somethin' after all."

"Don't know why you think this is funny," piped the shrill-voiced goblin. "Came back to do our stories over again, not patrol empty halls and chase candy. Why can't I be in class upstairs with the others?"

"Henchmen guard the castle, not go to class," groused the ogre. "Best git back to yer' post. Anyone breaks in and the School Master will shove us back inna graves we came from."

The goblin sighed and the two parted ways into opposing halls.

Behind the stairwell, Agatha didn't move. *"Class?"* What classes were taught in the School for Old? And more importantly, *who* was taking them?

On instinct, she tiptoed from her hiding place and up a staircase, quite sure that whoever the students were at this school were the same hooligans who'd defaced the portraits.

The classrooms were lined up in an airless corridor off the first floor of Malice tower, Agatha recalled, but as soon as she turned off the landing, she saw two spear-toting guards down the hall and ducked behind the banister.

Of course the classrooms are guarded, you idiot. But how else was she supposed to get a view inside?

She racked her brain for a plan, listening to the trolls pace up and down the hall, feeling a cold breeze raise goosebumps on her skin . . .

A cold breeze? In an airless hall?

She looked up. High over her head there was a hollow air shaft, boxed out of the ceiling.

Moments later, Agatha's bare toes clung to the banister like a balance beam, her clumps tucked into the waist of her breeches, as she reached for the sides of the vent, trying not to make a sound. She unfurled her fingers as far as they'd go, but they were still two inches short. Leaning on her tiptoes, she stretched her hands higher, higher, feeling her shoulders strain out of their sockets, and clawed her finger pads into the mildew coating the vent. Hoisting herself up with desperate strength, Agatha had almost jammed her head and neck through, when she felt one of her clumps sliding out of her shorts. Gasping, she swung one-armed from the vent like a monkey, lunging to catch it, only to see her shoe fall through the gap in the stair-case and crash far below with an ear-splitting boom.

Crap.

Instantly, she propelled herself back into the vent, nearly breaking her elbows, and crawled as fast as she could through the cramped stone shaft, hearing the trolls' stunned voices and footsteps racing towards the stairs.

Soon she didn't hear them anymore, only the swirling air in the vent churning past her. The light from the staircase dwindled and she was in pitch-dark, with no clue where she was headed, until she began to hear a growing clamor and glimpsed wintry gray light spraying into the vent from a grat-ing ahead. The buzz grew louder as Agatha drew closer, knees skinning along stone, before she flattened her belly against the grates and peered down through the slats.

Her mouth fell open.

Lady Lesso's old frozen classroom was teeming with

famous villains, stitched up and undead—at least 40 of them, hunched at desks, jammed under chairs, stuffed into corners, practically sitting on laps, so that there wasn't an inch of frosted floor untaken. She recognized many of these crusty, stitched-up Nevers, either from storybooks she'd read in Gavaldon, their gravestones on Necro Ridge, or the portraits downstairs. There was runty Rumpelstiltskin, the frog-faced Witch of the Wood, bloodshot Bluebeard, wizened old Baba Yaga, and even Jack's oafish Giant, looking bruised and battered from his encounter with Princess Uma's army.

No wonder we didn't see more of them in the Woods, Agatha thought. The villains had all been at their old school.

But doing what?

At the front of the classroom was a slender, ferocious-looking woman in a tattered silver gown, with a full face of makeup, a coiled bun of white hair, and skin stitched up like the rest.

"A month since the School Master brought us back to school and what do we have to show for it? Five old stories turned Evil. FIVE! We'll never make it to Woods Beyond with *five* stories. You heard the School Master. Every story changed brings us one step closer to the Reader World."

Agatha's heart stopped. Reader World? Woods Beyond? Was she talking about . . . *Gavaldon?*

"I have my own work to do, it seems," the old woman's voice harrumphed. "Cinderella is alive, out there in the Woods, and my worthless daughters have yet to locate her. Can't have another turn at a fairy tale unless you *find* your old Nemesis first, can you?" She glowered at two hideous undead girls in the corner. "Now, for homework the School Master asked each of you to pinpoint the mistake that made you lose your story the first time. Giant, let's start with you."

Jack's giant held up a storybook, open to a painting of him sleeping in his castle as Jack sneaked past him. "Nappin' on the job," he sulked.

"Is that what got you beat by Princess Uma and a buncha animals too? 'Nappin' on the job'?" Rumpelstiltskin snorted.

"Just 'cause you redone your story already don't mean you can be rude," the giant fired.

"Who's next?" Cinderella's stepmother snapped.

As the old villains continued presenting their worst moments, Agatha crept ahead to the grating over the next classroom.

Dozens of undead villains milled between corkboards blanketed in hand-drawn maps of the Woods, covered with red and blue pins and scraps of multicolored notes. At first, Agatha didn't recognize many of these witches and monsters . . .

Then her stomach plunged.

Near the far wall, Snow White's rotted old witch and Red Riding Hood's wolf, nursing a black eye and bandaged leg, were both having an intense conversation with a third villain Agatha had never met before: a man, tall and darkly handsome, despite his zombified skin, with curly black hair, a pirate's hat, and instead of a right hand, a gleaming silver *hook*.

"Wolf found them on Necro Ridge and I saw them here at Cottage White," grunted Snow White's witch, tapping a yellowed fingernail on a map.

"Which means League Headquarters must be north of Maidenvale," Captain Hook surmised in a deep, silken voice. "I'm guessing within a mile of Knobble Hill . . ." He smiled thinly, stroking his hook. "Mmm, thirteen heroes at once. Wouldn't that be *dandy?*"

Agatha's heart was in her throat. A mile from Knobble Hill? That's precisely where League Headquarters was! She had to warn Merlin as soon as she got back. But first things first; she had a sword to find—

Suddenly ogre howls rang through the castle like a fire alarm. The door burst open and a troll guard crashed in.

"*INTRUDER! Intruder in the castle! Double meals to who-ever finds it!*"

Villains raucously stampeded out of the room after the troll, leaving Agatha petrified. She skirted to the wall and skittered through the vent like a cockroach, stopping at each grating, catching glimpses of five classrooms of undead Nevers emptying into the hall with bloodthirsty whoops . . . until she saw Captain Hook again right under her, speaking to a tall, shirtless boy, gorgeous and lean with spiked white hair and alabaster skin.

Agatha froze.

Him.

And he was holding her clump.

"Troll found this," the young School Master snarled. "Agatha's inside this castle. And either that mincing prince is with her or he'll come to us once we capture her. I need you to command the rest and—"

He stopped cold. His eyes rose to the ceiling and Agatha dove away from the grating just in time. Hidden in shadow, she held her breath. *Keep talking . . . keep talking . . . please, please, please—*

"Search the dungeons and the belfry," the School Master's voice continued. "Leave no stone unturned."

Agatha almost fainted in relief. As long as he was here, away from the Storian, he couldn't know she was hiding right over his head.

"But I want Agatha *alive*. It's time I had a little talk with our dear princess," said the School Master. "Now marshal the men while I secure the museum. Understood?"

"Yes, Master," Hook said.

Agatha peeked through the grate and watched them part ways. Captain Hook, *the* Captain Hook, was looking for *her*? And not only him, hundreds of villains, just as famous and deadly? She was dead . . . more than dead . . . she was horse meat—

And yet, as she watched the mob of hooting villains combing the castle, something the School Master said was still gnawing at her.

Secure the museum.

He had the chance to find and kill her and he was worried about the museum? Of all the things in the castle, why would an invincible sorcerer possibly need to secure a muse—

Agatha choked and bolted upright, smacking her head into the vent. Scrambling onto her hands and knees, she started down the air shaft in the direction he went.

There was only one thing in the world the Woods' greatest villain needed to secure.

The one weapon that could destroy him and his minions forever.

A holy sword Agatha never thought she could find.

And now the School Master was surely taking her right to it.

Tedros used magic to whisk away Sophie's gag, because he was afraid she'd bite his face if he got too close.

"Better pray I *never* get out of these," Sophie spat, flailing against the velvet sheets binding her to the bedpost.

"Now hold your horses," Tedros growled, trying to salvage what was left of his shirt.

"Rafal will be here any moment, so I suggest you take your horses and scat if you don't want to end up dissected for Evil research. Where's Agatha?"

"Getting my sword from the School for Evil. You'll need it to destroy your ring—" Tedros started, only to instantly regret it when he saw Sophie's face.

"My *ring*? My *Queen's* ring?" Sophie shot back. "That's why you were ogling it on the shore? Because you want me to *destroy* it?"

"Uh, it's how we k-k-kill the School Master," Tedros stammered, knowing he was talking too much. "It's how you'll be free—look, we can discuss this later, once we get out of—"

"*Free?*" Sophie hissed, shielding her ring. "By killing the boy who *loves me*? By taking me away from the one place where I might finally be happy? So I can live Ever After following you and your princess like a dog?"

"Be reasonable, Sophie. You can't stay with the School Master! He's a monster!"

"His name is Rafal, he's different now, and for your information, we were supposed to have our first date tonight—"

"Where you'd probably end up drinking the blood of little children together," Tedros retorted. "Now hear me out before I gag you again—"

"Don't you dare threaten me," Sophie scorched. "You can't hurt me more than you already have, Tedros. You made Agatha pick you over me. You made her believe she couldn't have her best friend *and* her prince. You tried to send me back home alone to no mother, a rotten father, a haggish stepmother, stepbrothers who've already moved into my room, and a town where no one—*no one*—cares about me. You and your princess sent me to hell with a kiss, and just when I found my way to a boy who truly cares about me, to a happy ending that might finally be real . . . here you are riding in on your white horse again to take it all away."

Tedros gazed at his once-princess tied up on the bed. "Sophie, don't you get it? He isn't what he looks like. He isn't your true love. He's *Evil*. And if you stay with him, that makes you Evil too. There'll be no way back to Good this time."

Sophie's eyes sparkled. "Do you know why I wanted a fairy tale my whole life? Because a fairy tale means love that never ends. I thought that love was you, Tedros. Then I thought it was Agatha. But it's *him*. It has to be him."

Tedros stood up from the table. Sophie watched the prince move towards the bed, his hair haloed in torchlight, as he slipped onto the sheets next to her. Their legs touched as they sat in silence.

"You think we'd come all this way if we didn't love you?" he said softly. "We're your best friends."

Sophie turned away. "No, *Agatha* was my best friend. My only friend. I needed *her*, Tedros. More than I needed anyone. But you made Agatha choose between a boy and her friend. And now you're trying to make me choose too." Sophie shook her head, letting tears fall. "How could she do it? How could she just throw me away?"

"She made a mistake, Sophie," Tedros said. "When you fight for love, sometimes you think it's you against the world. You become scared. You see what isn't there. It happened to Agatha. It happened to me. And now it's happening to you."

She felt him reach up behind her, undoing her first bind.

"But there's nothing holding us back anymore," he said. "We can all be together now."

"Even fairy tales have limits," said Sophie. "Three people can't have an Ever After. Not without me being alone."

"You won't be alone, Sophie." She could feel his forearm caress her neck as it reached for the other bind. "You'll have two people who want to see you happy. And until we have you in our lives again, we can't be happy either."

"You and Agatha have each other. You don't need me."

"She and I could barely be in the same room together until we came to find you. We should never have left you behind."

She felt his skin on her wrist, the loosening of a knot. "This journey to find you and fix our past mistakes ended up making Agatha and I closer. *You* brought Agatha and I together, like you always have before."

The velvet cuff fell away, setting Sophie free. She stared into his eyes, his last words stinging her.

"Come with us, Sophie," Tedros said, tilting her chin up, the way he once asked her to a Ball. "Come with Agatha and me to Camelot."

Sophie curled into his chest, making him hold her. "Maybe you can't see it. But now you brought me and Rafal closer too," she whispered, almost to herself.

"What?"

"If I go with you, I won't find love again," Sophie said, nuzzling Tedros tighter. "My story proves it. I'm unlovable by anyone else. My best friend. My father. My prince. Not even Hort wants me anymore."

"Because you've forgotten what love really is. Good is the path to love, Sophie. Not Evil."

"Rafal is my only path now," she said, remembering what it was like to be this close to a prince . . .

"There has to be a way," Tedros pressed. "There has to be a way to make you come with us."

"No, it's too late . . ." Sophie inhaled his scent, trying to wrest herself away, trying to let him go. "Take Agatha and leave."

"Not without you," he said, his lips at her ear.

"I won't leave him . . . I won't leave my true love," Sophie fought, looking to Rafal's ring for strength.

Only now she saw something else on her finger . . . rubbed raw by the binds . . . her heart's only answer all along . . .

"Unless . . . ," she whispered.

"Unless . . . ?" Tedros breathed.

Sophie clasped his hand.

Tedros looked down and stiffened.

Because now he saw his name on her flesh too.

"Unless I had you back," Sophie said.

20

Last Stop on the Fairy Dust Express

A clock struck somewhere across the bay. 11:30.

Thirty minutes to find Excalibur. *What happens if I'm not at the gates by midnight?* Agatha thought, scuttling through the air shaft to follow the School Master. *Will Tedros come looking for me? Will he try to get into the castle?* She couldn't let that happen. He'd be walking into a death trap—

She stopped short.

Agatha stared at a wall of black rock sealing off the vent, as the sound of the School Master's footsteps receded into the buzz of villains hunting her.

Alarmed, she was about to turn back and search for another route to the museum, when she noticed there was a small gap in the vent before the

dead end. Agatha crept to the edge of the gap and looked down.

A black void.

Either she backtracked to the last crossroads in the vent and risked losing the School Master . . . or she took a stupidly lethal chance.

Agatha slid her legs over the edge of the gap.

She let go.

Gravity blasted her into free fall—then her backside clamped onto a smooth stone slide, rocketing her through darkness. Without warning, the slide swerved left and Agatha was thrown onto her side with no idea where she was going. There were no more gratings, no more rays of light, just merciless black, with the odd green flicker of a dead fairy, caught in the sealed-off maze. Crossing her arms over her chest, Agatha let go like a swimmer in a riptide as she veered at the sharpest, scariest angles, convinced this would all end in a gruesome death, before she shot off the slide like shrapnel, skidded onto a smooth metal surface, and halted face-first over a steel grating.

Ow.

Agatha pried off the slats, rubbing the welts on her cheeks. Through the grate, she could see an empty room underneath her, lit by a weak green torch. No one inside it, nothing on the walls, nothing on the sooty black floor. And yet, something about the place seemed familiar. Bending closer to the grate, she squinted across the room, until she made out an ash-spattered door and its simmering red letters:

THE EXHIBITION OF EVIL

Evil's museum.

Agatha bobbed to her knees. Given how quickly she crossed the castle, there was no way the School Master could have gotten here already, which meant . . .

I made it before him.

Sweating in the shadows, Agatha waited for him to come and lead her to the weapon that could kill him.

She waited.

And waited.

And waited.

A clock in the castle tolled once.

11:45.

Something stopped him on the way, she thought. But there was no more time to wait. In fifteen minutes, Merlin would be at the gates.

She grabbed hold of the steel grating, which dislodged easily from stone. She left her remaining clump behind and lowered down through the hole, hanging on to the sides of the shaft. Arms stretched, she kicked the air as if to dismount a swing and landed on her soles without a sound.

Agatha scanned the museum, once filled with relics of Evil's scant victories and now wiped clean. True, she hadn't expected Excalibur to be waiting on a table for her, but there was nowhere in this room that Tedros' sword could possibly be hidden. The floor was a single slab of stone, every case and frame was gone, every wall bare—

Not every wall, Agatha realized, moving towards the corner.

For on the far wall, hidden in shadows, there was one painting left.

Agatha stalked closer, her eyes adjusting to the dark, until she realized it was a painting she knew well.

In a village square, raging children heaved storybooks into a bonfire and watched them burn. Behind the village, a dark forest went up in flames, blanketing the sky with red and black smoke.

The colors were gauzy and impressionistic, the style unmistakable. It was the work of Professor August Sader, a blind seer who once taught History before he sacrificed his life fighting the School Master. Agatha recognized the scene as the last in his Reader Prophecy, a series of paintings once mounted in the Gallery of Good. As part of the Prophecy, Sader had predicted pairs of Readers kidnapped to the School for Good and Evil, leading up to her and Sophie. But there had been no more Readers predicted after them . . . instead, only this scene of Gavaldon's children burning its fairy tales as smoke clouds closed in.

And yet they weren't smoke clouds, Agatha remembered now from her first year, focusing harder on them. They were shadows, hulking and monstrous, invading the town . . . and as Agatha leaned closer, her nose to the canvas, she began to see familiar shapes in the smoke . . .

A giant's bald head . . . a wolf's toothy snout . . . a stepmother's coiled bun . . . a captain's round hook . . .

These weren't just shadows.

These were villains. Real villains.

All coming to Gavaldon.

Agatha backed up, hearing the stepmother's ominous warning: *"Every story changed brings us one step closer to the Reader World . . ."*

Before his death, Sader had seen this too: the School Master's Dark Army crossing into her village.

But why? What could the School Master possibly want in Gavaldon?

Terrified, Agatha studied the shadows harder, trying to understand . . .

But something else caught her attention in the painting now.

Behind the bonfire, in the recesses of the square, there was a tiny slash of gold beneath the canopy of Mr. Deauville's hollowed-out book shop. Agatha made out a pattern of diamonds on a golden hilt and the start of a wide silver sword, buried blade-first in an anvil. She rubbed her eyes.

No doubt about it.

Excalibur was *inside* the picture.

Flummoxed, Agatha ran her hand along the surface of the oil-painted canvas, hard and stubbly . . . until her fingers touched the sword hilt. All of a sudden, the texture was different: warm, smooth, and metallic. She pushed harder against the canvas and watched her nails slowly penetrate the tight, viscous surface, a strange wetness soaking her fingertips. Further and further her hand sucked in, all the way to the wrist, before Agatha began to see her fingers appear within the painting itself, reaching for the hilt of the sword. Eyes widening, she grasped Excalibur's handle from inside the picture, her knuckles locking a firm grip, and pulled as hard as she could. The sword flew out of the anvil like a flower out of water— Agatha reeled as hand and sword ejected from the frame, and the weight of the blade sent her toppling to the floor.

Slowly, Agatha raised her head and looked at Excalibur, still clenched in her fist. Then she looked up at the painting, where an empty anvil posed in front of Mr. Deauville's.

Oh my God.

She launched to her feet, thrusting her prince's sword into the torchlight.

I did it.

I really did it!

Mission complete.

With ten minutes to spare.

A beam of pride and relief ripped across her face and she whirled to the door, sword in hand, ready to mogrify out of this depraved castle —

Agatha dropped the sword.

"I never underestimate you, Agatha," the young School Master said, leaning against a wall, barechested in black breeches. "And yet you underestimate me. A sorcerer who defeats death, returns to youth, takes your best friend as my queen, and here you think that I can't hear your breath in a vent ten feet over my head . . . that I'd randomly announce my need to secure a museum . . . that I'd willfully leave the search for an intruder in my castle . . . all for no good reason . . ." The beautiful boy arched a brow. "Unless, of course, I knew you'd overhear it."

Agatha's heart imploded. "Then w-w-why didn't you just kill me in the hall?"

"For one thing, I've been suspecting for a while that a pesky old wizard has been advising you and your prince as to how to defeat me, and now I have proof my suspicions are correct. For another, I was curious as to whether Excalibur is really as powerful as Merlin believes. So I put a charm on the sword when I hid it in the painting, so that no one except me could retrieve it. Which means that if *you* pulled it out, Excalibur's magic indeed exceeds mine, at once able to recognize its allies and surely powerful enough to destroy the ring that keeps me alive. But I suppose there's also a third reason I haven't killed you just yet, Agatha. I thought you should meet the boy who's claimed your best friend's heart, up close and personal. You may call me, Rafal, by the way." He smiled, striding towards her. "Sophie does."

Agatha snatched the sword and flung it out at him, halting his advance. "Why did Sader paint the villains in Gavaldon? What's the painting mean?"

Rafal eyed the sword blade, bemused. "Agatha, can you recall what I told you when you and Sophie visited my tower first year? I gave you a riddle to solve and sent you back to your schools, but you were angry with me. You said I should prey on other villages and leave yours alone. Do you remember what I answered?"

Agatha could feel herself transported back to that very moment, his reply vivid in her memory . . . the old masked School Master, so different from this young boy in front of her, leaving her with a single question as she and Sophie free-fell into a sea of white . . .

A question that had tormented her for two years.

A question that never made any sense.

"What other villages?" she whispered.

"That's the one," Rafal grinned. "You see, Agatha, all this time you thought the Reader World was the 'real world' far away from the realm of magic . . . when, in fact, your world is *part* of the Endless Woods. For how can a land of stories exist without Readers to believe in them?"

Agatha paled. "Gavaldon is *in* the Woods?"

"Why do you think Readers from your village are the only ones kidnapped? Why do you think any attempt to escape your village leads right back to it?" said Rafal. "Yours is the one unenchanted kingdom of our world, but still *part* of the fairy-tale world—as much a part of fairy tales as Camelot, or Netherwood, or this school itself. It is why no class here is ever complete without two Readers: one who believes in Good and one who believes in Evil."

Agatha felt her brain whirring, trying to grasp the enormity of his words.

"Actually, the only access I have to Readers is to make sure they are fairly and safely represented at my school, like every other realm of the Woods," Rafal went on. "Our world needs new Readers to survive just as much as it needs new stories. That is why there are magic gates that protect Gavaldon from the rest of our world. That is why we call it the Woods Beyond. Because Readers keep our stories alive, long after the people in them are dead and gone. You could even say that Readers are the one force in our world more powerful than me. Because as long as there are Readers who *believe* in Good's power over Evil, Good will still win, even if I obliterate every Ever kingdom in the Woods. Because there will always be Readers, no matter what I do. Readers who put their faith in the Old stories, passing them down, forever and ever, keeping Good alive beyond my control . . ."

The young School Master paused. "And yet, what if Readers learn that the Old has been made *New,* just like all your fellow students? What if the one power to keep stories alive discovers that the Good stories they hold dear are all a lie? That Evil always wins, has always won, and always will? What then?" His sapphire eyes reflected the fires of the painting. "The gates to Gavaldon will open for the *true* ending to your fairy tale—an ending that will erase every Ever After down to the very last one . . . and put an end to Good forever."

Agatha was corpse white. "What's the ending? What do you want with Gavaldon?"

"Me?" Rafal cocked a grin. "Oh no. It isn't me you should be worrying about, Agatha. If there's one thing you should have learned from Evelyn Sader, it's that the most dangerous person in a fairy tale is the one willing to do anything for love. A description that fits your best friend, doesn't it?"

The School Master held out his palm and Excalibur flew out of her hand and into his. He smiled wider, handsome as the devil.

"And it just happens your best friend's love is *me.*"

"Me?" Tedros leapt off the bed. "Have *me* back?"

Sophie lifted to her knees on the mattress. "I know you chose Agatha over me, Teddy. I know she's your princess now. All I'm asking is that you keep yourself open before you decide for sure. The End isn't written yet, is it? I'll come with you and Aggie to Camelot. I'll do anything you want. Just give me another chance to be your Ever After."

Tedros looked like he'd been kicked in the pants. "I . . . I don't know what you're saying . . ."

"That if you're asking me to question my happy ending, so should you," said Sophie.

Tedros shrank against a wall, clutching the shreds of his shirt. He could see the Storian furiously capturing the two of them, alone in the School Master's chamber. "And if I won't?"

Sophie's fingertip glowed pink. "Then I'll choose Rafal and my loyalty will be to him. Which means I have to tell him you're here."

"Listen to yourself, Sophie. Listen to what you're asking me," Tedros pleaded. "You're dazzling, intelligent, and absolutely mental in every way and I can't imagine my life without you. From the moment I saw you first year, I thought you were my future queen. But we already tried to be together. No matter how good we might seem on paper, in the end, we're meant to be friends. Just friends. Like we were last year—"

"When you tried to *kiss* me?" said Sophie.

"That . . . that's irrelevant . . ." Tedros stuttered. "What matters is that Agatha and I are happy together—"

"Really?" said Sophie, sliding off the bed and moving towards him. "You said I was the one who brought you two back together. Which means you two had broken apart. Which means you two aren't particularly happy if it takes a third person to *fix* your love."

"Look, happy endings take time and work and commitment," Tedros retorted. "Mine and Agatha's won't be the last Ever After that wrestles and doubts and fights to hold on to love. Just look at your own."

Sophie paused. "You're right, Teddy. That's why I asked my heart to tell me my *real* ending. And this is what it said." She held up the ink on her skin, desperation creeping into her voice. "I want to love Rafal. I want to love anyone but you. You bring me nothing but pain and hurt and humiliation. Yet my heart only knows your name, Teddy. What else can I do but see if it's right?" She gazed at him through tears. "Our fairy tale brought us back together, here and now, because it wants a different ending. Why else would you be here alone without Agatha? Why else would you be the one to rescue me instead of my best friend?"

Tedros went rigid, thinking of all the twists and turns that brought him and Sophie to this very moment. The two of them alone, face-to-face, no disguises, no tricks, for the first time in two years. Then his cheeks went apple red. "I could never do that to Agatha. Neither could you, Sophie. You're not a witch, anymore—"

"And yet, Agatha and I had our own Ever After until you made *her* reconsider," Sophie said, treading closer. "So if asking you to open your heart makes me a witch, then you're one too, Tedros. Because you did the same thing to Agatha when she was *my* princess."

Tedros was speechless.

"But now it's time for all of us to face the truth. It's time for the last Ever After," Sophie pressed, cornering him. "Don't you want to know who your princess is without a doubt, Teddy?" She stared into his eyes. "Wouldn't your father want you to look closer one last time?"

Tedros' turned away, gritting so hard she could see the bones of his jaw. "You know nothing about my father," he said.

"Teddy, listen to me. I'll leave Rafal, just like you ask," said Sophie gently. "I'll destroy his ring and commit my heart to Good forever. I'll follow you and Agatha to your kingdom, fully accepting you might choose her and I'll end up alone, the sidekick to your happy ending. All I ask of you is a simple promise: that you'll give me another chance before picking your princess forever."

Slowly Tedros looked back at her . . .

"Sounds like quite a deal," said a voice.

They spun to the window.

Rafal glared at Sophie, Excalibur to Agatha's throat.

But his expression wasn't nearly as surprised as Agatha's.

Hort woke up when he heard teachers' muffled shouts upstairs. He couldn't make out more than a few words: something about Aric attacked? An intruder on the loose?

His first thought was to check if Sophie was safe. Then he

remembered she was in the old cretin's tower, far away from the castle, and he'd been so good at *not* thinking about her and now wasn't the time to regress.

He glanced at Chaddick and Nicholas asleep in their beds, handsome, beloved Everboys who girls once drooled over.

Hort smirked. Now the girls all wanted him.

He saw the way they goggled at his new muscles and flirted shamelessly in the hall, sizing him up like a lamb shank. He could have anyone at this school, Ever or Never.

And yet, as he leaned against the window, staring at the School Master's spire over the Blue Forest, Hort found himself wondering what it would be like to live there with Sophie. The two of them, ruling all of Evil together . . . A hot, burning feeling edged through his body as he imagined her in his arms for a perfect kiss—

He flushed pink, smearing away sweat.

No.

She hurts you.

She only hurts you.

You don't love her anymore.

Tearing his eyes away from the Forest, he clenched his teeth, sank to his pillow—and bolted back up.

A small pinpoint of gold glowed from the School Master's window.

Not just gold. Buff, brassy gold, halfway between flaxen and amber.

He knew this because he knew everything about Camelot's prince, down to the precise hue of his glow.

What he didn't know is why that prince's glow was in the School Master's tower.

Tedros grabbed Sophie by the waist and held his glowing finger to her throat. "Hurt Agatha and I kill your queen," he warned the young School Master, only to see Rafal press Excalibur deeper into Agatha's neck.

"Teddy . . . not a good deal . . . ," Sophie wheezed, straining for breath.

But the two barechested boys locked eyes across the chamber, gripping their hostages tighter.

Feeling the sword's cold blade, Agatha shivered with confusion. Here she was, counting on her prince and best friend to rescue her from a lethal villain. Instead, she'd arrived to find Tedros' shirt ripped open and Sophie asking to be his princess.

"I said let Agatha *go*," Tedros growled at Rafal, his torso red with heat.

"Oh-ho, *now* you're my prince?" said Agatha, against the School Master's cold, pale chest. "The prince who a second ago seemed rather open to testing out a *new* princess?"

"Stop it, Agatha," Tedros snapped, digging his lit fingertip into Sophie's throat. "Rafal, release her or—"

"Or what?" Rafal was strangely calm, staring at Sophie. "You'll kill a girl you've come all this way to save? A girl pledging her heart to *you*?"

There was no anger or vengeance in his face, only a cool evenness that left Sophie unnerved. "Rafal, I'm sorry," she said. "But I have to make the right choice this time. The right choice for *me*."

"Like betraying your best friend?" Agatha lambasted her, before turning on Tedros. "Or telling your princess to her face how much you love her and the moment she's out of sight, pretending she doesn't exist?"

"I was just hearing her out," Tedros fired back. "Sophie said she'd come with us if I gave her a second chance. With everything on the line, don't you think that's a worthy request?"

"A second *chance*?" Agatha scoffed. "After all we've been through, after everything we said to each other in Hester's room, now you want to try out another girl?"

"You're not getting it," said Tedros, temper flaring. "Why can't you ever trust me? Why can't you trust *us*?"

Rafal raised his brows. "And here I am asking the same of my queen. For the first time, I have something in common with an Everboy."

He grinned at the handsome prince and Tedros looked away.

Silence fell between the two couples. Even the Storian faltered, unsure who was defending who anymore.

"Don't mind me," Rafal prodded, smiling. "Who needs a villain when you three have each other?"

"Ignore him, Agatha—" Tedros started.

"If you want me to 'trust us,' then tell her, Tedros," said Agatha quietly. "Tell Sophie I'm your princess forever. Right here. Right now."

Tedros looked at her, dejected, as if they were talking past each other.

"You can't do it, can you?" Agatha breathed.

"Agatha, dear, I know we haven't seen each other in a while," Sophie jumped in, "but knowing the male species as well as I do, ultimatums only drive them awa—"

"I'd rather have my throat slit than talk to you," Agatha thrashed.

Sophie shut up.

"Agatha, I love you," Tedros said, firm and clear. "But all Sophie wants is for me to think twice before we seal our Ever After, just like we're asking *her* to do. That's fair, isn't it?" He turned to Sophie. "Promise me that if I give you a chance you'll destroy the ring. Promise me you'll destroy it as soon as we leave here."

Sophie waited for Rafal to get angry, to threaten her, but he looked oddly entertained.

She nodded, distracted by Rafal's smirk. "I promise."

Rafal snorted.

"See?" Tedros pressed Agatha. "All I have to do is be willing to follow my heart and everything will end happily."

Agatha could see his frustration, as if she was the problem here, not him. It only rankled her more. "And what about my heart? Tedros, how can you stand there and look me in the eye and—"

She froze, finally feeling the clarity of her prince's blue stare.

He was lying.

Tedros was *lying*.

The prince bound to his promises, bound to the truth, was lying for *her*.

He was telling Sophie only what she wanted to hear. He'd do whatever he had to in order to rescue their best friend from Evil's clutches and destroy that ring, including pretending to give Sophie a real chance at his heart.

This whole time Tedros had been trying to tell her the stakes were worth it. A ring destroyed. Good heroes spared. Her best friend saved. Her prince still hers . . .

And all Agatha had to do was go along with the lie.

So much for being 100% Good, she thought, resisting tackling and kissing him right there.

"Do you understand the terms?" her prince smiled, seeing the change in her face.

"You'll give Sophie a chance and follow your heart . . ." Agatha smiled back, her face glowing.

Sophie was beaming now too, glancing between them obliviously.

". . . straight to Camelot's future queen," said Tedros, eyes on Agatha.

Agatha's smile vanished.

Queen.

That word again. That word that never seemed real.

From the moment they came back to the Woods, she'd put off thoughts of ever making it to Camelot, assuming Tedros and her would break up first or she'd die rescuing Sophie or the Woods would go dark and kill them all. Indeed, the closer they got to finding Sophie again, the more she'd fought with Tedros, as if unconsciously trying to tell them they *couldn't* ever get to Camelot.

But here she was, on the cusp of her future as queen of the most famous kingdom ever known. As a queen who the people would judge so closely after Tedros' mother failed them. As a queen who must restore the legend of her crown.

And nothing standing in the way between her and that crown except one big little lie.

Right then and there, in a moment where Agatha had accused Tedros of doubting their future, only to see he was, in fact, rock solid . . . it was she who suddenly had the doubts.

Me. A queen? A _real_ queen?

Tedros saw her face darken and his smile dissipated too, as if he knew she'd stalled before the last hurdle.

"Aggie?" said Sophie's voice.

Agatha looked up.

"*I* still feel like his queen," Sophie said, reading her expression. "Which means something in our story's still wrong, isn't it?"

Agatha could see the unswerving belief in Sophie's face and her gut twisted deeper. *Something _was_ wrong.* For how could she and Tedros be The End if everything in her heart told her she'd never make a queen to Camelot, while everything in Sophie's heart told her she would?

Maybe that's why she and Tedros never sealed their happy ending, Agatha thought. Because something was broken between them. And maybe that something couldn't be fixed. Because that something was . . . her.

"Mmmm, now it's getting interesting, isn't it?" said a chilling voice.

All eyes went to the young School Master, his sensual lips in a twisted grin.

"Evil's queen, ladies and gentlemen, still vying for Good's throne," Rafal said, Excalibur's blade reflecting him. "But trust her at your peril, because in the end, she'll end up right back here, my ring on her finger, her heart belonging to me."

Sophie felt his placid stare and sweat trickled down her side.

"You don't know what will happen any more than we do, Rafal," said Agatha, still looking at her best friend.

"You're trying to talk reason to a murderer?" Tedros blurted.

Agatha's eyes never left Sophie. "Maybe she's right, Tedros. Maybe we have to think twice about our happy ending if we're ever going to find it."

Sophie looked at Agatha, stunned.

Tedros brightened instantly. "Wait . . . Agatha, you're saying that you're okay with Sophie's terms? That you *get* what I'm proposing? That—"

"—we question our happy ending, Tedros, just like you said," spoke Agatha, still looking at Sophie.

"That we all wipe the slate clean," Sophie said eagerly, looking at Agatha.

"The three of us," said Agatha. "This time with no secrets, no hiding, no guilt. We go in with eyes wide open and let the truth lead us to The End. That's the only way we'll know how each of us can be happy."

Tedros glanced between them, baffled. "Okay . . . this got

a little deep for me . . ." He smiled lovingly at Agatha. "But I knew you'd understand."

Agatha smiled back at him sadly.

He couldn't see she meant it for real.

Midnight tolled from distant castles, a deadline come and gone.

Agatha took a full breath, looking at her prince. "To new beginnings."

Tedros smiled at his princess. "New beginnings."

They both turned to Sophie.

Sophie smiled at Tedros. "New beginnings."

The three students' eyes held for just a moment . . . then all at once moved to Rafal.

The young School Master's smirk vanished. In a flash, he seized Agatha tighter to the sword, about to slice her throat—

"Now!" Tedros yelled.

Sophie shot Rafal's hand with a scorching pink spell and he dropped Tedros' sword in shock. Agatha caught it and rammed the hilt into his gut, sending him reeling into a bookcase, which crashed on top of him along with hundreds of colorful fairy tales. Agatha flipped Excalibur to Tedros, who slid the hilt into the back of his shorts, the flat of the blade against his spine. Instantly he, Sophie, and Agatha sprinted to the window and climbed onto the ledge—

"We need to get to Merlin," Tedros panted. "Mogrifying is our only chance!"

"The School Master can *fly*, Tedros! He'll catch us!" said Agatha, watching Rafal blast through the bookcase with magic. "We need something faster!"

"You came in without a plan to get me *out*?" Sophie said, the sounds of the bookcase splintering behind them.

"Was pretty sure we'd be dead by now," puffed Tedros. "What's faster than mogrifying?"

The bookcase over Rafal flew across the room, shattering against the opposite wall.

"He's c-c-coming," Agatha stammered, spinning back to her friends. "We have to leave right no—"

Her eyes bulged. Sweeping from the Woods towards the School Master's tower was a sooty black cloud, boxy and elongated like a passenger train, and strangely moldy in texture. For a moment, she thought it was smoke from a distant fire, until she saw the familiar twinkles sewn into the cloud, glittering like . . .

"Fairy dust?" Agatha said, agape.

And indeed, now she, Sophie, and Tedros all glimpsed the shadow *inside* the fairy-dust cloud: a shadow with flowing purple robes and a cone-shaped hat, flying and flapping his arms as he steered towards the window.

"If you don't come to Merlin, Merlin comes to you," the wizard trumpeted, bringing the cloud a few feet from the window ledge. "Quickly, children! Tink's dust won't last much longer!"

Agatha glanced back and saw Rafal starting to rise. She spun to Sophie and Tedros. "We have to jump into the fairy dust!"

"*Jump?*" Sophie squeaked, peering off the ledge.

"On three!" said Agatha. "One . . ."

"Two . . . ," said Tedros.

"Three!" they yelled—

Agatha and Tedros cannonballed into the thick of the cloud and felt a magic lightness buoy them into air, as if they'd lost all mass. As Merlin veered the cloud train towards the school gates, Agatha closed her eyes, abandoning to weightless flight. Tedros, meanwhile, couldn't stop somersaulting in midair, like an asteroid knocked from its path.

"How do I stop spinning!" Tedros howled.

"Relax your buttocks, dear boy!" Merlin called back.

Swimming through dust, Agatha grabbed on to the prince's wrist, stopping his orbit. Tedros smiled gratefully . . . then frowned.

"Where's Sophie?" he asked.

They twirled to see her standing on the windowsill, white as a ghost while the dust train floated away.

"Sophie, what are you doing!" Agatha cried.

"Jump *now*!" Tedros hollered.

Terrified, Sophie inched closer to the ledge and suddenly felt a clamp on her left hand. She spun to see Rafal holding on to her, calmer than ever.

"You'll come back to me, Sophie," he promised. "Leave now and you'll come back, begging for forgiveness."

Sophie saw the cold confidence in his pupils, reflecting her scared face. His grip on her hardened, her hand weakening in his . . .

"Sophie, come on!" a boy's voice called.

She turned and saw the golden, shirtless prince suspended in the sparkle cloud, beckoning her to his side . . . like the first day they ever met . . .

"I'll never be your queen, Rafal," Sophie whispered, a pink princess's song swelling in her heart. She turned to the young School Master. "Because I'll be someone else's."

Her pink fingertip glowed, lighting up *TEDROS* beneath Rafal's golden ring. The School Master reddened in surprise, his hand slipping off his queen's. Like a dove breaking free, Sophie leapt backwards out of his window, beaming radiantly as she floated into the last tail of glitterdust.

Agatha and Tedros swam through twinkling soot and caught Sophie in their arms, the three of them drifting over the bay like flowers in a sandstorm, as Merlin helmed the dust train towards the school gates.

Tedros draped his arms over the two levitating girls. "We're together," he marveled. "We're *actually* together."

"And finally on the same side," said Sophie, hugging him.

Watching Sophie and Tedros as friends for the first time, Agatha smiled tightly, at once relieved and on edge . . . until her face deadened.

"What is it, Aggie?" Sophie asked.

Agatha squinted at the beautiful, white-haired boy in the window, letting them escape. "He's not chasing us. Why isn't he chasing us?"

"Ummm, because everyone else is?" said Tedros.

The two girls spun to see two hundred undead villains exploding out of the School for Old: witches, warlocks, ogres,

giants, and trolls roaring and shrieking like banshees and hurtling after the fairy-dust cloud.

"Speed up, Merlin!" Agatha shouted at the wizard, who
was turned away at the front of the cloud.

"What, what? Can't be feeding you now, child," Merlin
bellowed, sucking on a lemon lollipop. "Tink's dust's already
lasted longer than I expected."

"Not feed! *Speed!*" Agatha blared.

But now the dust train sputtered with an ominous hiss
and broke apart like a weak mist, sending the three students
parachuting on sooty wisps to the shore, barely clearing the
corrosive bay. Shell-shocked, they looked up from the ground
and saw Merlin flying towards the gates in a piece of cloud,
blissfully unaware that he'd lost his passengers.

Horrified, Agatha glanced back and saw the zombie army
smashing towards them—

"RUN!" she yelled, bolting up onto bare feet and hot stepping towards the gates.

Sophie and Tedros thundered after her, the three of them
waving and screaming at Merlin, trying to get his attention.

"Why can't he hear us!" Agatha shouted.

"He's *old!*" Tedros barked.

Hobbling in her stilettos, Sophie lagged behind, an ogre
within arm's reach, before she slung off a high heel and pelted
him in the head, sending him spinning into a three-troll pileup.
Flinging her other heel into the pestilent bay, Sophie raced after
her friends, who were so far ahead she could hardly see them.
"Wait for me! Already the third wheel and we're still at *school*!"

Agatha and Tedros scampered side by side for the gates, whose green glow seeped through a patch of pine bushes. But as the gates came into full view, Agatha's eyes bulged in horror. "They're sealed, Tedros!"

"'Cause Merlin has Dovey's wand!" he moaned.

They craned up to see Merlin's cloud wisp crossing over the towering school gates, about to abscond safely into the Woods. Aghast, Tedros unleashed a two-fingered whistle—

Merlin flicked back a dismissive smile, only to see the caboose of his train missing and Tedros and Agatha on the ground inside the school gates.

"The wand, Merlin!" Agatha hollered. "Use Dovey's wand!"

Merlin frantically pulled off his hat, rifling through it and yanking out champagne bottles, throw pillows, an empty birdcage—

"God help us," Tedros breathed.

Agatha looked back and saw Captain Hook, Jack's giant, and Red Riding Hood's wolf closing in on Sophie, the latter's jaws snapping at her behind.

"Aggggieee . . . I'm hallllluccinnattinnggg!" Sophie squealed. "Therrre'sss faaamous villlainnssss chassinngggg meeeee!!!"

Agatha whipped back to Merlin. "*Hurry*, Merlin!"

The wizard pulled out a bowl of cashews, a chain of rainbow Christmas lights—"Oooh, these are lovely!"—before he heard Sophie's screams and glimpsed the wolf rip the hem of her dress as Sophie skidded towards her best friends, who were still trapped behind the gates.

Pursing his lips, Merlin dug deeper into his hat, his arm all the way in, and fished out Professor Dovey's wand with a relieved smile. "Goodness, this really should come with a case."

"MERLIN!" Agatha screeched.

Merlin wheeled and stabbed Dovey's wand at the glowing green gates, which slid open on command—

Tedros swept Agatha through in his arms and they collapsed together face-first into dirt.

"Close the gates!" Tedros wheezed at Merlin.

"*No!*" Agatha yelled.

Because Sophie was still bungling towards the opening, the wolf shredding more of her clothes with every second, and the rest of the villain army nipping at the wolf's heels, poised to stampede through the gate with Sophie. "DON'T STAND THERE LIKE LUMPS!" she shrieked at her friends. *"DOOOO SOMETHINGGGG!"*

Tedros drew his sword, but it was shaking in his hand. "There's too many of them!" he said to Agatha, watching Merlin awkwardly trying to turn his cloud around. "They'll tear us apart!"

Agatha saw Merlin flash the same panicked expression, because the prince was right. By the time Merlin turned, the villains would be picking their bones. The three of them needed a place to disappear . . . a place the villains couldn't get to . . . a cave or a tunnel or a—

"Wait!" she cried, waving at the wizard. "Your *cloak*!"

This time, Merlin understood. He stripped off his purple

robe, hurled it into the air like a kite, and with Dovey's wand, shot it down like a comet into Agatha's hands.

Standing in the gate opening, Agatha flung open Merlin's cloak like a bullfighter, the childish stitching of a night sky shimmering in the moonlight. She and Tedros climbed into the wizard's cloak, half their bodies magically disappearing into the silk, before the two Evers gripped on to the collar with both hands, like miners about to drop into a cave.

"Sophie, hurry!" Agatha shouted, holding open the cloak lining.

Sophie staggered through grass towards the gate opening, the wolf clawing into her petticoat, a giant about to throttle her from the left, Captain Hook hacking at her from the right—

Only there was another shadow coming from the other side of the shore . . . tall, muscular, and astonishingly fast, smashing out of the trees. "Oh my God! He's coming!" she choked, as she raced towards the magic cloak, waving madly at Tedros and Agatha. "Help! The School Master's coming!"

But it wasn't the School Master at all.

It was a pallid, dark-haired boy, weasel-quick and charging towards Sophie, black eyes aflame.

Agatha gasped. "Hort, *no*!"

Forces collided into the cloak, knocking Agatha into free fall. Losing consciousness, she looked up in horror as *four* bodies, not three, tumbled through a starry purple sky . . .

Then a blast of white sun blinded her and the universe went dark.

PART II

21

Peer Pressure

Sophie dreamt of the strange man again.

She was in the same pitch-black tunnel, her path barred by the towering gold ring.

Only this time something waited for her beyond the ring. It was Tedros, a king's crown of silver and diamonds upon his head. Bathed in sunlight, he stood before a white-rose altar in a royal blue jacket, the spires of Camelot rising behind him. Between his hands shimmered a matching queen's diadem, casting sun flares on his cheeks. The young king met Sophie's eyes and smiled.

Sophie lost her breath, gaz-ing at the crown in his hand.

This was it.

Her heart's wish come true.

All she had to do was

destroy the School Master's ring.

Without thinking, Excalibur was suddenly in Sophie's hands, the jeweled hilt warm against her clammy fingers. Lifting the blade over her shoulder, she crept towards the giant gold circle . . .

But as she drew closer, she saw a familiar reflection in its broad surface, blocking her from her prince. It was the dark, fiendish man she'd seen once before, with untamed hair, skin like rawhide, and a bulbous nose.

Sophie bared her teeth at him, undaunted. She hoisted Excalibur higher, poised to shatter the ring and the stranger inside it—

But the man's eyes stopped her cold: two onyx pools, dead and devil-like, as if daring her to strike.

Sophie's hands weakened on the sword.

"W-w-who are you?" she whispered.

The stranger grinned cryptically.

Paralyzed, Sophie looked between Tedros and the devil man . . . between a queen's crown and a gold ring . . .

Do it!

Do it now!

With a rousing cry, she raised the blade over the ring—

Two hands stabbed out and caught Sophie by the neck.

As she choked, the dark man smiled sadly from inside the ring, as if she'd given him no choice.

Then his eyes turned punishing and he ripped out her throat.

Agatha woke, gripped with terror, wheezing for air. Peeking down at her black-and-green uniform, it took her a few frantic breaths before she realized she was still alive and sopped in sweat on a hard, thin mattress. She looked up, but her surroundings were washed out by blinding red-orange light.

Camelot, Agatha panicked, shielding her eyes.

I'm in Camelot.

She squinted into the fiery glow—

A fat face shoved into it, splotched with rouge and emanating bacon breath.

"I ate your breakfast and there ain't no more, so don't bother asking," Cinderella spat and trundled away.

Agatha jolted to her knees to see she was back at League Headquarters, the burnt-red glare coming from a sliver of sunrise through the cave hole. The muggy, dusty den was a hive of activity, with all thirteen League members packing up and stripping the cave bare, readying for a company move. On one side, Hansel and Gretel were magically storing furniture in Merlin's hat, Peter Pan and Tinkerbell were stuffing a dozen satchels with snacks and tins of water, and Pinocchio and Red Riding Hood were scrubbing the last of the breakfast plates clean. On the other side, Yuba studied a spread of open storybooks, Princess Uma and the White Rabbit swept up scraps of black satin scattered on the floor, and Jack and Briar Rose pretended to be working while huddling over a notebook, finalizing their wedding guest list.

Amidst all this chaos, Hort lingered in front of the moth-eaten curtain shrouding the far cave wall. He was eerily still, biceps folded over his chest, as if standing guard over something. He met Agatha's gaze for just a moment, then narrowed his eyes coolly and glanced away.

Meanwhile, near Cinderella's mirror, Merlin was having an intense conversation with Tedros, who looked clean in taut white breeches and a cerulean shirt, the laces open down his smooth, bronzed chest, marred by a long scar near the heart. Agatha noticed Excalibur sheathed at the prince's waist, while Sophie was nowhere to be seen.

"What's going on?" said Agatha, approaching the prince.

Tedros turned, his stare brilliant and blank. "I'm sorry. Do I know you?"

Agatha gaped at him.

"I'm Tedros of Camelot, Heir to Arthur Pendragon, Guardian of Good, and Eligible Bachelor, seeking my future queen." He extended his hand. "And you would be . . ."

Agatha didn't take his hand. "Bachelor?"

"You wanted a 'New Beginning,' remember," Tedros joked, irritated she wasn't playing along.

Agatha felt sick, the events of last night flooding back. Her prince had thought she was in on the lie to pretend to question their happy ending . . . when deep down, Agatha knew they *should* be questioning it. She didn't want to be a queen. She wanted an ordinary life, away from the spotlight and people judging her and the pressures of having to look and act a certain way. That's all she'd ever wanted since she was a child in Gavaldon, condemned by its people as a "witch" and a "freak." Besides, who was she kidding? She couldn't be queen of a potato sack, let alone King Arthur's Camelot! Not without disappointing its people, who deserved a real queen who would restore the kingdom to glory. Not without disappointing its new king most of all.

"Right. Sure," she said, stiff as a board. "New beginning."

Tedros saw her making eye contact with everything but him. "Look, Agatha. Don't worry. Everything's fine. I just have to pretend to give Sophie a chance. So on that note . . ." He bowed dramatically. "Lovely to meet you Agatha of Woods Beyond, Daughter of Callis, and Friend of Sophie. I look forward to seeing whether you'll indeed make an acceptable queen." He kissed her hand and winked.

Agatha yanked her hand away reflexively.

Tedros gave her an odd look.

"If you two are finished with your adolescent theatrics, can we get back to saving lives?" a voice snapped.

Agatha turned to see Merlin glaring blackly.

"Lovely. Now, Agatha, because of your quick thinking last night, you managed to hide your friends in the Celestium, from where I magically transported all of you to League Headquarters," said the wizard. "You took quite a blow to your head in the process, so you were hardly coherent and desperately in need of rest. Indeed, you and Tedros had broken into Evil's fortress and accomplished everything I'd asked: namely, to find Sophie and Excalibur and extricate them both safely. I know how dangerous both these missions were, but we had no choice. Since Sophie's kiss brought the School Master back to life, *only* Sophie could undo that kiss by destroying his ring.

But now that we are in possession of Sophie, the ring, and the sword, she could finally send him and his Dark Army to their graves, and the three of you would be on your way to Camelot, your storybook closed."

Merlin paused. "But I'm afraid there's been a change of plans," he said to Agatha. "As you fell asleep last night, you whispered that our League wasn't safe—that 'they knew where we were.' I knew better than to question your babbling, given I'd witnessed the army of famous villains that chased you out of school. So we must move from our Headquarters immediately. The League will split up and hide throughout the Woods, while I escort you, Tedros, Sophie, and that surly, overmuscled Neverboy to a safe house where the four of you won't be found."

"Hort? We're taking *Hort?*" said Agatha, trying to keep up. "And why do we have to hide at all? If the School Master is dead, the League can all return safely to their kingdoms just like you said, and Sophie, Tedros, and I can—"

She saw Merlin's and Tedros' faces.

"Change of plans."

Agatha's stomach dropped. "The School Master's not dead?"

Tedros shook his head.

"Sophie still has the ring?" said Agatha.

Tedros nodded.

"Sophie's still *wearing* the ring?" said Agatha.

Tedros bit his lip.

"How is that possible!" Agatha exploded. "Did anyone talk

to her! Did anyone tell her what's at *stake*?"

"Ha!" Hansel pipped, rolling by.

Merlin smiled tightly at Agatha. "We tried this morning, dear. The entire League tried." He eyed Uma sweeping up the scraps of black satin. "Let's just say Sophie won't be destroying the School Master's ring anytime soon."

"I don't understand—" Agatha pressed. "She promised to do it once we left school!"

"Put it this way," said Tedros. "Last night, Sophie beat Hort with any utensil in the kitchen she could find, saying he'd ruined everything by coming with us and he better scram before she put the rolling pin up his you know what. But ever since we tried to make her destroy the ring, well, not only won't she destroy it, but now it seems she isn't in such a hurry to get rid of Hort after all."

Agatha followed the prince's eyes to the buff, black-haired boy standing sentinel in front of a curtained cave wall . . . and a human-sized lump in the curtain behind him.

"It's why he's coming with us," Tedros said grimly. "She says he's her *bodyguard*."

Hort barred her path. "Can I help you?"

"I need to talk to her, Hort. *Now*," Agatha commanded.

"No visitors," said Hort.

"Sophie, tell the ape to move!" Agatha barked over his shoulder.

"Are we going to talk about the ring?" squeaked Sophie behind the curtain.

"Obviously!"

"Then no."

Hort grinned at Agatha, bangs jagged against his forehead like lightning bolts.

Agatha glowered witheringly. "Tried to be her roommate, tried to be her best friend, and now you're her *slave*. Nice muscles by the way. If only a hot body cured spinelessness and servility."

Hort thrust his face in hers, flashing sharp, yellow teeth. "As soon as she's ready, I'm taking her back to the School for Evil where she belongs," he hissed, lowering his voice so Sophie wouldn't hear. "She's not staying here with these weird old fogeys or anywhere near that . . . that . . . *dingleweed*." He locked eyes with Tedros across the room and spat in his direction. Tedros made an obscene gesture at him.

But Agatha was still gazing at Hort's jacked-up torso and edgy haircut, her face softening in astonishment. "You really think you still have a chance with her, don't you? That's why you chased her. That's why you're still here."

Hort blinked back, as if she'd seen him naked. Then he sneered savagely. "If you don't get out of my reach in the next three seconds, I'll—"

"Hort, dearest?" Sophie's voice fluttered softly. "You can let Aggie through. But tell her she has to bring me new clothes and some nail polish."

Agatha barreled by Hort, elbowing him in the sternum, and threw open the curtain to find Sophie shivering against the wall, black gown torn to shreds, cheeks pale, hair rumpled, and makeup smeared all over her like a madwoman in an attic.

"If only the role of Bride of Frankenstein hadn't already been played," said Agatha.

"Aggie, my darling! My poopsie! You don't know what it was like!" cried Sophie, collapsing into her arms. "I never said I wouldn't do it. All I said is I needed a little *time*. And then they descended on me like wolves! Here I am, tickled pink to meet my childhood heroes, and instead Tinkerbell is stinging me, shrieking like a dog whistle, Hansel and Gretel are goosing me with wheelchairs and yammering in that Teutonic accent, Peter Pan is jabbing me with a cane and lecturing me on civic responsibility, and even Merlin—Merlin, who in storybooks is wise and just and kind—shoves Excalibur into my hands as the others yank and peck at me like magpies, trying to get the ring off my finger! And then! *Then!* That monstrous Cinderella corners me, stinking of a mummy untombed, and threatens in no uncertain terms to sit on me! Yes, you heard me, Agatha. A legendary princess threatening to put her voluminous buttocks upon my face and keep them there until I smash the ring. And you wonder why I find old people so repulsive! Well, now that ring is staying on my finger until kingdom come, you hear me? I will not reward bullying, terrorism, and worst of all, poor manners!"

Agatha was long used to Sophie's overblown monologues, but this one even left her pop-eyed.

"Sophie," Agatha said, attempting to collect herself. "Their *lives* are at stake. *All* of our lives are at stake. The School Master is rewriting famous fairy tales so Evil wins. Every old story Evil makes new brings him and his army one step closer to Gavaldon. That's where he'll destroy Good once and for all."

"Gavaldon? What does the School Master want with Gavaldon?" Sophie asked, picking at a plate of bacon on the floor. "Do you think I can trade this for a kale omelet?"

"Sophie!" Agatha seized her friend's shoulders. "This is a boy who stabbed you through the heart, nearly hacked Tedros in half, came back from the grave, and has a school of two hundred undead villains fighting for him. It doesn't matter what the School Master wants with Gavaldon. We don't want to find *out*."

Sophie gulped.

"So listen, *poopsie*. I'm going to get Excalibur and you're going to smash that ring just like you promised," Agatha said firmly. "Right here and now, with no one watching but me. Got it?" She grabbed the curtain to leave—

"I can't."

Agatha let go of the curtain.

"I can't do it, Aggie," Sophie whispered behind her. There was a steel to her voice, the frippery and friendliness gone.

Agatha slowly turned.

Sophie's face was a strange, tense mask, as if she'd prepared for this moment but was struggling how to play it.

"This isn't about manners, is it?" said Agatha.

Sweat beaded Sophie's brow. "I have dreams, Aggie. Dreams of this . . . man. A devil-faced man who I've never seen before. But if I try to destroy the ring, he kills me."

"Dreams? That's what's stopping you?" Agatha groaned in relief. She'd been sure it was something far worse.

"No, Aggie. This man in the dreams *knows* me. I can see it in his eyes," Sophie said, her voice still unsteady. "He's telling me I can't destroy the ring. At least not yet."

"It's just a dream, Sophie. Dreams aren't real."

"Before I ever came to school, I dreamed a beautiful, frost-haired boy would love me and that was real. I dreamed of you as my Nemesis and that was real too," said Sophie. "Dreams aren't just dreams, Agatha. Not in this world."

Agatha took in Sophie's anguished face. "So what are you telling me, then."

Sophie caressed the ring on her finger. "I know why the man stops me. He wants me to make sure it's right. Just like you and I agreed to make sure it's right back at school. Once I know it's right, I can destroy the ring."

"You're blathering, Sophie," said Agatha, exasperated. "Once you know *what*'s right—"

But now she saw Sophie wasn't caressing the ring on her finger. Sophie was caressing the name tattooed beneath it.

TEDROS.

Tedros.

Tedros.

Slowly Agatha's eyes widened, the rules of the game dawning on her.

Sophie would destroy the School Master's ring only once she had the thing worth destroying it for.

And not before.

"Aggie?"

Agatha looked up and saw Sophie watching Tedros through a slit in the curtain.

"It must have been hard to let your prince go. But it was *your* idea to start over, wasn't it? You agreed to give Tedros up. You agreed to give the three of us a clean slate to find love," Sophie said defensively. "And now all can still come to a happy end, Aggie . . . because of you."

Agatha's heart stoppered her throat. "It doesn't matter what I agreed. You promised to destroy the ring as soon as we left school—"

Sophie turned back to Agatha. "I'll destroy the ring. I'll kill Rafal like I promised. And all your Good friends, Old and New, will be safe forever," she said. "But I need Tedros to give me a chance like *he* promised. I need him to . . . kiss me. Because once he kisses me, he'll know I'm his queen."

Agatha couldn't speak, for she understood perfectly.

To save Good, she had to help Sophie kiss her prince.

To save Good, she had to help her best friend take her Ever After.

"But—but that's *cheating*!" Agatha fought, anger swelling. "You think you can blackmail me? What about what I want? What Tedros wants? You can't change what people feel!"

Sophie held her gaze. "I love you so much, Agatha. And I know how much you love Teddy. . . . But you? A *queen*?"

Agatha's anger seeped away.

"I saw the way you looked at him in that tower, Aggie," said Sophie. "You won't have Tedros to yourself anymore as a queen. You'll have to share him with an entire kingdom for the rest of your life. Just think: thousands of eyes on you, every second of every day, watching your every move, picking out every flaw, telling you that you aren't good enough. . . . Everyone will have their claws out for you, like Gavaldon all over again, only a thousand times worse. Tedros will spend every waking moment defending why he chose you as his queen instead of doing *real* Good as king. You'll close yourself off to protect him. You'll doubt whether he's happy. And it'll only be a matter of time before Tedros doubts you too. The tension will fester, the two of you at each other's throats, forgetting why you ever thought you were in love at all. And before long, Aggie, you'll steal away from Camelot in the middle of the night and set yourself free—just like Guinevere did, leaving your king all alone. Imagine what that would do to Tedros. To end up like his father, lonely and humiliated. It'd *kill* him." Sophie moved closer. "You can't be his queen, Agatha. You don't want to be. For his sake."

Agatha recoiled, breathless. "This isn't about me—this is about the ring . . . about your promise—"

Sophie touched her shoulder. "I know you'll want to tell him all of this. Maybe he'll even lie for you and pretend to give me a chance . . . but I'll know if he's faking it, Aggie. I'll know if his kiss is for real. So if you want the ring destroyed, I need you to help me win his heart—"

Agatha spun away, lurching for the curtain, but Sophie held her back. "When our storybook closes, you'll see this is how it was meant to be from the beginning. Tedros and me, King and

Queen of Camelot. You, our faithful friend and savior of Good, happy on your own like you used to be," she said. "I know what you must be thinking. That I'm still a witch. That I'm still Evil. But how else can three people have a happy ending? You never wanted to be a princess like I did. You never wanted a fairy tale or a boy's love or anything to do with boys at all. That's when you were happiest, Aggie. Never caring what people thought of you, never doubting yourself, never answering to anyone but yourself. . . . Don't you see? This is how each of us gets what matters most to us. This is the ending that *feels* right. The last Ever After to our fairy tale." She reached up, fingers shaking, and stroked her friend's cheek. "Look at me, Agatha . . ."

"Get away from me—" Agatha gasped, strangling for air. She broke free and fumbled at the curtains, grasping at the opening, only to tangle up in the fabric and crash through, face-planting in cave sand.

"Coulda talked louder for us," Peter Pan's voice grouched.

Agatha wiped away sand to see the entire League gathered behind Hort's body barrier, pretending not to eavesdrop.

"Old people don't have the best of ears, dear," Riding Hood chided. "Couldn't hear a word."

The others murmured agreement.

Then Agatha glimpsed Merlin in the far corner, tight-faced and tugging at his beard. Maybe no one else in the League had gleaned her and Sophie's conversation. But the wizard heard everything.

"So?" asked a deep voice.

It was Tedros, smiling hopefully next to Princess Uma.

"Is Sophie ready to do it?" he asked. "Is she ready to destroy the ring?"

Agatha saw him smile wider, convinced she'd accomplished what he couldn't. For all their fights and failings, her prince still trusted her more than he trusted himself. Agatha's heart melted. In this single, terrible moment, she loved him more than ever before.

Tedros saw the change in her face and his smile wavered. "Or . . . are we moving on to new hideouts?"

Over his shoulder, Agatha could see Yuba the Gnome tacking storybooks to the far wall. More old tales, at least ten of them, open to their last pages, new endings illuminated. Fair princesses slain, valiant princes gutted, clever children eaten . . .

Agatha's legs jellied.

The School Master was working faster now.

Old villains were on the hunt.

Agatha lowered her eyes to the League of Thirteen, all watching her intently—the greatest heroes of Good, in mortal danger of losing everything they'd worked for to Evil.

Was her Ever After worth all of theirs?

Was her own happiness worth so many lives?

And would she even be happy if she fought Sophie for Tedros?

Just like Guinevere, a voice echoed.

Just like Guinevere.

A sparkle of green distracted her from her thoughts, and

in Cinderella's mirror Agatha spotted the reflection of a single emerald eye spying on Tedros through the curtain.

Old villains on the hunt indeed.

Agatha waited for the fire to burn inside of her . . . the mettle to fight Sophie for her prince . . .

But it never came.

For as Agatha looked at thirteen heroes who needed her, she knew Sophie was right. She couldn't risk their lives by striving for a crown she doubted to her very core . . . for a kingdom she would inevitably fail . . . for a king who would see he'd made a terrible mistake.

How could she fight for something her heart didn't even want? Especially when there was a greater fight to be won?

It's why Sophie had known all along that Agatha would agree to her terms.

Because Agatha could never be Tedros' queen, no matter how much she loved him.

And because Sophie knew that deep, deep down, in the pit of her soul, Agatha was Good. And when put to the test, Agatha would sacrifice everything to stay true to that Good.

Even if it meant surrendering her battle to win the war.

Even if it meant giving up her prince.

Even if it meant her prince giving up her.

Slowly Agatha looked up at Tedros, holding back tears.

"We're moving on," she said.

22

Everything Old Is New Again

B y the time the weak warmth of sunrise left League Headquarters, the League was gone too.

Agatha stood with Merlin under a fungus-infected oak a few paces from the entrance hole, watching twelve old heroes go their separate ways into the Woods, satchels of clothes, food, and drink weighing down their backs. Peter Pan, Tinkerbell, and Cinderella journeyed to the west, Pinocchio and Red Riding Hood to the east, Jack and Briar Rose to the north, and Uma, Yuba, and the White Rabbit to the south, with Hansel and Gretel wheeling their rickety chairs behind them.

Tedros sidled up to Agatha. "Just when I was starting to feel fond of the old farts," he said, shivering in his unlaced shirt.

"You think we'll ever see them again, Merlin?"

"I hope so, dear boy. Because it will mean we're still alive," said the wizard, pulling two black cloaks from his hat and handing him one. "In the meantime, there are bigger questions to be answered." Merlin fixed subtly on Agatha. "Like when Sophie will destroy the ring."

"What do you think she's waiting for?" Tedros asked, struggling to button his tight cloak. "Um, are you sure this one's *mine*?"

Agatha stared at Merlin, silently asking whether they should tell Tedros the truth. Tell him Sophie had lied about destroying the ring. Tell him she wouldn't kill the School Master until he kissed her and saw what he'd been missing . . . until he took her as Camelot's queen . . .

But Merlin pressed his lips together, his eyes dulling, and Agatha knew what the wizard was thinking.

Sophie had warned her. She'd know if Tedros was faking his interest before he ever said a word. And if she did . . . there'd be no way back.

No, thought Agatha. If Sophie was to destroy the ring, she'd have to get Tedros for real.

Her gut twisted tighter.

Meaning Tedros has to fall in love with her for real.

"Well?" Tedros pushed, subduing his last button with a growl. "What is she waiting for?"

Your lips on hers, Agatha thought. *Your lips that kissed me on hers, your lips that taste like vanilla clouds on hers, your lips you vowed to me "Forever" on hers.*

Agatha turned. "She needs a safe place where she can rest and think," she said quickly. "That's what all of us need, to be honest."

"Relax, worrywart," said Tedros, massaging her shoulder. "I know you're not much of a liar, but this isn't grand theater. Just act insecure around me, like you don't know if you can be happy as my queen, and I'll act like I'm struggling to choose between you and her."

Agatha stared at him.

"M, you said the safe house is beyond the Frostplains?" Tedros asked. "That's a two-day journey northeast."

"And the trail's quite narrow through the Never Lands," Merlin added. "Given there are four of you now, we certainly can't travel in a pack with the Dark Army on the hunt . . ." He looked at Agatha keenly. "Which means we'll have to travel two by two, with each pair a good ways behind to avoid drawing attention."

"Fair enough," Tedros surmised, clutching Agatha by the wrist. "You lead the way, M, and I'll walk with—"

"Yoo-hoo, here I am!"

Tedros and Agatha spun to see two muscular arms thrust Sophie out of the cave hole like a dancer bursting out of a birthday cake. She bustled towards them in a belly-baring fire-red blouse, a black leather miniskirt, a billowing bearskin coat, and baby-pink fur booties.

Tedros' cloak buttons popped open.

Agatha dropped her satchel.

"Sorry, darlings, I needed time to wash this morning out

of my hair. Managed a bit of creative costuming with the curtain fabric, den rugs, and Cinderella's sewing kit. Turns out that hulk of a woman is willing to trade *anything* for leftover bacon," Sophie vamped as Hort crawled out of the cave behind her. "Now, what were you saying about pairing off? I remember when Teddy and I sat on a balcony over the Blue Forest and he told me about all these beautiful sights in the Woods. I was a boy then, of course. But now I'm a girl and he can show them to me firsthand—"

She stopped because she could see the prince trying not to look at her.

"It's the clothes, isn't it?" she said, blushing. "I just thought it's been a while since I could actually be myself—"

"No. You look really, really good. Trust me," Tedros said, forcing eye contact. "But I'm pairing up with Agatha. Merlin can set the pace ahead of us and you can follow with the weasel at a distance. He is your bodyguard, isn't he?"

Sophie's face fell. "Oh yes, that does makes sense, doesn't it?"

She looked at Agatha for the first time since they'd met behind the curtain. But there was no apology on Sophie's face, no sign of the guilt-racked Sophie who'd tried to justify taking her prince. Instead, Sophie gazed hopefully at Agatha, as if they were old friends working towards a new goal.

"It's just . . . ," Sophie started, "I'm quite sure Agatha would prefer you walk with me."

"What?" Tedros snorted.

Agatha glared back at Sophie, suppressing the instinct

to bash her head with a rock. Because Agatha knew Sophie was right: this was the decisive moment. If Sophie walked the trail alone with Tedros, then by the time they reached the safe house in two days, she could be that much closer to earning his kiss. That much closer to killing the School Master.

That is, as long as Tedros wasn't still holding on to his old princess.

"Agatha?" Tedros said, frowning.

She could see Merlin's eyes on her between Sophie and the prince. She couldn't dare waver. It was like a bandage. She had to commit to the pain and rip it off.

"Yes," she said on a breath. "Take Sophie with you, Tedros. I'll keep Merlin company."

Tedros' cheeks pinked, like an instant sunburn. "But Merlin loves to be alone! It doesn't make any sense. Agatha, this is two days in the toughest part of the Woods, with villains on the loose and sleeping in close quarters and protecting each other from whatever we might face—"

Agatha's expression didn't change. Tedros grabbed her by the arm, hissing in her ear so Sophie couldn't hear: "Listen, I know we said to pretend, but this is going too far! I'm your prince and I'm not letting you out of my sight. We need to be together—"

Agatha pulled away.

Now Tedros saw it in her face. That same halting expression he'd seen in the tower.

"Oh my God. You meant it for real, didn't you? You're questioning our happy ending for real," he whispered, his eyes wide. "But we're so close—Camelot's waiting for us—"

Agatha tried not to look at him, focusing instead on Sophie behind him . . . on the ring circling her finger . . . on the thousand of Good lives depending on that ring. "You and I had our time together, Tedros, and I'm not sure me being your queen will make either of us happy," she forced, turning from him so Sophie would hear. "Sophie took a lethal risk to leave school with you. You and she need space to get to know each other again."

Stunned, Tedros looked at ravishing Sophie, ogling him with a princess's ardor . . . then at Agatha, rigid in her black cloak. "You can't mean that!" he fought back. "You don't want all of Camelot to see you standing next to me in your crown? You don't want to be the face of a kingdom as its rightful queen?"

Agatha shook her head. "No," she rasped. "I don't."

It wasn't even a lie.

Tedros' hurt froze to ice. He matched her expression, stiff and guarded. "You're right. Maybe Sophie and I do need some time together," he said, and took Sophie's arm tight under his, his eyes searing Agatha the whole time. "Come on, Sophie. Let's go."

Sophie couldn't have looked happier. She smiled at Agatha gratefully—the same smile she had first year when Agatha promised to help her get Tedros' kiss.

Agatha didn't smile back. She plowed ahead on the trail so brusquely that Merlin had to hike up his robes and scurry after her.

As Sophie and Tedros dropped behind, Agatha could hear Sophie's voice lowered: "Odd that Aggie still calls you Tedros. Would have thought you two would have nicknames by now . . ."

Agatha pumped her legs faster so she wouldn't hear Tedros' answer.

Near the cave hole, Hort gaped at all this in horror.

"HIM? You're going with *him?*" he screeched, losing his rebel-cool facade. "What about *me?*"

"You follow behind us and ward off danger, darling!" Sophie called, without turning. "That's what bodyguards *do*."

Hort's chest puffed up, his rage about to blow, but it was too late.

Sophie was already cozied up to another boy—a boy Hort had come all this way to save her from—leaving the weasel alone in the dust.

Agatha peeked over her shoulder.

She'd checked a thousand times in the past four hours, trying to gauge if it was going well, but they were a mile back now, tiny halo-haired figurines against a misty, mustard-colored bog. She needed Sophie to destroy that ring. She needed Sophie to hold up her end of the bargain, after she'd forced Tedros to give her a chance.

But what if Sophie ruined it?

Suddenly Agatha felt like the old Agatha: the Agatha who'd studied spellbooks and fed Sophie lines as a cockroach and moved mountains to get Tedros to kiss her best friend and send them home. But her plans had failed then and it would fail now, if the new Sophie acted anything like the old Sophie. Because Tedros wouldn't kiss that Sophie, then or now.

Agatha anxiously glanced back again—

She tripped badly, her new boots slipping off the wet path into a marsh of black water. A ribbon of saw grass snapped against her cheeks like a whip. Gritting her teeth, she climbed back onto the muddy trail through the mossy, yellowed Boglands, chasing after Merlin, who had grown so impatient with her distracted lagging that he was no longer waiting for her.

But Agatha's mind couldn't stop churning. On the one hand, she and Merlin needed Tedros to kiss Sophie. On the other hand, she could puke at the idea of Tedros kissing that lying, back-stabbing, double-crossing—

Pain pricked her ribs, a twinge Agatha felt when her thoughts went wrong.

She'd been demonizing Sophie as the old Sophie, the Evil-witch Sophie, still scheming for a prince. But had she tried to see the story from Sophie's point of view? Behind the curtain in the cave, Sophie had looked so regretful, as if she knew what she was doing was wrong. Yet, as Sophie pointed out, all of this was Agatha's fault to begin with. She'd given Tedros a clean slate in the tower, even if Tedros hadn't known it at the time. She'd given *all* of them a clean slate when she'd balked at being queen. And with a clean slate, Sophie had done what anyone with a second chance at their fairy tale would do, just like those undead villains in the School for Old. They'd gone back to the moment in their story when things went awry.

And Sophie's moment was when she'd almost won Tedros' kiss two years ago, only to lose it.

All this time, Agatha had believed that she and Tedros were the true loves in this fairy tale. That Sophie was never meant to get the prince's kiss their first year.

But what if she's right? Agatha thought. *What if Sophie is Tedros' true love and we made a wrong turn? What if Tedros was never meant to be with me?*

Agatha's chest hollowed. Her face softened with understanding. The only way she'd ever know is if she let Sophie and Tedros be together. If she didn't hate Sophie for trying to be his queen, but instead *gave* her that chance, just as Agatha had promised her in the School Master's tower. For a month Agatha had Tedros to herself, which turned out to be a lumpy, potholed stretch of tension and misunderstandings, with a cloudy and doubt-riddled future. She'd had her turn at being happy with him and couldn't find The End. Now it was Sophie's turn.

And if their kiss is real? If his name on her skin is right?

If Tedros is really Sophie's true love?

Agatha held her breath.

Then I'm meant to be alone.

She stopped in her tracks and looked over her shoulder, but she couldn't see Sophie and Tedros at all now against the waterlogged landscape.

"Dear girl, it will be a very long road if you spend more time looking backwards than *forward*."

Agatha turned to see Merlin far ahead on the trail. Veiled

in fog, with a severe countenance, floppy cone hat, and a walking stick in hand, he looked like the Great White Wizard of epic storybooks, who had all the answers. Then a wasp landed on his nose and he fled up the path, shooing and cursing at it, his robes riding up over lime-green socks.

Agatha exhaled. Either Merlin had gotten too old to be a Great White anything or she'd gotten too old to believe in answers at all.

"What will happen to the League members?" she asked when they were side by side again. "Yuba was putting up more storybooks—all of them had new endings—"

"Eleven. Eleven more dead, including Jack Horner, Puss in Boots, and Anya, the Little Mermaid, all found in ripe old age and dispatched by Nemeses returned from the grave," said Merlin gravely, wiping his fogged-up spectacles. "It was only a matter of time before the Dark Army began to have more success in finding their old targets. But I trust the members of our League to survive in the Woods until Sophie decides to destroy her ring. Once upon a time, those same heroes were trained in a Blue Forest, just like you. The only difference is they made it to graduation without the world ending." He gave Agatha a droll smile.

Up until now, it had seemed too fantastical, too cartoonish for Agatha to think that the sun that rose and set every day for thousands of years was melting because of *them*. But the tenor of Merlin's voice suddenly made it real.

"What happens if it goes dark?" She peered at the small gold circle in the colorless sky, so faint she could look right at it.

"It's barely lighting the Woods anymore."

"When it drips its last light, the sun will sink into the horizon and our world will extinguish like a candle into the sea," said the wizard. "Every story must end, Agatha. That is how the land of stories stays alive. But your fairy tale *undoes* its endings: first you and Sophie, then you and Tedros. Well, now the moment is coming where your fairy tale either ends for real and earns its place in eternal lore—or becomes the last Ever After for us all."

"How long do we have?" Agatha asked, the boggy trail growing firmer and drier under her feet. "For Sophie to kiss Tedros, I mean?"

Merlin gave the sun a cursory glance. "It's melting faster. Three weeks at most. Might not last until the boy's coronation. But perhaps that's another secret we'll keep from him until the School Master is dead." He pulled a peach-flavored lollipop out of his hat, only to see it covered in mold. "Even the best magic seems to be losing its luster," he mumbled.

"It doesn't make sense," Agatha mulled as the trail sloped upwards. "Why didn't the School Master chase us? If he knew Sophie could destroy the ring, why didn't he try to keep her at school?"

Merlin gave her a curious stare, but said nothing.

Agatha didn't ask any more questions as they moved out of the Boglands and into Gillikin on the outskirts of Oz, the kingdom famous for its Emerald City. Gillikin's hills were steep and purple, blemished with dead, saffron-colored streaks, and the glittering green city in the valley was hardly visible behind yellow-bricked walls built to keep out the Dark Army.

Agatha looked back, trying to spot Tedros and Sophie down the slope, before she saw Merlin glowering at her and forced her eyes ahead. They hiked the purple hills for an hour, Agatha itching at what seemed a copious amount of unseen pollen, before Merlin spoke again.

"Agatha, since we have a while before lunchtime and I know you're sorely in need of distraction, may I ask you to recount for me the events of last night? I'm particularly interested in anything you may have learned about the School Master."

Agatha quelled her instinct to check on Sophie and Tedros one last time and drew a deep breath. She told Merlin every detail of what happened once he'd left them behind Evil's glowing green gates. She revealed how she and Tedros made up before they parted ways as Edgar and Essa, how they kissed as boy and girl instead of girl and boy, and how Hester saved her from a night with Aric in the dungeons. She explained how the menagerie atop Honor's rooftop was now Tedros' story instead of his father's, how she outwitted her reflection on Halfway Bridge, and how the old villains had defaced each other's student portraits. She spoke of the classes in the School for Old, including the villains' assessment of past mistakes and the maps pinning down the whereabouts of their Good Nemeses. She talked about finding Excalibur in Sader's painting, the School Master's revelation about the Reader World, and the beautiful, white-haired boy named Rafal, who remained calm and still at his window as he watched Sophie escape. And when she was finished, Agatha had to double over for breath, because she'd been so lost in her story that she hadn't realized they'd made it all the way to the highest hill in Gillikin, crested with a field of wilted tulips.

"Rafal said one day Sophie would come back to him," she puffed, waving away more pesky pollen. "Maybe that's why he didn't chase her. He doesn't understand how much Sophie loves Tedros."

"Or he understands *exactly* how much she loves Tedros," said Merlin vaguely, laying out a picnic lunch of chicken potpie and watercress salad atop the flattened flowers.

"What do you mea— Wait, we're eating *here*? In the middle of the day with zombie villains on the loose?"

"Gillikin fairies are an Ever's most dependable scouts." Merlin held up a handful of watercress stalks. "You'll keep an eye out for us, won't you, Gillies?"

Agatha watched him waving vegetables at thin air, convinced the old man had finally lost his mind. But then she noticed the watercress whittling down in his hand, as if magically being eaten by something . . .

"Invisible," said Agatha, flashing a bright smile. "It's not pollen! It's *fairies*!"

She looked up at the drab, gray air and imagined it aglow with thousands and thousands of diaphanous wings and tiny, fantastical little bodies. Once upon a time, she'd thought of fairies as girly, vapid insects (she'd swallowed one her first day at school), but now, she'd give anything to see the little Gillies, even for a moment. She held out her arm and felt them crawl all over her, chills of wonder goose pimpling her skin, her smile growing as she listened to their thrumming wings . . .

Then her smile evaporated. She could see Sophie and Tedros in the valley of a distant hill, their blond bodies close together as they walked.

"Merlin, am I . . ." Words stuck in her throat. "Am I . . . doing the right thing?"

Merlin studied Sophie's and Tedros' small figures, as he sipped on a goblet of wine he'd pulled from his hat.

"Let me tell you a story about Tedros' father, Agatha. Years after Tedros was born, King Arthur came to my cave one day demanding a spell to spy on Guinevere, his queen. He was quite sure she'd been straying from the castle at nights for some time and wanted to see where she'd been going. Now, Arthur's anxieties about Guinevere were not new. Even when they were students at the School for Good, he'd schemed and manipulated and done everything he could to ensure she chose him as her true love. At the time, there was stern competition from a young knight-in-training named Lancelot, who in addition to being bookish and an animal lover like Guinevere, also happened to be Arthur's best friend. Arthur certainly noticed the attraction between them, but he made sure Lancelot knew of his intentions towards Guinevere and that he would not be denied. Besides, as Arthur saw it, Lancelot couldn't hold a candle to him when it came to the things that mattered to a girl: looks, lineage, money, fame. . . . So when Guinevere and Arthur were tracked as Leaders, and Lancelot as a Helper to the future king, Arthur persuaded Guinevere he was the right choice for a husband. How could she marry Lancelot—now a knight for the king—when she could have the king himself? As Arthur put it, Camelot *needed* Guinevere: he would accept no other queen and it was her duty to Good to marry him. No girl could stand firm against such words, not when they came from a boy as dashing and determined and powerful as Arthur.

"The two were married in a resplendent wedding and soon had the beautiful baby prince Arthur wished for. And yet, even with the queen of his dreams, Arthur couldn't relinquish his suspicions. Just like he did as a teenager at school, he tried to control Guinevere, have her followed, and ensure that she loved him and only him. But still he couldn't sleep easy, as if he'd known he'd forced her hand. By the time he flung into my cave, ranting for a spell to verify her faithfulness, he was an angry and obsessed man, his soul possessed by fear and jealousy. That day, I told Arthur there was only one magic spell to cure his plight after all these years. . . . He had to let Guinevere leave the castle at nights and do exactly as she wished."

Merlin gave a rueful grin. "Arthur was apoplectic, of course. I told him that for ten years he'd tried to control his and Guinevere's fairy tale, denying Guinevere her own story, only for him to be nearly driven mad. A man cannot force his own destiny. A man can only hold it back. All these years he'd been terrified that Guinevere did not love him, but the only way he'd overcome that fear is if he enabled the truth. To restrain Guinevere from finding her real true love—whether Arthur or someone else—meant neither Arthur nor his queen would ever be happy; neither of them would ever know if their love was *real*. The wound would reopen again and again, the two of them punishing each other over a fairy tale arrested from its true ending."

The wizard drained the last of his wine. "Needless to say, Arthur found this all treasonous hogwash and left my cave vowing he was finished with me. Indeed, it's what led him to steal the sex-switching spell from my cave. Soon Guinevere had fled with Lancelot, Arthur had put a death warrant on his own queen's head, and I had to abandon the precious boy I'd raised from childhood, never to see him again."

Merlin finally looked at Agatha, his blue eyes glistening. "Now Tedros is reliving his father's story in front of our very eyes. Indeed, when he becomes king, he'll inherit the death warrant on his own mother. Everything old is new again, my dear. Only this time you are in Guinevere's place, unsure whether you can be her son's queen, just as she was unsure of being his father's. But Guinevere wasn't strong enough to be honest with Arthur, even if she knew she couldn't be happy at Camelot. By failing to be true to herself, she was as blame-worthy as the king. But you are a wise, wise girl, Agatha, and Tedros is lucky to have found you. For the difference between you and his mother is that you're willing to question your story as you live it—and thus stop history from repeating itself. You have a compass in your soul directed towards Good, even if it means setting your beloved prince free to the night and let-ting him test your love. Even if it means you may lose him at The End. Because neither you nor I knows what will happen, Agatha. Neither of us knows whether your doubts of being a queen are well founded or whether Sophie is Tedros' true love or whether Sophie will destroy the ring. But unlike Arthur that day he came into my cave, you are willing to let go of the old and accept the unknown of the new. And that is what will keep Good alive, whatever Evil may come."

Agatha was sobbing hard now, cleansing, sepulchral tears, as if she couldn't bear the weight of Merlin's words. He wrapped her in his arms, letting her cry, until he heard her blow her nose on his robes and had to shove a cup of pistachio pudding in front of her face to distract her. She laughed through her sniffles and rested her head on the wizard's shoulder, spooning at the sweet green cream. "I'm really not all that Good," she croaked. "The first day of school in those candied halls, I ate part of a classroom."

Now it was Merlin's turn to laugh. "So did I, my dear. So did I."

More laughter echoed behind them and they turned to see Sophie and Tedros arriving to the hilltop, both of them in stitches. "Here I am in a girl's body with a dye job so bad that Merlin had to be joking, and I'm just off a chocolate roller coaster steered by a rat, and I'd prepared this whole speech to give you, and before I can get one word out, one *word*, here you are, fee-fi-fo-fum, clubbing me in the head—"

Sophie was giggling so hard she had to clutch her stomach. "Well, if I'd known you had to touch one of Anadil's rats!"

"It peed on me the entire ride!" Tedros could hardly speak now. "The worst part is . . . the speech I had ready was really, really *good*!"

Sophie nestled into him, howling.

Agatha had never seen Tedros laugh this hard with her. She'd never seen her prince this joyful or relaxed. Even Sophie looked so free and guileless, as if she and Tedros had their own history and intimacy that Agatha hadn't known. Agatha felt nauseous, as if she should grab Tedros and pull him away from her—

But the echo of Merlin's words held her back like a wind. She felt old resentments give way to the new truth of the moment: the sight of her two best friends safe and happy, sniggering over a ludicrous story . . . and before she could help herself, Agatha was snorting too.

The prince looked up, startled, and stopped laughing.

"Goodness," Sophie said, following his eyes to Merlin and Agatha. "Either we're too fast or you're too slow."

"Knowing us, a little of both," said Agatha.

Sophie stared at her, breath held, waiting for the bitter punch line.

Instead Agatha smiled.

Sophie's face lightened as if she sensed a silent change between them.

Tedros, on the other hand, gave Agatha a frosty glance.

"Not too fast or too slow, as Goldilocks might say, but just right," said Merlin, pulling new plates of food from his hat. "Wanted you two to catch up with us and get a hot lunch. Tedros, here's chicken pie and some fresh greens for you and Sophie, while Agatha and I will resume our journey. Tomorrow, we'll meet at the safe house by sunset. Come, Agatha—"

But Agatha was peering into the horizon. "What's that?"

Sophie squinted across purple hills and saw Hort's shadow trudging along the trail. "Oh he'll be fine. His father was a pirate, for goodness' sakes—"

"No," said Agatha. *"That."*

She was watching a mirage far, far away, barely discernible against the gray sky. The colors were thin and impressionistic, like one of August Sader's paintings, but Agatha could make out the outlines of a village: turreted cottage houses, yellow schoolhouse, crooked clock tower, shielded by a protective bubble. . . . Her mouth fell open.

"Gavaldon. That's . . . *Gavaldon.*"

"The beginnings of it, at least," said Merlin.

Agatha gazed at him, suddenly understanding. "Every old story changed brings him closer to the Reader World. That's what he said."

"And he meant it literally," said the wizard. "It seems your fellow Readers are *reading* his new stories."

Agatha and Sophie both looked confused.

"You see, as long as Readers believe in the old fairy tales— and the power of Good to triumph over Evil—the School Master has no access to their world, other than to take two students to school every four years. Indeed, he confessed this weakness to Agatha himself," said Merlin, studying the mirage carefully. "But once Readers read the new stories and begin to lose their faith in Good, their world gets closer and closer to the School Master's grasp. With every hero's death, that protective shield will weaken . . . the mirage will sharpen . . .

until at last the gates will open to his Dark Army. For there is something in your village the young School Master needs to complete your fairy tale. Something he needs to destroy Good forever. And whatever it may be, it is something he will surely get . . . unless we destroy that *ring*."

Merlin, Agatha, and Tedros all turned to Sophie.

"I don't understand, Sophie," Tedros said, glaring at the gold circle on her finger. "What are you waiting for?"

Sophie bristled. "Teddy, look dear! What a lovely lunch Merlin's served us! You must be famished." She pulled him down to the picnic spread before looking up at Agatha. "You and Merlin best be on your way, shouldn't you, Aggie? Don't want any villains catching us here in broad daylight."

Agatha could see Merlin about to expound on the wonder of Gillikin fairies, but she nudged him and Merlin grinned oafishly, picking up the hint.

Later, as the two of them crossed the abandoned lake village of Urthur, hopping between what seemed like an enormous game board of waterpuddles, Agatha could still see Merlin smiling. She assumed it was because there was something primal about jumping over puddles reflecting the pink-and-blue sunset, clearing hurdles or missing by inches and splish-sploshing ice-cold water with giggly shrieks, like two children playing leapfrog.

But Merlin wasn't smiling at any of that.

He was smiling at Agatha.

Not just because it was she who'd known to give her friends

privacy on that hill instead of him or that it was the wizard now huffing and puffing to keep up with the student . . .

But because in the four hours since she'd left her prince and friend to their own story, his wise, young Agatha hadn't looked back once.

Two Queens

Sophie watched Agatha recede on the trail, smaller, smaller, until she was a speck on the horizon.

"Sophie, it'll take thirty seconds!"

She swiveled to Tedros. "Absolutely not. I'm not watching you *urinate* in broad daylight."

"Why can't you turn around—"

"And *listen* to it? As if I'm in a horse trough?"

"Sophie, if I don't pee I'm going to explode and I can't leave you alone on a hill, even with Gillie fairies scouting for us." Tedros inhaled a lump of chicken pot pie and shifted in his shorts, looking highly uncomfortable. "Suppose one of the zombie villains shows up?"

"Then I'll defend myself,

thank you. Besides I can think of nothing more villainous than you swaying back and forth, tugging at your pants like you're doing some baleful interpretive dance," said Sophie, reaching for watercress, only to see it magically devoured. "These fairies come a close second. Now hurry before Hort gets here and challenges you to a duel."

Tedros stood as Sophie nibbled on a watercress leaf. "Don't eat all the pie," he cracked.

Sophie smiled coyly and watched the prince dart down the slope. Beyond the hillcrests, she glimpsed the beginnings of Gavaldon behind a protective shield, and her smile flattened. Rafal's ring suddenly felt like a heavy weight on her finger.

I have to destroy it soon, she thought.

Old heroes were dying because of *her*, Good's stories were turning Evil because of *her*, Readers were in danger because of *her*. Smash the ring with Excalibur here and now and their fairy tale would end before Rafal ever made it to Gavaldon—storybook closed, sun restored, Good and Evil back the way they once were.

Sophie nervously picked at the pie.

She couldn't do it.

She needed that kiss first.

Once Tedros finally kissed her, he'd feel it in their lips like an answer to a riddle: that they were meant for each other from the first day they locked eyes at the Welcoming.

But destroy the ring without that kiss and she'd have nothing to ensure their Ever After. No matter how many heroes' lives were on the line, she couldn't throw away her own happy ending to save theirs. Martyrdom sounded Good in theory, but in reality, it was pointless, idealistic, *insane*. Even with all of Good in peril, no one in their right mind would willingly sacrifice their true love—

Agatha would, thought Sophie.

Agatha would do whatever it took to save Good, just like Agatha had found it in her heart to let her best friend and Tedros have a chance at Ever After, risking her own . . . while Sophie had tried to *kill* Agatha for the same offense.

I'm Evil. Sophie swallowed. *Definitely Evil.*

So what made her think she could end up with Good's greatest prince?

She caressed Tedros' name on her skin beneath the cold, metal ring.

Her heart had promised he was her true love.

And hearts don't lie.

"I was kidding about you eating the pie," a boy's voice said behind her, "but maybe I shouldn't have been."

Sophie glanced down and saw she'd drained almost all of it.

"Stress eating," she mumbled, and looked up to see Tedros looming over her, the sun shadowing his wind-chilled face. He pulled Excalibur from its sheath, the silver blade nearly blinding Sophie with its glare.

"One blow will take care of every last one of our stresses. That's all we need from you, Sophie. One hard blow."

Sophie started fussing with the picnic plates, scooping the leftovers into one. "We really should get on. The other two are far enough along by now—"

"I don't understand girls," said Tedros, plopping into crinkly tulips. "You leave Rafal, but you won't destroy his ring. You hire Hort as a bodyguard, but you want to travel with me. You act like you live on air and leaves, but you pillage a whole pie in twenty seconds. Not that I'm complaining. So many Evergirls won't eat in front of boys because they think it makes them look, I don't know . . . *human*? Trust me. Every boy would rather have a girl who eats."

"So that's why you and Agatha got along. I've seen that girl wolf down garlic-fried sausage," said Sophie, remembering how she'd abused Agatha for hours afterward over her breath. "Oh, Agatha," she whispered. "Silly, wonderful Agatha."

She looked up and saw Tedros flinch, as if the name had stung him.

The prince caught her staring and walked away. "You're right. Shouldn't linger until the weasel comes along."

"He'll be hungry, won't he?" said Sophie, bunching dead tulips into a mound and topping it with the leftovers plate, so Hort wouldn't miss it. "He really is a nice boy. Just wants to protect me from being hurt, even if he doesn't love me anymore. Poured his heart out in the steam bath at school. Well, after all I've done to him, making sure he has his lunch is the least I can do."

She scraped to her knees to get up and saw Tedros halted on the path, smirking at her. "What?" she asked.

"Who knew you had feelings?" he marveled, and hiked ahead.

Sophie pinked in surprise.

Maybe a wee bit Good after all, she thought.

"And who knew you took steam baths with *Hort?*" she heard Tedros say.

Thank goodness I have proper shoes for once, Sophie thought, pattering along the trail in snug, pink booties.

They'd been at it for six hours straight, with only a few short breaks to fill water tins and rest weary knees. (Sophie did a few yoga poses to stretch until she saw Tedros gawking and decided yoga was best done in private.) It was dark now and they could only see the trail by magical embers of white light Merlin had left behind like breadcrumbs. Before they departed Headquarters, he'd told them when they reached the last light crumb on the path, it was his signal to camp for the night.

From Gillikin, the trail had led them out of Ever strongholds into Never territory—Ravenbow by afternoon, with its steaming rivers of blood and castles of bone, then Magalae at sunset, with its rope bridges across crog-filled sludge pits, then Drupathi in the moonlight, a land of orange tree blossoms and papaya-colored fruit, completely out of place amongst the sinister Never Lands and withering Woods, until Sophie had glimpsed the dunes of dead flies beneath the trees and realized everything here was toxic.

All through the Never Lands, Sophie had seen pairs of eyes flickering beyond the trail, yellow, red, and green, accompanied by growls and hisses in the underbrush. Still, nothing attacked and she ventured that as long as they stayed within the boundaries of Merlin's light, they'd be safe from harm.

Tedros snorted. "Oh please, no one's afraid of an old wizard's magic. They're afraid of a young, strapping prince with his father's sword. Until Evil actually seals a Never After, they know Good still always wins."

"Tell that to once-dead zombie villains who have nothing to lose," said Sophie. "Do you know what safe house Merlin is taking us to?"

"Not a clue. Nowhere in the Woods is safe, if you ask me."

"What about that strange purple sky we hid in during the escape?"

"The Celestium? It's just a place for Merlin to think. Air's too thin up there to breathe for more than a few hours. Even if there was a safe house in the Woods somewhere, the Dark Army could easily find us. It has to be a place no one knows. A place Merlin's stashed secrets before." Tedros stopped and exhaled his frustration. "Will you really not tell me why you're still wearing that ring?"

"It's your birthday in a few weeks, isn't it?" Sophie pivoted deftly. "No wonder you're being extra careful about your choice of a princess."

Tedros hesitated, as if unsure whether to pursue the old subject or the new.

"I'm ready to be king," he said finally, tramping on. "Been parentless for years now, so I'm not of those sheltered brats, who'll put himself before his people like some young kings. Not that the people are expecting much. Camelot's been a bloody mess since my father died. His council is supposed to be running the realm until I'm sixteen and instead they're starving people, executing dissidents, and hoarding his gold. No matter. I'll throw them in the dungeons on my first day as king." He looked at Sophie. "We'll make my father's kingdom new again."

A kinetic shock lit up Sophie's body.

"We'll?"

Had it been a slip? Or was it deliberate?

She saw Tedros still looking at her, as if expecting her to contribute to a conversation she'd started. "Oh I'm sure we . . . you . . . yes, it'll be glorious, won't it?" Sophie bumbled. "But what about your mother? Last year you said there was a death warrant on—"

"Not something I think about," Tedros clipped. "Probably dead by now anyway. No one ever saw her or Lancelot again after the night they left."

Sophie raised her brows. "You're supposed to execute your own mother and it's not something you *think* about?"

"Look, my mother's a cold, selfish deserter, but she's not vicious," said Tedros, puffing on his thick blond bangs. "Last place she'd come back to is Camelot, knowing her son would have to kill her." His face clouded over. "Doesn't stop her from invading my dreams though."

Sophie knew what it was like to be haunted by a mother that was gone forever. "What was she like? Beautiful, I imagine."

"Not at all. That's the odd part. Dad was so much more handsome, dynamic, and fun. Mother was gangly, anxious, and mousy. Only came alive when she was talking about books or tending animals. Zero clue why Father or any other man fawned over her," said Tedros, grimacing. "But it serves Dad right for picking a girl who wasn't good enough. Lancelot was more on my mother's level. Had a horrible face, poor chap, but simpleminded and a sturdy knight. Mediocrity needs mediocrity, I suppose."

"I can't sympathize," Sophie sighed. "Could you ever imagine leaving someone charismatic and beautiful for someone perfectly average?"

She saw Tedros stiffen and glance away, as if shutting down this conversation.

Suddenly Sophie understood.

Tedros didn't need to imagine leaving someone beautiful and charismatic for someone average. He already had when he left her for Agatha their first year.

Sophie thought of the way he'd flinched when she mentioned her friend's name back in Gillikin—just like he was now, his cheeks blotched red.

"We'll" didn't mean him and Sophie.

"We'll" meant him and *Agatha*.

It didn't matter if he'd promised to give her a chance.

Words couldn't change a prince's heart.

A heart still in love with his old princess.

"I'm trying to imagine you as a queen," Tedros mused, as if he'd suddenly remembered she was there. "You'd probably have your own wing with twenty servants drawing you hot baths of goat's milk, massaging your feet every hour with fish eggs and pumpkin puree, and picking every last cucumber in the kingdom."

Sophie stared at him, aghast.

"Made Agatha tell me about your beauty routines," he quipped. "Helped us laugh after fights."

"Glad to see I'm the court jester!" Sophie lashed, tears rising. "Is that what you think of me? A slave to beauty, an empty ball gown, a bubbleheaded sidekick who isn't worth a second thought?"

"Sophie, you're wearing a short skirt on a winter *hike*!"

"Because you haven't seen me as a girl in a very long time and I want you to remember you loved that girl once!"

It came out before Sophie could stop it and she saw Tedros freeze on the path.

"You promised to give me a chance," Sophie breathed, dabbing eyes with her bearskin coat. "Even if you still love Agatha. You promised you'd give me a chance."

Tedros lifted Sophie's chin, his blue gaze honest and unblinking.

"I *am* giving you a chance, Sophie. I'm here with you, aren't I? I haven't mentioned Agatha once on our entire trip. You're the one who keeps bringing her up. But instead of worrying about her or worrying about what I see on your outside, maybe you should be trying to show me your inside." His tone was serious and mature. "So tell me, Sophie of Woods Beyond. What would *you* do for my kingdom as queen?"

He strode ahead on the path, between ripples of white-hot glow.

Sophie pursued him, pumping with hope. In the trail light, she could see the slashed ink on her skin beneath the gold ring. This was the moment she'd been waiting for since she'd lost Tedros to Agatha two years ago. The moment to show her prince a love so deep, it had carved his name into her. And if she could only find a way to make him feel that love as deeply as she felt it . . . then maybe, just maybe, words could change a prince's heart after all.

"At first, I thought all a queen does is choose china and throw cotillions and kiss babies at parades," Sophie began. "But when I was with Rafal, I saw the way the other students looked at me. I wasn't the old Sophie anymore, amusing and frivolous—I was the new Sophie, a girl who'd *made* something of myself. That's what made them resent me, I suppose . . . they didn't realize someone so young could be so extraordinary. It wasn't as if I was born special or enchanted like them. All I ever had was a pretty face and a hunger to have a *big* life. And yet, I spent so much time fretting about the scale of that life that I forgot to ask what it should mean. That's why I couldn't commit to Rafal in the end. He might offer me immortality, infinite power, eternal love . . . but it was Evil's love. And no matter how Evil he thinks I am, I still want to be Good, Tedros. Even if I have to war against my own soul until the day I die."

Tedros' eyes moved to her.

"There are two queens," she said, her voice stronger now. "There's the queen who doubts her crown. Choose her and you'll forever distrust each other, sparring and bickering, because in her heart of hearts, she doesn't want a queen's life.

Your father chose that queen and suffered until the end. Now you can go back to where his story went wrong and fix it. You can choose a queen who *wants* to be your queen. A queen who will fight for her people the way she fights to be with her king. The queen I couldn't be for Rafal, because I'm meant to be that queen for you."

Tedros stopped, gazing at her so intensely it was as if he was seeing her for the first time.

Heart throbbing, Sophie held his eyes, the mist of their breaths coalescing.

"If they see a king and queen doubting each other, they'll lose faith in you," she said. "But choose a new type of queen and they'll see how a king should be treated: with unconditional love, respect, and loyalty. No one will give you those things more than me, because unlike Agatha, I never doubted you."

"Sophie . . . ," he whispered, touching her waist.

Her body electrified, blood rushing to her head.

"Don't you see? I was your queen from the first moment we met," she said, leaning in. "The old story between us was right, Tedros. All we have to do is make it new." She closed her eyes, her lips reaching for—

"*Sophie.*"

Sophie's eyes shot open and saw Tedros, milk white, staring past her.

Two flesh-flaking, stitched-up zombies converged towards the path from opposite sides of the dark Woods. One was a stumpy, copper-nosed man with a bushy gray beard, a belly bulging from his half-sized shirt, and a black pirate hat on his bald head. The other was dark and sleek, with an even bigger hat over his swell of black curls.

It was only when he stepped onto the lit path that Sophie saw his big steel hook.

"Here we are looking for Peter Pan and we find Evil's queen instead," sneered Captain Hook. "Only I hear you've deserted your post, dear queen. Tell her, Smee, what we do to deserters on my ship."

"Stick their head on the mast 'til the birds done their way with it," Smee giggled, drawing a slim dagger from his breeches.

"And yet, despite your desertion, I'm afraid the School Master doesn't want you returned to him at all," said Hook, eyeing Sophie carefully. "He insists his queen is free to do as she chooses."

Sophie paled with surprise.

Hook turned to Tedros. "Said nothing about the boy, though."

The two pirates stalked towards the prince.

Tedros drew Excalibur with one hand and grabbed Sophie with the other. "Stay close to me."

Sophie gulped, watching the two men slinking towards them, blades shining in the path light.

Once upon a time, Tedros had been in mortal danger during a Trial as she stood by, too scared to fight. That was the exact moment her story had gone wrong. The moment she'd lost her prince to Agatha. *This is my chance*, thought Sophie—to go back and fix her fairy tale, just like she was asking Tedros to fix his. Fight for her prince and she'd win her kiss at last.

Tedros gripped Sophie tighter, pulling her to his flank, as the two Evil pirates inched within striking distance. As Hook raised his weapon over the prince, Sophie focused on her fear, feeling her fingertip glow hotter, hotter . . .

Then she magically whisked one of Merlin's white-hot crumbs into Smee's eye.

Smee shrieked, dropping his dagger, and Sophie tackled him off the path into the Woods.

"Sophie!" Tedros cried in horror—

Hook swung his blade at him and Tedros raised his sword just in time, steel clashing steel.

Sophie had never fought a full-grown man, so she wasn't prepared for Smee to tackle her back, pinning his fat, hairy belly against her as she kicked and scratched.

"Such a pretty girl," Smee snarled, the giggly tone gone. "Never any pretty girls in Neverland."

He sniffed her hair and Sophie slapped him so hard he gaped at her, clutching his cheek. For a moment, she thought she'd defused him, only to see him turn bloodred and seize her by the throat. His filthy nails dug into her larynx, as if she'd triggered something deep within him, a murderous rage consuming him.

"Not—supposed—to kill—me—" she gasped.

But Smee had forgotten or he didn't care and Sophie choked and sputtered, knowing she was going to die here, her prince only a few feet away. Out of the corner of her eye she saw Hook trap Tedros with his boot, slashing at Tedros' cloak as the prince squirmed and yelled. Cheeks blue, Sophie looked up at Smee, as she wheezed her last breath—

A fire-tipped tree branch ripped right through Smee's head, igniting his skull with blue flames.

Eyes wide, the henchman let go of Sophie, his head combusting at the stitches, as he flopped back into darkness.

Stunned, Sophie looked up at Hook, who'd moved off Tedros as he watched Smee's body consumed by blue fire. Slowly the Captain looked down the path at a broad-shouldered, raven-haired stranger, brandishing a glowing blue fingertip.

"I-I-I know that boy," said Hook, astonished. "That's Scourie's son. Born and raised on my very ship—"

But it was Hook's last words, for a sword ran him through and he dropped to his knees, mouth open in shock, before falling face-first on the trail.

Behind him, Tedros wiped his blade of zombie guts and rose gingerly, inspecting a patchwork of hook wounds in his right side, bleeding into his cloak. He breathed relief, as if none of them were mortal.

"I owe you my life, Hort," said Tedros, looking up.

Hort stepped into the moonlight, teeth gnashed at him. "I saved *her*. Not you."

Sophie saw the rage in Hort's face, the result of a full day alone with his festering feelings. Her eyes widened, suddenly understanding.

"But . . . but . . . you said you didn't love me anymore—" Sophie rasped.

Hort whirled to her. "I *lied*."

Lost in a fog, Sophie didn't know what to say. But she knew one thing for sure. She couldn't make Hort travel by himself any longer. Not when he'd saved her life.

Her time alone with Tedros was over.

I had it! He would have kissed me! she thought miserably. She glowered at Rafal's ring, undestroyed on her finger, feeling heavier than before.

Soon they'd resumed their journey, the three of them in a silent pack, for Sophie couldn't say anything to Tedros that Hort should hear, and Tedros and Hort had no desire to speak in the other's presence. And just when Sophie thought the tension could get no worse, she looked back distractedly at the horror show they'd left behind—

"Um . . . boys?" she croaked.

Prince and Weasel turned.

They looked past Sophie to see Smee's corpse in the distance, still burning off the path.

Hook's body was gone.

"But I stabbed him in the heart!" said Tedros, still defending himself the next afternoon.

"For the last time, zombies don't *have* hearts," snapped Hort. "Why do you think I set Smee on fire? It's the only way to destroy them—"

"Why didn't you say something then?"

"'Cause I was hoping Hook would kill you!"

"Please tell me we're getting close to the safe house," Sophie growled.

After losing Hook's body, they'd hurried along the trail like a spooked cabal, tracking Merlin's light crumbs to bubble-like caves that resembled the ones in the Blue Forest. There they'd camped until morning, each in their own den, with the two boys taking turns on lookout. By sunrise they were on the trail again, plowing through miles of the Frostplains' blue-iced tundra. Hiding under their cloaks, they braved relentless blizzards of snow and hail until at last they glimpsed something through the monotony of white.

It was a small, peninsular kingdom, built upon a bluff of rock, with pearl-white towers veiled by mist off stormy gray seas. The crash of waves echoed with violent booms, the entire kingdom shuddering down to giant iron doors, swinging open against the rock.

Crack! Crack!

Warily the three teenagers passed through the open doors, but there was no one there to greet them. Indeed, there seemed to be no one in the kingdom at all, only the magnificent white towers with no windows or entrances, arranged in a circle above a series of descending marble staircases. Squinting over the railing, they saw a vast lake at the bottom of the stairs, gray-watered and eerily still, leading into the tempestuous ocean.

"Did we hit a dead end?" Sophie asked.

Then she saw Tedros' face, blissful and calm.

"It's Avalon," he said.

"You've been here before?" Hort asked.

Tedros shook his head. "My father drew pictures of it in his will," he said softly, as he gazed down at the lake. "Said he wanted to be buried in 'Avalon's safe house.' Merlin brought us to my father's resting place."

"*This* is the safe house?" Sophie murmured as they went down a long staircase, trying to be sensitive to what Tedros was feeling. "It's just . . . it's freezing, the doors were wide open, and the towers had no way insi—"

She stopped at the sight of Agatha, sitting in dead grass at the edge of the lake, her back to them. To see Agatha by herself on the shore gave Sophie an unsettled feeling, as if the scene was incomplete . . . as if Agatha shouldn't be ending her story all alone.

Agatha turned at their footsteps. She smiled serenely, as if relieved her best friends were safe after the long journey.

Sophie's heart relaxed and she sidled closer to the prince. There was no reason to be unsettled. Agatha could be happy alone in a way that she never could.

"There you two are," yawned a voice and Sophie turned to see Merlin lumbering up from a nap against a rock. "Took you long enough. Oh and look, our bodyguard too," he said as Hort came off the stairs.

"The safe house is in those waters, isn't it," asked Tedros, stepping to the edge of the shore. "That's where my father is buried."

He tossed a pebble into the water and watched it sink.

Sophie frowned. "How can a safe house be in a—"

But now the waters were silently churning into a whirlpool where Tedros' pebble had sunk, mirroring the circle of towers above. The waters spun faster, faster, like a spinning wheel at work . . . so fast that a creamy white foam spewed from the pool's eye, building, thickening into a human shape . . .

A ghostly, silver-haired nymph in white robes floated out of the waters and into the sky, raising her head to her guests. She had chalk-white skin, a long nose, and big black eyes that fixed on Tedros, before her crimson lips curled into a smile.

"Never made another one quite like it," she said.

For a moment Tedros thought she was talking about him, only to realize she was looking at his sword.

"Excalibur . . . you made it . . . you're the Lady of the Lake!"

The nymph smiled, turning to Merlin. "Hello, handsome. It's been a while," she cooed in a low, husky voice. "Let me guess. You *need* something."

"Excuse me if you're a bit far out for social visits, but I wouldn't come unless it was a serious matter," Merlin replied.

"Another sword? A life-extension potion? Or a holy grail this time?" the nymph huffed. "Come to the lonely Lady and she'll do magic on command!"

"I need to ask for the same thing I asked for two others once upon a time," spoke Merlin, stark and firm. "That you hide these children in your shelter as long as they need it."

The Lady of the Lake stopped smiling. A fraught moment passed between the two sorcerers.

"Merlin, dear. You do know what you're asking," she said darkly.

The wizard's eyes flicked to Tedros for a moment before he looked back at the nymph. "Indeed."

Sophie glanced at Agatha, utterly lost, and Agatha shrugged back, just as befuddled.

The Lady of the Lake took a deep breath and gazed hard at the four students. "Well? Come on then, children. The waters are warm."

"*Waters?* You want us to swim?" Hort blurted, peering over the edge of the lake. "How are we supposed to live underwat—"

Merlin groaned and pushed him in.

Hort was sucked through the water with a blast of white light before he vanished under the surface entirely.

Agatha, Sophie, and Tedros all gawked at Merlin.

The wizard smiled. "Why do you think *water* was always the portal in Merlin's Menagerie?"

He thrust out his hands and the three students went flying into the lake headfirst. Light detonated in Sophie's eyes and she felt her whole body swarmed by gooey heat, water all around her and yet not touching her, like she was protected by an invisible womb. Deeper and deeper she sank into the lake until all at once the waters receded and she was on solid ground in a glare of sunlight, completely dry and curled up like a baby.

"Where are we?" said Agatha's voice above her.

Sophie craned to see Agatha with Hort and Tedros standing on a lush green moor, the grass so green and dewy it sparkled under the melting sun. Sophie stood and saw they were surrounded by more green heaths, with sheep, cows, and horses grazing freely, as if they'd found a haven from the dying Woods.

"Look," Agatha said.

The others followed her eyes to a small farmhouse across the moors.

"Must be our safe house," said Hort.

Tedros squinted. "Someone's coming."

Two people were walking towards them now, tan-skinned and weather-beaten, both holding hands. A bony woman with straggly brown hair and a broad-chested man with rough black curls.

"Hope they have hot water," said Sophie, smiling at her prince with relief. "I really need a—"

She stopped because Tedros wasn't smiling at all. Watching the strangers approach, his face flushed dead white, sweat streaking his temples.

"No no no no no—" he gasped.

Sophie spun to the strangers, confused, but the woman had stopped cold, her mouse-like face a mask of shock.

"God help me," she whispered.

Tedros stumbled back, grabbing Agatha's arm like a panicked child. "Wake me up . . . *please* . . . wake me up—"

"T-T-Tedros?" the woman stammered.

"I'm afraid your son and his friends need you, Guinevere," said Merlin's voice, as the wizard appeared out of a sun flare, striding onto the moor.

Tedros couldn't speak, wild eyes darting between Merlin

and the woman, his entire body shaking so much Agatha had to cradle him under her arm.

Sophie knew she should go to the prince, but she couldn't move. She was trembling at the sight of the dark-haired, coal-eyed man the same way Tedros trembled from his mother.

Because just as Tedros dreamed of Guinevere, Sophie dreamed of *him*.

The devil who appeared inside Rafal's ring.

The devil who stopped her from Tedros' crown.

And now the devil who had a name.

Lancelot.

24

Who Do You Belong With?

Tedros had been staring at the steaming cup of cinnamon-apple cider for nearly twenty minutes, but had yet to touch it.

Watching him, Agatha had been so worried about what he was thinking that she hadn't touched hers either. Nor had Sophie next to her, who was too busy giving Lancelot nervous looks, as the swarthy, pock-skinned knight lay plates and silverware for each of them.

"You must be famished, the lot of you," he said in a rumbling baritone. "Your dark-haired friend asked if he could have a bath. Funny lad . . . said he didn't want to stink up the table. What's his name again? Homer? Hodor?"

None of them answered.

"Hobbin, I think," said Lancelot.

Agatha could see Tedros' shirt wet with perspiration, his Adam's apple lurching up and down, the veins on his arms about to pop—

"Hort. His name is Hort," Guinevere said, bustling in from the kitchen with a dish of fire-grilled turkey and a bowl of rampion salad. In the torchlight of the farmhouse's dining room, Agatha saw she had Tedros' small, snub nose, his flat brows over electric-blue eyes, as well as his tendency to sweat profusely. Her hair was another matter: it was so tangled and twiggish brown that her small, pallid face was like an egg in a bird's nest.

"It's Tuesday and Lance and I cook for the week on Mondays, so we have plenty to go around," she said. "Until next Monday, that is. Doesn't mean you can't stay past Monday, of course. We're just not used to guests . . . or people for that matter. Sometimes Lance and I go days without talking at all." She sat down and waited in vain for someone to fill the silence. "Hope it's edible. Tedros always loved my turkey, even as a little boy. He'd come running the second he smelled it from the kitchen, even in the middle of his lessons with Merlin."

Tedros didn't look at her.

"Shall we start?" Guinevere said weakly, inching the dishes forward. "You've been on a long journey, so load up your plates. I can always make more."

No one ate.

No one spoke.

"Well, seems like you're all settled in, so I'll be on my way!" chimed Merlin, ambling in with his walking stick in hand.

Everyone looked up urgently, as if he were the last lifeboat leaving a ship.

"W-w-where are you going?" said Tedros.

"Just as you are safe here, I must ensure our other friends are safe too, including your fellow students at school," said Merlin. "No doubt the School Master has accelerated his plan, once the Storian revealed to him that you are under the Lady of the Lake's protection." He looked at Guinevere cryptically. "Apologies for not staying for dinner, my dear. Though I did go to the grove to pay my respects . . ."

Guinevere nodded, as if she understood what he meant.

"I'll see you soon, children," said Merlin, before he glanced at Sophie, his eyes finding the ring on her finger. "Hopefully with no more blood on our hands."

Agatha saw Sophie hold her breath as Merlin magically whisked a lump of turkey from the table to his hand and sauntered out of the cabin, the door swinging shut behind him.

Unbearable silence resumed.

Agatha tried to forget about Merlin's absence and Sophie's ring and Tedros' torment and focused instead on the house's logwood walls, the oval-shaped rooms with crackling fireplaces, the handmade leather couches and sheep-wool rugs, everything so cozy and lovingly crafted, as if two people, without friends, family, community, had made a home at the end of the world—

"White or dark meat, Tedros?" Guinevere's voice asked.

Agatha snapped to attention to see Guinevere pick up her son's plate and smile at him.

Her question hung in the air, the first challenge to the silence.

Tedros finally looked at his mother. "I can't do this," he breathed.

Guinevere said nothing as Tedros wrenched from the table, his cast-iron chair screeching against the floor.

Lancelot frowned. "Tedros, you don't have to talk to her, but at least eat your—"

"If you even look in my direction, you dirty fink, I'll split you in half," Tedros hissed.

Lancelot rocketed to his feet, but Guinevere clasped his wrist, guiding him back down. Lancelot said nothing as Tedros' boots snapped out of the room and the farmhouse door slammed behind him.

Instinctively Agatha jumped up to follow her prince—

"I'll go, Aggie," Sophie's voice said.

Agatha turned to see Sophie standing. Sophie gave her a subtle nod and left the table, but not before flashing Lancelot a last anxious look. Agatha heard the front door close once more and she lowered back to the table, her stomach in a knot.

The room was so quiet they could hear the sound of Hort's bath running across the house.

"Well, then," Agatha said, forcing a smile at her hosts, "shall we dig in?"

Guinevere and Lancelot both exhaled, as if keeping someone at the table was victory enough.

Agatha started on the turkey, so smoky and soft she closed her eyes with pleasure, trying to block all thoughts of what may or may not be happening outside . . .

"He's picked a lovely princess, hasn't he?" Guinevere said.

Agatha's eyes opened.

"'Sophie,' was it?" said Guinevere, shunting her straggly hair out of her salad. "Went after him so surely, like Tedros' father used to come after me. She must love him very much." Her voice wavered. "Not sure Arthur or I could have chosen any better for him."

"Well, they look enough alike, don't they?" grumbled Lancelot, mouth full.

"I just mean she carries herself like a queen. More than I ever did to be honest," said Guinevere, sniffling a laugh.

"She's perfect for the lad. People of the kingdom will fawn over her and she'll dote on him hand and foot," said Lancelot.

"Camelot will finally have a real queen," Guinevere sighed, putting on a smile. She turned to Agatha. "What about you, dear? Did you and Hort meet at school? Or was it the Snow Ball—"

"I'm sorry. Will you excuse me?" Agatha gasped. "I . . . I feel like I need some air—"

She pushed herself from the table and fled the cabin, leaving Lancelot and Guinevere, who'd never needed anything but each other's company, feeling suddenly alone.

Agatha didn't know where she was going; she just had to get away from that house. Clumping across the moors in steel-blue twilight, she took a long, full breath and noticed, for the first time, the air was warm. Gone was the raw winter chill, replaced by a humid breeze, just like the wind that blew through Merlin's Celestium.

Maybe this is the Lake Lady's thinking place, she wondered, clinging to any thought that didn't involve Sophie or Tedros. Nothing loomed ahead except flat, lucid evening and sky maps of stars and Agatha knew she could go on walking, forever and ever, never finding an end.

She slowed to a stop and peered back towards the house. Beyond it, animals commingled, with a few pigs amongst the sheep and cows, while horses chased each other in the moonlight.

The moon lit up something else too: Gavaldon against the horizon, already clearer than it was a day before. And now there were visible holes in the glassy shield around it.

More stories rewritten.

More old heroes dead.

The School Master was getting closer to his ending.

But what was it? she thought. *What did he need in Gavaldon?*

Something he needs to destroy Good forever, Merlin had said.

Agatha chewed on her lip, wrestling this most important riddle of all—

That's when she saw them. Two goldilocked figures by a small oak grove, indistinguishable in the dark.

Agatha was reminded of a moment two years ago during Forest Group sorting when she caught Tedros and Sophie flirting against a tree. It was the first time Agatha had ever seen her best friend look happier than she did when she was with her. Now the sight of Sophie with the same prince, neither in a rush to find nor include her, brought the feelings roaring back. A sick, primal loneliness reared its head—

Only this time Agatha didn't run from the pain.

Slowly she let the loneliness in, holding it, studying it as it clawed at her heart like a monster at the door.

What am I so afraid of?

She'd spent her whole life alone before that June morning four years ago when Sophie first came with a basket of face creams and diet cookies, offering to make her over. She'd been *happy* alone, like a bird trapped in a cage who'd never seen the sky. But as they grew closer and closer, Sophie had opened Agatha's wings to a love so strong she thought it would last forever. It was she and Sophie against the world.

But on that first day of school, watching Sophie with a prince, Agatha realized how blind she'd been. The bond between two girls, no matter how fierce or loyal, changed once a boy came between them.

She and Sophie had tried to go home after that. They'd tried to get back to the way they used to be. But it was as impossible as returning to being a child once you'd already grown up.

All this time, Agatha couldn't understand why Sophie had chosen to be with Rafal to begin with . . . why Sophie would choose to be with a boy so Evil. But standing there, alone in the dark, Agatha suddenly felt for her best friend. Because when Agatha kissed Tedros and vanished him home with her, Sophie no longer had someone who put her first. Her two best friends had left her for each other.

Tedros too had once felt that pain, watching her and Sophie

kiss before they vanished home.

Now Agatha was the odd one out. For if Sophie and her prince ended up together, their first loyalty would be to each other and their new kingdom. She'd still be their friend, of course, but it would be different. For the first time, there would be a part of Sophie and Tedros that Agatha could no longer share. The two of them would have each other. And she would only have herself.

The ache inside her amplified as if she was getting closer to the fire.

It wasn't just her best friend or her prince she was afraid of losing.

It was the old Agatha.

The Agatha who knew how to be alone.

That's why she'd held on so tightly to Sophie as a friend . . . then to Tedros as her prince . . . doubting them, testing them, distrusting them . . . but still holding on.

Because somewhere along the way she'd stopped trusting herself too.

Pain smashed through the barrier and flooded her heart. Agatha closed her eyes, unable to breathe, as if she was drowning—

"Heard I took you to the Snow Ball and didn't even know it," a voice said.

She turned to see Hort, barechested in long underpants, his hair dripping wet.

Maybe it was her wrought expression or the red in her cheeks, but Hort awkwardly covered his chest. "Uh, she's washing my clothes. Don't fall in love with me or anything," he mumbled.

Agatha took one look at his worried face and exploded into cackles, tearing and laughing at the same time.

"Oh eat my dust, will you!" Hort barked. "You know full well you're impressed by what you see!"

Agatha wiped her eyes. "Oh, Hort. One day people will read our fairy tale and you'll be the one they love the most."

She started walking away.

"I didn't lose my clothes this time! I *gave* them to her!" he called out. "And I'll have my own fairy tale, one day. With a happy ending and everything. I can prove it—"

"Really? How's that?"

"'Cause I found something you won't believe."

Agatha stopped walking and turned.

The weasel flashed a wicked grin. "Want to see?"

Sophie had been standing next to Tedros in the oak grove for nearly ten minutes, but the prince didn't say a word. He was staring at a beautiful glass cross, rising out of the ground between two trees. Garlands of fresh white roses draped the cross, along with a small glowing five-pointed star resting against the base. There were more of these five-pointed stars around it, ashy and burnt-out, as if Merlin returned to lay a new star whenever the old had grown cold.

Sophie nuzzled into Tedros' side. "Is this where your father's buried? It's pretty."

Tedros turned to her. "Sorry, do you mind if I do this alone?"

Sophie scalded pink. "Of course—I-I-I'll see you at the house—" She spun on her heel, tripping over a dimmed star, and bungled out of the grove.

"Sophie?"

She looked back at the prince.

"Thanks for checking on me," he said.

Sophie nodded briskly and hurried away.

Without the light of Merlin's star, she couldn't see anything outside now, except the outlines of the house a quarter of a mile away. She tromped across the moors, cheeks still simmering.

Everyone had made her so frantic about the ring, so guilt-ridden and jittery, that she'd only been focused on getting Tedros' kiss as fast as she could. She'd forgotten her prince wasn't a prize to be won or a finish line she could barrel through. Had she even considered how he was feeling? Tedros was trapped indefinitely with the mother who'd abandoned him and the lover she'd chosen to spend her life with instead. How could he possibly look at Guinevere, let alone talk to her, let alone stay in her house, without wanting to kill her? Especially since it was completely within his *right* to kill her, according to his father's decree?

Sophie shook her head, mortified. Tedros was probably dying inside, his heart shredded by emotion, and she'd floated in like a gas bubble to tell him his father's grave was *pretty*.

Agatha would never have been so selfish or stupid.

Sophie sighed dismally as she neared the farmhouse. She'd set out on this journey to rewrite her fairy tale, only to repeat the mistakes she'd made the first time. Tedros couldn't be pushed or rushed or wheedled into a kiss. Even back on the trail, she'd been the one who tried to kiss him, which was no doubt one of the reasons why it hadn't worked. Her prince had to come to *her*. Until then, she'd wait patiently, even if heroes were being slaughtered, even if the sun was drip, drip, dripping until they all dropped dead.

Sophie gritted her teeth. If heroes were dying, it wasn't *her* fault, was it? Wasn't it a hero's *job* to win their story, even if it was happening the second time around? Why should she take the blame if they got old and useless? Let them take care of their stories and she'd take care of hers.

Because this was her fairy tale.

This was her happy ending.

And this time she was getting it right.

She pulled off her dirty shoes as she came up the porch. They'd all appreciate her in the end, of course—once she'd sealed her Ever After with her prince and relighted the sun. *Everybody* would win because of her hard work. In the meantime, Tedros could have all the space he needed. She'd be a patient ear to him, a perfect guest to her hosts, a good friend to Agatha: helpful, convivial, polite, like the girl who once kept track of her Good Deeds. With a deep breath, Sophie arranged her face into a smile and pushed her way into the house, fluttering back towards the dining room—

She stopped cold.

Lancelot was alone at the table, eating an apple.

"W-w-where's everyone else?" she asked.

"Gwen is cleaning up and Horbst went to check on Agatha."

He chomped into the apple and slid her a cup of smoky red-brown liquid. "Gwen made a pot of her famous licorice tea."

Sophie turned for the door. "I should see if they're okay—"

"You're scared of me, aren't you? Been giving me cagey looks all night."

Sophie froze. Lancelot was staring at the ring on her finger as if he'd noticed it for the first time.

"They'll find their way home, I'm sure," he said. "Sit and have your tea."

His tone left little doubt as to her options. Sophie sat opposite him, her stomach queasy.

"Guinevere was just touting what a perfect queen you'll make for the young prince. The kind who'd make Arthur proud." Lancelot bit into his apple, studying Sophie.

"Funny thing, actually. You see, every Christmas, Merlin comes to the house to give Gwen news of her son. Last year, I remember he told us Tedros had found the princess of his dreams. Thoughtful, fiery, compassionate girl . . . a soul of pure Good, who loved him as much as he loved her. Only I could have sworn the name of that princess didn't sound anything like 'Sophie' at all. Lousy with names so I knew I must have remembered it wrong. Gwen never misses a thing, so I mentioned it to her just now in the kitchen, figuring she'd set me straight. Strange, though. Gwen said I was *right*: Merlin had named Tedros' princess as 'Agatha,' but even Gwen agreed the old codger was losing grip on that famous brain of his, 'cause clearly *Sophie* was the one who was the boy's princess. Not just from the way you went after him at dinner, but Gwen noticed you had Tedros' name tattooed on your finger, which also happened to be bearing Tedros' ring."

Lancelot's dark pupils glinted. "Only now that I'm seeing it, I'm wondering how Tedros could give you a ring made of Evil's gold."

Sophie's heart hammered, like an alarm set off.

"Black-swan gold, to be exact," said Lancelot. "Every black swan has a single gold tooth at the back of its mouth—gold which has nefarious properties when it touches human skin. Since the very first tale, black-swan gold has been hunted by Nevers as a powerful weapon, the same way Good has long sought steel from the Lady of the Lake. For centuries, Evil murdered these swans and plundered their gold, killing every last one. Still, Evil had all the black-swan gold it could ask for . . . before King Arthur led his knights on a quest to destroy it. A quest on which I rode by Arthur's side, finding and smashing treasure after treasure, until there wasn't a shred of black-swan gold left in the Endless Woods." Lancelot grinned. "Except, it seems, for the one circling your finger."

Sophie stood up. "It's dark out there—I should check on Tedros—"

"The effects of black-swan gold are unmistakable," Lancelot went on. "Once you wear it upon your skin, it commits your heart to Evil, no matter how hard you try to be Good. It is like a wicked compass that steers you towards sin, without you even realizing it. Wear it long enough and it will convince you it knows the secret of your Ever After . . . that it knows what your heart really wants . . . that it can even *prove* who your true love is. Ask it a name and the magic ring will carve the answer you seek upon your skin, like a guiding light—but that answer will only lead you right back to Evil, where you began."

Sophie was numb now, trapped in her chair.

"Stories go wrong when people think their own happiness is bigger than anyone else's," said Lancelot. "Arthur knew Guinevere loved me, and still he put a ring on her finger, even knowing she wouldn't be happy as his queen. In the end he left the wreckage of a family and two *real* loves exiled forever. I, too, lost a best friend, for Arthur was like a brother to me. But at least Gwen and I live the truth now. We have each other, as it should have been from the beginning. What does Arthur have? He's dead and his queen's ring long destroyed, for Guinevere couldn't wear a ring that didn't belong to her in the first place. Not when she belonged with someone else."

Sophie saw Lancelot staring harder.

"Which begs a question of our queen-to-be," he said, rising from his seat. He put his big, meaty hands on the table and leaned towards her. "You're wearing a ring that doesn't belong to your prince, young Sophie . . ."

The dark knight drew closer, closer, until Sophie saw his devilish, cold-eyed face reflected in the gold on her finger.

"So who do *you* belong with?"

The door swung open and Guinevere came in, with a small basket.

"Oh! Sophie, thank goodness. I put some turkey and greens in here for Tedros. He'll eat it if you give it to him, surely. I don't want him to go hungry tonight on my account—"

Sophie didn't hear words, only blood throbbing in her ears.

"I know what you must think of me, Sophie, all of it deserved," said Guinevere quietly, seeing her face. "Just know that if he never forgives me, if he never speaks a word to me again . . . I'm thankful he's found his true love. Merlin told us how much Tedros fought for his princess—how much *both* of you fought to be together. So I can be at peace, knowing my son won't repeat my mistakes." Guinevere smiled at the ring on Sophie's finger. "Because both of your hearts only wish for each other."

She stroked Sophie's cheek and left the basket in her shaking hands.

As Sophie watched Tedros' mother return to the kitchen, she glanced back sickly at Lancelot—

But the knight was gone, as if it'd all been a dream.

"What is it?" Agatha asked, trying to track Hort's muscled frame in the dark. "What'd you find?"

"You'll see. You all think I'm such a weenie. Big mistake," said Hort, itching at his long underpants as they treaded deep into the oak grove. "Huge."

Squinting back at the house's lit windows, Agatha could see Sophie and Lancelot talking in the dining room. She turned to Hort. "Wait, this doesn't involve you turning into a werewolf, does it? You never last more than ten seconds—"

"*Man*-wolf. And it's *better* than that. Trust me. Besides, haven't practiced my talent in a while, so I only last five seconds now. I don't get it. How do other man-wolves last so long? Is there some special diet or potion for stamina? I asked Professor Sheeks, but she sent me to the Doom Room for being cheeky."

Agatha followed Hort towards the sparkle of a pond at the grove's edge, reflecting the moonlit mirage of Gavaldon.

"Now that Sophie's not with the School Master anymore, how can he still win your fairy tale?" Hort asked, studying the outlines of the town. "Doesn't he need love on his side?"

"That's the odd thing. He hasn't chased her even though he can't win without her," Agatha answered as they stopped at the pond's edge. "He admitted it to me himself. That's why he needs her as his queen so badly. She's Evil's only hope to win."

"Then he's too late."

Agatha stomach plummeted. "Oh . . . so Tedros might, um . . . kiss her? N-n-not that I care. But you were on the trail with them, so I'm just curious how they were getting alon—"

"I wasn't talking about Tedros," said Hort.

Agatha saw him grin down at his reflection in the pond and she rolled her eyes. "Oy, Weasel Boy, if you brought me out here to ogle you in a mirror—"

But now she saw what he was looking at, shimmering deep beneath the surface . . . small bullets of light, shooting upwards like a comet tail, getting closer, closer, until a thousand tiny white fish splashed through, spitting streams of water.

"Wish Fish? You found *Wish Fish*?" Agatha said, wiping her face and kneeling at the shore. "Princess Uma taught us about them first year!"

"Told you it was better than a man-wolf. Touch the water and they'll dig into your soul and find your greatest wish," said

Hort. "Nevers were supposed to do the lesson the day after the Evers did it, but then you set the fish free, started an animal stampede, and nearly burned down the castle. School didn't get new Wish Fish after that."

Agatha stroked the bobbing mouths of the little white fish, feeling their tickly kisses. "Suppose these want to be set free too?"

Yet as she gazed into their big, black eyes, she didn't see any traces of the same yearning. "I used to be able to hear wishes," she said to Hort. "Maybe I lost my talent like you."

"Or maybe they've just been fish too long to remember they were once human," said the weasel. "In any case, I'm going first."

He stuck his finger in the water.

Instantly, the fish zipped off in different directions, turning black, silver, and gold, as they assembled themselves into a picture. For a moment, Agatha had no clue what she was seeing, until suddenly the mosaic of fish clarified, as if coming into focus, and she raised her brows in surprise.

The fish had drawn Hort and Sophie's sunlit wedding at the edge of a lake as a mob of well-wishers cheered them on. Both the bride and groom wore black, the only concession to the fact this was an Evil occasion as opposed to a Good one.

"It's lovely, Hort," Agatha said, feeling let down, "but it's just your wish—"

"That's what I thought," Hort replied, "until I saw *that*."

He pointed to the corner of the fish's painting, where two guests holding hands—a teenage boy and girl—looked happiest of all for the new couple. The boy had a crown of silver and diamonds upon his golden head. The girl wore a matching crown in her black hair.

Agatha lost her breath.

"It's me and . . . Tedros," she whispered.

"And I'd *never* wish for you to marry that prat," snorted Hort. "I hate him too much to wish him the slightest happiness, let alone a queen with as much class and integrity as you. So if that's inside my wish, it means it's already going to happen. It means this whole picture is deeper than a wish, Agatha. It's the *truth*. I'm going to end with Sophie and you're going to end with Tedros. That's our happy ending. The four of us together. No one left out."

Agatha's eyes bulged, pink streaks rising on her cheeks. *Oh my God. . . . This is it!* She could have grabbed Hort and kissed him. This was the answer they'd been waiting for . . . the way out of this tangled fairy tale . . . the Last Ever After revealed once and for all. Sophie with Hort and she with—

Slowly the color seeped out of Agatha's cheeks.

"No . . . it can't be the truth, Hort," she croaked. "Because I'll never marry Tedros. And Sophie will never love you."

The glow in Hort's face snuffed out.

"Sophie loves Tedros. And unlike me, she never doubted that love," Agatha said, hunched in the grass next to him. "All I *did* was doubt Tedros. The more time he and I spent together, the more I couldn't understand why he wanted me when he could have a *real* princess. That's why I wanted to keep him in Gavaldon. In my mother's house, he wasn't a prince. He was a scared teenage boy, as lost and confused as I was. But here, in the Woods, Tedros is different: he's true to himself and lives with a purpose. In his heart, he's already a king—a king who needs a queen just as confident and self-assured as he is, who can lead his people to hope again. That's not me. I'm still learning to like what I see in the mirror and accept that someone can actually love me for who I really am. I'm not a leader. I'm not . . . special."

She gazed at her crowned self in the painting. "When we were at school in the wrong bodies, Tedros said he was afraid of me seeing him once the prince is stripped away. That I'd see he's nothing special . . . just an ordinary boy. But that's the Tedros I love. Because the real Tedros—the prince who will grow into a strong, powerful king—will see one day that I'm no different than his mother. I never wanted a prince or a fairy tale. I never wanted a big life. I'm just a girl struggling to be ordinary."

She looked up at Hort, eyes wet. "But Sophie? Sophie believes she deserves a prince. Sophie *wants* to be queen. Enough that she's willing to risk the future of Good for it—"

"Which is exactly why she *can't* be Good's queen!" Hort fought, nodding at his Wish Fish. "Don't you get it? You belong with Tedros and I belong with—"

"Then why can't I see my future together with him? If I belonged with him, why can't I see myself as this girl in your wish? I'm meant to be alone, Hort. That's why I'll lose him. Because I need to learn to be happy on my own. Like my mother was. That can be an Ever After, can't it?"

"You haven't lost him," Hort pressed, still looking at his fish. "It's never too late in a fairy tale!"

Agatha sighed wistfully and touched his cheek. "Even fairy tales have limits, Hort. Both of us have to let go. Let Sophie and Tedros live their Ever After. For your own happiness."

Hort scorched pink. "For my own *happiness?* That's rich coming from you," he sneered, yanking his finger from the water, dissolving the painting. "You're the one forcing Tedros to love Sophie, just so she'll destroy that ring. I heard what she said behind that curtain in the cave. At least I'm willing to fight for my happy ending. You're giving away your true love to someone he doesn't belong with and expecting him to live with it forever! Tell yourself all you want that you're not good enough for him, Agatha. Tell yourself you're doing it to save Good. Tell yourself any excuse that lets you sleep at night. But we both know you're just too afraid to fight for the person you belong with. And you know what, princess? Even if I hate the boy to his bones, that doesn't sound Good to me *at all.*"

Hort stalked away, leaving Agatha alone by the pond.

She watched him go, her heart wasting to a small, dark hollow.

Soft burbles echoed behind her and she turned to see the Wish Fish, white-hued once more and bobbing at the pond's edge for her turn.

"Please help me, little fish," she said softly.

The fish's eyes twinkled with moonlight, like a thousand wishing stars.

With a breath, Agatha dipped her finger in the water and

waited for her heart to give her an answer . . . the way Sophie's heart had led her so clearly to Tedros . . .

Tell me what I really want, she asked.

Instantly the fish began to turn different colors . . . pink, blue, green, red . . . vibrating and shaking madly, like corn kernels in a fire—

Agatha closed her eyes, knowing the fish were about to paint the answer . . . her path towards goodness and happiness, once and for all . . .

Her lashes fluttered open.

The Wish Fish hadn't moved.

Like fading flowers, they drained to white, looking up at her, tired and defeated.

Agatha smiled sadly, remembering what her teacher once decreed of such a result.

"Foggy mind," she whispered.

She caressed the fish goodbye and followed Hort's receding shadow back towards the house.

Neither Hort nor Agatha had noticed there was a third person by the pond the whole time, sitting behind a tall oak.

The blond prince never moved from his spot, even when the sun rose the next morning like a golden ring and cast him in precarious light. Instead, he lay against the tree and listened again and again to the echo of everything he'd just heard, a single tear shining on his face.

25

The Scorpion and the Frog

For the next week, Tedros was a ghost.

No one saw him during the days—not in the house, nor on the moors, or near the oak grove—and no one had the slightest clue if or where he slept. Guinevere fretted her son would starve, until Agatha gently suggested they leave a basket of food on the porch for him in the evenings. By the morning, it was always gone.

To Agatha, his disappearing act was at once a terror and a relief. On the one hand, the sun was getting smaller every day, leaving the moors streaked in permanent pink and purple sunset. The world was bar-reling to an end and the prince who could save it with a kiss was nowhere to be found.

And yet, it also meant for the first time in weeks, Agatha didn't have to *think* about that prince. The two of them had become inextricable, the way she and Sophie had once been. Every thought she'd had these past few weeks had been consumed with Tedros: worrying about Tedros, fighting with Tedros, making up with Tedros—Tedros, Tedros, Tedros, until she'd run herself ragged living life from both their points of view. With the prince gone, she suddenly remembered she was a full human being without him. And indeed, if being alone was her ending to come . . . then now was the time to start preparing for it.

By the sixth day, she and the group had settled into a routine, like a ragtag family. Hort spent his days with Lancelot doing chores around the farm. From morning until night, they'd milk cows, till the vegetable garden, gather eggs from chickens, shear sheep, bathe the horses, and manage a frisky goat named Fred who chased any animal of female persuasion halfway across the moors. Caked in sweat, smelling of hay and manure, Hort seemed elated to be useful to such a virile man, and they looked almost like father and son with their oily black hair, puffed-up chests, and swaggering gaits.

Guinevere, meanwhile, had the house to manage, with an endless amount of laundry, sewing, cooking, and cleaning on account of the extra guests, all of which she did eagerly, rejecting any offer of help, as if she needed the work to distract her from her thoughts.

Which left Agatha and Sophie on their own.

For the first time since they lost their Ever After, the two girls didn't have a boy between them. Trapped on these heaths with nothing to do, it was like they were back in sheltered

Gavaldon, with a world of princes and fairy tales far far away.

While Hort slept on the couch in the den, the two girls had to share a bed in the small guest room. Each morning, they'd have bacon and eggs with Hort, Lancelot, and Guinevere, do their best to tidy up before Tedros' mother shooed them out, and spend the rest of the morning walking the moors or riding horses together.

The first week, they seemed to have forgotten how to be friends at all. At night, each girl rolled to her side of the bed and murmured something half-hearted. During walks and rides, their stilted conversation revolved around what might be for lunch, the abundance of farm animals, and the weather (which given the magical location, was invariably the same). Agatha noticed Sophie was edgy and preoccupied, constantly peeking at her ring and Tedros' name tattooed beneath it. Whenever Lancelot crossed their path, Sophie pretended to fix a fingernail or adjust her shoe, avoiding eye contact. Sometimes, Agatha would catch her tossing in her sleep, murmuring disconnected phrases: "Don't listen to him" . . . "black-swan gold" . . . "hearts don't lie," before Sophie would wake up shaky and red faced and seal herself in the bathroom.

Agatha, meanwhile, still couldn't get comfortable around her old friend. While traveling with Merlin, she'd convinced herself that letting Sophie end with Tedros was the Good thing to do—first, because Sophie would destroy her ring and kill the School Master; and second, because if she couldn't be the queen Tedros needed, shouldn't Sophie have her chance?

But Hort's words at the pond had put a dent in her

convictions. For one thing, while Sophie aspired to rule one of Good's kingdoms, here she was holding Good hostage over her ring. Even if agreeing to her terms would save Good's future . . . it still *seemed* Evil.

More importantly, could Sophie really make Tedros happy? Tedros might appear strong and swaggery, but deep inside he was gentle, lonely, and soft. How could Sophie know every part of him? How could she take care of him? The more Agatha tried to envision their Ever After, the more she had a sinking feeling, as if reliving an old story. As if she were Lancelot now, surrendering Tedros to Sophie, like the knight had once surrendered Guinevere to Arthur. What Good had come of that in the end?

As the days passed and Tedros didn't return, each girl seemed to slip further into private doubts, speaking less and less to the other . . .

Then came Nellie Mae.

For the past six days, Agatha had been riding a horse named Benedict, which she'd chosen for his scrawny legs, rumpled black coat, and hacking cough.

"Goodness, Aggie, don't you read storybooks?" Sophie said after Guinevere had opened the stable of riding horses that first day. "Black horses are untrainable, untamable, and *mean*. Besides, he sounds like he's on death's door. What in the world possessed you to pick him?"

"Reminded me of myself," Agatha said, rubbing his neck and finding a handful of fleas.

Sophie, meanwhile, had chosen an elegant, chestnut-skinned

Arabian mare named Nellie Mae, with a striking white tail.

"So much character in her eyes," Sophie admired. "For all we know, she belonged to Scheherazade."

"Schehere-who?"

"Oh Aggie, didn't they teach you *any* princess history at that Good school?" Sophie said, mounting her horse. "Not every fairy-tale princess is creamy white with a small nose and a name like Buttercup or—"

Agatha didn't hear the rest because Nellie Mae had bolted from the stables like a demon out of hell.

For the rest of the week, Sophie tried in vain to control her mare, which kicked and neighed and spat at her, only obeying Sophie if she strangled it by the reins . . . while Agatha calmly rode Benedict as if coasting down a river.

Still, day after day, Sophie refused to switch Nellie Mae, as if admitting her poor taste in horses would somehow invalidate all her life choices. But this morning, after Nellie Mae stomped on her toe, farted in her face, and spent a good deal of time walking in a circle, Sophie finally turned to Agatha. "She's as difficult as me, isn't she?"

Agatha snorted. "You're worse."

"What is it with me and foul-tempered animals?" Sophie mewled as Nellie Mae swayed back and forth, trying to fling her off. "Is this because I didn't take Animal Communication?"

"Problem is you're fighting it instead of trusting it," said Agatha. "Sometimes there's more to the story than *you*, Sophie. You can't pick everything at first sight, just because it looks good, and then force it to be with you, like a handbag or a dress. Relationships are more complicated than that. You can't control the story from both sides."

"Wouldn't you try to control your story if everyone told you your heart was Evil, when you know it isn't? Wouldn't you try to prove them wrong?" Sophie fought, gripping the reins. "I have a Good heart, just like you, and I trust what it chooses for me. I *have* to. Because if I don't, what do I have left?"

Agatha met her eyes. Neither of them were talking about horses anymore.

Sophie stroked Nellie Mae's head. "I *am* ready for a relationship, Aggie. You'll see." She whispered into the horse's ear. "Right, Nellie Mae? We're a team for Good, you and I. I trust you and you trust m—"

Nellie Mae bucked Sophie so hard she flipped backwards and landed face-first on her horse's rump, before Nellie Mae took off across the moors.

"Aggggieeeeeeeee!" Sophie screamed.

For a moment, Agatha relished the sight of Sophie dragged into oblivion, her nose in the horse's buttocks, her buttocks on the horse's head, before Agatha realized that if she didn't stop them, Nellie Mae wouldn't *ever* stop.

With a firm kick to Benedict's side, Agatha raced after Sophie's horse, while Hort and Lancelot hooted from the sheep's meadow, thoroughly entertained.

The problem, of course, was that as kind as he was, Benedict lived life at a glacial pace and saw no reason to move any faster, especially given how little regard he had for both Sophie and Nellie Mae. But now Agatha glimpsed a deep swamp patch ahead of Sophie's horse, bounded by a fallen tree the size of a boulder.

Nellie Mae accelerated towards the tree, perhaps seeing a chance to rid herself of her rider once and for all.

"Sophie, watch out!" Agatha yelled.

Sophie looked up and gasped—

Nellie Mae leapt over the tree, throwing Sophie headlong into swamp mud, before the horse landed gracefully on the other side and galloped into the sunrise.

Sophie heard Agatha's horse trotting up. "Now do you take back the part about me being more difficult?" Sophie groaned, caked in mud.

Agatha looked down from her horse and held out a hand. "No."

"Fair enough," Sophie sighed, pulling up and climbing onto Benedict behind her.

As they rode towards the house, Sophie gripping onto her, Agatha felt her friend's head rest on her shoulder.

"Still rescuing me after all these years, Aggie," Sophie whispered, nuzzling in.

"Have you ever heard of a fairy tale called *The Scorpion and the Frog*?" Agatha asked.

"Obviously. Do you not know it? Really, as much as I like Clarissa Dovey, her curriculum seems woefully thin." Sophie cleared her throat. "Once upon a time, a scorpion desperate to cross a stream sees a frog safe on the other side and asks him for a ride. The frog doesn't want to help, of course, because he says the scorpion will surely sting and kill him. The scorpion replies that to kill the frog would be foolish, for he can't swim, and if the frog dies, so will he. Convinced of this logic, the frog offers the scorpion a ride . . . but as they start to cross the river, the scorpion instantly stings the frog. 'You fool!' the frog croaks as he sinks. 'Now we both shall die!' But the scorpion only shrugs and does a jig on the drowning frog's back. 'I could not help myself,' the scorpion says—"

"It's my nature," Agatha finished.

Sophie smiled, surprised. "So you do know it!"

"Better than you can imagine," Agatha said sharply.

Sophie didn't say another word for the rest of the ride.

By the next day, the girls had fallen back into their old friendship, with Agatha grumbling at Sophie's monologues, Sophie teasing Agatha over her clumsiness, and the two of them bickering and giggling like teenagers in love. The days rolled by, into the second week, and still there was no sign of the prince, except for the missing baskets of food each morning. And yet, his absence brought Sophie and Agatha closer and closer, whether they were drinking cherry punch in front of a fire, exploring the moorlands, or gabbing and snuggling with each other well after the rest of the house was asleep.

"Why do you think Lancelot and Guinevere have a guest room at all?" asked Agatha one evening, as they shared a picnic basket in a wild garden about a mile from the house. "It's not like they can have guests. Except Merlin, I suppose, but he prefers to sleep in a tree."

Sophie stared at her.

"The things you learn when you're camping with someone," Agatha smirked, picking at a slice of Guinevere's almond cake. "Do you think she and Lancelot wanted a child together?"

"It would explain the puerile choice of wallpaper," groused Sophie, sipping at homemade cucumber juice.

"But what's stopping them? Been more than six years since Merlin hid them here."

"Maybe Guinevere realized she didn't want a child with a man whose personality is as odious as his hygiene," Sophie snipped.

When they were finished, they treaded farther into the flower garden, reveling in the hazy air and feeling of safety, as if they were in a bigger, better version of the Blue Forest.

"I've been meaning to tell you something," said Agatha, sucking the honey out of a honeysuckle. "When we came back to the Woods, Tedros and I found a portal through your mother's grave on Graves Hill. But there was no body in it. And when we came out the other side—"

"My mother had a villain's grave on Necro Ridge."

Agatha looked at Sophie, thrown.

"The things you learn when you're camping with someone," Sophie smiled. "Tedros told me everything that happened before you both rescued me. But it doesn't make sense to me either, Aggie. It has to be the Crypt Keeper's mistake. I know your mother didn't tell you she'd been at school, but my mother *would* have told me. She never went to the School for Good and Evil. She never went into the Woods. I'm sure of it. So the Storian couldn't have written her fairy tale. Because my mother died right in front of me . . ." Sophie stopped, voice faltering. "Like yours died in front of you."

Agatha's throat dried out.

"I'm so sorry, Aggie," Sophie rasped.

Agatha felt old emotions rise as Sophie wrapped her in a smothering hug. For the first time since she left Gavaldon, Agatha wept for her mother.

"Callis loved you so much," Sophie whispered, rubbing her friend's back. "Even if she hated me."

"She didn't hate you. She just assumed we wouldn't stay friends once we got to our schools," Agatha said, wiping her eyes.

"She also assumed you'd be in Evil and me in Good," said Sophie.

"Would have solved everything, wouldn't it?" said Agatha.

The two girls laughed.

"Everyone thinks we're so different, Aggie," said Sophie. "But we both know what it's like to lose someone who truly understands us."

Agatha lay her head on Sophie's shoulder. "And to find someone too."

Now it was Sophie's turn to cry.

"We should get back," sighed Agatha finally. "Think Guinevere and Lancelot have enough headaches without us disappearing too."

As they walked home, Agatha took Sophie's arm.

"What do you think of those two, by the way? For two

lovers who changed the course of a kingdom, they're quite . . . domestic."

"That's sugarcoating it," Sophie said, grimacing. "If she'd stayed with Arthur, imagine the things Guinevere would be doing with him right now: planning the Easter Ball or welcoming neighboring kings for dinner or managing the royal court. And here she is, folding a man's shirts and taking pleasure in it. Arthur would have been better off with someone like my mother, who knew she was meant for a grander life."

"I only saw your mother once or twice in town when I was really young," said Agatha. "But I remember she was beautiful, like a gold-haired nymph."

"It's been seven years, so I can't even picture her face anymore," said Sophie. "The more I try to remember it, the more it shape-shifts, like I'm trying to recapture a dream. But she didn't leave the house much. Didn't have any friends either except Honora, until . . . well, you know. That's how I know she never went to the school or into the Woods at all. Because she never would have gone back to Gavaldon. She despised that place."

"Like mother, like daughter," Agatha quipped.

"The difference between me and her is that I got out," said Sophie, her tone steeling. "I'll have the grand life she always wanted. I'll have an Ever After big enough for the both of us."

Agatha smiled tightly and they lapsed into silence.

As the two girls neared the farmhouse, they glimpsed Gavaldon lit up far away like the northern lights, the protective shield around it pocked with holes of various sizes, none bigger than the size of a melon. Through the holes, they could see the green turrets of the cottages rich and textured, the clock on the crooked tower sharp and clear, and groups of children in the square, noses buried in storybooks. They could even see some of the shop windows, including Mr. Deauville's Story-book Shop, now reopened and teeming with kids.

"They're reading the rewritten storybooks," Agatha realized, remembering Merlin's warning. "Every time Evil wins, a fairy tale rewrites itself. That's why Gavaldon's opening to the School Master and his Dark Army. Readers are *believing* in the power of Evil."

Sophie swallowed. "Uh . . . how long did Merlin say we had before the Woods went dark?"

"No more than a week now," Agatha warned, eyeing the ring on Sophie's finger. The End was right *there* . . . and yet so far away. "Meant to ask you. The other night, I saw you and Lancelot talking in the dining room. What did he say to you?"

Her friend stopped walking, but said nothing.

"Sophie?"

Sophie's eyes were still on Gavaldon. "It's coming, isn't it?" she said softly.

"What is?"

Sophie turned. "Each of us thinks we know who's Good and who's Evil. You, me, Tedros, Rafal . . . even Lancelot. But all of us can't be right, Aggie. Someone has to be wrong."

Agatha shook her head. "I don't underst—"

"What if we could go back to the beginning? When it was just me and you." There were hot spots on Sophie's cheeks, desperation in her voice. "It was our first Ever After, Aggie. Can't it be the last?"

Agatha gazed at her starlit, hopeful friend, framed by the vision of their old home.

Gently Agatha took Sophie's hand and looked into her eyes. "But it wasn't, was it? Our Ever After didn't last."

Sophie let go of her, sadness weakening her smile. "You still think I'm that same girl. You think I'm the one meant to be alone."

"No—that's not what I meant—" Agatha countered.

"Say it, Aggie," Sophie asked, lips quivering. "Tell me you and Tedros deserve the Ever After. More than Tedros and me. More than me and you."

Agatha broke into a sweat.

"Tell me you want to be Camelot's queen. That only you can make Tedros happy forever," said Sophie, eyes welling. "Tell me and I'll destroy the ring tonight. I promise."

Agatha flushed in surprise. She searched Sophie's face and saw she was speaking the truth.

This was The End.

This was the way out of the fairy tale.

All she had to do was say the words.

"Say you're a fairy-tale queen, Agatha," Sophie coaxed.

Agatha opened her mouth—

And yet no words came . . . only the image of her in a Wish Fish painting, wearing Tedros' crown . . .

"*Say* it, Aggie," Sophie pressed her.

Agatha imagined herself as that classic, regal leader . . .

worthy of standing beside King Arthur's son.

"Say it and *mean* it," Sophie demanded.

Agatha struggled for air. "I . . . I . . . I'm . . ."

Shallow gasps faded into the wind.

"But you can't say it, can you?" Sophie whispered, touching Agatha's cheek. "Because you'll never really believe it."

Agatha felt hot tears blind her, her voice padlocked inside—

But now there was someone else coming towards her across the moors.

A blond, broad-shouldered boy, holding a single pink rose.

Freshly bathed and shaven, Tedros glided towards Agatha in a loose, milk-colored shirt and black breeches, Excalibur sheathed on his belt.

Only he wasn't looking at Agatha.

His eyes pinned on Sophie as he stopped in front of them, his mouth a sensual grin.

"Can we go somewhere, Sophie? You and me?"

Sophie smiled and glanced at Agatha plaintively, as if asking her permission . . . but she'd already let Tedros take her hand.

As he led Sophie away from the house, Agatha waited for her prince to look back at her.

He never did.

Standing there, alone on the moors, Agatha watched the two shadows nestle closer, before Tedros slipped his rose into Sophie's palm. Gazing at her prince, Sophie clasped it to her chest and whispered something to him. The future king smiled and guided her ahead, their silhouettes melting into the moonglow, as if a door to Ever After had opened . . .

Then they were gone, like the last beat of light in Agatha's heart.

"Here I was expecting you to swing in on a vine, bearded, dirt-smeared, and thumping your chest like Tedros of the jungle," Sophie ribbed as they treaded through darkness hand in hand. "A bit disappointed, actually."

"Stopped at the house and cleaned up," the prince said tersely.

"You've been gone more than a week. What have you been doing all this time?"

"Thinking."

Sophie waited for him to elaborate, but they walked more than an hour before he said another word. His clean-smelling hair tickled against her neck and the prince led her so firmly that a hot flash rippled up her spine. Sophie's other hand cupped the soft pink rose, making sure it was still there. Once upon a time, at a Welcoming, Tedros had thrown his rose to see who would be his true love, and she'd failed to catch it.

But Sophie had the rose now.

A muffled roar echoed ahead and she looked up to see the moon reflect off a broad river bounded by walls of dark rock. The river slipped ahead calmly before it plunged down a cavernous waterfall, too deep to see the bottom. Beyond the waterfall, there was nothing but the moon's white glare.

"Leave it to you to find the ends of the earth," said Sophie.

"In here," said Tedros, pulling her towards an opening in the river rock.

Sophie crammed into the hole, trying to find her grip without crushing her prince's rose. As she came through, Tedros clutched her waist and helped her stand to full height. For a moment, she couldn't see anything. Then she heard the scrape of a matchstick and watched Tedros light a tall candle he must have taken from the house—

Sophie gasped.

They were in a shimmering sapphire cave, the walls made entirely out of the rich blue gem. Bands of flawless sapphires distorted her face back at her like a hall of mirrors. A blanket and pillow lay in the corner and crumbs of food littered the ground, along with a few discarded baskets. Clearly this had been Tedros' camp for the past week.

He spread the blanket and helped Sophie sit down before he cozied in beside her, his leg touching hers, and placed the candle in front of them.

"Noticed you and Agatha spending a lot of time together," he said.

Sophie peeked at his arched brow and knew better than to ask how much he'd been spying on them from afar. "Well, you had your time with Agatha and you had your time with me. Isn't it fair that she and I had our turn? Especially if it's the last time before things . . . change." She gave him a coy look.

Tedros nodded, picking at the candle wax. "Of course."

"We were worried about you, Teddy. Out there on your own. It must have been overwhelming to be thrown in that house with—"

"I don't want to talk about an old story, Sophie. It's the new story I care about."

He turned, his stare piercing. "When we were on the trail, you said there were two types of queens. The one who wants to be a queen and the one who doesn't. I asked what you would do as my future queen—"

"Before we were rudely interrupted by zombie pirates," Sophie simpered.

Tedros didn't smile. "It was the wrong question. I should have asked you *why* you want to be my queen."

Sophie's shoulders relaxed. Finally, they'd finish what they started in the Woods. No nerves, no setbacks this time. . . . Everything was in her hands now. All Tedros wanted was the truth.

She looked up at the jagged sapphires over their heads, reflecting the two of them like a thousand crowns. Then Sophie took a deep breath and began to speak.

"I used to dream of princes. Magnificent balls filled with hundreds of beautiful boys and me the only girl. I'd walk the line examining them, trying to pick which one would be my Ever After. Every night I'd get closer and closer, only to wake up before I found him. How I dreaded that moment when my eyes opened. To be in a world of magic and romance and Goodness and then robbed back into a drab, pointless life seemed so . . . *wrong*. I didn't belong in a cottage lane with fifteen houses exactly like mine. I couldn't marry some shop-keeper or cobbler's boy and slog at the bakery each day just to feed our children. I wanted to find real happiness, where The

End didn't mean getting old and useless and being crammed in a graveyard with everyone else. Agatha thinks all this sounds like heaven, of course, but she wants to hide in an ordinary life. I'm special. I'm *different*. I'm meant to have my name remembered more than Snow White and Sleeping Beauty and girls who were just pretty and passive and waited like dolls for their princes to arrive. I'm meant to live in people's hearts for Ever After, no matter how old my story gets. Because unlike all those other Good girls, I found a happy ending for myself. *I* made it happen, no matter how many people tried to take it away from me. That's why I want to be a queen, Tedros. Because no matter what anyone said, I always knew I was one. Searching for her king."

Sophie stroked his cheek. "And here you are."

Tears sprang to Tedros' eyes.

"I told you," Sophie smiled. "I told you we belonged together from that very first day."

Her prince took her by the waist. "Thank you for telling me the truth, Sophie."

"And was the truth . . . enough?" she asked, red-hot.

Tedros nodded, his fingers moving up her back. "You only left out one thing . . ."

She inhaled his sweet breath. "What's that?" she whispered, leaning in.

Tedros held her neck and slowly pressed his lips to hers, soft as a cloud. With a gasp, Sophie fell into his kiss, heart pumping against his chest.

At last.

At last!

She tasted every morsel of his perfect mouth, waiting for the rapturous swell between them that would seal their end . . . for a spark as electric and strong as love could bear . . .

But all Sophie tasted was dead hollowness, as if kissing a stone.

Shaken, she seized Tedros tighter, kissed him harder, but she felt nothing from his side, nothing from her side, absolutely nothing at all, as their lips grew lifeless, repelling each other, until finally she pulled away.

Tedros glowered at her, ice-cold. "You left the part out about being my queen because you love me."

Sophie's heart was a black hole.

"I'm not your true love, Sophie. I never was," said the prince. "We don't belong together."

Sophie sputtered for breath. "But . . . but—the ring—" She glanced down at her hand urgently, only to see the stain of Tedros' name vanish beneath the gold, as if it had never been there at all.

A loud clink jolted her and she turned to find Excalibur on the ground next to her.

Sophie looked up at Tedros, tramping out of the cave.

"By the time I come back, I want it destroyed," he commanded.

Then he forged into the night air and veered out of sight.

Slowly Sophie looked down at the ring, flickering beneath the candle.

Rage ripped through her blood . . . rage so thick and primal it made her whole body rattle—

She tore the ring off her finger and hurled it at the sapphire wall, before it crashed into dirt across from her.

Lancelot was right.

The ring had lied to her. It had carved the name of a prince who she never belonged to. It had knowingly led her down the wrong path. It had made an utter *fool* of her.

And so had the boy who'd given it to her.

Teeth gnashed, she grabbed Excalibur with both hands, picturing Rafal's twisted grin. Evil's Master would learn his lesson for betraying her.

Sophie raised Good's sword high over the ring and brought it down with a scream—

The blade stopped a sliver short.

But <u>had</u> he betrayed her?

Why would Evil's ring lead her to Good's prince in the first place?

And why would Rafal let her go off with that prince without chasing her?

She thought of Captain Hook, who had orders not to return her to the young School Master. She thought of the beautiful frost-haired boy at the window, watching her leave. She thought of his omniscient blue eyes and serene face, his last words floating as she fell away . . .

"You'll come back to me."

Eyes widening, Sophie slowly put the sword down.

Rafal hadn't betrayed her.

He'd set her free, just like Agatha had set her and Tedros

free . . . so that all of them could find the truth for themselves.

A truth Sophie had been running from for a very long time.

The gold ring was warm to the touch when she picked it up from the dirt and slid it onto her finger. For a moment it glowed red, as if sealing a new bond between them, and she glared down at her reflection in its surface.

There would be no destroying the ring tonight.

Or ever.

For the reason she'd known what was missing in Tedros' kiss is because she'd already felt it once with someone else.

Someone who loved her for what she truly was.

Someone she'd been too scared to love back.

Because if she did, it meant she and Agatha were *both* queens—each afraid to accept their fate.

But unlike her best friend, Sophie was ready now.

Alone in candlelight, she closed her eyes and made a wish . . .

For a prince . . . a castle . . . a crown . . .

Evil this time, instead of Good.

A chill swept through the cave and blew the candle out.

Agatha lay in infinite darkness, praying for sleep. She lasted only a few minutes before she sat up and lit the candle on the bed table.

Her eyes caught the small mirror on the wall and she saw her tired face, raccoon circles around her eyes, and the slouch in her shoulders.

How long ago it seemed she was a princess.

She was about to ball up under the covers and try to sleep with the candle burning, when she heard faint music and giggles from behind the house.

Rising to her knees, she peered through the window to see Guinevere dancing in the garden as Lancelot played the piccolo, dancing beside her. Lancelot took her arm as they twirled and laughed, the two of them celebrating the end of each song with a kiss.

Agatha watched, mesmerized. All this time, she'd thought of them as woeful exiles, banished to purgatory and surely bored stiff of each other after six long years. Instead, they were swaying and kissing at midnight for no reason at all, like two punch-drunk teenagers. It didn't matter where they were, who was around them, what they had and what they didn't.

They still had each other.

They still had love.

Agatha colored with shame. Here she was, surrendering her prince because she was too afraid to fight for her own self-worth. And not only that, she was pretending she was doing it to protect Good's old heroes. What would those old heroes think of her now? A true princess didn't hide from her fate behind the shield of Good. A true princess knew fate wasn't just hers—but her prince's too. By not being with Tedros, she was ruining both of their lives. Gavaldon or Woods, royals or peasants, Good, Evil, Boys, Girls, Young, Old . . . none of it mattered as long as they were together.

She didn't have to be a queen. She had to be *his* queen.

And that, she knew how to do.

Without thinking, she was staggering out of the bedroom and down the hall. She flung open the front door and darted down the porch steps to the dewy moors. She squinted into the dark night, heart breaking . . .

Because it was too late. Tedros and Sophie were long gone.

Crestfallen, she hung her head and trudged back towards the door.

A soft crunching sound crackled in the distance.

Agatha looked up and saw a hulking outline far across the heath moving towards the house.

She slunk forward, eyes fixed ahead as they adjusted to the darkness.

"Hort?" she called out.

But now she recognized the heft of the walk . . . the long, muscular arms . . . the thick belt on his waist, missing a sword.

Tedros' gaze locked on her as he strode towards the house.

Before she knew it, Agatha was sprinting towards him and Tedros sprinting towards her. Stumbling in the dark, Agatha could hear herself panting, choking up, as his shadow hurtled towards her, faster, faster, until they collided like stars and Agatha fell. Tedros swept her up in his arms as she laughed and he kissed her long and hard, like he'd never kissed her before—

"You think I don't know you, Agatha," he whispered. "You think I can't see who you are."

"It's not enough for you to see it, Tedros," said Agatha. "I have to see it too."

"And now my whole kingdom will see it. The greatest

queen who will ever live."

Agatha stared into his eyes, so clear, so convinced. "But I'm just me—I'm just a girl . . . and you . . . you're . . ."

"You think I know how to be a *king*?" Tedros blurted.

"What? But you always act so—"

"Act. *Act!*" He shook his head, voice breaking. "Tell me you love me, Agatha. Tell me you'll never give me up again. Tell me you'll be my queen forever—"

"I love you, Tedros," Agatha wept. "I love you more than you know."

"Say the rest too!"

"I—"

But there were no more words, as tears streamed down their faces and mixed on their lips, the sugar and salt of love.

Far across the moors, Hort waited a long time after Tedros left the cave before he made his move. He'd followed the prince when he'd brought Sophie here, so it was unsettling to see him leave the cave without her. Skulking out from behind a tree, Hort stole through the opening, his fingertip glowing, until the sapphire walls blinded him with their glare.

"Sophie?" he called, shielding his eyes. "Sophie, where are you?"

But all Hort found was an unused sword and a spatter of black feathers, as if she'd been rescued away by a swan.

PART III

26

In Darkness Comes a Queen

When Sophie woke up in the School Master's tower, there was a dress waiting for her on the bed, spotlit by the dawn.

Now she stood at the window in the strapless black velvet, tight to her skin, with a long, flowing train that made her look like a sinister bride.

Across the bay, green fog snaked over the quiet black castles of Old and New, hazy beneath a morning sun no bigger than a yellow marble. *So peaceful,* she thought. All these years, she'd clawed and strained and agonized to be Good, trying to bully her way to Ever After. But as she looked

out at her Evil kingdom, Sophie realized she never should have tried at all. Two years ago, the School Master had put her in the school where she belonged—the school she was meant to one day rule. And if she'd just embraced that fact instead of denied it, if she'd just loved herself the way she was, she would have saved herself a world of pain.

She glanced down at her arms. "No warts or wrinkles yet. When will I, um, turn into a . . . you know . . ."

Rafal came up beside her, wearing a black velvet coat with a mandarin collar that matched his velvet trousers. "Professor Manley begins his first day of Uglification class by explaining why villains must be ugly to succeed. Ugliness releases you from the surface—from the prison of vanity and your own looks—and sets you free to embrace the soul within. The first time you turned into a witch, your soul needed you to be ugly so you could see beyond your beauty and access your own Evil. But you're a different witch now, Sophie. You accept yourself as you are, inside and out. Ugliness would serve you no purpose. Just as it serves no purpose to me."

She expected to feel relief at keeping her beauty, but instead felt a strange hollowness, as if what she looked like no longer mattered after all she'd been through. Her eyes moved to the ring on her finger. "It's black-swan gold, isn't it? You knew it would lead me to Tedros."

His mouth tightened, as if deliberating whether to find out how she'd learned this or to let go of anything that might have happened during the time she had strayed. "Let's put it this way," he said at last. "As long as you didn't destroy it, I knew it would lead you back to *me*."

"And what if I had destroyed it?" she asked, turning to him. "What if Tedros loved me?"

"A kiss of true love has to go both ways, remember? I'm quite sure the prince felt as little from your kiss as you felt from his." His face softened. "Besides . . . I'd rather you'd have killed me than deserted me forever."

Sophie looked down, quiet. Then she looked back at the beautiful, young School Master. "I'm sorry," she said. "I'm sorry for leaving—"

He put his finger to her lips. "You're here now. That's all that matters."

"You're not angry with me for betraying you?"

"How can I be angry when your betrayal made us stronger? If anything I should be thankful. That is, if it's you I'm meant to thank at all."

"What do you mean?"

Rafal bit his lip thoughtfully. "Your friend Agatha used to have a rare talent—the ability not just to hear wishes, but to grant them too. Her first year, she wasted her talent on pointless concerns: setting a few fish free, befriending a gargoyle, standing up for some wolves. . . . But now I suspect she's learned to use it on something more worthwhile." He stared into Sophie's eyes. "*You.*"

"What?" said Sophie, jarred. "How could she—"

"Your wish was to have Tedros kiss you, was it not? And it was Agatha who gave you and Tedros the clean slate to let that kiss happen. Perhaps she even went one step further, giving you your kiss with a prince like a genie from a lamp, knowing all along that Tedros would feel nothing and return to her in the end—his love for her stronger, because it'd been tested. That'd be something now, wouldn't it? Granting your wish in order to fulfill her own."

Sophie furrowed. "I know Agatha and Agatha doesn't think like that—"

"Not consciously, perhaps. But her soul spins towards Good the same way yours does towards Evil. Maybe she even thought in your heartbreak and anger at losing your prince, you'd turn your back on me too and destroy my ring. Good would have its perfect Ever After, clean and efficient, all because of a princess's secret talent."

Sophie's face calcified. "So she wanted me to end up *alone.*"

"Indeed," the young School Master smiled. "Only she hadn't counted on you discovering the difference between me and Prince Tedros of Camelot."

Sophie gazed into his riddling blue eyes. "What's that?"

Rafal's hand found her waist, pulling her in, and he pressed his lips to hers. His mouth was delicate yet firm, and from the moment it touched hers, Sophie felt her thoughts go silent, rapturously silent, like a dark bomb had imploded in her head. Then came her heart, rioting between fire and chills, as if it'd found its other half. He'd kissed her before, but this time she kissed him back harder, and as a breeze blew her hair over both their young faces, in streaks of sun-tinged gold, she knew there was no more guilt or doubt or shame, because she'd found love . . . everlasting love . . . as beautiful as it was Evil . . .

Rafal's lips floated off hers.

"The difference is to a girl like you, Evil feels *good*," he said.

Sophie could hear the Storian behind them, inking their kiss in a vibrant splash of color.

"And it's time I finally felt good, isn't it?" she grinned, feeling the dark stirrings of her heart.

She kissed her beautiful boy again, biting his lip so hard she tasted blood. "I'm your queen now, in heart and soul," she whispered.

Rafal licked his lips with pleasure and ran his hands through her hair. "Only one thing still missing, then . . ."

The dress was no accident, it turned out. He'd planned the whole ceremony while she was sleeping.

Now Sophie waited outside tall double doors inside the old Evil castle, her chest drumming with anticipation.

With a baleful creak, the dark-wood doors slid open and eerie off-key music began, like a wedding march played backwards. She looked up at two black fairies perched on the door, sliding their green stingers across tiny violins.

"Are you ready?" his voice said.

She turned to Rafal, his young face framed by a wall of defaced old portraits in the leaky stair room.

"Yes," she said.

His fingers slipped through hers and he led her through the open doors.

Everyone in the Theater of Tales stood up as Master and Queen paraded down the long silver aisle. Once divided into

Good and Evil, the vast, torchlit room was now fully devoted to Evil, Old and New. On one side of the aisle, the Dark Army of zombie villains watched from crumbling wooden pews, bounded by scorched walls spattered with green mold. Most of the old villains wore crossbone pins over their hearts, except for some of the most famous, including Red Riding Hood's wolf, Cinderella's stepmother, Jack's giant, and Captain Hook, alive despite the bloody sword wound in his chest. Hook flashed Sophie a cheeky smirk and she stiffened, reminding herself she was his queen and he could do nothing to hurt her.

"Crossbones mean they've killed their old Nemesis and rewritten their storybooks," Rafal whispered, noticing her expression. "Pesky old wizard's been hiding the most famous heroes in his so-called League. That's why the shield over your world has yet to fall. But they're running out of time. Soon Merlin and his League will come to us."

Sophie felt a hot glow of satisfaction at the thought of those foul old freaks being slain, after the way they'd bullied her in their cave.

"Readers are believing in the power of Evil, my queen," he said. "The shield hangs by a thread now. Any one of those famous heroes dead and Readers will surely lose their last faith in Good. The shield will break and then *you* will seal Evil's victory once and for all."

"How?" Sophie whispered back. "What do we need in Gavaldon?"

But Rafal only smiled.

Over his shoulder, Sophie glimpsed the other side of the

theater and her young Ever and Never classmates, who'd trekked across the Bridge from the old Good castle, and were standing in ivory pews made of polished bone. The last time she saw them, they looked defiant and resentful of their new Evil school. Now all of the young students were goggling across the aisle at the old villains, finally seeing what the School Master had been hiding in the other school and looking completely scared out of their wits. But joining the two schools wasn't the only thing that had brought the New students into line. Because as Sophie peered closer, she saw her former classmates had been sectioned into three groups.

In the front were the tracked Leaders, with gold swan pins over their hearts and new forest-green berets on their heads—Beatrix, Ravan, and Chaddick amongst them. In the middle pews, she spotted Reena, Nicholas, Arachne, and Vex amongst the tracked Henchmen, with silver swan pins and no hats at all. And behind these sidekicks, to Sophie's astonishment, was the final group: the lowest-ranked students, with bronze swan pins, who'd already begun the process of mogrification. Kiko sniffled back tears, trying to hide limbs covered with white goose feathers; Tarquin snorted through a pig's nose; Millicent itched at the deer antlers growing out of her red hair; and Brone's arms were already sprouting fresh, green leaves.

Serves them right, Sophie thought, *for being hopelessly incompetent.* She assumed Dot would be amongst the Mogrifs, turned into a chocolate-guzzling cow, but she couldn't spot her in any of the groups. Or Anadil for that matter, or . . .

Where were the witches? Sophie wondered, scanning the room.

But the only other people in the room were the Evil faculty against the back wall, with the Good teachers still nowhere to be found. Professor Manley and Professor Sheeks looked blissfully proud of their student-turned-queen, as did Castor, whose ferocious canine head had been reunited with his brother Pollux's on their dog's body. (Pollux waved at Sophie and dabbed at his eyes with a handkerchief, pretending to be happy for her.) Next to them, Sophie could see Lady Lesso, seemingly pleased she'd returned to Evil, while her son and fellow Dean stood at her side—

Sophie recoiled. Because Aric didn't look like a Dean anymore at all. He had a blackened eye, deep claw marks across a swollen nose, and the word "CREEP" had been slashed into the skin of his forehead and was only just starting to heal. He glowered back at Sophie, as if daring her to keep gawking.

Sophie turned away and caught her first glimpse of the raised stage at the front of the theater. The stone surface was cracked down the middle as always, but now there was a frost-blue mist seeping through the crack from beneath. If it was for magical effect, it was rather pitiful, Sophie thought, given the heft of the occasion. *Unless it isn't magic at all.* . . . As Rafal led her up the steps, she squinted through the crack, trying to see if there was something below the stage—

But then Sophie noticed what was *above* the stage.

A black crown of spikes floated high in the air, glimmering in the green flame light of a skull-shaped chandelier. It was the same crown she'd seen herself wearing in the E-V-I-L murals back at the old Good castle, her smiling, painted self wrapped in Rafal's arms.

Sophie matched the smile now, clutching her handsome love, as they took center stage. Two years ago, the Circus Crown dangled above this spot the same way, awaiting the winning student of the first-year talent contest. She'd won her crown that night by disavowing Good and embracing Evil . . . just as she would tonight.

Only this time, she wasn't alone.

So much for Agatha's wish, she smiled bitterly.

So much for Agatha at all.

As the whole theater watched, Rafal magically lowered Evil's crown onto Sophie's head, before he gently fit it in place and kissed her on the forehead. His cold lips clashed with the iron at her temples, still warm from the chandelier flames, and she closed her eyes, imprinting the feeling and moment into her memory. When she opened her eyes, the young School Master was turned to his audience.

"Light fades over our Woods and darkness rises. And in darkness comes a queen," he declared. "Like every true love, Sophie and I have gone through harsh trials to find and commit to each other. But doubt and pain have only made us stronger. Now we are as unshakable as any two Evers who loved for Good. But our love, bonded by Evil, is still not enough to win our Never After. For Evil to find its first happy ending in two hundred years, a happy ending that will bring forth a Golden Age of wickedness and sin . . ." He stepped to the edge of the stage. "We need each of you."

The theater was dead quiet now.

"In seven days, the Woods will go dark," said Rafal. "We must enter the Reader World before the seventh sunset or all our lives will be at an end. With the most famous heroes yet to be killed, Readers still cling to their faith in Good. But that will soon change. For now that my queen has returned, the forces of Good have no choice but to attack our castle. Killing me is the *only* way they can win. I assure you, then, that Merlin and his heroes will charge our School for Evil before the week is done. Our mission is to kill these old heroes and break the Readers' last faith in Good. That is our path into their world where we will seal Evil's victory once and for all. Until Merlin's heroes arrive, however, every one of us—young and old, Ever and Never, Leaders, Henchmen, and Mogrifs of future and past—must work together to defend our school. Our Deans of Evil and teachers shall lead our preparations and you *will* obey them."

He clasped Sophie's hand. "In the past, Evil has lost every war because it had only something to fight against, rather than something to fight for. But now you have a queen who has given Evil a true chance at glory. A queen who once sat in the very seats in which you sit. A queen who will fight for you the way you fight for her."

Rafal's face hardened. "And if anyone dare question that queen, then they will suffer the fate of all those who have failed their allegiance to Evil . . ."

The stage began to rattle, as if shaken by an earthquake, and Sophie teetered against Rafal in surprise. All at once the stone stage tore apart at the crack, cold-blue mist spewing through the widening gap, until it cleared over a deep chasm and Sophie could see beneath the stage.

Hidden in the bowels of Evil's old castle was a cavernous frozen dungeon, with hundreds of bodies encased in ice. The first face Sophie saw was Professor Emma Anemone, eyes shocked wide under manic, blond curls, sealed in an ice tomb cut into the dungeon wall. Next to her, Dean Clarissa Dovey had her own glacial grave, her silver bun and rosy cheeks blurred by the ice—though Sophie noticed a shattered hole at the edge, where Anadil's rat must have burrowed through and borrowed Dovey's wand the night Agatha and Tedros broke in.

"The Brig of Betrayers holds all those who've shirked their loyalties to Evil throughout the history of our school—including the old faculty of the School for Good, who were each given the chance to teach for their *new* school and all refused," said Rafal.

Pollux sniffed grievously from the back of the stage, expecting acknowledgment.

Rafal ignored him. "And lucky for you, today we have three fresh inmates to the Brig . . ."

Shrill squeaks echoed above him and the audience craned up to see Hester, Anadil, and Dot, bound together with rope, lowered over a pulley from the rafters by giggly Beezle.

"These three so-called Nevers conspired to let our enemies through our gates, while one even mutilated our own *Dean* with her Evil-given talent," said the School Master, leering at Hester and her demon as both writhed against the suffocating binds. "Yet even the most guilty betrayers deserve a fair trial, before they're condemned to the Brig for an *indefinite* sentence . . ."

The three witches were hardly paying attention now, for they'd caught sight of Sophie, returned to the School Master's side with her menacing crown.

"So I leave their fate to my queen, who, in addition to being intimately familiar with the accused, once even shared a room with them," said Rafal, turning to Sophie. "So what do you say, my love? Spare them? Or condemn them?"

Sophie saw the witches hone in on her, silently pleading for mercy. Even Hester, who'd rather pluck out her own eye than show weakness, looked scared out of her wits.

How much we've been through together, thought Sophie, she and the Three Witches of Room 66. For all their tempestuous ups and downs, she'd almost come to think of them as friends.

Almost.

For these were the friends who'd always believed she'd end up alone . . . friends who pushed Agatha to side with her prince over her . . . friends who'd spied on her inside her own school . . . friends who'd never been there for her when she needed them most . . .

And now they expected *her* to be their white-knight hero when they needed her.

Sophie's face went cold. If there was one moral to her fairy tale, it was that the witches were right all along. Nothing good ever came of her trying to be Good.

"Condemn them," she said.

"No!" cried Dot—

Rafal smirked at the terrified witches. "Then I'm afraid this is goodbye." He raised his finger to sever the rope over the Brig—

"Never was fond of goodbyes," piped a voice above him.

Rafal looked up.

Merlin smiled down from the rafters, holding Beezle by the throat. "Mama!" the dwarf shrieked—

Rafal stabbed out his finger, but Merlin shot first and a blast of fire exploded down the rope, hurling Rafal and Sophie off the stage and rocketing Beezle like a cannonball into the pews. From the ground, Sophie's eyes fluttered open and she saw zombie villains stampeding the stage, Rafal lurching to his feet, the smoke over the rope clearing . . .

But Merlin and the witches were long gone.

The young School Master roared his fury and led the crush of villains from the theater to hunt the fugitives—

Sophie scrambled up from the floor to join them, only to stall in her tracks. For there was something in the lap of her dress, something that wasn't there before.

A small five-pointed star, smoking bright white against black velvet . . . like a wizard's reminder of Good left behind.

As the sun ascended over the moors, Agatha leaned against an oak tree in a baggy brown shirt she'd borrowed from Lancelot, her hair greasy and bedraggled, her stomach groaning with hunger. She glanced down at a diadem of silver and diamonds, shimmering from a small wooden box in Guinevere's hands.

"Did Lance give you that? It's lovely, I think, but I'm clueless about jewelry and clothes and anything that involves, you know . . . girls," she said groggily. After being up half the night with Tedros and scavenging a few hours of sleep, the prince's mother had dragged her from the house this morning, insisting she had something to show her. If Agatha had known it'd be about frilly headpieces, she would have stayed in bed.

"It is a bit formal, though. The type of thing you'd wear to a Ball or a wedding, so not exactly practical for gallivanting on the moors . . ."

Agatha's voice trailed off. Where out here would Lancelot get silver and diamonds? Did he go spelunking into gem mines between shoveling horse poo and milking goats?

Half-asleep, she peered at the diadem and its loops of diamonds dangling off the silver circlet. It didn't seem new at all, for that matter. And the closer she looked at it, the more a squeezing feeling rose through her throat, because suddenly she was sure she'd seen this piece before . . .

In a pond's moonlit reflection . . .

Shining bright inside a Wish Fish painting . . .

Fixed atop her very own head.

Slowly Agatha raised eyes to Guinevere, who looked regal and imposing despite her weathered face and grubby housedress.

"This is . . . this is your . . ."

"I'm afraid it's yours now," said Guinevere. "Formal and impractical, as it may be."

"*Mine?* No, no, no—not mine at all—" Agatha croaked, backing into the tree.

"When Lance and I spotted you and Tedros together last night on the moors, I was so cross with myself," Guinevere sighed. "I should have known Merlin had the names right that Christmas, if only from the way you stared at me during supper when I got it wrong. How could I be so daft? I suppose sometimes it's easier to see the simplest answer instead of the truth. That has always been hard for me." She smiled sternly, holding out the box. "But now there will be no more mistakes."

Agatha gaped owlishly at the crown and flicked the box shut. "Look, I can't take this! I'm not queen yet! I'm not anything yet—I haven't even taken a bath—"

"Good cannot wait anymore for its queen, Agatha," said Guinevere, hardening. "Last night, your friend Hort went searching for Sophie and discovered she'd vanished from our safe haven and magically returned to the School Master."

For a moment, Agatha thought she'd misheard or that this was all a sick joke, but nothing in Guinevere's face suggested either. "What? Sophie went back to *h-h-him?* But that's impossible—there's no way to leave this place—"

"The Lady of the Lake can only protect those who ally themselves with Good. All your friend had to do was wish to rejoin the School Master and he could break through the lake's enchantments and rescue her," Guinevere replied. "Poor Hort was gutted after he found her missing. Said he'd do anything to kill the School Master and get her away from him. So he stayed up with me and Lance and told us as much of your and Sophie's story as we needed to know. And from what I've heard, Agatha, I have no doubt that your friend has committed to be Evil's queen with all her heart. You must take your place as Good's queen with the same resolve and belief. Or you and my son will not stand a chance."

Agatha said nothing, the words "my son" hanging between them.

A long moment passed. Slowly Agatha's fingers crept into Guinevere's palm and cracked open the wooden box just a sliver. "You, uh, kept your crown all this time?"

"Arthur's crown remains at Camelot until Tedros claims it," the former queen replied patiently. "But I rode with mine the night I fled the castle, hoping the guards would assume I was on official business and wouldn't wake Arthur from his sleep. All these years I wanted to destroy the crown so that Lance and I could forget that part of my story ever happened. . . . But the truth is, I'm still a queen and I'm still a mother, Agatha. Nothing can change that, even if I hide away from the world. And as the holder of the crown, one of my duties to my kingdom, my son, and myself, no matter how much I've failed all three, is to pass that crown on."

Her voice faltered and she composed herself. "I know I can never have a relationship with my child. I don't deserve to. But I still have to protect Tedros as best I can. And the only way I can do that is by making sure he has the queen that Arthur never had. A queen who isn't just sure of her crown, but is ready to fight for it when the time comes."

Her hand slipped down and lifted the diadem out of the

box. Agatha could feel her heart throttling as Guinevere raised it into the sun.

"And that time is *now*."

Agatha expected more protest to sputter out of her and her body to pull away . . . but instead she stayed in place, something changing inside. Looking up at Camelot's crown, Agatha felt fear and tension melt away, as if the queen's words had called up a part of her deeper than herself. Fire and purpose ripped through her, like armor beneath her skin, usurping the old Agatha and steeling her shoulders and chest.

Guinevere was right. This wasn't about her anymore.

This was about two sides, warring for love.

She and Tedros fighting for Good. Sophie and the School Master fighting for Evil.

Once upon a time, she and her best friend tried to find a happy ending together. Now only one of them could come out alive.

Right then and there, Agatha knew why she couldn't have an ordinary life.

She was never meant for one.

Because as long as her story was about her—her worth, her love, her future—she resisted her fate, as if living for herself was too much responsibility.

But the moment she saw her fate was bigger than her . . . as big as Good itself . . . she finally felt free to embrace it.

Slowly Agatha lowered her head to the queen as strands of light silver sprinkled over her forehead and a glare of red sun exploded against diamond edges.

Agatha looked up to see Guinevere clasp her hands to her mouth, fixed in a dazzling smile.

It was the only mirror Agatha needed.

Suddenly Guinevere paled, her smile gone—

Agatha spun to see Tedros across the field, watching them.

"I'll go—" Guinevere started.

"No . . . stay," her son ordered.

He moved towards Agatha in a grass-stained shirt and rumpled breeches, his eyes on his princess. "Everyone just . . . stay."

As he approached, Agatha could smell dew and sweat on him and see the sleepless circles under his eyes. He ran his fingertips over the diadem, remembering its every bump and crevice, but his focus was still on her, his hand drifting down from the crown to her cheek to her mouth. Without a word, he bent and kissed her, long and slow, as if to make sure it was still the old Agatha inside and out.

"You're not allowed to take it off," he whispered.

"Not even a 'good morning' before you start bossing me around," said Agatha. "Besides, are you trying to give orders to a queen?"

"Oh, so *today* you're a queen," Tedros said, pulling her closer.

"Late bloomer if you haven't noticed," said Agatha.

"Well, even so . . . a king is still a king."

"Which means that your queen is *beneath* you?"

"No, only that you should do as you're told."

"Or what?" Agatha chortled. "You'll put a death sentence on my—"

She saw Tedros' face and her whole body went cold.

Both of them turned to Guinevere, still there, white as a ghost.

"What's this?" Lancelot's voice blustered, as the knight galumphed into the grove with Hort. "A coronation we're not invited to?"

"I'm never invited to anything," Hort muttered.

Neither Tedros, Agatha, nor Guinevere acknowledged them.

"Well, it's about time that blasted crown came to some use after all the trouble it's caused us," Lancelot added. "Though you might want to give the girl a proper dress while you're at it. Diamonds don't go well with that shirt."

Nobody laughed.

"A swimming start to the morning," the knight cracked. "Well, make your wish, Agatha, and be done with it. Time for lunch and there's still chores to be done."

Agatha looked at him. "Wish?"

Lancelot frowned. "At a proper coronation, you make a wish for your kingdom once you're anointed with the crown. It's the closing rite of the ceremony. Surely Gwen told you that much."

"I'm afraid I've done a poor job, then," Guinevere said softly, looking at her son.

Tedros held her gaze for a moment and turned away.

"Then I should make my wish, shouldn't I?" said Agatha, studying her prince. She stood up straighter. "I wish that all of us can sit down and have lunch together."

Tedros' eyes snapped to her.

Guinevere froze to stone. Lancelot and Hort both held their breaths.

Agatha stayed locked on her prince, waiting for his answer.

Tedros said nothing, staring back at Agatha in her new crown.

The grove was quiet.

Tedros turned to his mother.

"Well, what are you making?" he asked.

Guinevere went apple red. Then her face crumbled and she shook her head, flooding hot tears. "It's—it's Monday—I-I-I don't have any food—"

"Hear that, boy?" said Lancelot. "Mum ain't got any food. That's what the death sentence was really for, wasn't it?"

Everyone gaped at him in horrified silence.

Then Agatha burst into cackles.

Seeing her, Tedros tried to resist, but started snickering too.

His mother was sobbing so hard she couldn't breathe, years of pent-up emotion pouring out of her. "It's not . . . not funny—"

The prince hung his arm around her and held her tight as she heaved into his chest. "We'll handle it, Mother," he whispered. "Everything's going to be okay."

Watching Guinevere and Tedros together, Agatha felt overwhelmed with emotion. They needed time alone, without anyone else—

"Leave making lunch to me and the boys," she said quickly, eyeing Lancelot as she took Hort's hand.

"Me?" Hort blurted. "Why can't the pampered prince do it? I didn't get a wink of sleep and then spent half the morning wrangling hogs while you and him spent last night snuggling in the barn, doing God knows wha—"

Agatha dug her nails into his wrist, making him yelp. "We'll be back with food soon," she said, dragging him off.

"You'll need a lot more than you think," a voice called.

Agatha turned to see a parade of silhouettes striding out of sun flare over the moors.

Merlin led them, followed by Hester, Anadil, Dot, Peter Pan, Tinkerbell, Cinderella, Pinocchio, Jack, Sleeping Beauty, Hansel, Gretel, Red Riding Hood, Yuba, the White Rabbit, and Princess Uma, all filthy, weary, and gawking around the magical moors as if they'd crossed through a portal from hell into paradise.

"I'll take care of the lunch menu," said Merlin, "though we'll have to endure some grumbling from my hat. He's only just recovered from serving breakfast. But we have a lot to discuss and there isn't much ti—"

The wizard stopped hard at the sight of Agatha in her crown. So did everyone behind him, a rapt silence overtaking the moors.

Merlin smiled, his eyes big and blue. "In darkness comes a queen," he whispered.

Slowly the old man bent down to one knee before Agatha and bowed his head. So did all his charges behind him, young and old. Then Guinevere, Lancelot, Hort . . . until Tedros gazed at Agatha squarely and sank to his knee too.

In that moment, beneath a dying sun, with an army of heroes kneeling before her, Agatha made a second wish. That she would be the queen that Good needed her to be.

"I don't see the big deal," Cinderella mumbled so everyone could hear. "Looks like a giraffe in her granny's crown."

But as they all walked towards the house together, the League's heroes sniffling quietly, Agatha could even see a tear in the old princess's eye.

~ 27 ~

Rebel Hearts

"What if Merlin marshals the Ever kingdoms against us?" Sophie heard Professor Manley ask.

"For the last time, Bilious, Good *defends*, not attacks; the Ever kingdoms will not fight us if we do not fight them," Rafal's voice growled. "Besides, they know better than to risk their people for a few decrepit heroes. Not that this will save them, of course. Once Sophie and I prove that Evil can win, we'll destroy the Ever kingdoms one by one."

"And what if more of our students turn out to be spies for Good?" asked Professor Sheeks.

"What if Princess Uma brings an animal army?" pushed Pollux.

"If you're worried about our students'

ability to fight *animals*, then I wonder what business you have being a teacher at all," the young School Master fired. "As for spies, Sheeba, I believe the threat of imprisonment in the Brig will deter any further rebellion."

"'Cause that worked real well tonight," Castor murmured.

Sophie wasn't paying attention to them as she inspected the food laid out at the back of Lady Lesso's old frozen classroom. Rafal had promised they'd serve lunch at the faculty meeting, but all she'd found was a stinking heap of cold mackerel, burnt potatoes, and crusty cheese.

She glimpsed her reflection in an iced wall and almost didn't recognize herself. Gone was the panicked, needy girl who'd chased a prince to Avalon and in her place, an imperious queen in a spiked crown and maleficent gown. Ever since yesterday's coronation before famous villains and former classmates, standing in homage to their new leader, Sophie had begun to feel like her old self. She glanced down at Merlin's white star, which she'd buried in her pocket. No doubt he'd left it to make her rethink her allegiance to Evil. Instead it had only recommitted her. Because like Agatha, that hoary, two-faced wizard had *used* her all along. He'd pretended to rescue her because he wanted to see her happy—when he'd just needed her to destroy her ring. Like Agatha, he didn't care if she ended up alone. She was nothing but a means to an end. A gullible stooge. A cog in Good's wheel.

And that didn't seem Good to her at *all*.

Oh, what she would have given to see that scheming meddler thrown into the iced dungeons, with his stupid cape and infernal hat and doddering quips. Next time, she'd handle sealing prisoners in the Brig herself.

Her eyes refocused on the pitiful buffet and she glanced back at the seated teachers—Professor Manley, Professor Sheeks, Castor, Pollux, and Lady Lesso—who each had full plates of putrid food. Dean Aric was the only one missing from the gathering.

"I say the biggest problem we have is that we crammed all the Evil students into the old Good school and those numpty Nevers don't know that castle from their own arse," Castor grouched. "Keep locking themselves in closets and falling down secret passageways. How can they protect a school if they don't know where anything is—"

"The biggest problem we have is the *food*," Sophie's voice boomed.

Everyone in the room turned.

"If this is what's served at a faculty meeting—to the queen herself—what are the *students* enduring?" Sophie said, sitting beside Rafal on Lady Lesso's old ice desk. She slipped her arm under his. "Now that I've been crowned, I have the right to make a few changes around here. And you can't very well lead an Evil army that's bloated and malnourished, can you, darling?"

For a moment, the young School Master looked just as dumbstruck as the teachers. Then he touched Sophie's cheek. "Of course, my queen."

"Lovely," said Sophie. She glared at Pollux. "Do something about the food."

Pollux looked as if he'd been pelted with manure.

Lady Lesso cleared her throat. "Rafal—"

"You mean *Master*," said Sophie.

Lady Lesso's eyes flicked to her. The Dean gave her an amused look, as one might give a puppet claiming to have a mind of its own.

"Master," she simpered, back to Rafal, "I think what the rest of my colleagues are trying to say is that one cannot approach the coming war like an impetuous *child*. If Hester and Anadil, two of our best Nevers, turned out to be spies for Good, how can we trust the rest to be faithful to our cause? Tracking them into their future groups might sedate their instincts to rebel, but it cannot address their deeper loyalties. When faced with the choice of fighting with us or against us, we cannot predict what many of them will do, particularly those Evers whose families have fought for Good their whole lives. And speaking frankly, *Master*, to believe otherwise is to let your new youth impair your judgment."

Sophie flared. "Quite sure Rafal and I know more about what young people think than *you* do, Lady Lesso."

"Really?" The Dean fixed on her, the amusement gone. "Because all I see is a school full of students who will turn on you the second they get a chance."

Sophie felt Rafal's arm tighten. He suddenly looked like an unsure teenager instead of an all-powerful sorcerer. How could he let the teachers question him like this?

Sophie puffed her chest. "Lady Lesso, I find it offensive that you would impugn our Master's leadershi—"

"What is it you're proposing, Lady Lesso?" Rafal asked, ignoring his queen.

Sophie went quiet.

"I propose that you avoid the students fighting for you at *all*," said Lady Lesso. "Take the old villains into the Woods and ambush Merlin's forces before they reach our gates. Let the Dark Army finish them off before they ever get to school. The students will remain barricaded at school under our control."

"It is the most sensible plan," said Professor Manley, as if he and Lady Lesso had already discussed it. "Our students would only hamper your army."

"It will prevent spies or sabotage," said Professor Sheeks, clearly privy to the plan.

"And it will save students' lives," added Castor, apparently part of the team too.

(Pollux frowned, as if it was the first he was hearing of it.)

"So the old villains will fight the battle while the young students lounge *here*?" Sophie glowered, incredulous. "And I assume you, our virtuous and valiant faculty, will avoid the front line too?"

"Can't very well leave the students unsupervised, can we? Given their *dubious* loyalties," Lady Lesso glowered back, as if she wanted to gag Sophie with her crown.

Rafal smiled dryly at the teachers. "This isn't about loyalties at all, is it? You don't think we'll win. Now that I have youth on my side, you think I might lose this war."

"Youth also brings with it reckless optimism and a willingness to risk the lives of fellow youth. Neither of which are useful in war," said Lady Lesso. "A war where half your own forces may not be on your side."

Rafal held her eyes, but Sophie could see he was questioning himself even more now. She wanted him to punish Lady Lesso, to show his full strength as Evil's leader . . .

The young Master picked at his collar and looked away dismissively. "I'm afraid you've wasted your breath, Lady Lesso. Truth is, I'd already decided upon leaving the students at school before you ever mentioned it."

"I bet," Castor mumbled.

Sophie touched Rafal's waist. "Leaving the students *behind*, darling? Are you sure—"

The door crashed open and Aric stormed in.

"Can't believe you let them get away after what that demon-skinned wench did to me," Aric fumed, the "CREEP" slashed into his forehead glowing bloodred. "Told you we should have gutted them and served them in meat pies at supper."

"Because *that* would surely inspire loyalty from their fellow students," Lady Lesso scorned. "You and the young School Master should replace our entire faculty with hot-headed, teenage boys. You could rename the towers Brashness, Arrogance, and Thuggery."

Aric shoved his face in hers and grabbed her by the throat. "You think because you scared that demon off me, you can talk to me like that? You think because you called a few teachers to help your wounded 'little boy,' all is forgiven?" he snarled, spit flying. "Well, I blame *you* for that witch-spy attacking me in the first place. You taught her these past two years, so clearly something went wrong in her education if she attacks her own *Dean*." Aric squeezed her neck harder. "But you're the Old Dean and I'm the New, mother. Which means when you're out, I'm in and this school goes my way. And trust me when I say you'll be out sooner than you *think*."

Lady Lesso gurgled for breath—

"Aric, I'd prefer you kill your mother after the war is over," said Rafal.

Sophie noticed his tone was dead serious.

Aric sensed this too, for he smirked at his mother and whispered in her ear. "And before I kill you, I'll kill your old fairy godmother friend too. Dovey, is it? I'll tear out her heart with my bare hands and make you watch." He released her quickly and pulled back. "Of course, School Master. Please go on."

Lady Lesso showed no emotion, but when her son turned to his seat, Sophie saw her eyes flicker with terror and her hand brush the marks he'd left on her throat.

"Then our plan for war is set," Rafal resumed. "Once Merlin and his heroes approach, the old villains will ambush them in the Woods, while the young students defend the castles, under the teachers' supervision. You will not tell the young students they're staying behind in the coming war, of course. For the next week, they will train rigorously for combat alongside the old villains. This will ensure they're prepared in case any of Merlin's heroes make it past the Dark Army onto school grounds. As to who will be Training Leader of both schools—"

"*Me,*" Aric and Lady Lesso both spouted.

Rafal ignored Lady Lesso and began to nod at Aric—

"I have a better idea," said Sophie.

Rafal, Aric, and the rest of the faculty all turned to her.

"Hope it's as good an idea as the food one," Castor muttered, drawing snickers.

"HOW *DARE* YOU," Sophie hissed.

The room went still.

"I am your *queen*," said Sophie, slinking towards the teachers. "Not a student, not a teacher, but a Master of both. Just like the young Master who sits in front of you and yet you continue to disrespect. No wonder our students doubt their loyalties to Evil when they have old, bitter teachers who see no value in youth or a young Dean who can't even protect himself." She leered at Aric as she circled the teachers like a shark. "But that will change starting today. Because now they have *me*.

"When I was first appointed as a teacher, I resisted it. In my heart I still felt I was supposed to be Good. That's what Readers like me are taught, after all: Never lose your faith in Good, no matter how lost you are. And yet, the Good towers may have once been named Valor, Honor, Purity, and Charity . . . but when I was lost, it was Evil that extended me those things. The rules say Good defends, forgives, helps, gives, loves . . . but in my story, it's Evil that's proven these rules true. And suddenly I understood what Rafal has been trying to tell me all along. That some hearts are rebel hearts, pumping with anger and darkness and pain the way others pump with light. And yet, even if my heart beats for Evil, that doesn't mean I can't find love. That doesn't mean I can't find happiness. It just means I have to find love with someone who embraces my darkness instead of fighting it. Because that's the love that will change the world. That's the love that will win this war. And that's the love we must teach."

Sophie paused, letting these words echo in the quiet room. "I was with Merlin, Tedros, and Agatha the past two weeks. I was face-to-face with all those wretched heroes in their cave. I know their weaknesses and how to beat them. And if you still doubt me, then perhaps you should remember that the last rite of any coronation is a queen's wish for her kingdom. I didn't have a chance to make my wish then, but I'll make it now. My wish is to do what I couldn't do the first time I was at this school: to lead this war against Good and know that righteousness is on *our* side. All of you may not trust Evil can win this war. You may choose to stay behind with the students and cower from the future. But not me. I'll prepare our Dark Army for war. I'll stand with Rafal at the front line. I'll do whatever it takes to show the world that Evil can win. Because this isn't just my fairy tale now. It's all of ours. And in the end, my life is worth risking if it means more rebel hearts will finally have a happy ending."

Her cheeks were red, her chest thumping.

The teachers gazed back at her. They weren't snickering anymore. Instead their eyes shined with a new hope, as if Evil finally had a chance indeed.

Rafal clasped Sophie's hand. "Well, then," he said proudly. "I believe we've found our Training Leader."

Sophie gave him a regal smile and turned to Lady Lesso,

expecting her to be just as proud of how far her former student had come . . .

Only Lady Lesso didn't look proud of her at all.

Once lunch was served, Merlin cleared his throat and prepared to speak, but no one paid the slightest attention. They were far too busy with the food.

With more than twenty people to serve—thirteen old heroes, three young witches, a former queen and her knight, a future queen and king, and a loveless weasel—Merlin's hat had hidden away in the kitchen, letting out shrieks of stress, until one by one, silver platters began magically floating through the swinging door. Soon the dining table was a smorgasbord of colorful, cosmopolitan delights: truffled crab salad, curried venison with beetroot jelly, shredded duck in a citrus marinade, peppered-ham pizza on roasted pitas, a yogurt-and-mint olive tapenade, fennel and wildflower salad, and a chocolate bouchon cake with crispy honeycomb.

With the old League heroes starving from their travails in the Woods and the youngsters deprived of breakfast by the morning's events, the dining room quickly turned into a battle scene, so crowded and muggy with jostling bodies and hands stabbing for pizza and cake that Agatha didn't even bother looking for Tedros. Nor did she search for her prince after lunch, for she'd eaten too much and too fast and had to hide behind a sofa in the den where she could clutch her belly and burp in private. Glancing up, she saw everyone else had the same idea; each nook and cranny of the farmhouse was filled with a young or old body, nursing indigestion or passed out in a food coma.

Agatha yawned and closed her eyes, about to join the comatose, when she heard three backsides plunk to the floor.

"After everything we did to get you in and out of that school, after risking our lives for you, you couldn't even get Sophie to destroy the *ring*?" Hester's voice attacked.

Agatha opened her eyes. "I tried, Hester—"

"First of all, you can't talk to your friends in a diamond crown. It's pretentious," said Anadil.

Agatha had forgotten she even had it on. She quickly pulled off the diadem and shoved it behind her back.

"Can I wear it for a bit?" Dot asked, mouth full of pizza turned to chocolate. "I bet it'll look nice on me."

"If it can fit around that head," Hester mumbled.

Dot hurled her pizza at her, smacking Hester in the cheek. "Do you know how unfair that is, you contemptuous git! You made me gain weight in order to stay in the coven and now you're making fun of me for it? Are you that insecure that you needed me to be fat to feel okay about yourself? Well, you picked the wrong piggy tail to pull, honey. I love myself no matter what I look like, so nothing you say to me will ever make me feel ugly again. Because unlike you, Hester, I'll never be ugly *inside*."

Hester gaped at Dot like she was a rabid bear. "Agatha. Give the girl the damned crown before she stays this way forever."

Dot snatched the diadem out of Agatha's hands and

admired herself in a brass urn as she jammed it on (upside down and backwards, but no one said a thing).

"Now where were we," said Anadil. "Oh right. The part where Agatha fails us all."

Any pleasure Agatha took from Dot's tirade evaporated. "Listen, I thought I could convince Sophie to destroy the ring. We'd even gotten close again in the last few days. It was like she was the old Sophie and I was the old me and I thought she'd listen . . ." She remembered their last moments together and guilt rushed through her. "I had my chance. I should have taken it—"

"You don't have to defend yourself, Agatha. The truth is it doesn't matter what you would have done," Hester said with awkward sympathy, clearly smarting from Dot's words. "We've warned you since the day you got here. All three of us did. Sophie was sorted into the School for Evil for a reason. And no matter how much you love her or try to change her, that's where she was always going to end up."

"We just didn't think it'd be as the School Master's *queen*," said Anadil. "How we're going to make Sophie destroy his ring now . . ."

A quiet doom fell over the witches' faces and Agatha realized why everyone had ignored Merlin when he'd tried to speak before lunch. They wanted a few precious moments before they had to face the truth.

The truth that Sophie destroying her own ring was the only way to kill the School Master and stop him from killing *them*. And now that Sophie had returned to Evil, there was no hope of her destroying that ring at all.

"Did you see her when she came back?" Agatha asked softly.

"Saw her the way we saw you when we first came through the portal: wearing her new crown," said Hester.

"Only with four hundred more people in the audience," said Dot, still making kissy-faces in the urn.

"She did look beautiful, I have to say," Anadil added thoughtfully. "Paraded into the Theater of Tales on a handsome boy's arm, just like the old Sophie, who believed her destiny was so much bigger than everyone else's. The strange thing was how calm and composed she was. Not like that warty, deranged witch who savaged anything in sight. It was as if Evil had finally opened her path to a happy ending."

"As if Evil had the right to win," nodded Dot.

"As if Evil was Good," Hester finished.

Agatha thought of Sophie, who just a few days ago had nuzzled her head against her as they rode across the moors. Sophie, her prissy, pink-dressed best friend who fantasized about being a princess for Good. Sophie, who would draw glass castles, ponder her future prince's name, and mull what her Evil archenemy would look like—while Agatha had been branded as Evil from the day she was born. She'd retaliated by ironically playing along, wearing black and lurking in her graveyard and nursing her hateful little cat . . . until the irony wore off and even she believed she'd end up a witch.

Now here they were. She, the queen for Good. Sophie, the queen for Evil.

"How'd we get so lost?" she breathed. "How can two best

friends end up at war against each other, even though they still love each other?"

"Because each of you is fighting for something bigger than yourself now," said Hester.

Agatha hung her head. "I miss the days where my biggest worry was surviving makeovers in Beautification."

"Speaking of makeovers, anyone notice Hort's looking even juicier than he did at school?" chirped Dot, biting into the cocoa-pizza she'd swiped off the floor. "Saw him when we came in and he has this swarthy tan from working the moors and mud stains on his cheeks, like he's Captain Lumberjack or something. But you know how I like woodsy types, with my crush on Robin Hood and all. Anyway, I sneak behind and give him a good sniff and notice he smells like a man now, nothing like that boy who used to wear frog pajamas and reek of baby powder, and all I could think was since there aren't too many rooms in this place, I wonder if I can get Merlin to put me and him in the same—"

"Over my dead body," bellowed Hort, who stuck his head out from around the corner.

Hester glared back, demon twitching. "That can be arranged."

Hort muttered something obscene and vanished behind the wall.

Hester saw Dot goggling at her. "What now?"

"Did you just *defend* me?"

"Only because you look so stupid in that crown," Hester grumped.

All the girls laughed, even Dot.

"What'd I miss?"

They looked up at Tedros, licking yogurt off his fingers.

"Ugh. The old ball and chain," Hester moaned.

"Nice to see you're as awful as always, even when you're working for our side," said the prince.

"Let's go," said Hester to her coven-mates as she stood up. "The smell of spoiled prince makes me sick."

Anadil and Dot followed her, but not before Tedros swiped at Dot's head and snatched back the crown.

He waited until the witches were out of earshot and peered down at Agatha. "I don't, uh, you know . . . smell, do I?"

"Hester thinks Reaper is *cute*," said Agatha.

"Point made." Tedros sat down next to her, still in his grass-stained shirt and ragged breeches, but he'd taken a bath, because his hair was wet and he smelled of the tea-scented soap Guinevere kept by the tub. He leaned over and fixed the crown back on her head.

"I knew you'd do that," Agatha sighed. "I'm not even a real queen, Tedros. For one thing, you have to be crowned king first—"

"I will be in a week."

"If we're alive, which is looking more and more doubtful," said Agatha. "And even if you are crowned king, I'm too young to be a queen . . . officially, I mean . . . you know . . ."

"No one's asking you to be official. Yet," said Tedros, straightening her crown. "But you *are* my queen. No one but you. And I like seeing you wear it. Because as long as you do, I know you still love me. And given our history of miscommunication, physical cues are helpful."

Agatha snorted.

"This is where you tell me how I can show my love," Tedros prodded.

"Uh, romance isn't really my thing," said Agatha, resting her head on his shoulder. "Every year, there's a Valentine's Day dance in Gavaldon. One year, I got so annoyed by all the couples I set off a flaming skunk bomb and cleared the place."

"I hope they punished you for it."

"They were too scared I'd boil their children in a witch stew."

Tedros put his arm around her. "Remind me never to give you something for Valentine's Day."

Through the archway, Agatha could see Guinevere in the dining room, collecting dirty dishes by herself.

"There's nothing I'd want anyway," she said. "Only gift I'd ever want is to talk to my mother one more time."

Tedros looked at her.

"Though if you could find a time to talk to your mother, just the two of you, that would mean nearly as much," said Agatha.

Tedros looked away. "I think I've come far enough on that front."

"You asked me for a way to show your love," said Agatha. "I didn't know it had limits."

Tedros didn't answer and Agatha didn't press him. Soon

both of them were asleep in each other's arms.

By three o'clock, Merlin's hat had finished floating around the den, serving coffee and tea, and one by one, everyone began to drift back to the dining room, where the wizard was sitting at the head of the table. No one sat with him. Instead, the old heroes hugged the walls and the young students crouched on the floor, engaged in idle chatter, while the wizard just waited patiently. When an ominous silence fell, the old heroes quickly began filling it with stories of how they'd survived these past two weeks.

Peter Pan and Tinkerbell, for instance, had bunkered with the mermaids of Neverland, while Cinderella and Pinocchio had hidden in Rapunzel's tower, reasoning that if Rapunzel was already dead, then the old villains certainly weren't going to frequent the place.

"Her tower is a museum now, like Snow's house, so there's a rope that lets tourists climb all the way inside," said Pinocchio. "Shoulda seen Ella climb, swinging and slamming against the tower like a wrecking ball. Kept whistling for birds to help, but with all her squawking and cursing, they just stood back and let nature take its course—"

"If nature took its course, you'd be *firewood*," Cinderella snarled.

Hansel and Gretel had used a similar strategy, for they'd returned to their witch's old gingerbread house, also an Evers' landmark now.

"Zombie witch is stupid but not so stupid to think we go

back to her house," explained Hansel. "My idea, of course."

"*Your* idea! Only thing you did was eat half the roof!" Gretel barked.

Agatha noticed Hester gnashing her teeth as she listened to this. . . . Suddenly Agatha's eyes flared, remembering the witch's defaced portrait in the School for Old. "Hester, that's *your* house!" she whispered. "Your mother was that witch! She's alive—somewhere in the Woods—"

"She's *not* alive, Agatha. She's a zombie under the School Master's control," Hester hissed. "I'm not stupid or sentimental enough to think whatever dead-eyed goon he's brought back from the grave is my *mother.*"

"Hester, I know you pride yourself on being strong," Agatha whispered worriedly, "but how can you just sit here with them talking about her like that? They *killed* her!"

Hester glowered at her. "The biggest mistake a villain can make is to get caught up in revenge. Hansel and Gretel were two hungry kids trying to survive in the Woods. Mother thought she'd captured another pair of greedy, gluttonous brats, only to grossly underestimate them. Hansel and Gretel killed her because they had to. It wasn't personal." She glanced back at the old siblings. "Doesn't mean I can stand the sight of 'em, of course. But it also doesn't mean their story has anything to do with mine anymore."

Agatha could see Dot and Anadil gazing at Hester with awe, and for a moment, Agatha wondered whether in this room of heroes young and old, Hester was the greatest hero of all.

"Shouldn't have been so mean to her before," Dot whispered to Agatha. "Must be hard having me as a friend when I'm the kinda girl her mother used to eat. I mean, if I'd gone to her house that day instead of Hansel and Gretel, her mother would still be alive. Gretel saved Hansel 'cause she loved him, where I'd have ended up alone and cooked to a crisp. That's why I'm not an Ever. Don't have anyone who'd care enough about me to save me."

"That's not true," said a voice.

Dot turned to see Hester looking right at her.

"That's not true at all," Hester said.

Dot blushed.

Agatha forced her attention back to Jack and Briar Rose's story, if only to hide a sniffle.

On they went, each hero regaling the room with raucous tales of survival—Red Riding Hood, Princess Uma, Yuba and the White Rabbit—until twelve had gone and only one remained. Then, and only then, did the room fall silent for good.

Slowly everyone turned to face the head of the table, their smiles gone.

Merlin took off his hat.

"Seven days," he said. "That's as long as the sun will light our Woods, based on Yuba's calculations. *Seven days*. If we wish to survive beyond them, we have no choice but to attack the School for Evil and the School Master knows it. He knows Good will always fight for life. And I'm afraid we have no choice but to fall into his trap." The wizard sighed. "At the same time, so many of our fellow heroes have been slain in the Woods that the shield over the Reader World is barely intact. If any one of our old League members die, I suspect it will fall at last. The School Master will invade their world and claim the secret ending he's been after all along. An ending he believes will destroy Good forever."

For a moment, no one spoke, taking this in.

"I don't understand. Isn't killing these two duffers enough?" asked Cinderella, pointing at Agatha and Tedros. "It's their fairy tale. Why does he need the Woods Beyond?"

"It's a good question and I wish I knew the answer," said Merlin. "Though I have no doubt he'll kill Agatha and Tedros too when the time comes."

Agatha and Tedros exchanged tense looks.

"I think it's clear the School Master wants this fairy tale to be so cruel, so Evil, that Good has no power left beyond it," said Merlin. "He's already rewritten so much of our past. Now he's after our future. He believes that whatever ending he has planned will make Evil invincible."

"And you have no idea what that ending is, Merlin?" Princess Uma pushed.

"Only an inkling and nothing I would share," said Merlin. "Until I know for sure, however, our only hope is to catch Sophie and make her destroy that ring."

Agatha felt nauseous, trying to remember her best friend was leading the enemy now.

"So how do we do *that*?" asked Red Riding Hood.

Merlin smiled. "We charge the school, of course."

The old heroes eyed each other warily. "Well, which Ever kingdoms are joining us?" asked Jack. "We'd need Maidenvale, Gillikin, and Avondale at the very least—"

"None," said Merlin.

"What?" Briar Rose blurted.

"None of the Ever kingdoms are joining us."

The room was very still.

"Merlin," said Peter Pan. "The School Master is young and strong. He has two hundred old villains who can't be killed by anything other than fire, along with a school of young students—"

"Leave that problem to *me*," said Merlin. "In the meantime, I expect the League to work with our young heroes—Agatha, Tedros, Hort, Hester, Anadil, and Dot—and prepare them as best as you can for the villains they'll face, given you once battled these same villains yourself. We leave for war one week from tonight."

"But we're old bones!" Hansel blustered.

"And they're young idiots!" said Gretel. "It's impossible!"

"It's idiocy!" said Cinderella.

"It's a massacre is what it is," said Red Riding Hood.

"The other option is to lay down and die," said Agatha, launching to her feet.

Everyone turned to her. Tedros gave her a surprised look, as if she had far more courage than him at the moment.

Meanwhile, Agatha felt sweat puddling beneath the crown. She'd stood up before she actually had anything to say.

But then she saw Guinevere in the corner. The old queen

nodded at her with a steely smile and Agatha felt her voice again.

"My mother died to let me live," Agatha said, still watching Guinevere, as if she was feeding her the words. "For most of my life, I made the mistake of thinking she was clueless. I figured she was old and out of touch and couldn't possibly know how hard it was to be young. Never paid much attention to her, just like me and Tedros discounted all of you when we first came to your cave."

"Discounted?" Peter heckled. "Your boyfriend called us a retirement home for the about-to-be-dead!"

"Well, you had your own opinions about us, too," said Agatha. "You thought what my mother did: that young people are careless and thoughtless and have it easy."

The old heroes grumbled agreement.

"But in the end, my mother knew how to keep me *safe*," said Agatha. "She didn't just save me from death . . . she also sent me to you. Not to a warrior kingdom, not to a young League of Knights, but to a group of legendary old heroes she knew would protect me. And she was right, wasn't she? That's why I put my faith in you, no matter how little you have in yourselves or in us. Because I might not have listened to my mother while she was alive. But I'm listening to her now."

Agatha leveled eyes with the League. "Me and my friends will tell you everything we know about the young School Master and his new school. In return, we need you to tell us how to defeat your old enemies. Let Merlin worry about our plan for war. Our job is to listen to each other, Ever and Never,

young and old, no matter how puny our army is. And if anyone doesn't want to be a part of that army, then leave now and
see how you fare in the Woods alone."

Merlin stood up.

All eyes shot to him.

"Oh goodness. I'm not leaving," he said. "Hips are a bit
stiff."

Laughter rippled through the room.

Agatha saw Tedros smiling at her, his expression soft, as if
her words about her mother had meant as much to him as they
had to her.

"Well then, now that our new queen has set the tone, the
real work begins," Merlin declared. He swished a finger across
the table and tiny marble figurines of each member in the
room appeared on top of it. "Each young student will train
with an old hero . . ."

Agatha crammed between Hester and Hort, trying to get
a view of the table as Merlin paired up the figurines, announc-
ing the training teams: Dot with Red Riding Hood, Anadil
with Jack and Briar Rose . . .

Agatha couldn't focus. Her crown was itching terribly and
she looked up, hoping Tedros was far enough away that she
could take it off—

Only she couldn't see Tedros anywhere.

And now that she was scanning the room, Guinevere
wasn't there either.

She heard the front door latch in the hall and glanced back
to see a boy's shadow through the window curtain, leading his

mother out to the moors alone.

Hester elbowed her. "Pay *attention*."

Agatha spun to the table. The wizard was glaring right at her, saying something about her mentor and her assignment in the war to come . . .

But Agatha couldn't stop smiling, because for the briefest of moments, she felt like a war had already been won.

~ 28 ~

Who's Helping Who

The thing Tedros liked about girls is that they always started the conversation. Most of the time, his job was just to listen, ask questions, and try to understand what in God's name was going on in their complicated little heads. He rarely had any idea what girls were talking about or why they made everything so torturous in their logic, so playing the role of the strong, silent type usually gave him time to catch up.

But this was different. This was his mother. And he was the one with the storm in his head.

Which meant he was *definitely* going to have to start this conversation.

The breeze over the lush moors was brisk enough that Guinevere had to cling to her lumpy sweater, but Tedros was

sweating like a mule, tugging at his shirt, wishing he could take it off. His chest pummeled like a pressure cooker and the silence between them was only making it worse. He didn't even know where he was taking her—there wasn't some hallowed landmark that would make this any easier—so without warning, he plopped down midstride into the grass, still fidgeting with his sleeves.

Guinevere calmly sat down beside him.

"When we met the Lady of the Lake, Merlin asked her to hide us the way she'd hidden someone before," said Tedros, not looking at her. "Which means Merlin helped you escape from me and Dad."

"Merlin knew I was unhappy for a long time," said Guinevere.

"Father adored you," Tedros shot back. "He decorated the castle with your portraits, brought you the most extravagant gifts from his quests, and lavished you with attention and affection. He never raised his voice to you or laid a hand on you or deprived you of anything and now you're acting like he was some madman in the attic. So what if he had a few bad habits? No relationship is perfect. Look at me and Agatha—"

"The difference is that Agatha loves you back."

Her answer disarmed him. Tedros exhaled. "Mother, you couldn't have been unhappy enough to abandon your own *son*."

"I know. That's why I stayed with your father much longer than I should have," Guinevere replied. "Believe me when I say I was well educated in the values of Good. I'd been trained by a Dean far less progressive than yours to put king and kingdom first. I knew full well that no one would forgive a queen who absconds with a knight from her king's court, and for good reason. Even if Lancelot was my true love, the idea of going off with him felt childish, selfish, and deeply Evil. I had a duty to keep my family together."

"Exactly," said Tedros.

"It wasn't as if I could take you with me," said Guinevere. "That'd be unfair to you, to your father, and a kingdom that needed its future king—"

"Not just unfair, but unconscionable," Tedros piled on.

"Which is why I told all this to Merlin, hoping he'd condemn such sinful thoughts and force me to focus on the life I'd chosen, not the one I kept imagining." His mother paused. "Instead he asked me if I so desperately wanted to leave Camelot, why I was still there."

Tedros looked at her, agog.

"Why? Because you have a child! You have a husband! Because that's what you're *supposed* to do! How could he ask you such a stupid question! It's a matter of right and wrong!"

"I was even harsher," his mother concurred. "I said only a man would have so little regard for a woman's sense of duty. How irresponsible to think this was simply a matter of choice. I couldn't just dump my old life and start a new one. How would I wake up every day knowing I'd left a son behind? He's my child! He's my blood!"

"He needs you," Tedros fought—

"He needs my *help*," Guinevere finished.

Both of them were quiet, looking into each other's eyes.

"What did Merlin say?" Tedros asked tightly.

Guinevere's eyes glistened. "He just looked at me and said: '*Who's helping who?*'"

Tedros shook his head. "I don't under—"

But he did. His soul did. Tears stung his eyes, washing away his anger.

"To stay with your father would have ruined my life. And it would have ruined your life too," said Guinevere. "Arthur may have been a wonderful king to his people, a loving father to you, and a faithful husband to me . . . but I loved someone else, Tedros. I'd always loved someone else. And if you found out I'd clung to an unhappy marriage for your sake, you would carry that weight forever. You would know that your mother chose to disavow her own happiness on your behalf. And as much as I wanted to give up my life and stay by your side, I couldn't make that choice for you. Not for a boy with as much courage and compassion as you. Part of your journey was to come to see your mother for who she truly was, not who she pretended to be. Most children would never get past the resentment and wither from the pain. But Merlin knew you were different. He said my leaving wasn't just necessary for my own fate, it was the essential seed of your fate too. It would make you look closer and find *real* love. It would make you the king you needed to be. And even though leaving would strike us both with an indelible wound . . . one day, you would find a way to forgive me."

Tedros was a mess of tears. "You were my mother. . . . You were my whole life. . . . I wanted to die when you left—"

"But you didn't," said Guinevere. "And I didn't either, even if I thought I would. For months, I pounded at the moors and screamed at the sky, begging the Lady of the Lake to take me back to you. But Merlin had forbidden her. He came every Sunday that first year to soothe me and tell me stories of what you were up to: how you'd sit in on the advisers' meetings and ask them questions about the kingdom; how you'd hide your vegetables under your rice so the nursemaid wouldn't notice; how you'd sit with Arthur every night after I'd left, even if he wouldn't say a word to you . . . and how you cursed me for days and weeks after he died. I'd make Merlin tell me every detail again and again until I cried myself to sleep."

She smiled wistfully. "He came less and less as the years went on and soon only on Christmas. But on that one day, I'd feel like a child again, listening to the tale of my own son growing bolder and stronger, his mother's absence fueling his desire to make something of himself. And soon I began to feel bold and strong too, knowing I finally had an honest love instead of a love forced by duty. It didn't matter if Lancelot and I would be alone for the rest of our lives; it didn't matter if we were cast out in disgrace . . . because we'd found *real* Good, instead of a lie, and honored the truth of our stories. Listening to Merlin speak of you, year after year, I started to feel I was living with you, even if I wasn't there, growing younger and younger in spirit while you grew older and older—until here we are, humbled by the blessings of Good, our two stories connected once more. Only now I see Merlin was right. Just as your father made you strong and responsible, my leaving Camelot also made you the man you are. It made you sensitive, independent, and resilient and led you to your perfect queen. Naturally, it also made you a bit raw and bullheaded—"

"Like Father," Tedros sniffled.

"No," said Guinevere sharply. "Your father would never be sitting here with me the way you are right now. Your father could never see that deep down, everything I did was to give all of us a chance to find real happiness. He believed happiness meant something very different. He was a different kind of man . . . a different kind of king. But you can see what he can't, Tedros. That even though your father and I are flawed to our very core, we came together by the grace of our stories to make the most perfect child in the world. And for that, all of our pain is worth it."

Tedros couldn't speak anymore. His mother clasped him to her chest, letting him cry, his muscles fighting and fighting her until at last they surrendered and he curled against her like a little boy. They stayed that way a long time, until his heaving breaths calmed.

"Does that ogre treat you well?" he croaked, nose running.

Guinevere laughed. "As well as an ogre can treat a lady."

"'Cause if he doesn't, I'll gouge out his eye," Tedros puffed.

"I appreciate your chivalry—"

"If he so much as looks at you the wrong way—"

"How many times you gonna threaten to kill me before you cock up and do it, boy," a voice growled.

Tedros whirled to see Lancelot approaching, while the rest

of the Ever-Never army were gathered in the distance outside the house.

"Though you might want to wait a bit," said the knight, "considering Merlin just paired the old and young ones up and chose me as your training leader."

Tedros frowned.

"Come on, lad," Lancelot smirked, beckoning him towards the others. "Time to show us what you learned at that god-forsaken school."

Guinevere smiled. "Be gentle with him, Lance."

"Wouldn't dream of it," Lancelot said with a wink.

Tedros stayed by his mother's side, watching the knight catch up with the others.

"Go on, now," Guinevere urged. "You and your queen have a war to win. Can't be wasting time with an old housewife."

Tedros turned. "You'll be home when I get back?"

The question was so silly and obvious . . . and yet his mother knew what he meant.

"I'm not going anywhere," she answered flatly.

Tedros nodded, averting his eyes. He rose and started to jog after Lancelot before he stopped and looked at her one last time.

"I love you, Mother."

He sprinted ahead, ensuring Guinevere didn't have time to say it back.

She didn't need to.

Him saying it was enough for the both of them.

It wasn't long before the first death.

Lady Lesso had been warning from the start that having New students fight Old, bloodthirsty zombies was recklessly stupid, but Sophie felt like the young students had been pampered enough. First, Rafal had protected them from the front line of the coming war. Then, he'd moved war preparations to the School for New, since the old Good castle was warmer and better lit. Then he'd abolished the Doom Room, allowed open access to the Groom Room, and even halted further tracking, ensuring half-mogrified dimwits like Kiko wouldn't be fully turned into animals and plants until after the war.

Enough was enough, Sophie scowled. She was Training Leader and the training fights would continue as scheduled, no matter what anyone said. It didn't matter if the old villains were injuring and torturing the new students. Evil had a *war* to win, and Evil only learned to be Evil through suffering and pain.

That's how she'd learned, after all. And now her classmates would too.

She'd planned the entire training schedule herself. For the next six days, four hundred villains, Old and New, would be divided amongst the various Evil teachers and rooms. During each class, there were no lectures, no tests, no challenges. Instead, teachers would supervise one-on-one fights between an old zombie and a young student in accordance with a class theme. Each student's schedule consisted of the following sessions:

EVIL ARMY TRAINING

Session	Faculty
1: WEAPONS FIGHTING	Castor
2: SPELLS FIGHTING	Prof. Bilious Manley
3: TALENT FIGHTING	Prof. Sheeba Sheeks
4: DEVIOUS FIGHTING	Pollux
5: LUNCH	
6: MENTAL FIGHTING	Lady Lesso
7: HAND-TO-HAND COMBAT	Lord Aric

From the very first class, screams of young Evers and Nevers rang through the hall. An ogre chased Reena with an axe during Weapons, a witch burned a hole in Vex's thigh during Spells, Jack's giant threw Chaddick down the stairs in Talents, and Red Riding Hood's wolf *ate* half-feathered Kiko before Pollux made him choke her out. Meanwhile, Aric's Hand-to-Hand Combat sessions produced so many gashes and concussions and broken bones that the fairies set up a makeshift infirmary in the foyer, supervised by Beatrix, who scurried about in a panic, dispensing healing elixirs and spells out of old library books.

As the days went on, Sophie began to relish the students' misery and the growing number of bodies in the infirmary, as if her heart, once fueled by love and hope, was now only fueled by other people's pain. She woke up craving the first

screams of the morning and felt forlorn when the day's training ended and the students limped back to their rooms. By the
third night, she was staying up late to make her own draws of
who would fight each other the next day.

"Think I'll put Beatrix against Hook," she said, perched
in the windowsill, as she scribbled onto a piece of parchment.

Rafal eyed her across his chamber as he changed shirts.
"The point of training is to prepare the Dark Army for war.
Not batter young students, who won't be on the front line."

"That wasn't my decision," Sophie murmured.

"Our students are Evil's future, Sophie. We have to protect
them until they're fully trained—"

"And that's what I'm doing. I'm training them."

"By breaking their bones and spirits? I'm not sure they see
it that way."

"I'm not sure I care," Sophie murmured.

"Says the girl who used to care desperately what other
people thought of her."

Sophie looked up. "I care what you think."

The young School Master smiled. "I think you're forgetting
that once upon a time, you were in their shoes."

Sophie frowned and went back to her list. "Actually, I don't
care what you think."

Rafal was about to say something, but Sophie preempted
him. "You put me in charge, didn't you?" she clipped, without
looking up. "If you have doubts, then replace me."

She heard the young School Master sigh, but he spoke
nothing more.

The truth was, deep down, Sophie wished she could feel bad for her fellow classmates. But she felt nothing. It was as if a part of her heart had simply switched off. She didn't know when it had happened. When Tedros' kiss turned rotten? When she learned Agatha had used her to get closer to her prince? Or was it when she finally looked at herself in Evil's crown and felt strong and in control for the first time in her life? Perhaps it was all of these and more . . . a lifetime of rejections by Good, casing her heart inch by inch until it sealed to stone.

And indeed, with each passing day, she noticed her skin was paler, her voice steelier, her muscles harder, with her ice-blue veins almost translucent through her skin, matching the chill inside of her. Though still in her young body, she felt like one of the old, dead-eyed zombies, drained of humanity. Even her kisses with Rafal had changed. His lips no longer felt cold.

By the fifth day, Sophie had disbanded the infirmary, since students had started faking injuries to avoid having to fight. Even the most intrepid Nevers trudged into the ring with their hands up, offering no resistance before their zombie opponent punched them, slashed them, or blasted them across the castle. Sophie was furious at first, but she knew the young students would eventually pay the price for such cowardice.

And indeed, when Beatrix accosted her in the hall after lunch, face shining with tears, screaming that a student had been killed, Sophie couldn't help but feel whoever it was had deserved it.

"Saw it from our window—it was an ogre . . . threw

someone off the belfry . . . into the bay—" Beatrix gasped.

"It's what happens when you don't fight back," said Sophie, without stopping.

Beatrix grabbed her arm. "But aren't you going to see whose body it is? It must have come from Castor's class—"

"There won't be a body if it was thrown into the bay. Slime would eat it right up," said Sophie airily. "I suppose it erases the need for a funeral."

Beatrix gaped at her, trembling. "All you ever wanted was to be Good. And now . . . you're as bad as *him*."

Sophie pulled Beatrix's hand off her arm and walked away. "I'll take that as a compliment."

It turned out the student thrown off the belfry wasn't a student at all, but Beezle, who'd been cheering for an ogre in his fight against Ravan, only to stumble into the middle of the ogre's charge and end up head butted over the railing. (Castor led a short memorial before first session the next day in which no one shed a tear.)

By the afternoon, Sophie was making her rounds as usual and noticed for the first time that the New students were actually performing *better*. Whether Beezle's death had scared them into action or they'd had enough of losing or their survival instincts had finally kicked in, the young Evers and Nevers fought back with a vengeance against the old villains, using an array of black magic that Sophie had never seen. Vex cast himself into a noxious wind to beat off the wolf, Kiko turned part of the floor to acid, burning a hole in a witch's feet, while Chaddick morphed into a deadly germ and infected his troll opponent. All three of them still lost in the end, but by the morning of the sixth day, the School for New had their first victory, when Beatrix summoned crows that pecked out Cinderella's stepsisters' eyes. The zombie-girls managed to recover them from the pesky birds, so they'd no doubt have their revenge on Beatrix later . . . and yet, Sophie wondered. Where had the students learned such black magic? Certainly not from the School Master, who'd restricted the teaching of sorcery at the School for New, either because he didn't trust the young Evers and Nevers with it or because he viewed such sorcery as a direct threat to his own.

So it had to be a teacher, Sophie thought. And yet, none of them took credit for the rise in the students' performance. Instead, they thought *she* was responsible for it. Once doubtful of her training methods, now all the teachers gave Sophie approving looks.

All the teachers, that is, except for one.

Sophie waited until a break between sessions to knock on the door of Professor Dovey's old room. When the locked door magically opened, the pumpkin treacle walls were still intact from the Good old days, but now they were cracked from end to end, like a mirror that might shatter at any moment.

Lady Lesso was poring over a scroll at Professor Dovey's old sour-plum desk, the plums all rotted to black pulp.

"Interesting choice of rooms," said Sophie, sitting on one of the students' desks and glancing around.

She heard sniffling, oddly guttural, and looked up to see Lady Lesso hastily wipe her nose and adjust herself at the desk.

"I didn't choose it," she said, eyes still on her scroll. "As the senior faculty member, I let the others pick their rooms first. Professor Dovey's was the only one left."

"You must miss her," said Sophie smoothly. "Clarissa was your best friend."

Lady Lesso raised her violet eyes. "I'm not sure you've earned the right to call a Dean by her first name."

"A *former* Dean," Sophie said. "And I am her superior as I am yours, so I can call anyone what I like. I'd call you by your first name too if I knew it, Lady Lesso. You aren't a teacher to me anymore. You're an *employee*."

"My, my." Lady Lesso grinned at Sophie's pale face and stone-mouthed expression. "It's like looking in a mirror at my younger self. Even sound like me."

She went back to her scroll, producing another strange sniffle that made her readjust her chair. "Regardless, since *no one* knows my first name and Professor Dovey is frozen at the bottom of a dungeon, I suppose this is all rather irrelevant. Though I'm quite envious of Clarissa, given she doesn't have four hundred students to supervise now, with Young, Old, Ever, and Never all attending class in one castle. So if you don't mind, I'll get back to my lesson plan before next session starts—"

"Speaking of your lesson plan, what *is* it you're teaching them exactly?" Sophie asked. "You're the only teacher who locks her door during training so that I can't stop by."

"Nor can my son, and given the School Master has made it abundantly clear he'll let Aric kill me, locking my door seems the least I can do. As for what I teach them, I'm preparing them for war, just as you instructed, my *queen*."

"Is that so? I've stood outside your door after class ends and never once has a young student come out looking like they've been in a fight."

"Because teaching them to fight means teaching them to protect themselves," Lady Lesso glared. "Particularly when the fight is an unfair one."

Sophie smiled wryly at the Dean. "It was you, then, wasn't it? You taught them black magic to fight against the old villains." She paused, confused. "And yet the old villains were still in the classroom the whole time."

"I put them to sleep while I taught the others," said Lady Lesso. "A simple mist of Sleeping Willow. When they woke up, it was as if they were never in class at all. Surely you remember the effects of it from your first-year Trial."

Sophie's jaw clenched. "You had no right to disobey orders!"

"It worked, didn't it?" Lady Lesso replied swiftly. "The young students are brimming with confidence. The old villains have been forced to raise their level, since the new students are giving them a fight. The teachers now fully support you as their leader. Even Rafal no longer looks as if he'd made a mistake in letting love guide him."

Sophie said nothing.

Lady Lesso let out a long sigh. "Sophie, my dear. You think I'm working against you, when helping Evil to win has been my life's work. After all, I was the one who told you there were spies for Good plotting against you within this very school.

But ever since you returned, I've feared that your emotions are too volatile to lead our army. I could feel the young students resisting you instead of respecting you. You cannot beat young souls down into believing in Evil. You yourself only gave Evil a chance when it gave you something to fight *for*. By helping the students fight back, I empowered them for the first time since they stepped foot in their new school. I helped them see that, Ever or Never, trusting in Evil is their only hope to survive."

Sophie looked skeptical. "So why didn't you tell me what you were doing?"

Lady Lesso leaned in. "Because I wanted Rafal and the teachers to credit the reversal in their performance entirely to *you*."

Sophie stared at her.

"Remember what I told you when we spoke in my office," the Dean said. "I want you to be a legendary queen. I want you to make Evil great again. And most of all, I want you to be happy. Because you deserve the life I never had. You deserve a love that's *right*." Her eyes sparkled with warmth. "So maybe you don't see me as a teacher anymore. But I'll always see you as my student, Sophie. And when you lose your way, I'll be there in the shadows, your Evil fairy godmother, pushing you towards your destiny like a wind behind a sail. Even when you lose sight of what that destiny is."

Sophie could see there was more Lady Lesso wanted to say, but she was holding back. Instead, they just gazed into each other's eyes, Sophie's throat tightening. It was the first emotion she'd felt in days.

Fairies shrieked through the halls.

Sophie stamped out the emotion, like the embers of a flame. "Well, I don't need your help," she said, moving towards the door. "And I don't need a 'fairy *godmother.*' This is my school, not yours, and if the young students are going to fight with black magic, well, now I'm going to let the old villains use weapons. Only fair, isn't it? And when you hear the students' screams, you'll know it was your doing—"

"Sophie."

She stopped. "What is it, Lady Lesso?"

"You couldn't kill Agatha and Tedros when they came to rescue you," Lady Lesso said quietly. "What makes you think you can kill them now?"

Sophie turned, ice-cold. "The same reason I returned to Evil. A heart can only fight the wind so long before it learns to embrace it."

Lady Lesso watched her leave, the black train of Sophie's gown slithering behind her like a snake.

"Well said, my child," the Dean smiled. She went back to her work. *"Well said."*

It wasn't long before young screams pierced the hallway again, much worse than before.

Sophie had made good on her promise.

29

Failed Assignments

Far away, in the bright sunshine of a safe haven, Agatha brainstormed ways to murder Cinderella.

Merlin had paired her with the abominable princess, just as he'd paired up each of the other young students with an old hero. Agatha knew the wizard was going to team her with that over-rouged hellion, if only because Hester, Anadil, or Hort would have put an axe through her head. (Dot wasn't an option; Cinderella would have squashed her like a fly.)

Agatha couldn't appeal the assignment, for Merlin had left the farmhouse after the group's lunch meeting and hadn't been seen since. At the outset, Agatha genuinely believed she could learn something from the former princess. First, Cinderella wasn't as old as the rest of the heroes. Second, they'd both had Professor Dovey as a secret fairy godmother and third, given what she knew of Cinderella's storybook, hadn't they each overcome their own self-doubt to find true love?

But as open as Agatha tried to be to her mentor during their training sessions, by late in the week, the only thing she'd learned was to count to ten every time she had the urge to disembowel her.

"IT'S A WAND, YOU HOPELESS HALF-WIT," Cinderella barked, jowls flapping. "FIVE DAYS OF THIS AND YOU CAN'T EVEN HOLD IT STRAIGHT!"

"Because you're making me nervous!" Agatha yelled, trying to steady Professor Dovey's wand at the White Rabbit, patiently leaning against a tree while he snacked on a cheese biscuit.

"IMAGINE HOW NERVOUS YOU'RE GONNA BE WHEN AN ENTIRE ARMY'S TRYING TO KILL YOU!"

"If I could just speak to Merlin, he'll see he shouldn't have picked me for this—"

"TOO BAD MERLIN AIN'T AROUND!"

"But why do *I* have to do it?" said Agatha, the wand shaking so much she could feel her queen's crown quivering. "Why can't someone else?"

"'Cause for some ungodly reason, Merlin thinks *you're* the one to make Sophie destroy her ring!" Cinderella blared. "I, on the other hand, think we should fillet and fry you and serve you to Evil as a peace offering."

Both glowered at each other, fuming.

"Listen to me, you overgrown milkweed. There's no use fighting this war unless you can make Sophie shatter that ring," Cinderella growled. "And I say the only way you can do that is by giving her the choice between living and dying. But you have to be willing to hurt her in practice, otherwise you won't believe it when the time comes. And if you don't believe it, *she* won't believe it."

"But why do I have to hurt a rabbit?" Agatha argued, pointing at the one against the tree.

"Agatha," said Cinderella, trying to control her temper. "If you can't hurt a rabbit, how would you hurt your best friend?"

"Can't I just stun him with a spell? Why do I have to use a wand—"

"'CAUSE SHE'S NOT GONNA BE AFRAID OF A STUN SPELL! SOPHIE WON'T BE AFRAID OF ANY STUPID SCHOOL SPELLS!" roared Cinderella. "She'll be scared of Dovey's wand if she thinks you're ready to shoot her with it, and Dovey's wand works the same way all magic does in our world: by intention and conviction—both of which Merlin seems to think you have, despite all evidence to the contrary."

Agatha gritted her teeth and exhaled. "Once, all right? I'm only doing this once!"

Cinderella threw up her hands. "So far you've been doin' diddly-squat, so once would be an improvement!"

Agatha ignored her and slowly raised the wand at the White Rabbit once more. She pictured armies clashing around her . . . the entire fate of this war resting on her shoulders . . .

She held her breath, gripping the wand tighter.

It's for Good.

Just once for Good.

But now, instead of the rabbit, she saw Sophie looking back at her with emerald eyes and rosy cheeks. The Sophie who'd tried again and again to be Good, only to end up Evil.

This is how it would end: standing in front of Sophie, willing to kill her . . . wanting Sophie to *believe* she could kill her . . . so she could help her be Good one last time.

Good and Evil in a single wand stroke.

Love and Hate.

Friend and Enemy.

But all Agatha could see was the Friend.

"I can't," she whispered, lowering the wand. "I can't hurt her."

The White Rabbit calmly finished his biscuit.

Cinderella snatched the wand from Agatha and shot a blast of light at the rabbit, slamming him so hard against the tree that he was knocked out. The old woman dumped the wand in Agatha's hands and glared at her.

"And to think, for a moment, I'd mistaken you for a *queen*."

She tramped towards the house, leaving Agatha alone.

They weren't the only team with growing pains.

At first Dot resented being paired with old Red Riding Hood. ("Just 'cause we both like cake doesn't mean we'll get along," she grouched to Anadil.) Things got worse when Red

Riding Hood didn't seem to have anything to teach her.

"Well, you can't outrun the wolf or beat him in a fight and he won't fall for any stupid tricks," mulled Red Riding Hood. "Best if you just do what I did when I was your age and scream for help. Maybe there'll be a woodsman nearby."

"That's your advice? Wait for a woodsman to possibly pass by?"

Red Riding Hood blushed, lost in her memory. "A handsome woodsman, who smells of leather and earth . . ."

"Look, Miss . . . *Hood*, the second that wolf sees you, he's going to come for you and try to rewrite your happy ending. I can't let that happen," Dot snapped, stifling the urge to bond over their similar taste in men. "If he kills you, the School Master will break the shield into the Reader World. You heard Merlin. Doesn't need more than *one* of you heroes dead!"

Red Riding Hood tapped a finger to her lips. "Chocolate, isn't it? That's your villain talent?"

"Oh for heaven's sake, do you know how much energy it takes for me to turn a toad or mouse into chocolate? I can't possibly turn a whole wolf—"

She saw Red Riding Hood grinning. "Who said I was talking about a *whole* wolf?"

As her jolly old mentor explained her plan, Dot found herself smiling wider and wider, suddenly realizing why Merlin had paired them in the first place. And indeed Red Riding Hood's plan was so good that by the time they'd perfected it four days later, Dot was pretending they'd come up with it together.

Meanwhile, Hester had been teamed with Hansel and Gretel, which was as awkward as it sounds.

"You said you didn't have a problem with them—" Anadil started.

"I meant I can be in the same house without killing them! Doesn't mean I can *train* with them!" Hester yelled.

The wheelchair-bound siblings had a similar revulsion to helping the daughter of the witch who'd tried to eat them. ("Does this one cook children too?" Hansel asked Gretel.)

Yet, despite their rocky start, the three of them soon found common ground.

"We are not friends, yes?" Hansel said to Hester. "But all of us want same thing: your mother back in grave."

"For the last time, that *thing* is not my mother," Hester retorted.

"Mmmm," said Gretel thoughtfully. "And yet not-your-mother still sees you as her daughter . . ."

Hester's eyes widened, catching on.

"What?" said Hansel, glancing between them. "What I'm missing?"

But now Gretel and Hester were grinning at each other. "The plan is clear, young witch?" said Gretel.

"Crystal," said Hester.

Gretel beamed at Hansel. "Merlin gave us smart one, eh?"

Hansel still looked lost.

"Smarter than your brother at least," Hester cracked.

Gretel gave her a high five.

Across the oak grove, Anadil was rankling over having to

train with both Jack and Briar Rose. ("They're in love. Can't blame Merlin for wanting to keep them together," said Dot. "They can't even take a poo apart!" Anadil miffed.)

In addition to having to deal with double mentors (as well as their geriatric displays of affection), Anadil also had double the villains to deal with: Jack's giant and Rose's Evil fairy. And for Anadil, who'd been trying so valiantly to prove she was more than just Hester's sidekick, the extra burden was worth it. It didn't matter if she had to put up with two lovey-dovey mentors. It didn't matter if she had to work twice as long and twice as hard as everyone else. Kill two villains and no one would call her a henchman ever again.

But it was Hort who had the worst pairing of all. He'd been so focused on wooing Sophie these past few weeks that he'd failed to notice that one of the old men stalking about the farmhouse was his mortal enemy.

Pan.

Pan!

At first he couldn't believe it, since Peter Pan was the boy who'd vowed never to grow up, let alone grow bald, wrinkled, and frail. But then he saw Tinkerbell perched on the old man's shoulder and his stomach went cold.

To be matched with the hero who'd slain his father during the Battle of the Jolly Roger, the hero who'd left him an orphan at the age of six, the hero who he'd shadow-dueled in daydreams all his life . . . well, it nearly stopped the poor boy's heart. And yet, after the shock subsided, he never felt rage, only an empty despair. For in his dreams, Hort had always imagined Peter young and cocksure, a bumptious, trash-talking sprig he could kill in a fair fight. But now, watching Pan so old and ordinary, Hort lost the will to fight him at all.

Right then and there, he understood what made him different from the Evil School Master they were about to face. Because unlike him, Hort could see when a story was over and it was time to move on.

So that first day of training, he and Peter slit their palms and made a blood oath to mutual respect. Hort vowed to slay Captain Hook and put him back in his tomb. And in return, Pan promised to stand beside Hort at his father's grave when the war was done and won.

Neither Cinderella nor Agatha showed up to training on the sixth day.

While the others went out to the oak grove after breakfast, the old princess stayed in her nightgown and roasted marshmallows over the fireplace in the den. Agatha just lay in bed, curled towards the window, watching Lancelot and Tedros clash swords across the moors.

Her prince had come so far with his mother since that day they'd gone off together. He sat beside Guinevere at meals now, helped her scrub dishes, and took her on private walks in the gardens each night. In fact, his kindness towards her touched Agatha so deeply that she had to stop herself from mentioning it, for fear of making Tedros self-conscious. (She'd learned that if you compliment boys for something they've done, they go out of their way never to do it again.) But Tedros' willingness to let go of old resentments and start anew with his mother made Agatha realize that he wasn't just a worthy prince and a loving son . . . but he'd make a wonderful king too.

Agatha naturally assumed, then, that once paired with Lancelot for training, Tedros would extend the same kindness and openness to the knight as he had to his mother.

She was wrong.

Face red-hot, Tedros slashed and hacked at Lancelot with his father's sword, only to be beaten again and again. Not just beaten, but humiliated, with Lancelot nicking Tedros' ear every time he won a round, lopping off a bit of his hair, or smacking him on the backside with the flat of his blade. No doubt Merlin paired the two together knowing Tedros would benefit from the great knight's sword skills, but by the sixth day of their sparring the prince was a deranged beast, stabbing Excalibur wildly at the knight and grunting and salivating, as if fighting not just for his pride now, but for his father's, for his kingdom's—

Lancelot beat him even worse than before.

When Tedros ended up face-first in a pile of horse manure a few bouts later, Agatha couldn't watch anymore. She took a long bath and sauntered down to the kitchen, hoping there was food still left.

"Shouldn't you be out training?" Guinevere asked, laying out a spinach omelet and mug of tea for her.

Agatha eyed Cinderella lounging in the den with curlers in her bluish hair, stuffing a cheese biscuit with roasted marshmallows. "You know how well things are going with Tedros and Lancelot?" She turned back to Guinevere. "They're practically lovers compared to us."

"I NEED ANOTHER BISCUIT," Cinderella boomed from the den. "THIS ONE BROKE."

Agatha ignored her. "I really need to speak to Merlin," she said to Guinevere. "It's been six days. Surely you know where he is—"

"If you haven't noticed, Merlin isn't particularly forthcoming about his thought process or whereabouts," said Guinevere.

Agatha looked out the window at the silhouettes of her old and young friends in the distant oak grove. "He hasn't even told us how he thinks we can win this war. The School Master has both the Dark Army *and* the students. We're outnumbered twenty to one."

"Merlin wouldn't send children off to war unless he had a plan," Guinevere smiled.

"Or unless he was desperate," said Agatha.

Guinevere's smile wavered. She poured Agatha more tea. "Well, at least he's left his hat!" she said, with forced cheer. "Otherwise I have no idea how I'd manage meals for such a mob. Poor thing is a bit run-down." She glanced at the hat drooped over a houseplant and snoring softly. "Everyone seems to be helping our war effort. Except me, I mean."

"You're managing almost twenty people in your house, including a half-dozen cranky old heroes and their meals, laundry, dishes, and demands. That isn't just helping the war effort, that's *leading* it," said Agatha. "If anything, I'm the disappointment. Merlin trusted me with the most important assignment of all and I can't even do it. And if I could just tell him, then he'd know there's no way I can get Sophie to destroy that ring and no way for us to win this war if it's all left to me."

Guinevere raised her brows. "Convenient he left, then, isn't it?"

Agatha was thinking the same thing.

No one else seemed as concerned by Merlin's absence, perhaps assuming that he was off forging a flawless plan to take on Evil. But once another dinner came and went without the wizard returning, panic began to set in.

"We're running out of time and we can't fight all of Evil by ourselves!" Hort fretted, as he, Agatha, Tedros, and the three witches shared a midnight snack of chocolate cookies (they started as gingersnaps before Dot had her way with them). "For one thing, we don't even have weapons! Lancelot hardly had use for them out here, so all we have are a couple of his rusty old training swords and a few carving knives that won't stop a rat, let alone zombies that can only be killed by fire. What are we supposed to fight with? How are we supposed to win?"

"Win? How do we even *get* to Evil if Merlin doesn't come back to let us through the portal?" said Hester.

Hort gaped at her. He swiveled to Agatha. "This is your fault! You give some highfalutin speech about young and old working together, making us all feel guilty, when Merlin never even told us the plan!"

"*My* fault?" Agatha shot back. "Merlin said 'Leave it to me' as if he'd return with some giant army to fight behind us!

How was I suppose to know that a week later, there's no Merlin and no army—"

"And there'll *be* no army," said Anadil. "The Ever kingdoms won't help us, remember?"

"It isn't just numbers," said Hester. "Before we broke Agatha and Tedros into school, we spent weeks with Merlin working out every detail. The stakes are far higher now and he's nowhere to be found."

"What if he's hurt?" Dot asked, paling. "What if he's *dead*?"

"Don't be stupid!" Tedros huffed. "He'll be back soon. Everything's fine."

But Agatha noticed the prince was eating his third chocolate cookie, which meant everything wasn't fine at all. She clasped his hand to comfort him and noticed it slick with sweat. Tedros drew it away.

"Hot in here," he said, even though it wasn't.

Agatha tried to look supportive.

"I'm not scared," Tedros said loudly. "Even if Merlin doesn't come back, I'll command the Lady of the Lake to let us through. I can lead this war all on my own!"

"After Lancelot beats you into another pile of crap, you mean," snorted Hort.

Tedros ignored him and took another cookie.

Through the archway, Agatha could see the old heroes gathered around the dining room table, the tiny, paired-up figurines still in place on the surface. The League members were no doubt having a similar conversation about Merlin's disappearance.

"I say we all go to sleep," Dot yawned. "Sleep always fixes things."

No one had a better plan.

Hours later, Agatha curled up in a blanket on the floor of the guest room, listening to the house rumble with every tone of snore and snuffle imaginable. She'd given the bed to Dot, Anadil, and Hester, who spooned and slept on each other like puppies, occasionally knocking one of their pillows down onto Agatha's head.

It wasn't like she could sleep anyway. All she could think about was whether Merlin had made a fatal mistake leaving her and Tedros in this safe house for so long. It'd been almost three weeks since the Lady of the Lake had stashed them here. They'd been lulled into the languid pace and tranquility of Guinevere and Lancelot's life, forgetting that out in the Woods, legendary heroes were dead and Readers like her were losing their faith in Good. Here on the moors, the sun was strong and bright, the food was plentiful, and they were safe from Evil . . . while in real life, darkness was falling, an Evil army was rising, and her best friend was fighting at the School Master's side. What would it be like when they went back through the portal? Would she and Tedros be ready for what they'd find?

If they went back through the portal, that is.

If Merlin ever returned for them.

Her heart flurried faster and she knew that if she didn't find a way to sleep now, she wouldn't sleep at all. She pulled her blanket tighter, about to roll over—

Only there was something odd about the blanket. It was

thicker than usual, with furry, velvety fabric that smelled like a musty cabinet. As her eyes adjusted to the dark, she saw the purple inseam . . . the lining stitched with silver stars . . .

Agatha gasped.

Chest pounding, she yanked the wizard's cape over her head and felt herself floating through violet sky before she landed softly on a cloud . . .

Merlin was waiting for her.

Agatha sat cross-legged in white mist beside him, her shoulder touching his. For a short while, neither of them said a word, basking in the vast silence of the Celestium. Just being next to the wizard again made Agatha feel calmer, even if he did look alarmingly thin.

"Where have you been?" she asked finally.

"Visiting a dear old friend."

"For six days?"

"We would have stayed together far longer if we had the time," said Merlin wistfully. "I do wish I had my hat, though. Never realized how difficult it is to procure a decent meal without magic. I suppose that's why people find companions eventually; it makes it easier to manage the burden of food when there's two of you. Then again, living life alone comes with its benefits. Like learning self-reliance or traveling on a whim or washing your hair only once a year."

Agatha waited for him to get to the point.

"It is marvelous up here, isn't it?" he sighed, gazing into star-spattered emptiness. "Almost makes me forget the things I've seen—Good's old heroes, slain and discarded, their bodies left in the Woods to rot. Some as famous as Thumbelina and Aladdin, others never known by their proper name, but only as the 'Clever Tailor' or the 'Wily Beggar Boy.' I buried as many of them as I could, but we'll have to give them proper graves in the Garden of Good and Evil when the time comes."

A haunted sadness clouded his face, his thoughts still somewhere in the Woods. Agatha knew she should be just as sad for these dead heroes, and yet, all she could think about was finding a way not to join them.

"Merlin," Agatha prodded gently. "You are aware that you left us here and never explained how to beat an army twenty times our size—"

"I'm well aware, Agatha. But what's most important to me now is whether you've made any progress in how you're going to convince Sophie to destroy her ring."

"I can't do it, Merlin. You told us that Sophie has to destroy the ring by choice. Threatening to kill her doesn't give her a choice at all, nor does it seem Good."

"Is *that* how Cinderella told you to get Sophie to destroy the ring?" Merlin said, aghast.

"Um, she spent the last five days trying to get me to torture the White Rabbit."

Merlin groaned. "Should have known that's why she wanted Dovey's wand. A bit of a guerrilla, that girl; no doubt a product of her upbringing. Yes, I'm afraid bullying your best friend to get what you want isn't just morally questionable, but utterly useless. As I've said, the School Master is only destroyed if *Sophie* destroys the ring. If Sophie dies without destroying the ring, the School Master loses his true love in body, but not in spirit. Meaning he'll lose his immortality and be mortal like the rest of us, but still very much alive, with an army of villains at his command, and nearly impossible to kill. Hardly the end that we seek."

He paused thoughtfully. "And yet Cinderella is onto something. Sophie is Evil's queen now. You will not convince her to destroy the ring by appealing to her Goodness. You have to confront the deepest Evil in her and prove she has a reason to do so."

Agatha looked at him.

"But you will only have one chance," said the wizard. "Use it *wisely*."

Agatha thought about what she'd do with this one chance . . . but still, nothing came.

"Merlin, before you left, you said the School Master is looking for something in Gavaldon. Something that will destroy Good forever. Do you know what it is yet?"

"I'm afraid I've been as successful with my assignment as you with yours," the wizard smiled dryly. "And yet, I keep coming back to something you said to me when we were traveling to Avalon. That the School Master suggested it was *Sophie* who would destroy Good in the end . . . not him."

Agatha remembered what Rafal told her in Evil's museum. "He said the most dangerous person in a fairy tale is the one willing to do anything for love."

Merlin tugged at his beard, spectacles slipping down his nose.

"Do you think it has something to do with Sophie's mother?" Agatha nudged. "We never did find where her body is. Could the School Master have her?"

"Perhaps it has do with Sophie's mother or perhaps it has to do with much, much more," said Merlin. "Remember what I told you the last time we were here. For hundreds of years, Good has had love on its side, making Good invincible against Evil. But *why*? Because the School Master killed his own brother in the pursuit of power, proving that Evil could never love. To balance that one terrible deed, the Storian has made Good win every single story, as long as it has real love on its side. But now that Rafal has Sophie as his queen, he believes that her love is finally enough to redeem the murder of his brother."

"But that doesn't make any sense," Agatha countered. "Even if he does have Sophie's love, that doesn't erase the fact he killed his own blood."

"Precisely," said Merlin. "So the question remains: what is it he expects Sophie to do for him at the end of this story? Does he think *she* can redeem that original sin? And if so . . . is that why he chose Sophie as his true love in the first place?"

Agatha's gut twisted. "Merlin, whatever it is he's planning, we can't win. Not without help. Don't you understand? We're just a few students and rickety old heroes!"

Merlin wasn't listening. "What if we have the whole story wrong, Agatha?" he said softly. "What if he can prove killing his brother was never a crime at all? That love is the greatest Evil instead of the greatest Good? What then?" His body straightened. "Then Good would become Evil and Evil would become Good, wouldn't it? Just like he promised . . ."

Agatha shook her head. "Merlin, you're not making any sense—"

He flinched as if he suddenly remembered she was there. "This was thoughtless, wasn't it, bringing you here in the middle of the night when you haven't had a wink of sleep, especially with all that's to come. Come, come, off to bed—every minute counts—"

Agatha frowned. "But wait, how are we supposed to fight him? How are we supposed to . . ."

But she was yawning now, and she knew he'd done something to her, for her body grew numb and her head so heavy that she sank through the cloud like an anchor. She thrust out her hand for Merlin, striving to stay awake, trying to grab hold of him, but all she felt was a fistful of stars as she fell into the dark, and the warm taste of sky in her mouth.

Voices swelled sharply out of the void and Agatha's eyes opened.

She was sprawled on the floor in one of Guinevere's blue tattered blankets. The witches were gone from the room, their bed neatly made. Through the window, she could see the inky night sky, with no sign of the sunrise.

Agatha followed the voices towards the den and glimpsed her friends, young and old, packing burlap sacks with crackers and fruit and tins of water, while devouring last bowls of oatmeal. Everyone was clad in thick black cloaks, buzzing in hushed whispers, except for Guinevere, who was still in her

nightdress, packing a bag for Lancelot while the knight polished his sword. As Agatha inched into the den, she noticed
that the group was no longer divided into old on one side
and young on the other as usual, but into the various mentor groups—Hort with Peter Pan, Anadil with Jack and Briar
Rose, Hester with Hansel and Gretel, Dot with Red Riding
Hood . . . before Hort caught sight of Agatha and he and Pan
went quiet. All the other pairs did too.

Merlin sauntered into the den from the dining room, sipping a mug of coffee.

"Tried to keep our voices low, my dear. Wanted to give you
a bit more rest."

In her sleepy daze, Agatha didn't understand.

But then she felt someone touch her shoulder.

She looked up at Tedros, clean and beautiful in a black
cloak, Excalibur strapped to his back. He clasped her hand
with a scared smile.

"It's time," he said.

~ 30 ~

Apologies and Confessions

Agatha knew they were all doomed when Tedros tried to convince Lancelot to stay behind with his mother.

Tedros knew as well as Agatha did that they needed the knight to join their army in the war to come. So for him to beg Lancelot to remain at the house meant Tedros knew they were all going to die. For as much as the prince despised the scalawag knight, he couldn't bear the thought of his mother losing him.

Not that his wishes mattered in the end. Guinevere wouldn't hear of it.

She said her goodbye to Lancelot out on the moonlit moors, just as she did with the rest of her guests, taking the time to give brisk hugs to each, as if they were all popping off to a shop and would be back by lunch.

It was only when Guinevere hugged Agatha that the old queen

lingered. Agatha could see her lips trembling and the wet sheen of her eyes.

"Take care of my Tedros," Guinevere whispered.

"I will," said Agatha, trying not to cry.

Something cold touched her head and Agatha looked up at her prince as he fit her crown back on her.

"You left it in your room," he said, with a droll smile. "An oversight, I'm sure."

Then he met his mother's gaze.

Agatha could see each of them overwhelmed with emotion . . . a mother and son who'd battled so much pain to come back together, only to be pulled apart once more.

"Let me come with you, Tedros. Please," Guinevere pleaded. "I can fight—we'll be together—"

"No," said the prince. "It's the one thing Lancelot and I agree on."

Guinevere shook her head, tears falling.

Tedros hugged her to his chest. "Listen to me. You'll be at Camelot for my coronation. Once Agatha and I close her storybook and the School Master is dead. That's where your story will end, all right? Not here, but Camelot, where you'll be a mother . . . then a grandmother . . . and you'll have so much love for the rest of your life. . . . You can even bring the ogre."

Guinevere sniffled a laugh. "Promise me, Tedros. Promise me you'll come back."

"I promise," Tedros rasped.

But Agatha knew he was lying.

Guinevere spotted something over her son's shoulder and pulled away.

Agatha and Tedros turned to see Merlin leading his League of heroes, young and old, towards a floating portal of white glow atop a distant hill.

Lancelot climbed through first, evaporating like a shadow into the sun, before the old and new heroes followed him into the light, one by one . . . until only Merlin was left, raising consoling eyes to Agatha and Tedros across the moors, as if he wished he could let them stay.

"Has to be morning by now, surely," said Tedros to Agatha, peering through the darkness of the Woods, as they tried to keep up with the pair in front of them.

"Then where's the sun?" Agatha asked, searching a horizon of fast-moving black clouds with a pinprick of light pulsing through it. "All I see is the North Star and storm clouds—"

Only they *weren't* clouds, as Agatha looked closer.

It was smoke, emanating from somewhere far ahead, directly in the path of where Merlin was leading their army. Huddled into a black cloak, Agatha stood on tiptoes, squinting over the pairs in front of her, but she couldn't see where the smoke was coming from.

"Lift me up," she nudged Tedros.

"What?"

"On your shoulders."

Tedros frowned. "Just because you're wearing a crown doesn't mean—"

"*Now.*"

The prince sighed. "And I thought Sophie was high maintenance."

He swung her up onto his shoulders, grunting softly as she clasped her arms around his cloak collar, her clumps digging into his chest. She could see Hort and Peter Pan paired in front of them and hear Cinderella and Pinocchio a ways behind, trading jokes at the sight of them.

"Someone's whipped," said Pinocchio.

"Finally as tall as his father," Cinderella groused.

Tedros gritted his teeth, laboring under Agatha's weight. "How much longer you need up there?"

Agatha leaned forward, the lattice of tree branches brushing against her crown, as she gazed far into the darkness, tracking the smoke.

It was coming from a fire.

Far into the black horizon, a tall tower of yellow-red flames raged into the sky. As the blaze licked higher and higher, it lit up the surroundings: a crooked clock tower, the shops of a square, turreted cottage rooftops, and the rest of a crystal-clear village, glowing in the flame light beneath a tattered shield . . .

Gavaldon.

Gavaldon was on fire.

Suddenly, she remembered the painting in the Exhibition of Evil . . . August Sader's last vision of a giant bonfire in the middle of the village . . .

"No, it's not on fire. They're burning the *storybooks*," she whispered, clutching Tedros tighter. "Sader knew they'd burn the books."

She could see the shield over Gavaldon riddled with small holes and quivering in the wind, as if about to shatter at any moment.

"They're believing in the new endings, Tedros. Merlin was right. They're losing faith in Good . . ."

"I don't get where M is taking us," Tedros murmured, not listening to her. "The school is to the east, and your village is to the west. If Merlin keeps us on this path, we'll run straight into the Stymph Forest between them."

"Stymph Forest?"

"Where stymphs come from. You know those bony birds we used to have at school before the crogs ate them all," said Tedros impatiently, sweating under her. "Merlin's insane if he thinks we'd last a minute in there. No one in their right mind ever goes in that Forest, because the School Master controls the stymphs."

"I thought stymphs hate villains," said Agatha.

"Because the School Master's *trained* them to seek out Evil souls. Only time anyone even gets near the Stymph Forest is on November 11, every four years, when the new Nevers are picked for school. Families have picnics on the perimeter and watch the stymphs blast out of the trees to kidnap kids and bring 'em to Evil castle."

From Tedros' shoulders, Agatha could see the dark stretch of woods that separated Gavaldon from the faint outlines of the School for Evil.

She'd been in that Forest before.

That night more than two years ago, when the School Master took her and Sophie from Gavaldon . . . he'd dragged them into the Endless Woods, where a stymph hatched out of a black egg, snatched them in its jaws, and flown them off to their fateful schools.

But why would Merlin be taking them to the Forest where their story began? They were supposed to be attacking the School for Evil. They were supposed to be finding Sophie, so she'd destroy her ring—

If Agatha could convince her to, that is.

Quickly she looked into the sky, trying to distract herself from her impossible task. How long did they have until the Woods went dark anyway? And why hadn't the sun risen yet?

Her eyes drifted back to that tiny speck of light, trapped behind the smoke clouds. As she focused harder, she saw it was dripping: orange pieces of flame that scorched through the smoke and extinguished midair.

"Not the North Star," she rasped. "Tedros, that's the *sun*."

Tedros glanced at the sky, irritated. "Don't be daft. The sun can't be that small—" His expression tensed. "Can it?"

Agatha knew he'd just realized the same thing she had last night. They'd been away from the Woods too long.

Slowly he lowered her back to the ground. "Seven days. That's what Merlin said, didn't he?"

"Meaning the sun will die at sunset . . . *tonight*," said Agatha.

"Meaning tonight the storybook closes," said Tedros. "One way or another."

They looked at one another, the same shade of pale.

"I won't let anything happen to you," he promised.

Agatha nodded. "I know."

But she was the one lying now. Not even a prince could protect her from what was coming.

Tedros forced a gallant smile, hugging her into his flank. "Of all the tales in all the kingdoms in all the Woods, you had to walk into mine."

Agatha feigned a smile back, holding him tight, as they followed Merlin and the rest of Good's army towards the dark Stymph Forest.

When they'd come through the portal into the Woods, the first thing Agatha and Tedros noticed was how cold it was. After three weeks in the springtime haven of the moors, the return to a sunless winter sent them both into shivers, even under their thick cloaks. But worse than the cold was the new, nasty smell: a stink of dead trees and decomposing animals that made her and Tedros shield their noses with their sleeves for the first hour, before they got used to it.

As the morning dragged on, no warmer or brighter, the group continued on the path, two by two, old with young— except Agatha and Tedros, who paired with each other to avoid their respective mentors. At first, the teams were lulled into a sense of safety by the deserted Woods. The Ever kingdoms had sealed themselves away, just as Merlin predicted, while the Never kingdoms like Ravenbow and Netherwood knew better than to attack Good's army, however small, until the School

Master proved that Evil could win.

The safe feeling didn't last much longer.

Soon the pairs began to notice makeshift graves off the path, topped with smoking white stars on which Merlin had written fallen heroes' names. Walking with the White Rabbit, Yuba made a note of them in a small notebook and whispered a prayer for each. By the time he and the rest stopped for lunch a few hours later at a dried-up pond, they all had the same grim faces, knowing they were drawing closer and closer to graves of their own.

And yet, they still had faith that their leader had a plan to save them. So when Merlin lit a fire in the middle of the pond-bed and handed out turkey sandwiches, his audience settled into the dirt, relieved they were about to finally, *finally* hear how a small gang of heroes and students could beat an Evil army twenty times their size.

"Sometimes I wonder," Merlin declared, licking a bit of mustard off his upper lip, "where exactly does the food come from? Is there a fourth dimension where a magic hat goes to fetch it? Or does it simply summon turkeys and bread out of thin air? In which case, what is this sandwich *really* made of?"

Forty eyes gaped at him.

"Merlin," said Lancelot, simmering, "it's clear we're headed straight for the Stymph Forest, otherwise you would have turned us east hours ago. Is there a *reason* we're going there instead of the school?"

"Certainly," said Merlin, digging in his hat for a toothpick. He didn't elaborate.

"So? What is it?" Peter Pan snapped.

"The Stymph Forest is where the School Master plans to attack us, of course," said Merlin, as he picked his teeth. "Shall we have some coffee? Though twenty mugs of it is a bit much to ask, given all of you are no doubt fussy about how you take your milk and sug—"

"Merlin, for God's sakes!" growled Jack.

"When I said, 'Leave the plan to me,' I meant it," the wizard retorted. "All of you have enough to worry about without the intricacies of war: a war that will be all for naught if even *one* of our most famous heroes dies. The shield over the Readers is almost broken now. Peter, Cinderella, Jack, Sleeping Beauty, Red Riding Hood, Hansel, Gretel, Pinocchio—you are all that's left between the School Master and the end of Good as we know it. So let me worry about the battle plan while you and your young lieges worry about how to keep all of you *alive*."

Tedros gave Agatha a sharp look, questioning whether leaving the plan to Merlin sounded as faulty to her as it did to him.

Agatha cleared her throat. "Merlin, you just said you're taking us into the Stymph Forest because the School Master will attack us there. Given the School Master controls the Stymph Forest, don't you think that warrants *some* details?"

"Details?" Merlin asked, pursing his lips. "How's this. The School Master plans to ambush us with the old villains before we get to school. Given I know this before it happens, I had to choose where I want this ambush to take place. The Stymph Forest seemed the best option."

Rumbles rolled through his audience.

"He's finally lost it," Tedros mumbled to Agatha.

"Merlin, first off, the Stymph Forest is the worst place we can go if it's under the School Master's control—" Lancelot snorted.

"Forget the stymphs," Hester jumped in. "He's ambushing us? With two hundred zombie villains?"

"How would wizard even know they ambush us?" Hansel scoffed.

"For once Hansel is right," Gretel agreed. "'Ambush' means attack with *surprise*, so if there is no surprise, then there is no ambush—"

"What's surprising to me is that our future queen is worried about me," Merlin boomed, eyes still on Agatha, "when *she* is the one ultimately responsible for winning this war and yet has no idea how to make Sophie destroy her ring."

Everyone shut up.

Agatha slowly looked up at Merlin.

"Either the School Master dies or we die, Agatha," the wizard impressed. "So if I were you, I would be wholly focused on Sophie instead of *stymphs*."

His echo resounded across the Woods.

Agatha could see Tedros staring at her.

The rest of the group frowned at her too, dead silent.

"Might as well kill ourselves now, then," Cinderella cracked.

Agatha twirled to her. "Or kill you since you're a vile, black-hearted *beast* who no one can stand!"

Cinderella went beet red.

A stillness fell over the group, with everyone looking away.

Agatha glanced at Tedros, but he couldn't meet her eyes either.

Merlin lumbered to his feet, brushing his hands of crumbs. "Another reason I've stayed a bachelor all these years . . . ," he said, heading towards the path. "The joy of eating *alone*."

"I'm not apologizing," Agatha declared.

Tedros chomped on an apple, ambling beside her.

"I'm not. She deserved it," Agatha pushed, trying not to look back at Cinderella with Pinocchio, a ways behind. "You would have done the same thing."

Tedros didn't answer.

"Look, if you're going to make a scene about it, I'll apologize, but only if she apologizes first," said Agatha.

Tedros gnawed at the apple core and tossed it aside. "What is she apologizing for, exactly?"

"Tedros, she's done nothing but torment us since the day we met her."

"None of it bothered you before. If anything, you've gone out of your way to be civil to her until ten minutes ago."

"Because I can only take so much!"

"Or because you found a convenient whipping girl during a moment of self-doubt."

"What?"

"Agatha, do you remember first year we were in Dovey's Good Deeds class and you told me I was dumb as an ass and then—"

"You threatened to *kill* me?"

Tedros pointed at himself. "Self-doubt." He pointed at her. "Whipping girl."

The prince cocked a smile. "Takes one to know one."

Agatha folded her arms. "Well, you didn't apologize to me back then, so why should I apologize to her?"

"Because you're a better person than me, obviously."

"Is that the defense you're going to use in every argument from now until we die?"

"Works, doesn't it?"

Agatha groaned. "Fine. Given that it's impossible to get her alone at the moment, I'll wait until there's a more suitable time and plac—"

"Hey, Long Nose!" Tedros shouted to Pinocchio. "Mind walking with me for a bit?"

Pinocchio grimaced. "I'd rather not, given your air of entitlement, but seeing you're a spoiled brat who will heckle me with emasculating taunts if I don't, I'm sensing I don't have a choice," he said, shuffling towards the prince.

Tedros blinked at him. "It must be exhausting to always tell the truth."

"Why do you think I'm not married?" said Pinocchio, walking off with him.

And just like that, Agatha was alone with her mentor.

She expected the old princess to attack her and make a public spectacle of this, but instead, Cinderella trudged ahead, slouched and shifty-eyed, looking like a shamed child.

"Um, hello again," said Agatha, a bit thrown. "I wanted to say sorry. I guess I felt defensive and took it out on—"

"You think I'm a bad person," Cinderella mumbled. "Everyone thinks I'm a bad person and that I'm bitter and frigid and rude. But no one in this group will ever understand, least of all you."

"That's not true," said Agatha. "People used to think I was pretty rude too. Truth is I was afraid of their judgments, until I learned to—"

"Oh, no one gives a hoot what you learned," Cinderella grouched. "You got it all wrong anyway. This ain't about me being scared of stupid judgments or people like you. Forget I said anything. I accept your apology and now you can go away, all right?"

She crossed her arms and looked away, done with this conversation.

Agatha sighed. "All right."

She started to leave . . . but then she heard it. A quiet voice inside of her.

Don't go.

Only it wasn't her voice.

It was Cinderella's.

Once upon a time, Agatha could hear the wishes of souls in need. Since then, she thought she'd lost her talent.

But perhaps she hadn't lost it after all.

Perhaps she'd just stopped listening.

Slowly Agatha turned back to the old princess.

"Tell me," she said.

Cinderella looked at her, startled. "Still here, are you," she said, trying to sound annoyed.

"Look, Merlin thinks we can help each other," said Agatha. "And I have a feeling you know why."

Cinderella shifted her eyes to the ground. "What's the point?" she muttered softly.

"Please," said Agatha.

They walked in silence for a long time.

"I never thought in a million years I'd get into the School for Good," said the old princess. "I grew up with a stepmother who told me I was ugly and stupid and paunchy and wasn't worthy to scrub her toilet, let alone be an Evergirl. 'Cinderella,' she named me: the girl who would be lucky to marry a stableboy. All her attention was focused on her two daughters, who she knew would marry eligible princes after graduating from the School for Good. So when *I* got a Flowerground ticket to school and my stepsisters didn't, I felt so ashamed, as if there'd been some great mistake. Surely someone would see it was my sisters who belonged there, not me. But then I got my uniform and schedule and portrait on the wall . . . and there I was, a real student just like the others. Ella. Sweet, cinderless Ella of Charity, Room 24.

"But I wasn't happy at school. By the end of my first year, I was horribly homesick. Because here's the thing no one knows about me: I *loved* my stepsisters. And they loved me! The storybooks never tell you that, because it would mess up everything, wouldn't it? I mean, sure, they were silly and spoiled and prince-obsessed, but they were also clever and bawdy and sassy like me. Plus, they'd saved my life. When my father died and I was orphaned to my stepmother, she'd wanted to sell me to Bluebeard, who was looking for a new wife at the time. But knowing that Bluebeard had a reputation for hacking up his wives, my stepsisters came up with the idea of making me the housemaid instead. I could tell they felt guilty about having me wash their underpants, but I was happy as a clam, knowing they'd spared me from a terrible end. Besides, they usually were at my side while I did the sweeping and cooking, telling me all about the legendary School for Good and how glorious it would be once they got their Flowerground tickets, along with relaying the latest town gossip and carping about their troll of a mother. The three of us were so *close*. So to then be whisked off to school without them, especially when I always thought of that school as theirs . . . well, by the second month, I was moping over a bucket of ice cream before bed every night, wishing I could go home."

She took a deep breath. "But graduation finally came and while other students went off into the Woods in search of their fairy tales, I dashed back to my stepmother's cottage in Maidenvale. At first, my sisters wouldn't speak to me, still furious that I'd 'stolen' their place at school. But I was careful never to mention my life as a student and in time, they began giving me chores all over again. Meanwhile, my stepmother tore up any letters that arrived from my schoolmates and burned my old uniforms and textbooks, and soon it was like I'd never gone to the school at all. Which was a relief, honestly, because I was just happy to be laughing with my sisters like it was old times.

"But my stepmother was a jealous wretch and began warning her daughters to keep their distance from me—I was a wolf in sheep's clothing and would one day betray them, just like I had when I'd taken their spots at school. The bonds between girls who weren't blood could *never* last. My stepsisters didn't believe her, of course. I was family to them. And the truth was, I wanted them to be happy. After seeing my father marry that she-devil and seeing all the stupid energy that Evergirls put into boys at school, I was more than happy to leave marriage and love and princes to my stepsisters, while I lived life in their shadows, perfectly fine with their company and my own."

Cinderella paused. "So you have to understand, when Professor Dovey came to my house on that famous night and granted my wish to go to the Ball, she—and everyone else who knows my story—thought I wanted to go to the Ball to meet the prince. I *never* wanted to meet the damn prince! I wanted to go to the Ball because I wanted to see my *stepsisters* meet the prince! Their whole lives had been building towards the night Prince Keelan would see the eligible girls of the kingdom. And after all those years of me listening to them gush about what they'd say to him and what they'd wear and how they'd win his heart, now they'd finally get their turn in front of him. How could I not be there! They wanted me there too, of course, but they couldn't dare admit it to stepmother. You should have seen their faces when I cornered them at the Ball and revealed myself, magic slippers and all. Just as I'd played down my time at school to keep us together, now they saw again how much I really loved them: for I'd used a magic wish to see their moment with the prince."

Her mentor's eyes slowly dimmed. "When Prince Keelan

chose me, I could see the shock in their faces, as if in a single moment, they realized they should have listened to their stepmother all along. The things they called me in that moment, with so many people listening, were so horrible that I can never forget them. I tried to explain to them that I didn't want the prince—I even ran away from the Ball to prove it. But princes always find their princesses, even when they don't want them to. He tracked me to my stepmother's house like a snoop and fit me with the glass slipper I'd left behind. When he proposed to me, I gave him one condition: my stepsisters would come and live at the palace with me, because if I was marrying a man I hardly knew, at least I could live it up in style with my best friends. But he'd seen how my sisters behaved towards me at the Ball and when his men fitted me with the slipper. He couldn't see in them what I did. Instead, he demanded I choose: either I'd go to the palace alone as his wife or be left behind at the house with my sisters forever. He gave me until the morning to decide and left with his men."

Cinderella paused. "That night, my stepmother tried to kill me in my bed with an axe, but my prince had hidden outside my window, knowing I wasn't safe under her roof. He killed her on the spot with his sword and swept me away. The last thing my stepsisters ever saw was me riding away with the prince they'd both dreamed of, their mother dead on the floor."

Cinderella teared up. "First I took their place at school. Then I took their prince. Then I took their mother. How could they see the Good in me now? How could they see me as anything but an enemy?" she rasped. "For years, they plotted against me until my prince had them both killed, without my knowledge. When I discovered what he'd done, I left him forever. Because what my stepsisters never knew was that I would have stayed the next morning and given up my crown for them. Because *they* were my Ever After. More than any boy could be. And if I had to be alone the rest of my life in order to keep them in it . . . I would have. But it was all too late."

She finally looked at Agatha, racked with pain. "That's why I told you to just stick that wand to Sophie's head and threaten her and make her do what you want. That's what my story taught me at least—might as well be a big fat bully and get what you want, 'cause love doesn't mean anything in the end. Not when a boy's gonna swoop in and ruin it forever." She broke down in sobs.

"Oh Ella," Agatha whispered, tears sliding down her face.

"It's why I'm never happy," Ella wept, the harshness gone from her now. "Because everyone thinks my fairy tale was about finding a fairy godmother and a dress and a prince, when I never wanted any of that! I just wanted my stepsisters to be happy! I just wanted to keep my best friends!"

Agatha touched the old princess's back and let her cry as they walked in silence on the path.

"You really love Sophie?" Ella asked finally. "After everything she's done?"

Agatha nodded, suddenly overtaken by emotion. "As much as you love your stepsisters."

Ella stopped on the path, a quiet awakening in her eyes. "*That's* why Merlin paired us together. Because I let my story go.

I gave in to despair and anger and let it steal my life from under me. But you can fix my fairy tale by fixing yours, Agatha. You can still fight for Sophie. You can still fight for your friend."

Agatha shook her head. "I don't know if there's any of Sophie left to fight for, Ella."

Her mentor touched her cheek. "You can't give up, Agatha. Not yet. Show the world what I couldn't. Love that means just as much as a boy's. Love that's stronger than blood. Do it for the both of us."

Agatha gazed at Ella and for the first time the dark fear inside of her gave way to a ray of light . . .

Then Cinderella's expression changed.

Agatha turned and saw the entire group stopped on the path, gawking at her and her mentor, as if they were a lion and rabbit having a garden party.

"Oh good grief, the fools think I've gone soft," Cinderella growled.

"I'll tell them I groveled for forgiveness," said Agatha.

"And pledged your eternal servitude too," snapped Cinderella. "Now get back to your blasted prince before you completely ruin my reputation."

With a wink, she gave her charge a swift kick in the buttocks, and Agatha couldn't help but smile as she stumbled away, wondering how different her life might have been if she'd just learned to say sorry more often.

31

Spies in the Stymph Forest

By the time they made it to the outskirts of the Stymph Forest, the sun's shrinking glow was firmly in the east.

"Only a few hours until the sun sets," Tedros said nervously, his hand moving to Excalibur as if to make sure it was there. "Even Lance keeps looking at the sun like he knows we're doomed."

"Lance. He gets a nickname from you and I don't?"

Tedros glanced at Agatha. She cracked a smile.

"It's not funny," he said, seeing the entrance to the Stymph Forest ahead. "There is no escape this time. The dark is coming, Agatha. This is The End for us. The *real* End—"

"I know." She squeezed his hand, still affected by Cinderella's story. "So let's try to hold on to every last bit of light that we can."

He stared at her. "Now you decide to be romantic? *Now?*"

Agatha stopped smiling. "Look, Merlin has a plan, all right? He *has* to have a plan."

In front of them, the other pairs began to slow down as they approached the gates of the Stymph Forest. At the entrance stood two colossal elm trees, as tall as castle towers, with their trunks bowed towards each other and dead branches whittled into the shape of a bristling black swan, beak open, feathers beating, so lifelike in its impending attack that Agatha felt herself clutch Tedros tighter as they crossed beneath it.

She shook off her fear. "I mean, it's *Merlin* we're talking about, the Merlin of legend and myth, who never fails Good in times of crisis—"

"Except when he deserts us for six days, forgets to recruit a real army, drags us straight into School Master territory without weapons, and doesn't teach us a single fire spell to kill any of the two hundred zombies about to eat us."

Agatha swallowed.

They couldn't see anything now, for the Stymph Forest was so dense with sky-high elms that it scrubbed out the last pinprick of sun. Agatha waited for someone to light a torch or a fingerglow, but no one took the initiative, as if it was less frightening to be in the dark than to see what was lurking in the trees. With no other light source, the nineteen heroes folded in a tight hive behind the wizard, whose hat led the way with its glowing white stars.

The deeper they drew into the Stymph Forest, the more they began to smell the acrid smoke seeping from the bonfire in Gavaldon beyond the Woods. Instinctively, the younger members shielded their older mentors, remembering their duty to protect them and keep the shield over the Reader World intact. Anadil's rats spread out across Anadil's, Jack's, and Briar Rose's shoulders like bodyguards; Hester and Lancelot wheeled Hansel and Gretel through the pebbly dirt; Yuba stuck by the White Rabbit, whose night vision was quite acute; Dot and Red Riding Hood hewed to Princess Uma, insisting a teacher of Animal Communication should know how to manage stymphs ("Stymphs aren't animals; they're *beasts*," Uma moaned); and Hort held out a rusty training sword, guarding Peter Pan and Tinkerbell.

Slowly their eyes drifted upwards, pinned to the trees, and as they adjusted to the darkness, they began to make them out . . . bony, vulturous shadows, eerily still on the elm branches, not making a sound.

"They're watching us," Lancelot murmured.

Merlin stopped suddenly, causing a pileup behind him and an array of hissed curses and crushed toes. The wizard peered ahead.

"Gretel, why is wizard stopping—" Hansel started.

"Shhh!" Gretel retorted. "Listen . . ."

That's when Agatha heard it too.

The low thunder of marching, reverberating through the Forest.

Far away, pulses of bright green glow pierced the blackness like blinking stars . . . first a few . . . then a dozen . . . then hundreds, lighting up all at once before vanishing back to dark. With every second, the pulsing lights grew closer, matching the crescendo of footsteps—*left, right, left, right*—until Agatha wasn't sure whether it was the light following the march or the march following the light. As the flashes grew bigger, brighter, she honed in on the green detonations, like mini-fireworks, holding just long enough to illuminate the trees in the distance . . .

And the bodies coming towards them.

The Dark Army skulked into the Stymph Forest in perfect rows, carrying axes, swords, and spears. Over their heads floated a cloud of black zombie fairies that kept the beat of their march with their glowing green tails, extinguishing and rekindling again and again. With every flash of light, the army strobed closer, as if time was skipping forward, and soon Agatha could make out their dead-eyed glares, stitched-up skin, and infamous faces.

Peter Pan and Tinkerbell shrank against a tree at the sight of Captain Hook and his curved steel blade; Cinderella clutched Agatha's arm when she saw her wicked stepmother with a rusty axe; Jack pulled Briar Rose close, glimpsing his club-wielding giant and her dagger-carrying fairy; Hansel and Gretel wheeled to the rear of the pack to hide from their zombie witch; and Red Riding Hood shifted from cowering behind Dot to cowering behind Lancelot when she snagged a look at her salivating wolf.

"Merlin, this is where we 'leave it to you'!" Hort called out.

If Merlin did answer him, it was drowned out by the swell of the villains' march. Agatha searched for the glow of the wizard's hat, but the Forest was too dark and the heroes huddled too close.

"Looks just like when I saw him in Granny's nightdress," Red Riding Hood rasped, watching the wolf in the front line, only fifty yards away. "Ate me in one swallow then. But I'm a grown woman now. Which means he'd have to *chew* first—"

"I'd take a wolf's teeth over a hook any day," said Peter Pan anxiously.

"My stepmother has an *axe*!" Cinderella boomed.

"You win," said Hansel.

"It's not your stepmother, okay? They're not any of your old villains," Hester retorted. "They're zombies. They're not *real*."

"They look plenty real to me," Lancelot growled, drawing his sword.

Hands shaking, Tedros pulled Excalibur, as the Dark Army marched closer. "Lead the way, Sir Lancelot."

"Look who's suddenly showin' me respect!" Lancelot snorted. "You, who spent all week blathering that you could win this war without my help!"

"You don't know me well enough to know that I spend half my life saying stupid things and the other half apologizing for them," said Tedros. "Please, Lance. You're the greatest knight who's ever lived. Surely you've faced tougher battles. . . . Surely this isn't as bad as it looks?"

The knight could see Agatha and the rest gazing at him with the same hopeful expressions.

Lancelot glanced up at two hundred villains brandishing weapons, thirty yards away now . . . then back down at his army of defenseless Evers and Nevers, crotchety old heroes, and a prince who held the world's greatest sword but still wasn't much good at using it.

"Not as bad as it looks," he said. *"Worse."*

The Dark Army halted their advance, twenty yards from the knight. The fairies lit up to full blast as the villains sneered across the forest, eyes red and murderous, mouths clamped in flat, lifeless lines. They raised their weapons in the fairy light, waiting for the order to charge.

"Think I just wet myself," peeped Hansel.

"M-M-Merlin?" Agatha spluttered, fixed on the zombies. "Merlin, tell us what to do!"

"That'll be difficult, 'cause Merlin ain't *here,*" said Hort.

Everyone spun around.

Merlin was gone.

Agatha and Tedros gripped each other in horror. "We're *dead,*" they gasped—

From the sky came a blast of wind and they looked up to see two shadows, embraced in flight, float down through the trees.

The boy touched down first, his white hair spiked as sharp as the black crown of the girl he held in his arms. He wore a sleeveless black shirt that showed off his porcelain skin and lean muscles, and long black breeches that hung low on his hips, revealing a piece of his rippled stomach. The girl was as pale as he was, her cheeks and lips so colorless that for a moment Agatha thought her a marble statue, until she pulled away from the boy wearing a black leather catsuit that hugged every curve of her frame. She moved towards Agatha, her hair a gold wave beneath her jagged crown, her skin so tight against her bones the veins glowed through, and her mouth curled in a cold, nasty smile.

But it was only when Agatha saw the green of her eyes, the wicked emerald green, as bright as the fairy tails around her, that Agatha knew who the girl was.

"Hello, darling," said Sophie.

Agatha's throat felt like a vise, trapping her voice. Her vision blurred, Sophie lapsing out of focus, as if Agatha's whole body was rejecting the moment, searching for the ends of a dream. She could hear nothing, only a furious ringing in her ears. Darkness curled in at the corners of the scene and she knew she was losing consciousness; her legs weakened, her heartbeat fizzled, the world funneling to black . . .

Only there was light through the darkness now, gold like a beacon . . . a gold light like the one that glowed from her own finger when she needed it most . . .

But it wasn't coming from *her* finger.

It was coming from the Evil Queen's.

The ring.

Make her destroy the ring.

Agatha felt the mulch beneath her feet again, the bleak night air, her eyes refocusing ahead . . .

And there she was. Sophie, as Evil and dead cold as the boy she'd chosen.

But Sophie still the same.

"Agatha of Woods Beyond. The girl who never wanted to be a princess," said Sophie. "And here she is with a *crown*."

Agatha held her ground. "Evil has a queen. So too does Good."

"If I have a prince, you want a prince. If I have a crown, you want a crown. It's what I love about you best, Aggie. Always a step behind me." Sophie looked past her at ragged, frightened Tedros, before her gaze moved to Rafal, immaculate in fairy light. "Until I do it *better*."

Tedros took Agatha's hand and scowled at Sophie. "You call *him* better? A demon? A devil's spawn?"

"Oh Teddy. Don't be transparent," said Sophie. "We can make you a paper crown if you like. For the boy not yet a man. The prince not yet a king."

Tedros flushed. "Well, perhaps you were too busy admiring your own crown to notice you're missing half your army!" he scoffed, struggling to sound intimidating. "What happened, lost 'em on the way here?"

A sharp laugh echoed and Rafal sauntered forward. "Oh I'm quite sure my queen would have preferred we attack you with full force, little prince. Now that she has her crown, she makes me look quite soft in comparison. But our students represent Evil's precious future. I wouldn't risk a single one of them when

Evil's past is perfectly able to destroy you all on their own."

Agatha followed his eyes to the Dark Army, teeth gnashed, impatient for their Master's signal. She thought of Reena, Chaddick, Ravan, and all the other students she'd come to know, trapped in the School for Evil. One day, Rafal would ensure they ended up as dark-hearted and ruthless as these undead killers hungry for war.

But then Agatha remembered Kiko . . . lovely, sweet-faced Kiko, who just wanted everyone to find happiness and love . . . who could never be Evil no matter what anyone did to her.

"Evil will never have a future," said Agatha, thinking of her kind Evergirl friend. "Not when there are those who want to be Good."

"And no one wanted to be more Good than me, Aggie," said Sophie. "But no matter how hard you try to make an Evil heart Good, it won't take. *You* know that, or you'd never have given me a chance with your precious prince. You knew full well that I'd make a fool of myself." Sophie's pupils gleamed. "But to make a Good heart Evil . . . oh that's child's play, Aggie. Because Good hearts are like the softest underbelly, ripe for Evil to rip through. Just ask your friend, Kiko, who I heard crying last night, wishing she still had her 'best friend' Agatha to talk to. Quite popular, weren't you, in your time at school, darling? Too bad your 'best friend' won't be able to talk much longer. She'll end up making a nice wicked goose, when her Evil education resumes and her mogrification is complete."

"You know what they say," Rafal said, smirking. "Even the

purest Good excels at Evil when it might end up as Christmas dinner."

The two of them burst into snickers.

Agatha tensed, thrown by the glee in their laughter. With their ghostly skin, ice-blue veins, and sharp cheekbones, they looked so much alike now.

"Well, there'll be no goose and there'll be no Christmas dinner," Tedros blustered. "Because we're winning this war."

"Are you?" Rafal said bitingly. "With your formidable League of . . . *Nineteen*? Seems you lost your wizard, though there's so *many* rallying to your cause that it's hard to keep up. My, my, how will I ever kill the *one* hero I need to break the shield?" He scanned the meager group huddled against the trees: eight famous old heroes quailing in fear, four young Never turncoats, a languid white rabbit, a potbellied green fairy, an animal-language teacher, and a feeble old gnome . . . before his eyes fell on Lancelot, sword in hand, watching the conversation between this young foursome with a confused look on his face.

Rafal's smile darkened. "A *complication*."

"Who the devil are you?" Lancelot blustered, squinting at the snow-haired boy. "And when does the School Master get here?"

"That *is* the School Master!" Hort hissed. "I told you he turned young!"

Lancelot's eyes bulged in shock. "Good God, why didn't anyone say so?"

In a split second, he launched forward, with a running

start, and hurled his sword like a tomahawk at Rafal's head. Caught off guard, the young School Master raised his hand too late. Sophie let out a cry of surprise—

The sword blade smashed into Rafal's forehead, cleaving right through his skull.

Villains froze. Heroes held their breath.

The Stymph Forest was as silent as a corpse.

Lancelot scratched his ear, stunned by how easy it all was, before he flashed a boastful smile. "Hooah! See that, boy? One shot and the cad goes down! School Master dead. Storybook closed. Now where's our bright sunshine—"

His smile eroded.

Rafal was still standing there, a sword in his head, a cheeky grin on his face. Slowly the blood seeped back into the wound around the sword before the young School Master reached up, took a hold of the hilt, and drew the blade out of his skull. The hole in his head sealed up, smoothing to fresh, young skin, as Rafal wiped the blood off the steel edge with his bare palm, his eyes never leaving Lancelot.

Sophie too was grinning now, stroking the gold ring on her finger, which had kept her true love alive.

"Our friend seems to have misplaced his sword," the young School Master said to her.

"Tends to have a habit of meddling in other people's business, if I remember," said Sophie. "Especially mine."

"Then perhaps you'd like to be the one to return his weapon?" Rafal asked.

Sophie gripped the sword by the hilt. "Would be my honor."

Slowly she lifted cold eyes to Lancelot, her fingertip glowing pink. "Never liked him much anyway."

She fired her glow to the knight's blade and shot it like a bullet across the Forest—

Lancelot didn't even have time to breathe. His own sword rammed into his shoulder, cutting clean through skin and tissue before spearing into the tree trunk. The knight let out a lion's roar of pain, pinned to the elm like a piece of meat.

Sophie cozied up to Rafal. "Complication *solved*."

Agatha and Tedros were white as death. All the other heroes cowered against the trees, watching their greatest warrior whimper and flail, immobilized by his own weapon.

Rafal caressed Sophie's cheek. "Like I said, my queen makes me look *soft*."

Agatha could see the dark pleasure in Sophie's face and the yellow, catlike glow in her pupils. Suddenly her hope to make her friend destroy her ring seemed numbskulled and naive. Merlin had warned her: there would be no easy path to Ever After. Because there was nothing she could say to make Sophie destroy that ring now . . . nothing she could say to bring her back to Good. . . .

Because there was no Good in Sophie anymore.

"Help me, boy," Lancelot cried out to Tedros. "Help me loose!"

Tedros didn't budge.

Agatha could see him watching Lancelot on the tree. The sword was buried at the top of the knight's shoulder, away from vital organs and clotting the wound from bleeding out. As long as Lancelot stayed there, he'd be in excruciating pain . . . but safe. Because the second Tedros helped Lancelot off that tree, Lance would make another charge for Rafal and end up dead on the spot. Villains didn't offer mercy more than once. And whatever happened to Tedros from here, whatever he had to sacrifice to help Good win—even his own self—he'd make damned well sure of one thing: Lancelot would go back to his mother *alive*.

The knight saw the change in Tedros' face. "Tedros, *no*! Don't fight them alone!"

But the prince was looking at Agatha, who'd taken Tedros' hand, her teeth gritted, silently telling him he wouldn't fight Evil alone.

He would fight it with her.

"Tedros . . . please!" Lancelot begged.

The prince's fear hardened to steel. Hand in hand with Agatha, he turned back to Sophie and Rafal, the scared and tremulous boy gone.

Rafal looked thoroughly entertained. "They think this is one of their old storybooks, my queen. Join hands, fight for love, and everything will go Good's way . . ."

"At least Evil does love with dignity," Sophie scoffed, studying their joined hands. "You two are like one of those cakes drowned in frosting so no one will notice it's spoiled."

Agatha lost her poise. "A cake you did everything possible to get for *yourself*, remember?"

"And I did, thanks to you," Sophie replied coolly. She smiled at Tedros. "It just didn't taste very good."

"You're a witch," Tedros hissed. "A witch who's even uglier than the warty, bald-headed one you were before. Lucky that you found a freak as empty as you. Another black hole of a soul."

The venom in his voice took Sophie by surprise. Her cheeks blushed, before they paled again. "And yet we love each other just like you and your princess, Tedros. Nothing you say can make my love with Rafal mean any less. Nothing you say can take away our happy ending."

She pulled in tight to Rafal, who kissed her gently on the head.

"Unless it's hate, not love, that keeps you together," said Agatha, watching them. "And hate can never win."

"Never *win*?" Rafal arched a brow. "Your steadfast wizard flees like a child the moment he sees our army. Your trusty knight proved even less useful . . . and yet still you're pretending as if you have a chance?"

Sophie glared at Agatha, fury building. "That's the problem with Good, isn't it? It tells you to believe in hope and faith, when those are just *phantoms*. Evil tells you to believe in the truth—the truth that's staring at you in the face, no matter how scared you are of it. And here's some truths for you. I was dreaming about Rafal all along. I was in the right school all along. I could have been happy being myself, instead of trying to be something I wasn't. And if I'd just accepted that, I'd never have tried to be your friend in the first place. Because the only reason I knocked on your door with my big smile and my basket of cookies was so that a School Master would think I was

Good. I was using you, Agatha. You were my Good Deed to get what I wanted. The same way you've used me to get closer to your prince. So don't stand here and tell me what Rafal and I have isn't love. What you and *I* had wasn't love. Because that was a lie from the beginning."

All Agatha could hear was the sound of her own breaths, for Sophie's eyes were like fireballs, scorching through hers.

"But then again, you have hope and faith on your side, those never-failing weapons," Sophie said cuttingly, "when all we have are axes, armies, and youth on ours."

"Is that all we have, my queen?" Rafal asked playfully.

Sophie read his face. "How could I forget?"

Fingertip searing pink, she thrust it skywards, directing the cloud of fairies higher into the trees and lighting up the Forest overhead.

Thousands of bony, fleshless stymphs snarled down from the branches with their eyeless sockets, cawing with high-pitched screams at the sight of their Master and his new queen.

Agatha and the heroes shielded their ears from the terrible shrieks, but Rafal just hummed along, as if listening to beautiful music.

"They can scream all they like," Tedros growled, trying to endure the sounds. "Stymphs won't attack the Good. You only trained them to attack the Evil."

Rafal tried not to laugh. "What I admired most about your father when he was a student was that he never thought he was more than he was. He knew he was about as sharp as a flint stone, so he kept his mouth shut and made up for it with a pretty face."

Tedros reddened, looking unnerved.

"You, on the other hand, despite having even less brains than Arthur, have somehow convinced yourself that you have something going on in that exquisite little head of yours," Rafal cooed. "Must have your mother's blood. Always thought she was quite the know-it-all."

"Whoever birthed you would slay herself on the spot if she knew you had *her* blood!" Tedros spat. "I'm proud to be my mother's son."

Rafal's stare chilled him to the bone. "Well, she won't have a son after tonight."

Agatha felt Tedros tense against her.

"And as for those *stymphs* . . . they are indeed trained only to attack the Evil," Rafal said, leering at the prince. "But the Woods are no longer the Woods you once knew, little prince. Good used to be the side with happy endings. Good used to be the side with true love's kiss. Good used to be the side with Evers fighting for it. But Evil has all those things now. Evil has become the *new* Good."

He raised his arms to the stymphs with a malevolent smile. "Which means to them . . . *Good* is the new Evil."

The young School Master bared his teeth. *"KILL THEM!"*

The Dark Army roared with bloodlust and charged for the heroes—

Rafal held his hand up and they skidded to a stop.

He was still staring at the stymphs, who hadn't moved from their posts. They weren't screeching anymore either.

"I said . . . *kill them*," Rafal bellowed.

The birds didn't flinch.

The Forest was quiet.

"Yoo-hoo! Over here!" a voice pipped.

Slowly Rafal raised eyes to Merlin, high in an elm tree, astride a stymph. "You see, I'm afraid Evil isn't the new Good, my dear boy. Not if your Evers *and* Nevers are both on Good's side."

At the top of every tree in the forest, shadows toting bows and arrows slid out onto the branches from behind the tree trunks. With a swish of his hand, Merlin magically lit all their arrow tips on fire, illuminating the archers' faces.

Agatha and Tedros blanched at the sight of her classmates—Chaddick, Mona, Arachne, Vex, Reena, Millicent, Ravan, and Kiko, beaming despite her goose-feathered limbs—along with nearly two hundred other Evers and Nevers, their flaming arrows pointed at the Dark Army.

"I peed again," Hansel said, alongside his fellow gaping League Members.

Sophie was the color of ash. She looked at Rafal, who was just as dumbstruck. "Impossible . . . ," he breathed.

"They were at s-s-school—with the teachers—" stuttered Sophie. "Lady Lesso barricaded them inside—"

"Just like she did inside her classroom every session this past week, preparing her students to fight for Good," said Merlin cheerfully. "I should know, my dear. I was there, teaching the class with Lady Lesso while the old villains were asleep. The sleeping spell was my work, of course; as your friends will tell you, I have a specialty in putting things to sleep, whether the thorned trees outside the school gates, visitors to my Celestium, or a sadistic fleet of zombies. And here you thought Lady Lesso was teaching them black magic tricks for your idiotic training fights! (That was Beatrix by the way, who found the spells in her old library books, while supervising the infirmary.) But it proved a useful smokescreen for what Lady Lesso was really up to, once you became suspicious and visited the Dean's room. Not that Lesso lied to you—she *was* helping the young students fight the old villains . . . just for a much bigger fight than your pointless classroom brawls. I was hiding under her desk the whole time you were there by the way, trying to disguise my sniffles. Terrible allergies to sour plums."

Sophie couldn't find air. "You . . . I heard you . . ."

Agatha and Tedros were just as floored. *That's why Merlin was gone all week*, Agatha thought. *That was the old friend he said he was visiting . . .*

Hester, Anadil, and Dot weren't his real spies.

"It was Lady Lesso," said Sophie, realizing it too. "She was the spy all along—"

"Playing Evil's fervent champion and your loyal mentor until I needed her. And with your return to Evil and the darkening of the Woods, that time finally came," said Merlin.

"You are a fool, old man, if you think a bitter, feckless hag of a Dean can make a difference in your fate," Rafal sneered.

"Given Lady Lesso has been Evil's greatest Dean of all, I'll happily play the fool," said the wizard. "For even she knows that Evil cannot exist without Good, the two of them in constant tension, refining and defining each other as nature's balance. Try to erase Good and you only tilt the balance more in Good's favor. Which means despite all your efforts, you haven't made Evil the new Good at all. . . . You've made Evil as old as it ever was."

The wizard smiled at Rafal. "And it seems you've trained your stymphs all too *well*."

He let out a piercing wolf whistle and with a rousing war cry two-hundred strong, the students leapt astride the birds and dive-bombed the birds off the trees, launching flaming arrows at the old villains—

Arrow blades ripped through their targets, igniting zombie bodies on fire.

Chaddick spiraled his stymph straight into the Dark Army, skewering three ogres with a single arrow . . . Beatrix managed a flying loop before she sparked fire to Snow White's witch with an arrow to the neck . . . Arachne took out a cyclops' eye with a straight shot and spinning dive . . .

Agatha watched a fleet of Nevers spray arrows into more zombie heads, utterly flabbergasted. Neither stymph-flying nor archery was ever taught at school. How had students as bumbling as Brone or Mona or Millicent become bird-riding, weapon-firing warriors in a *week*?

But it was only when Agatha saw Kiko, flying wildly with absolutely no direction, her hand puttering on her bow, unleashing an arrow miles off target, that Agatha realized what was really happening. For all of a sudden, Kiko's stymph magically leveled and her arrow magically veered, before tearing through a troll's throat and setting him aflame.

Slowly Agatha looked up to see Merlin high up in his tree, waving his palms like a symphony conductor, managing the stymph and arrow flights of his Ever-Never army with a sorcerer's touch. *Leave it to me*, he'd insisted all along. For if the School Master would bring forth an army under his control, so too would Merlin.

He swished his arms once more and four unmanned stymphs with bows and fiery arrows in their mouths throttled towards the ground, scooping Hester, Anadil, Dot, and Hort onto their backs, who immediately began taking aim at zombie targets and letting arrows fly.

"If Daddy could see me now . . . ," Dot cheered, lancing a headless horseman through the chest.

"He'd ask why we're fighting for Good," Anadil crabbed, taking out two Harpies.

"Always the party pooper, Ani," said Hester, firing arrows as her demon flung firebolts from its mouth, igniting zombies on the spot.

"No wonder Good always wins," Hort marveled as he flew above them, watching Merlin correct the witches' shots. "You guys cheat!"

For a moment, Agatha felt a surge of relief, knowing the wizard was in command of Good's whole army—well, almost the whole army. The old heroes were trying to charge into the fray, but were held back to the trees by Princess Uma, Yuba, the White Rabbit, and Tinkerbell, who knew even one of their deaths would break the Readers' shield. Meanwhile, Lancelot yelled for the wizard to help him off the tree, but Merlin was so distracted trying to orchestrate his army that he flicked his hand in the knight's direction and accidentally buried the sword deeper into his shoulder. As Lancelot hollered in pain, Agatha started towards him, but stopped short—

Tedros.

Where was Tedros?

She whirled to see him, Excalibur in hand, charging towards Rafal, whose back was turned. Agatha held in a scream as Tedros raised his sword—

Rafal spun just in time, shooting a bomb of black glow which Tedros barely deflected with his blade.

"Always so impulsive, little prince," the young School Master snorted. "And now you've taken yourself into battle against someone who can't be *killed.*"

"When I'm done, you'll be in so many pieces, I'd like to see you *try* to put yourself back together!" Tedros roared.

As the two clashed viciously, Rafal firing more death spells and Tedros repelling them, Agatha could see her prince already losing ground. The School Master was rifling spells so fast and blasting away trees with such force that Tedros was diving behind stumps to avoid being toasted alive.

Agatha couldn't breathe. Her prince was going to die. She had to help him! *But how?* The School Master was invincible. There was no way to save Tedros unless—

The ring.

She looked up urgently and saw Sophie, crimson with rage, firing spells at stymph birds and crashing them with their riders to the ground. Sophie sensed something and froze still, before she turned and saw Agatha glowering at her . . . at the ring on her finger . . . her jaw set with determination. Slowly the two friends locked eyes.

Sophie took off, fleeing through the Forest.

Agatha started chasing, then heard Tedros cry with pain. She whirled and saw him crawling through flaming bodies, clutching his singed arm, as he tried to dodge Rafal's spells.

At the same time, the Dark Army was starting to regain a foothold in battle, thanks to Jack's giant, knocking down stymphs with his fist, while Captain Hook slashed his weapon, sending students careening to the ground. Merlin's gestures were increasingly frantic, and he had the same anxious look that he'd had when he'd lost control of his fairy-dust train.

Agatha swiveled to Tedros and saw him using a stymph corpse as a shield against Rafal, as the School Master closed in. Petrified, Agatha spun and saw Sophie getting farther away—

Either she went to help Tedros or she went after the ring.

She looked up to the sun's glow sinking in the dead-east. There wasn't much time—

"Let me free!" Lancelot's voice ripped through the chaos. "The boy'll die without me!"

Agatha's eyes veered to him, speared to the tree. The knight was caked with blood, his hair ragged and beast-like, his face filled with primal rage.

"*I* fight," he snarled at her. "*You* go after her."

Agatha knew there wasn't an argument. In a heartbeat, she hurdled over burning bodies and yanked the sword out of the knight's shoulder.

Lancelot howled in agony and relief before he stumbled forward and snatched the sword out of her hands.

"Get her back here," he panted, squeezing her arm hard.

"But Tedros . . . what about Ted—"

"He'll be here, safe and sound, with Excalibur ready to destroy the ring when you return. I promise you, Agatha: I *will* keep the boy safe. But we need you to bring Sophie back," Lancelot pressed. "Don't fail me and I won't fail you. Understood?"

Agatha nodded, breathless.

He shoved her away and she hurtled after Sophie into the trees. She peeked over her shoulder at Tedros, trying to repel Rafal's death spells with a broken stymph bone, before she saw Lancelot storming towards them, the gang of old heroes at his back.

"Do we fight or do we cower!" Lancelot yelled.

"We fight!" the League roared.

They followed him into battle as Agatha ran away from it, Good's last and only hope to survive.

32

The Meaning of Evil

With the light of the black fairies and flaming arrows illuminating her path, Agatha launched after Sophie, who was sprinting eastwards towards the edge of the Stymph Forest. Sophie had a good thirty-yard lead on her, but the farther she ran, the more the lights receded from the Good-Evil war, and soon Sophie was stumbling through the dark in her black-leather catsuit, trying to find her way out of the Woods.

"Wait!" Agatha shouted, unable to see her anymore. If

she lost Sophie here, she'd never find her before the sun set. "Sophie—"

A pink blast of light blazed towards her head and Agatha dove just in time. She looked up to see Sophie racing ahead.

Where is she going? Agatha thought, holding out her own gold fingerglow like a lantern.

But then she saw it, through the gaps of skeletal branches overhead . . . the outlines of the two school castles.

Agatha stopped cold.

Sophie was Queen of Evil. She could open and close the school gates now, like any of the teachers. Which meant if Sophie crossed before Agatha caught her, she'd slam the gates shut.

Agatha exploded forward, trying to make up ground, as the two of them broke out of the Woods and into a grove of purple, giant-thorned trees separating the Stymph Forest from the School for Good and Evil. The lethal-sharp thorns stirred languidly, as if woken from a deep sleep, and Agatha knew she only had seconds before they spotted her. Ahead, Sophie was nearing the school gates, but Agatha suddenly couldn't see her anymore as deadly thorns started stabbing down in front of her like falling stalactites.

"Sophie!"

Agatha hurdled and dodged thorns, feeling the ground caving in as more and more thorns smashed holes around her. A thorn sliced from the left and she slid beneath it, only to have one gash her arm from the right; Agatha bit back the pain and fumbled forward, eyes locked on Sophie as the gates magically opened for her and started slatting shut the second she surged through. Agatha skidded towards them, still ten yards away, knowing she wasn't going to make it. The gate was closing too fast—

She glanced back and saw another thorn lashing down like a wave, about to impale her against the closing gates—

Only one play to make.

With a gasp, Agatha turned towards the thorn. Just as it hit her heart, she skirted its edge and leapt onto its side, like a hapless Tarzan, as the thorn reared up in surprise over the school gates. Agatha clung to the leathery purple thorn stem for dear life, swinging her legs through the air as she glanced down at the knife-edged gate spikes beneath her. The thorn coiled and flapped higher, about to shake her off. This was her last chance—

Agatha dug her nails into the stem, kicked her legs for momentum and flung herself off the thorn, over the gates, and shielded her head before she landed hard on her tailbone in a pine shrub. Any elation at being alive was scrubbed out by her throbbing backside. She lumbered to her feet to chase Sophie once more—

Agatha froze.

Sophie glared back at her from the shores of Halfway Bay.

Before Agatha could move, a pink spell slammed into her chest, flattening her to the ground.

The shock of being attacked with a stun spell by her best friend gave way to an onslaught of pain. It was as if she'd been stomped on by an elephant or bashed in the chest by a streaking comet. For a second, she forgot who and where she was. All she could think about was air and finding a way to get it inside of her, but her lungs were paralyzed, rejecting her breaths. She tried to inhale through her mouth, but her ears were ringing with a tone so shrill and piercing that she clenched her teeth and closed her eyes, waiting for it to end. It only got louder, compounded by crippling nausea. Every second brought a new surprise, like a house of horrors, until she realized the biggest, most obvious problem of all: she couldn't *move*.

She tried to crack open her eyes and see what was behind her, but her head felt like it'd been hacked open with an axe. Her field of vision was upside-down and shaky, her eyes watering too much to see any more than a dim, blurry fog. All she could make out through the quaking darkness was a blur of green coming off Halfway Bay—

And a black shadow, upside-down, running through it towards the old Evil castle.

Agatha could feel her heart trying in vain to pump blood to her muscles. Sophie . . . she had to follow Sophie. . . .

Only she was still nailed to the dirt.

How long do stun spells last?

She'd seen students recover from them easily in Yuba's class and during the past two Trials. That's why the teachers never taught a counterspell: stunning was so innocuous that even the most belligerent first year couldn't wreak havoc with it. So what had Sophie possibly done to make this spell so noxious and hateful . . .

Magic follows emotion.

Agatha's breaths shallowed. Sophie had hit her with every-thing raging inside of her: fury, frustration, revenge . . . she'd turned an ordinary spell into a missile of hate.

And there was only one counterspell to hate.

Magic follows emotion.

Agatha pictured her beautiful, brave prince in the Stymph Forest, fighting a deadly School Master. She focused on valiant Lancelot, who just wanted to go home to his one true love. She thought of noble, incorrigible old heroes, rushing into battle to repel old villains, who were starting to gain the upper hand. She looked up into the sky and watched the faint plumes of smoke blowing in from a shield over Gavaldon she couldn't let break . . .

They need me.

They need me to destroy the ring.

Gold heat surged to her fingertip and a rush of air inflated her chest. With a cry of pain, she curled up into a fetal position and lurched to her knees.

For the first few paces, she could only crawl, her vision so misty and poor that she almost floundered straight into the bay's lethal slime. Squinting up the hill at the old Evil cas-tle, she could see Sophie propelling through the main doors. Agatha knew how vast the inside of Evil castle was; if Sophie got too far ahead, she'd never find her before nightfall—

Panicked, she glanced up at the sky over the bay and saw the needlepoint glow sinking east.

A couple hours at most.

Agatha willed her way to her feet, her hands and arms

still locked up, her legs still spasming with pain. She limped past the bay, lumbered up the muddy hill towards the castle entrance, and shambled through the wide open doors. She'd find her. . . . She *had* to find her . . .

Her feet staggered onto the stone floor of the foyer before she slid down a wall of old portraits, drained of strength.

The castle was dead quiet, with the only sound a leaky drip that trickled down the portrait frames.

Sophie was long gone.

Head hammering, Agatha scanned the deserted halls off the foyer . . . the stairs in the anteroom leading to the towers . . .

I can't move. Not anymore.

How can I find her if I can't move?

She leaned against the wall, trying not to panic, trying to see straight—

Voices.

She heard voices. Carrying softly from the other side of the tall double doors at the end of the stair room.

Nauseous with pain, Agatha squirmed forward on her stomach like a seal, her hands and arms still paralyzed. Pouring sweat, she shoved her face to the doors and peeked through the gap between them.

Inside the dark Theater of Tales, Lady Lesso and Professor Clarissa Dovey were kneeling on the stone stage, hovering over the giant crack, revealing the deep, frozen Brig of Betrayers beneath. Thick, glowing blue mist billowed from inside the glacial dungeon, lighting up the Deans' faces. From her vantage point at the west doors, Agatha could make out Dovey using her wand to melt one of the ice tombs on a dungeon wall, as Lady Lesso tried to extract Professor Emma Anemone from inside it by hacking at the ice with the tip of her stiletto heel.

"Do the part around her mouth last, Lesso dear," said Dovey over Professor Anemone's muffled shouts. "I could do without hearing Emma speak until absolutely necessary."

Dovey's silver bun of hair and beetle-winged, green gown were drenched, no doubt the result of having been freed from her own ice tomb. Yet, her smile was as luminous as ever, as if she'd forgotten her frozen torment the moment she was reunited with her friend and fellow Dean.

Meanwhile, in the back corner of the misty blue pit, Agatha could make out a new addition to the Brig—Aric, tied up and gagged, thrashing on the dungeon's deep, snow-coated floor. Despite his muscles and height, there was nothing intimidating about him now as he whimpered and shivered on his side, "CREEP" still scarred into his forehead.

"Mother, please!" he garbled into his gag, but Lady Lesso ignored him.

"Couldn't we seal him in his dormitory, like we did the other Evil teachers?" Professor Dovey asked, frowning at her sputtering wand. "We just need to keep them out of the way until the war is won—"

"Aric will stay in the Brig," said Lady Lesso.

"Mother, I'm sorry!" he cried, trying to chew through his gag, but Lady Lesso still wouldn't look at him.

"He is your son, even if he is vile," Professor Dovey appealed. "And to leave your son in the Brig all alone seems rather—"

"I'm beginning to doubt my decision to free you," Lady Lesso snapped.

Professor Dovey pursed her lips and refocused on melting the tomb, only to see her wand fizzle again. "Goodness, what *did* Merlin do to my wand? If I hadn't been frozen stiff, I'd never have let that rodent take it from me—"

"Then I would have taken it from you myself," said Lady Lesso, tightening her braid.

Professor Dovey stared at her.

"Who do you think let the rodent *in* the Brig, Clarissa? Who do you think showed it where you were!" Lady Lesso groaned. "Really, I hope old age doesn't sap my brain as much as it has yours."

"If it does, I'll be there to remind you what you just said, dear."

"You'll be *dead,* Clarissa."

The sound of the two Deans bantering made Agatha want to run to them and tackle them both in a hug, but her arms were still numb and her body crumpled on the floor, too weak to kick open or pound on the door. She tried to scream, but no voice came out, clotted inside her throat.

Helpless, she watched her Good fairy godmother lean over the side of the pit with Lady Lesso and finally pull Professor Anemone from her ice grave, while Aric flailed and sniveled below.

"I still don't see how a Beautification professor is going to help us during *war,*" Lady Lesso panted, as she and Professor Dovey heaved their colleague onto the stone stage before collapsing on their sides.

"Emma is a *friend*, Lady Lesso," Clarissa puffed, dabbing at sweat. "A friend who actually had the courtesy of telling me her first name."

"Even my son doesn't know my first name and I prefer to keep it that way," said Lady Lesso. "Though if I had a name as bloodless as *Emma*, that would be reason enough."

Even Professor Dovey chortled.

The wild-haired Beautification professor sat up in a soggy heap and pulled out a pocket mirror, blinking wide eyes at her streaked makeup and sallow complexion. "Is this what it's all come to? Mighty Good reduced to a shadow of its former self?"

"A shadow we will *fight* for, Emma," Clarissa declared, dragging her up towards the east doors, across the theater from where Agatha was watching. "Now hurry! We have to get to the Stymph Forest and help Merlin. The sun is almost set—"

"Wait," said Lady Lesso.

She paused at the edge of the glowing Brig, glaring down at her son, tied up on the snow-covered floor of the dungeon. "Clarissa, are you sure no one can open the Brig except Evil's Deans?"

"Evil's Deans and their superiors, and only then from the outside. Neither me nor my Good colleagues could open it," said Dovey, looking at Aric sadly. "Nor can we once you seal it. Even if we wanted to."

Aric spat out his gag. "Please! I won't hurt you, Mother!" he sobbed, pulling at his binds. "Please don't leave me alone again! I'll be nice from now on. . . . I'll be a good son . . ."

Lady Lesso's glare wavered, taking in his terrified face.

"Are you sure, Lady Lesso?" Professor Dovey asked. "Surely he can change. Surely a mother's love . . ."

"That's the difference between Good and Evil, Clarissa," the Evil Dean said softly. "We know that love isn't always enough for a happy ending."

She looked at her son, jaw clenching.

Aric read her face. "Mother, *no!*"

Lady Lesso thrust out her finger and the ceiling of the Brig started closing as Aric screamed in horror, with a desperate childlike wail that filled the theater.

For a moment, Lady Lesso started shaking, her eyes glistening with tears. Then she felt Clarissa's hand take hers, so tight and warm. The Evil Dean steadied herself, wiping her cheek.

"Come on, girls," she said sternly, turning away from Aric's cries. "Merlin needs us—"

Pink light ripped past her and crashed into the Brig, magically stalling its walls. The impact tore a chunk of ice off Professor Anemone's old tomb, which fell and bashed Aric in the head, knocking him out.

Shell-shocked, Lady Lesso, Professor Dovey, and Professor Anemone slowly turned to see Sophie standing at the east doors, her fingertip glowing pink.

"You're not going anywhere, Lady Lesso," she said, dead cold.

Agatha choked outside the west doors.

She could see the ring gleaming on her friend's finger . . . the ring she had to destroy to save her prince's life. . . . Thinking of Tedros, Agatha hobbled up for the door handle, wanting to throw herself inside—

But what if she startled the teachers? What if Sophie used the moment to attack them?

She wouldn't have the strength to fight or help them if things went wrong. Despairing, Agatha held herself back.

"Take Emma and go to the Stymph Forest, Clarissa," said Lady Lesso.

"Lady Lesso—" Professor Dovey started.

"Now," Lady Lesso commanded.

Clarissa didn't argue. She grabbed Professor Anemone's hand and hurried out of the theater through the east doors.

Alone in the Theater of Tales, Sophie and Lady Lesso faced off in the green torchlight.

"You said you wanted me to be a legendary queen," Sophie boiled, shaking with rage. "You said you wanted me to make Evil great again. You said you wanted me to be *happy*."

"And I do," said Lady Lesso.

"Then how could you betray me and the one boy who *makes* me happy?" Sophie snarled, prowling towards her.

"Because in all of your years at my school, Sophie, I've only seen you happy in the company of one person," said Lady Lesso calmly, holding her ground. "And it isn't Rafal."

"Well, in case you weren't paying attention, Tedros and I aren't exactly getting alon—"

"It isn't Tedros either."

Sophie stopped her advance.

"With Agatha, your soul is complete, Sophie," said Lady Lesso. "Without her, you'll never be at peace."

Agatha's eyes widened through the door, matching Sophie's expression.

"But you said she's my Nemesis," Sophie scoffed. "You told me to kill her if I could—"

"Because I knew you couldn't," said Lady Lesso. "Agatha *is* your Nemesis. But only because you've always believed she has the happy ending *you* deserved. Everything you've done in your fairy tale has been to try and take that happy ending, whether trying to get Tedros for yourself or trying to replace him with Rafal. But what if you had that fairy tale all wrong, Sophie? What if a boy was never your happy ending? What if your happy ending was inside you all this time?"

The Dean gazed at her. "Then Agatha isn't your Nemesis at all, is she? For a Nemesis is someone who gets stronger as you get weaker, while you and Agatha make each other stronger. Each of you has taught the other about real love. Without you, Agatha could never have opened herself to Tedros. And without Agatha, you could never find the true ending to your fairy tale—which is to let her go to Camelot with Tedros and know that her happiness is *yours* too. Don't you see, Sophie? Your only Nemesis in your story is *yourself*. Because to find true love with another soul, like Agatha has, first you have to find it within. To find a happy ending with someone else, first you have to find it alone. Just as Agatha once did before she met you."

Sophie shook her head, rage building. "Alone? You think my happy ending is *alone*? I thought you and me were alike. I thought you were *Evil*."

"And I am. Certainly more Evil than you," said Lady Lesso. "Except the difference between me and you is that I know what Evil means."

Sophie smirked bitterly. "Being a spy for Good?"

"Accepting Good as our equal," said Lady Lesso.

Sophie's smirk erased.

"That's what Evil's love really is, Sophie," said the Dean. "Knowing that Good has the right to thrive and fight for happiness, just as much as we do. Because in the end, Good and Evil are two sides of the same story: every Good comes from Evil and every Evil from Good. Just as your mother's death made you want to find real happiness. Just as Agatha's Ever After with a prince will help you find yours on your own. That is the *balance* that sustains our world. The balance that let the School Master stay young all those years, loving his Good brother as his equal, even if he was his enemy . . . before he forgot the power of that love. Just like you have forgotten too."

"What would you ever know about love? Look what you did to your own son!" Sophie mocked, blotching red. "All because you were scared he'd kill you—"

"Not me," Lady Lesso said, smiling sadly. "I was *never* scared he'd kill me. I was scared he'd kill the one real love I have in this world."

Sophie stared at her, disarmed.

"Why do you think I was Merlin's spy in the first place?"

said the Dean. "Because it meant when the time came, I'd get to set Clarissa Dovey free. My best friend. *My* Agatha."

Sophie ashened. "You . . . you betrayed Evil for a *friend?*"

"Like you must, when the time comes," said Lady Lesso. "Because that friend's happy ending will be your own, if you can let yourself find peace in being alone. That's how this storybook will close. That's your real ending, Sophie. And *that's* a Never After worth fighting for."

Sophie's face froze, her lashes blinking faster.

At the west doors, Agatha watched them, her head lightening, her muscles unlocking, as if Lady Lesso's words had taken away her pain. She could see Sophie's big emerald eyes, gazing at the Dean, and for a moment, she caught a glimpse of her old friend inside of them.

But then Sophie's pupils hardened, the yellow fire returning, and she sneered back at Lady Lesso. "I don't *have* a friend anymore," she hissed. "I have love. I have real love that will last forever. I'll *never* be alone."

"If only you could see yourself as you are now, Sophie," said Lady Lesso, her voice tender and maternal. "Because you've never been *more* alone."

Sophie bared her teeth and fired a blast of pink glow at the Dean's head, but Lady Lesso deflected it easily, ricocheting the spell into Sophie, who stumbled towards the edge of the pit. Losing balance, she held out her hand towards Lady Lesso, as she teetered backwards—

Lady Lesso didn't take it.

Sophie plunged into the dungeon mist, landing on her ribs

in the cold sweep of snow.

Balled up on her side, all Sophie could hear were here own frigid breaths and the echo of Lady Lesso's footsteps clacking away through the east doors.

She rose gingerly, back aching and looked up at the walls of ice tombs, fogged over by the warm air seeping in from the theater. Still shaken by her run-in with the Dean, she squinted down long rows of glowing blue graves, extending right and left beneath the stage into dark oblivion. Clawing her hands into the shards of Professor Anemone's old tomb, she stood on tiptoes, looking for a way out of the Brig, but the walls were at least eight feet high.

"Help . . . ," a voice whispered. "Help me . . ."

Sophie turned to see Aric, hands and feet bound, stirring in a dark corner of the Brig. His temple was streaked with blood where the ice had bludgeoned him.

"Please . . . ," he croaked. "I'll get us out of here. . . . Just cut me loose . . ."

Sophie had no fondness for the boy, but she didn't have much choice.

Without hesitating, she bent down and burnt away his binds with her glowing fingertip. Aric stretched his legs, growling with pain.

"Give me a boost off that broken tomb, so I can get to the stage," he said. "I'll pull you over once I'm up there."

"No, you give *me* a boost. I'm going first," Sophie retorted.

"There's no way you can pull me up over that stage," Aric shot back.

"Aric—"

"We don't have *time* for this, Sophie."

Sophie exhaled angrily. She dug her shoe tip into the edge of Professor Anemone's old tomb. "Use my leg. Hurry."

Aric placed his heel on her thigh, gripped on to a broken spear of ice, and propelled himself up the ice wall. Sophie gnashed her teeth in pain, sustaining his weight on her thigh for a split second, before he muscled his way over the edge of the ice and crawled onto the stone platform above.

"Pull me up!" Sophie barked. *"Hurry!"*

Aric bent towards her. Then he stabbed out his glowing finger at the dungeon ceiling, which instantly started closing again, faster than before—

"What are you doing!" Sophie cried.

Aric's violet eyes flashed through the mist. "If it wasn't for you, I would have led training. And the war would already be *won.*"

He bounded off and out of sight, the sound of the east doors slamming behind him.

As the Brig hemmed in on her, Sophie felt her finger burn with fear. She shot a blast of light at the dungeon ceiling to keep it open, but the sides were closing too fast. She tried again, but she couldn't focus her emotion like last time. Lady Lesso had left her unsteady—panic and doubt were making her fingerglow flicker—

You've never been more alone.

She couldn't get the words out of her head.

"Help! Someone help me!"

But the stage was seconds from sealing over. She'd be trapped in the tombs. No one would know where to find her, even Rafal, even . . .

"*HELP*! SOMEONE HELP! PLEASE—"

A shadow suddenly fell over her.

Sophie looked up at a blue-lit silhouette, extending her arm into the pit.

"Grab on to me!" the familiar voice yelled.

Sophie gaped at Agatha, stunned.

"Hurry, Sophie! Before it closes!"

Instantly Sophie seized her hand, as her best friend started pulling her up to safety . . .

Sophie's grip slipped and she crashed back down. Petrified, she lunged up, clasping Agatha's hand again—

Too late. The crack was almost sealed. Agatha would never get Sophie out in time. Either Agatha let go of her or Sophie would be crushed by the sides of the stage—

"Don't leave me here!" Sophie rasped, holding on to her. "Please!"

Desperate, Agatha looked down at Sophie's hand in hers . . . the School Master's ring shining gold on her finger, like the last glow of sun over her prince fighting for his life . . .

Don't fail me and I won't fail you, Lancelot echoed.

Agatha wouldn't.

On a breath, she squeezed Sophie's hand tight and leapt over the edge into glowing blue mist, pulling her friend back down into the frozen dungeon before it sealed shut above them with a resounding crack.

~ 33 ~

An Unexpected History Lesson

With the ceiling closed and no warmth seeping in from the theater, the dungeon turned lethally cold.

The two girls stumbled to their feet and recoiled against opposite walls, lit by the frosty blue light of the tombs. Each held out her glowing fingertip, trying to catch her breath as they glared into the other's eyes.

"What are you going to do? Kill me?" Agatha panted, 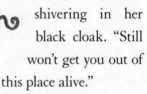 shivering in her black cloak. "Still won't get you out of this place alive."

"And *you* can?" Sophie scowled, fingertip smoking through the frigid air. "You who will do anything to make me destroy my

ring? Chase me, bully me, hurt me . . . bet you have a wand in that pocket, ready to hold to my head. Go on. Threaten me, Aggie. Threaten me with life or death. I'll die rather than destroy this ring for you."

Agatha went quiet, weak from the stun spell and the cold. She looked past Sophie at the long rows of graves leading into the darkness. She couldn't help but snort at the irony of it all.

Sophie simmered. "You think this is funny?"

"It's just . . . this is how Tedros and I started when we came back to rescue you," said Agatha. "Trapped in a grave."

"And now you're here with me, trying to find a way to rescue him," Sophie snarked. "Always rescuing, Aggie. Always so Good. How could I ever match up?"

"Friendship isn't a competition."

"Says the friend who made it one," Sophie retorted, pointing her fingerglow at Agatha's heart. "You and your old minions want me to destroy my true love, so you can keep yours. What if I destroy *you* instead?"

"He's not your true love," Agatha said, struggling to stay calm. "He's using you to get his ending."

"Just like you're trying to use me to get yours," said Sophie, finger glowing hotter. "Even if I end up alone."

Agatha matched her gaze. "My ending has you in it, Sophie. Even if I'm with Tedros. I'll never leave you behind, no matter how Evil you are, how many boys come in our way, or how old we get. We're stronger than Good and Evil, Boys and Girls, and Old and Young. We're best friends."

The fury drained out of Sophie's face. "And yet, we can't find a happy ending together, no matter how hard we try," she said, softer now. "Every path leaves us trapped."

Agatha clung to Cinderella's words. "Don't give up on us, Sophie."

"Do you know what you're asking me, Aggie?" Sophie's fingerglow dimmed, her eyes shimmering like cut emeralds. "You're asking me to throw away my Ever After for yours, and still be happy. You're asking me to end just like my mother, only worse, because you want me to come *live* with you two. It would be like Cinderella's stepsisters shacking up with her and the prince at the palace like one big, blissful family, Happily Ever After. You know why we never saw that in a storybook? Because it *could never happen*."

Agatha stared at her, her own fingerglow dimming too.

Sophie's face hardened again. "But it would also be foolish to kill you right now," she said, ice-cold. "Help me find a way out of here and maybe you'll see your precious prince again."

She tightened the ring on her finger and headed further into the Brig.

Agatha's heart withered, watching Sophie's black-leathered silhouette recede into the mist.

Where was Tedros right now? *Is he even alive?*

The sun must be on its last drips, no more than an hour left . . .

No. I can't think like that.

A hero always finds a way out.

Tedros would find a way out.

Agatha took a shallow breath and forced herself after Sophie.

"There must be a secret door somewhere," Sophie's voice echoed.

Agatha couldn't keep up, her legs still throbbing, her teeth starting to chatter. Limping behind, she scanned the coffins sunken into opposing walls, filled with those who'd betrayed their duties to Evil. Professor Espada, the Swordplay teacher . . . Professor Lukas, the boys' Chivalry teacher . . . Albemarle, the spectacled woodpecker in charge of the Groom Room . . . each freshly entombed when they'd refused to serve the young School Master's new school. Lesso and Dovey hadn't had the time to rescue them, but all three were still alive and healthy, their wide eyes blinking through the ice like trapped puppets. Guilty that she didn't have time to free them either, Agatha slunk further into the Brig, promising herself she'd come back if she could. At least they were still alive, she thought, because now she could see older coffins ahead, murky and cobwebbed, with dead bodies decaying inside of them. Each was labeled on the outside with a small steel placard, blank and awaiting inscription.

Yet as Agatha moved past the grave of a rotting teenaged boy with curly black hair, she suddenly noticed the placards weren't blank at all. There were carvings embedded in the steel . . .

A series of raised dots, small as pinheads, arranged in neat rows.

Her heart drummed faster. Blind Professor August Sader

couldn't write history in words like a normal historian. But he had *seen* history in a way no one else could and found a way to help his students see it too, using magic dots like the ones Agatha was looking at right now. Breathless, she couldn't resist brushing her fingertips across them—

A swoosh of silver air rocketed off the placard, contorting into a floating human silhouette, three-dimensional and the size of a fairy. Professor Sader grinned back at Agatha as he hovered in midair, wearing his customary shamrock suit, his wavy silver hair neat and clean, his hazel eyes twinkling with life. For a moment, Agatha beamed in surprise, thinking he was looking at her, before Sader's focal point scanned past her, addressing a larger audience.

"The next betrayer on our tour is Fawaz of Shazabah, a henchman ordered by an Evil sultan to hide a magic lamp where no one could find it, before Fawaz secretly tried to keep it for himself. The sultan caught him and had him killed, before he was brought here to the Brig for permanent display. You won't need to know *which* sultan he betrayed for your second-year exam, but keep your eye on Fawaz, who plays a crucial role in how Aladdin came to find his magic lamp . . ."

Of course he didn't see me, Agatha sighed, quickly moving on. One, Sader was blind; two, he was dead; and three, he was nothing but a phantom now, on a recorded loop. No doubt he'd left these placards behind for future History classes after he foresaw his own death, just as he'd once amended the class textbooks to include his obituary.

Agatha couldn't see Sophie anymore through the mist.

What would Sader have told me to do?

Sun setting . . . shield falling . . . Tedros struggling . . . a ring on her best friend's finger the only way out . . .

A happy ending is right under your nose.

That's what he'd say.

Tears sprung to her eyes. He'd always felt like a father to her. Sometimes in her dreams, she'd see him, with his silvery hair and light eyes, looking down at her, with the gentlest of smiles. But when she woke up, she knew he wasn't real, just as he wasn't real now. Just as there was nothing under her nose except darkness and snow.

As she hurried past more tombs, she ran her fingers over the placards, so she could see his face pop up again and again, the voices overlapping as Sader's phantom explained each one, until the entire dungeon chorused with Professor Sader's deep, measured tones. It didn't matter if he wasn't real, Agatha thought. There was something soothing about hearing him, as if she was safe and protected as long as Sader was talking . . .

Only she could see Sophie's shadow again now, looming in front of one of the graves ahead. Agatha's gut tightened.

"Did you find a way out?" she pressed. "Is that a secret doo—"

Sophie didn't answer.

She was staring at a beautiful woman in a silky white dress, her eyes closed inside her coffin, her face serene, like a princess waiting to be kissed. Unlike the other decaying corpses, she had flawless, vanilla skin, luscious lips, and the most beautiful long, blond hair, like hand-spun gold. From the pallor of her mouth and the waxy complexion of her skin, it was clear she was dead and embalmed long before she was ever placed into her frozen grave.

"Who's that?" Agatha said.

Sophie didn't answer.

Behind them, Sader's recorded voices had all gone quiet.

Agatha frowned. "Sophie, we don't have time to sit here and ogle random dead women who happen to look like you—"

Her heart dropped. *No.*

"That's . . . that's *her*?" Agatha blurted. "That's—"

"My mother," said Sophie, her voice flat and numb. "Her body was here in the Woods all along. The grave on Necro Ridge wasn't a mistake. Someone must have moved her here."

"But that's impossible!" said Agatha, before she looked up at Vanessa again and saw just how much she resembled Sophie. "Isn't it?"

"Only one way to find out," Sophie rasped.

Agatha followed her gaze to the placard on Vanessa's tomb and the silver dots carved into the steel.

"Her story is inside those dots," said Sophie shakily. "The answer to why she has a headstone on Necro Ridge. To why she's here in Evil's dungeon."

Sophie looked at her friend. "And maybe to why the both of us are in this fairy tale together."

Agatha held her breath, watching Sophie reach out a quivering hand and brush her fingers across the dots.

A cloud of silver leapt off the placard, melting into Sader's miniature silhouette once more. Only this time he was no longer smiling or at ease. His shoulders were stiff, his jaw tight, and his glassy hazel gaze locked on them.

"We don't have much time, girls. If you're seeing this, then my visions held true and you are nearing the end of your story."

Agatha reddened. "But Professor Sader, what happens at—"

"Dead seers still can't answer questions, Agatha, though I knew you would ask one *because* I am a seer and foresaw it. But from now until this recording runs out, neither of you will interrupt me again. There is no time for interruptions."

Agatha and Sophie glanced at each other.

This means everything turns out happily, Agatha thought, hope swelling. *Sader sees the future . . . he knows we come out alive—*

"I do not know how your fairy tale ends," Sader said starkly.

Agatha snapped back to him.

"My visions stop after you and Sophie appear in front of me, listening to this very message. From here, I do not know whether you live or die, end as friends or enemies, or whether either of you will find a happy ending at all."

Agatha felt hope shrivel away.

"What I do know, however, is that you cannot find the ending to your fairy tale unless you know how it began," said Sader. "And it began long before you two ever came to the School for Good and Evil. Every old story sets off a chain of events that leads to a new story. Every new story has its roots in the old. *Your* story most of all."

He conjured a storybook twice as big as his fairy-sized

body and let it float towards the girls. It had a red cherrywood cover, just like *The Tale of Sophie and Agatha* that the Storian was writing in the School Master's tower right now. Only as Agatha looked closer, she realized this wasn't her and Sophie's fairy tale. The title of this one was:

The Tale of Callis & Vanessa

Agatha saw Sophie's whole body seize up.

"She *was* in a fairy tale," Sophie gasped.

Sader spread open the storybook to its first page. A puff of mist erupted over it, along with a ghostly scene of an ordinary cottage. "And now it's time for you to go inside," he said.

Agatha and Sophie stared at his tiny image, confused.

"I was never fond of my sister Evelyn's spells, but there was one that I quite liked," Professor Sader explained, with a growing grin. "Because say what you will of her, when Evelyn Sader told you a story . . . she made you feel like you were *there*."

He raised the open storybook and blew on the phantom scene. With a fizzling swish, the scene shattered into a million glittered shards and crashed over the two girls like a glass sandstorm. Agatha shielded her eyes, her body drifting through space, until her feet touched ground next to Sophie's. Slowly they both looked up.

They were standing inside the cottage they'd seen on the page, the air thick and hazy around them, giving the room a vaporous feel, as if it wasn't quite real. Agatha recognized the effect at once, for this was how Evelyn Sader had brought them into her adulterated fairy tales a year ago. Now August Sader had brought them into one they never knew existed.

Agatha scanned the intimate kitchen and white, round dining table . . .

"Wait a second—" she started.

"This is *my* house," said Sophie, realizing it too.

Agatha furrowed. "But if it's your house, then who's *that*?"

Sophie followed her eyes to a skinny black-haired girl in the corner, scowling out a window. She had a sharp nose, big brown eyes, and thin pink lips. She couldn't have been older than sixteen.

"It's . . . *you* . . . ," said Sophie, studying her. "Only not you."

Definitely not me, thought Agatha, because this girl had a cruel mouth and a vicious gleam in her eye. There was something dark and venomous about her that made Agatha afraid of her, even if she was just a phantom. She'd never seen the girl in her life. She had no idea who she was and why she was in Sophie's house. But one thing was for sure. Whatever the girl was looking at through the window had her unwavering focus and utmost contempt.

"Once upon a time, in a land beyond the Woods, there lived a girl named Vanessa," said Professor Sader.

Sophie and Agatha froze dead still, eyes wide, breath misting.

Neither looked at the other. Neither spoke.

They gaped at the dark-haired girl, who looked starkly different than the blond-haired woman they'd just seen in the frozen tomb.

Because if *this* was Vanessa, then they had this story all wrong.

"Vanessa was a foul, miserable soul, who thought herself far better than the town she lived in," said Sader. "Perhaps she would have made a fair student at the School for Evil, except for one ray of light amidst the darkness of her heart . . ."

The scene magically zoomed in, so now Sophie and Agatha could see what the girl was looking at through the window . . .

A young and strapping teenager strutted by, with thick, wavy, golden blond hair, a tall, sturdy frame, blue-green eyes and a devil-may-care smile.

Stefan, thought Agatha, struck once more by his resemblance to August Sader, even as a young boy.

But it wasn't Stefan who Vanessa was glowering at, as he passed by her house. It was the plump, scraggly-haired, sweet-faced girl walking with Stefan, hand in hand.

"Honora," Sophie whispered.

Sader continued: "Since the day she laid eyes on him, Vanessa had been in love with young Stefan. Not that they knew each other. Vanessa fantasized about him from afar, waiting for him to rescue her from her dreary life. Day after day, he was her only source of happiness. This despite the fact their souls were mirror images. Where Vanessa was calculating, controlling, and disdainful of her fellow villagers, Stefan was jovial, gregarious, and a favorite of the Elders. Not that he didn't have his faults: Stefan was rakish and carefree in a way that made mothers keep their daughters away from him. But if Vanessa thought this cleared the way for Stefan to choose her, that would soon change. For Stefan had fallen in love with a girl named Honora, who despite her plain looks, had his same blithe and playful spirit. Stefan had eyes for no one else."

Vanessa glared harder at Honora, who was ruffling Stefan's hair, until Honora noticed Vanessa through the window. Vanessa quickly pretended to be doing dishes.

"Needless to say, Vanessa saw no such Goodness in Honora, and thought of her only as an Evil witch. Vanessa spent most of her days plotting how to tear the witch and Stefan apart, before she hatched the perfect plan. For what better way was there to get closer to her true love than to make *friends* with the witch?'"

The cottage vanished around them, instantly replaced by the town square, where Vanessa and Honora walked hand in hand through the lanes, as Stefan traipsed beside them.

"And Honora, who was just as affable as Stefan, was more than receptive to a new best friend. Meanwhile, Vanessa finally had her chance at the boy of her dreams . . .'"

Vanessa scooted closer to Stefan on the path and smiled up at him . . . He shifted away, ignoring her.

"Only there was one flaw in Vanessa's plan: Stefan didn't like her. And there was nothing Vanessa could do to change that," Professor Sader declared.

The town square melted away and now Vanessa was kneeling in the graveyard at night, near the Forest's edge, praying into the darkness with clasped hands.

"So young Vanessa did the one thing storybooks taught her to do when you love someone who is out of reach. She wished into the Woods for a magic spell that could help her win her one true love."

The scene started to evaporate around the two girls.

"Yet Vanessa's isn't the only love story that matters in this fairy tale . . . ," Sader's voice echoed.

Phantom colors melted in around them and now they were in the School Master's tower, as the masked sorcerer flew in through his window, carrying a young, attractive woman in his arms, with short brown hair, big, beautiful eyes, and tanned, gangly limbs.

"Because while Vanessa prayed for Stefan's heart, the School Master was trying to win Callis'."

Agatha choked on her own tongue. *"Callis?"* She ogled the woman's elegant posture, olive-brown locks, and bright, freckly skin. "But that can't be Callis. It doesn't look anything like—"

Something hopped out of the woman's black dress onto the floor.

A tiny, bald, wrinkled kitten.

Reaper.

Agatha blanched.

Merlin had told her part of this story—that the School Master sought her mother's love—but the woman in his arms didn't look anything like her mother . . .

Or did she?

For as Agatha looked closer at her wide, lucid eyes and long nose, she started to see bits and pieces of her mother, like a sculpture that had been deliberately altered.

Something floated back to her that Merlin had said her first time in the Celestium with him . . . something about Callis being quite pretty, before Tedros snorted incredulously . . .

Agatha watched the School Master bring the woman deeper into his chamber, Reaper pattering beside her.

It was her mother.

But then why didn't it look like her?

She broke out of her trance, for Sader had already moved on.

"The School Master was curious about a new teacher, Callis of Netherwood, who the Storian had chosen for its latest tale shortly after she took a position teaching Uglification at school. According to the Storian, Callis had long dreamed of finding her one true love, even though she taught at the School for Evil. In truth, Callis was having doubts as to whether she was Evil at all. So when the School Master took a shine to her—a School Master everyone thought was Good at the time—Callis saw her way out. A chance to switch sides to Good and find her true love at last."

The masked School Master pulled a golden ring from his pocket and took one knee before her. Slowly she reached for the ring . . . and stopped cold.

For now, as she looked closer at the ring, she could see the inky, black streaks swirling beneath its gold, like a poison waiting to latch on to its wearer.

"Until she realized what the School Master *really* was."

The scene flashed to Callis fleeing through the dark Woods in the rain, a bald, wrinkled kitten wrapped in her arms.

"She held him off for a night, but the next evening after

classes, she made her escape. She had to warn Merlin that he'd been right about the School Master being Evil and using her as a weapon against Good. All Callis had ever wanted was *real* love, and instead she'd found a villain trying to use that love to start war. She cursed herself for not accepting Merlin's help when he'd tried to see her at school. There was no time to find the wizard now. Once the School Master realized she'd escaped, he'd surely find and kill her, since she'd discovered the secret behind his mask. Except there was nowhere to hide that he wouldn't find her. Nowhere that he didn't have power over . . ."

Callis suddenly stalled, hearing a chorus of low, urgent whispers floating in the wind.

I wish.

I wish.

I wish.

"Like all witches, Callis could hear the pleas of those truly desperate enough to pay a price. Yet this wish wasn't coming from the Woods, but *beyond* it, where the School Master had no power. Callis wouldn't ask a price for choosing to answer this wish, she told herself—only a chance to turn the page and live a life free of Evil. Answering this wish would be her very first Good deed. And so a witch who dreamed of her one true love followed the wish . . ."

Callis tracked the whispers to Necro Ridge and an unmarked, open grave at the top of the hill. She dug through the bottom of the empty grave, Reaper helping her, deeper, deeper, deeper . . .

". . . all the way to a girl in the Reader World, dreaming of *her* one true love."

As Callis came out the other side of the grave, she found herself in Gavaldon's graveyard, standing in front of a dark-haired girl kneeling in the weeds. Slowly Vanessa looked up at Callis and smiled, knowing her wish had been granted at last.

All at once, Sophie and Agatha were back in the School Master's tower, as the masked sorcerer studied the open storybook on the altar table, the Storian frozen above it.

"During this time, the Storian had been writing Callis' fairy tale, but when she vanished, the pen went still, as if it'd lost the connection to her. Suspecting he'd been betrayed, the School Master commanded his stymphs to find Callis and bring her back to him alive. But when they didn't retrieve her and there was no sign of her going to Merlin's side, the School Master assumed Callis was dead. His suspicions were confirmed when the Storian abandoned her fairy tale and moved on to another. To the School Master, Callis' story was over and forgotten."

The scene disappeared and the girls were in pitch-darkness, Sader's small figure levitating over them.

"But unlike the School Master I had the power of sight, which meant I could see what happened after the Storian stopped writing. For unbeknownst to the School Master, Callis wasn't dead and her story *wasn't* over. Not in the least."

Sophie and Agatha glanced at each other, shaken.

"After leaving school, Callis wanted nothing to do with Evil or witchcraft ever again. But she hadn't given up on her dreams of true love. Seeing how safe and quaint Gavaldon was, she harbored fantasies of starting over and finding a new start as a Reader," Sader went on. "Yet, she still owed Vanessa a wish, since choosing to answer that wish had given her safe haven from the School Master. Callis promised herself it would be her very last deed of magic before she settled into ordinary life. And so she made the love potion that Vanessa had desperately wished for. But Callis warned her: it would only last one night, for matters of love were too delicate for magic, and use of a love spell for any long-term goals would only lead to the unhappiest of endings. Magic always had its price."

A new scene melted in and Sophie and Agatha were in a crowded pub, as Stefan caroused with his friends.

"Vanessa paid no heed," Sader said.

Stefan put his drink down on a table and a hooded shadow slipped by and poured a vial of smoky red liquid into it, just before Stefan picked it back up.

"She tricked Stefan into drinking the spell and he instantly fell in love with her. And even though the spell soon wore off, as Callis had warned, the potion had a far more enduring effect. For it wasn't long before Vanessa knocked on Stefan's door and told him she was bearing his child. Which meant by Council Law that he had to marry her."

The scene changed to Honora and Stefan arguing heatedly on Honora's porch.

"Furious, Honora broke ties with Stefan. How could he betray her trust? And with her best *friend*, no less? Stefan swore it was black magic. He had no love for Vanessa, and when he'd returned to her house to confront her, he'd noticed a strange houseguest huddling in her room. It was *she* who did it, he told Honora. The stranger. He could see the guilt in her eyes. That witch had cast a spell over him—he was sure of it! How could Vanessa do such a heartless thing? Trap him into marriage with a child? An innocent child? He feared the spell would backfire somehow. . . . But Honora wouldn't listen. Stefan begged her not to give up on him, but it was no use. No matter what he said, Honora didn't believe his story and wanted nothing further to do with him. So Stefan took his story to the Elders instead."

Now the girls were outside in the square at night with a mob of onlookers, watching Callis tied to a torchlit pyre, as the three bearded Elders presided from the stage.

"The Elders believed him, for Stefan had always been a beloved son. Moreover, the Elders had been leading witch hunts for years, searching for anyone who might be responsible for the child kidnappings that continued to happen every four years. So when Stefan pointed his finger at Callis—a strange, unmarried woman they'd never seen in town before—the Elders finally found their witch."

The executioner reached for the torch over Callis' pyre. Sophie and Agatha could see Stefan at the side of the stage, glaring at Callis as the executioner lowered the flame to the wood sticks under the witch. Callis' face flooded with tears of terror and regret; she'd tried to do one last act of magic in exchange for the chance at a life of Goodness and love and now she'd be slaughtered as an Evil witch instead. As she wept for the mistakes of her life, the flames spreading under feet, Stefan watched her, his own face beginning to soften.

"When he saw her in that moment, a human-hearted soul just like him, Stefan realized he didn't have it inside of him to be responsible for another's death," said Professor Sader. "Though he still believed Callis was a witch, he recanted his story and agreed to marry Vanessa in order to save Callis' life. Per the Elders' conditions for sparing her, Callis had to move to the graveyard and stay out of the townspeople's affairs forever. She could never marry a man from town, never have a shop in the square or a house in cottage lane . . . but she would keep her life, even if it was a loveless one. As would Stefan, who in the process of saving her, had doomed himself to a loveless life with Vanessa too."

Agatha couldn't breathe, watching Stefan free Callis off the pyre. "The debt," she whispered. "That was the debt she owed him."

Sophie shook her head. "But she looks so different from your mother, Aggie."

"So does yours," said Agatha.

Both girls turned back to the story as the scene melted into a lavish, sun-drenched wedding at the town church. Stefan stood at the altar next to a pregnant Vanessa.

He'd never looked more miserable.

"Stefan married Vanessa, while Honora's parents soon forced her to marry the odious butcher's boy. Now Vanessa had everything she'd always wanted. Her one true love and his child on the way to keep him. The girl he once loved married off and out of their lives. A perfect fairy-tale ending. Or so she thought. Because Vanessa hadn't counted on one thing . . ."

The church dissipated and now the girls were on Graves Hill in the middle of the night. Grim-faced, Stefan shoveled dirt to fill the last of two small graves. Vanessa watched him, weeping.

"Stefan's fear that the spell would backfire came true. Vanessa gave birth to two boys. Both born dead."

The scene shifted and Sophie and Agatha were back where they began: in Sophie's cottage, lit by a red sunset, with Vanessa glowering through her kitchen window. Her eyes were on Stefan in a hooded coat, hustling down the lane, before Honora snuck him into her cottage.

"In the years that followed, Vanessa tried everything she could to have a child with Stefan, but her efforts failed again and again. Soon, Honora suspected that Stefan was telling the truth all along: Vanessa had tricked him into marrying her. With Honora just as unhappy with her husband as Stefan with Vanessa, Honora and Stefan began to see each other in secret once more."

Brightness leeched out of the scene and now the girls were in Agatha's house on Graves Hill, watching Vanessa fuming at Callis.

"Vanessa visited every doctor in Gavaldon, who all agreed she'd never have a child. Enraged, she returned to Callis and demanded a new potion that would help her bear Stefan's baby. Unless she had his child—a child that could prove their love was real—Stefan would never believe in their marriage. Callis refused, insisting she was done with magic forever and just wanted to keep to herself, per the Elders' orders. But Vanessa threatened her: she said she'd go to the Elders and tell her she'd cursed her to never have children; that she was cursing other townswomen as well; that *she* was the one responsible for the kidnapped children . . . Callis knew then that there was no stopping Vanessa. Her only choice was to help her."

The scene skipped ahead and the girls watched as Vanessa drank a smoking black tonic from a wooden bowl.

"Callis warned her that magic could not force the union of souls into a child, as love does, just as magic could not force true love itself. Try to unite two souls into one child through magic and you would only split those souls even more," said Sader. "But just as before, Vanessa didn't listen, determined to have Stefan's baby. And soon enough, a healthy child was growing inside of her."

Night fell darker over the house. Vanessa was in painful labor now, as Callis comforted her.

"'The Miracle Child,' the doctors named it. Vanessa promised Stefan it would be a boy as handsome as him. Seeing Vanessa carrying his child again and how much it meant to her, Stefan tried to give his wife another chance. In his heart, he knew sneaking off to Honora's was wrong, for they'd both taken wedding vows to other people. Besides, it didn't matter what Vanessa did in the past; they were about to be a *family*. She was his wife now and forever and that meant if Vanessa had his baby, he would love it and its mother as much as he possibly could. Stefan even let himself name the child before it was born: 'Filip' after his own father," said Sader. "And in time, the night came where Vanessa finally had Stefan's child, thanks to the secret power of Callis' magic. Only it wasn't a boy at all. It was a fair, luminous girl that looked just like Stefan."

Weak and sweating, Vanessa stroked the blond, beautiful girl in her arms, before she suddenly felt strong pains again—

"But just as the witch predicted, the souls of Stefan and Vanessa never fused, for there was no love between them. Each soul produced its *own* child, which meant Vanessa delivered not one baby, but two. This second girl, then, looked nothing like Stefan. Instead, she looked just like her mother."

Vanessa gasped as Callis held out the baby: raven-haired, with bulging big eyes and a hideous face. Vanessa recoiled in disgust, shoving it back at the witch.

"She ordered Callis to dump the baby in the Woods and leave it there to die. She could never take such an *ugly* child home to Stefan, she scoffed, before bundling up her beautiful, blond daughter and hurrying off, sure that everything between her and her husband was about to change," said Sader. "But Callis, who only saw beauty in the girl Vanessa threw away, kept the child for herself. She named her Agatha, which meant 'Soul of Good.' Finally, after so many years of loneliness, Callis of Netherwood had found her one true love."

Callis glanced into a mirror as she studied the child's big, insect-like eyes. Slowly, Callis magically made her own eyes bigger.

"To ensure no one asked questions as to whether she was the child's mother, Callis gradually transformed herself over the years, using her Uglification skills to look more and more like Agatha. Soon the villagers began to notice Callis' child lurking on the hills, a practical duplicate of her. The Elders asked Callis questions, of course, but she gave no answers, and in time, the town simply shunned the young girl just as they shunned her mother."

Morning streamed through the house's rickety windows, as black-haired, sallow-skinned, scraggly Callis read storybooks to her black-haired, sallow-skinned, scraggly daughter.

"When new fairy tales appeared in Gavaldon year after year, with Good still winning every story, Callis began to question whether she had it all wrong. Perhaps the School Master hadn't been Evil at all. She even wondered: had she made a mistake by not taking his ring? As the years went by, she began to wish that her daughter would be taken to the School for Good and Evil so that Agatha could have a future filled with magic, adventure, and love, instead of being trapped in a lonely, ordinary life because of her mother."

The scene flashed to Stefan in his cottage, sitting at the dining table with Vanessa and young Sophie. He was eying his three-year-old daughter warily, no tenderness in his face.

"Meanwhile, as young Sophie grew, Stefan had an instinctive stiffness towards her. He tried so hard to love her: taking her to Battersby's for cookies, reading her storybooks at bedtime, smiling when passerbys said his young Sophie looked just like him. . . . But deep down, all Stefan could see in his daughter was Vanessa's soul."

Now Stefan was carrying lumber to the mill. He paused on the path, noticing five-year-old Agatha playing alone in the weeds on a nearby hill. She looked up at Stefan and smiled toothily. Stefan smiled back.

"And yet, when he'd see the strange urchin girl that skulked around Graves Hill, he'd feel such affection towards her, even as the other mill workers noticed her striking resemblance to Vanessa," said Professor Sader. "With two girls born to her, one ugly, one beautiful, Vanessa had kept the one she thought Stefan would love. The one who would bring her closer to him. But it was the one she threw away who imprinted herself on Stefan's heart."

Stefan's scene disappeared and the girls were alone with Vanessa in her bathroom, filled with hundreds of beauty potions, creams, and elixirs, as she thickened her lips with a special paste, made her eyes green with herbal drops, and dyed her hair golden-blond with a homemade brew. Seven-year-old Sophie mimicked her mother, rubbing honeycream from a bottle into her own cheeks.

"Vanessa couldn't understand why Stefan still seemed cold to her, even after Sophie's birth. *Was Sophie not pretty enough?* she thought. *Am I not good enough either?* Panicked, Vanessa obsessively tried to make herself more beautiful. Her daughter too. But no matter what she did, Stefan seemed to shirk from the both of them."

Sharply, the scene pivoted to Vanessa standing with young, ten-year-old Sophie at the kitchen window, each of them blond and gorgeous, watching Stefan playing with two young boys in Honora's front yard. Vanessa no longer looked angry anymore. She looked defeated and heartbroken.

"Eventually, Vanessa died alone, while her true love abandoned her for a girl she once thought an ugly witch. She lived to see Honora have two children of her own. Two boys Vanessa *knew* were Stefan's until the day she died, even if Honora pretended otherwise. She knew it from the way Stefan loved them. From the way Stefan held the boys at Honora's husband's funeral after he was killed in a mill accident. And from the way Stefan stared so distantly at Sophie, the daughter he had at home."

As Stefan played with Honora's children, he looked up and saw Agatha, hunched and gangly, stalking up Graves Hill. He smiled fondly.

"Yet Stefan never forgot about the girl in the graveyard, who he looked for whenever he passed by . . . because deep inside, she felt more like his child than any of them."

The story washed away like a painting in the rain, and Sophie and Agatha were in vast, silent blackness, listening to the sound of their matching breaths.

"Two sisters," said Sader's voice. "But sisters in name only, for there was no love in their making. Two souls, forever irreconcilable, since each soul was a mirror of the other: one Good, one Evil. Indeed, if fate ever brought these girls together, they'd be mortal enemies, even as their hearts yearned to find a bond. There would be no path to happiness, just as there had been no path to happiness for their parents. They were old souls made new, doomed to hurt and betray one another again and again, like Stefan and Vanessa, until they too were torn apart forever. And for anyone to think these two girls could defy that ending and find an Ever After together . . . well, that would be a fairy tale, wouldn't it?"

Slowly the Brig filled in around them and the two girls were in the frozen dungeon, their bodies slack, their faces ash white. Professor Sader floated in front of Vanessa's tomb, gazing back at them.

"But *I* had hope, even if I couldn't see what your ending was. Look at how far you've come already, against all odds. That's why I moved your mother here, so you could see the truth about your story. That's why I sacrificed my life for the both of you. Because by breaking all the rules of our world, you have the chance to save it when we need it most. To find a bridge between Good and Evil. To put love first, whether it's a Boy's or Girl's. To shatter the chain between your parents' Old story and your New one. No one knows if you will succeed, children. Even me. But the Storian chose you for a reason and it's time to face it. No more running. No more hiding. The only way out is through your fairy tale."

His hazel eyes sparkled with tears. "Now go and open the door."

Professor Sader smiled at the two girls one last time. Then his phantom dissipated to darkness, like the last tears of a sun.

34

The War of All Things

Neither girl could look at the other. They just stared at Vanessa, dead and beautiful in her frozen grave.

"We're sisters," said Sophie, a strange flatness in her voice.

"But *not*," said Agatha softly. "Family but not family. Blood but not blood. Together but apart." She could feel a wave of emotions trapped behind her heart, too big and powerful to let in. "That's why I saw Sader in my dreams like he was my father," she rasped. "Because he always reminded me of your father. Somewhere, I knew I was Stefan's daughter all along."

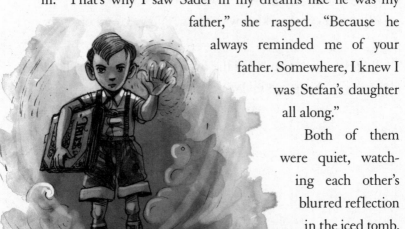

Both of them were quiet, watching each other's blurred reflection in the iced tomb.

"Sophie?" Agatha finally looked at her. "We have to go. We have to go right now."

Sophie didn't meet her eyes. Her muscles were tense, her entire body on edge.

"Did you hear me?" Agatha pressed. "We have to g—"

"It doesn't change anything, Agatha," said Sophie coldly, still staring at her mother.

"What? Sophie, it changes *everything*—"

"No," she retorted. "It proves I was Evil from the start. That my mother was never Good and cursed me to relive her miserable little life, rotting away alone while you get a happy ending with Tedros the same way my father gets a happy ending with Honora. Good gets Good; Evil gets nothing. Except I have the chance to change my ending. Now, more than ever, Rafal is my only hope to not end up alone. To not end up like *her*."

She shoved past Agatha and started jostling random tombs. "Bloody hell! There has to be another door somewhere."

Agatha watched her, stunned. "Sophie, don't you get it? Choosing Rafal only makes you *more* like her. Your mother did Evil in order to force love and look what happened! Choosing Rafal will only leave you more alone in the end—"

"Aggie, you're acting like I care about your opinion," Sophie spat, pounding on graves. "You heard what Sader said. There is no love between us. There is no bond. You're Good. I'm Evil. And now we'll see who makes it to The End first. Either Tedros gets you to Camelot or Rafal and I seal our Never After. Only one of us wins our fairy tale."

"Sader also said he believed in us," Agatha said, accosting her. "He *died* for us—"

"Just like my mother died knowing she'd never found love," Sophie said, elbowing her away. "Evil souls don't *find* love. First lesson at the School for Evil. Evil souls are meant to end up with no one."

"I won't let that happen to you," Agatha fought back.

"Really? Because you, Tedros, and I will be a happy *three-some*? Because I'll be your Evil little *pet*?" Sophie hissed, punching tombs. "Don't you get it? My soul is broken! I'm messed up, sick in the head, rotten to the core! I'm *damaged*. I'll never find the kind of love you did because I'll never be happy inside. All these years, I wanted to be like the mother I thought I had—an angel of Good and light—and instead, I see I was *always* like her. Unlovable down to the pit of a bad, bad soul."

"You aren't her," Agatha said, tailing behind. "Deep down, you're nothing like her—"

"Are you *deaf*? Did you hear her story?" said Sophie, hitting tombs faster now. "I made friends with you so I could get a prince, just like my mother made friends with Honora to get my father. I tried every trick my mother did to find love—love spells, beauty potions, wishing on stars—only to end up hated and alone, while my best friend gets everything. And just like my mother, I'm going to end up dead in a frozen dungeon, with all these other cowards, who were too weak to accept they were Evil."

She whirled to Agatha, splotched with rage. "So you better believe, if I get out of here, I'll do anything it takes to keep my true love, no matter how Evil. *Anything*."

A high-pitched *ping!* rang through the Brig.

All the steel placards on the tombs lit up with blinking, bright blue arrows that pointed towards a glowing tomb, before its coffin door magically popped open.

Lady Lesso's recorded voice blared from all sides: *"The student exit has been opened. Kindly exit the dungeon with the rest of your class and return to school. The student exit has been opened. Kindly exit the dungeon with the rest of your class and return to school."*

Agatha gaped at the lit-up coffin.

"Now go and open the door."

Sader's last words. He must have put a charm on it to unlock once they'd gotten close enough—

Her thoughts broke off because Sophie was already sprinting towards the glowing grave.

"Sophie, wait!" Agatha said, racing after her. She couldn't let her get to Rafal—

But Sophie was already thrusting herself into the empty coffin and shoving through a false snow wall at the back of the grave. Agatha tried to grab Sophie from behind, but Sophie flung her away and Agatha reeled off-balance. She recovered and lunged after Sophie through the wall, propelling into the freezing block of white.

As she came out the other side, Agatha shook the snowflakes out of her eyes and hair to see she was in a dark, leaky tunnel, sloping steeply uphill. Sophie was way ahead, almost to the door at the end. Agatha hurtled after her, hearing the echoes of Sophie's stuttered breaths and rustling leather catsuit as she wrestled the handle. When it wouldn't budge, Sophie threw her shoulder against it as hard as she could, before Agatha tackled her against the door, slamming it open with a tumultuous groan as both girls tumbled through—

Agatha's head cracked hard against a stone floor. By the time she wobbled to her knees, eyes blearing open, Sophie was gone. Agatha lurched up to the big, empty room lit by a weak green torch. A room she'd been in before.

The Exhibition of Evil.

She hustled towards the museum's exit, not wanting to let Sophie get too far ahead—

A sharp hiss slashed through the silence. Agatha froze on her heels.

Slowly she turned and spotted a small, dark shadow huddling on the floor beneath Sader's last painting of Gavaldon.

"Reaper?"

The bald, mashed-up creature hissed at her again before it glared up at Sader's painting with copper-yellow eyes.

Agatha rushed towards him and scooped him into her arms—

He bit her wrist and she dropped him with a yelp. Reaper turned back to Sader's painting, his slit-like pupils locked on the scene.

All Agatha's questions of how her cat had gotten into the school, where he'd been the past few weeks, or why he was in Evil's museum fell away. Because right now, Reaper wanted her to look at the painting on the wall. As she leaned in towards the canvas, Agatha saw why.

The scene was different than it was before.

It was darker, with only a needlepoint of light left in the top corner. And where the shadows of villains once closed in on Gavaldon as the villagers burned storybooks in fear, now there were *actual* villains coming through the trees as they battled the young and old heroes back. The only thing separating the villains from Gavaldon was a thin, hole-riddled shield, about to break.

Agatha bolted straight. Once a vision of the future, Sader's painting was now magically tracking the present. She was watching the war between Good and Evil as it unfolded . . . and Good was *losing.*

Urgently, her eyes scoured the scene for Tedros, but Sader had always painted with hazy, impressionistic brushstrokes, no detail to the faces at all.

I have to get to Sophie, she panicked.

But how? Sophie had too much of a head start—

Reaper meowed again, still fixed on the painting, as if whatever answers she was looking for were inside its frame.

What hadn't she seen?

She put her nose closer to the canvas, her fingers running across the oily surface . . . until they stopped.

The empty anvil from which she'd drawn Excalibur was tucked beneath the canopy of Mr. Deauville's book shop, far away from the action of the war.

Reaper growled, urging her on.

Of course, Agatha thought.

The School Master had enchanted the sword to hide it in Sader's painting . . .

Which meant he had to enchant the anvil too.

And if he enchanted the anvil . . . then maybe . . .

Heart rattling, Agatha slowly slid her right hand through the tight, wet surface of the painting until she watched her fingers appear in the painting . . .

She felt the cold, hard metal of the real anvil under her palm.

Her hand wasn't just inside the painting. Her hand was in Gavaldon.

A portal.

Reaper curled around her leg, ensuring he'd be along for the ride. Agatha smiled down sadly.

"Thanks for helping me, Reap," she whispered, prying him off. "I'll be back for you when it's safe. I promise."

As her cat whimpered, Agatha grabbed the anvil tighter and pulled herself headfirst into the painting. Her whole body was swallowed into hot, wet darkness, before her face poked through another tight, wet barrier and into cold night air. Still levitating horizontally, Agatha grabbed hold of the anvil with her second hand and yanked the rest of herself through the portal wall, the heel of her last clump popping out before she collapsed onto sooty cobblestones.

When Agatha raised her head, the first thing she saw was hordes of screaming villagers fleeing for cover. Trapped in the stampede, Agatha rolled like a log under Mr. Deauville's awning, just missing being trampled, before she ducked behind the anvil. Peeking over it, she could see people of Gavaldon cramming into the church, shuttering themselves in shops, and chaining themselves in cottages. Once upon a time, she'd witnessed the same scenes as parents tried to protect their children from the School Master. Now, it wasn't just the children they were hiding from him.

Agatha rose from behind the anvil, gazing out at the Woods, a half mile away.

It was exactly as she'd seen in Sader's painting. Flames streaked through the distant trees, illuminating legions of zombie villains as they battled old heroes and students out of the Woods, backing them towards an invisible barrier that separated the forest from Gavaldon. From inside the town, Agatha couldn't see the enchanted shield the way she'd seen it inside the Woods. She only knew it was there because an ogre slammed a stymph out of nearby trees, sending it whizzing into the shield and ricocheting to the ground, toppling the young rider on its spine.

Agatha squinted harder, trying to make out faces through the trees, but like Sader's painting, all she saw was a blur of bodies and fire. Scared, Agatha searched for the sun, but couldn't find it through the clouds of smoke.

How much time was left? Twenty minutes? Fifteen? Less?

All at once, it overwhelmed her. She'd never find Sophie in time. She'd never make her destroy that ring. She'd die here, useless and cowering, beneath a storybook shop. Panic ripped through her blood—

Don't give up.

Cinderella's voice echoed inside of her like a heartbeat.

For the both of us.

Air slowly came back into Agatha's lungs. Her mentor was right. Either she helped her Good friends win this war . . .

Or she would die with them.

But first she had to get past that shield.

Steeling with determination, she sprinted towards the Woods. As she tore through town, she passed a father sending his wife and son up a ladder to hide in a chimney . . . a mother and daughter sealing themselves in a barrel . . . and one of the Elders, herding children into the schoolhouse, with Radley amongst them, balancing a fishbowl as he scooted inside. Agatha scanned the scattering villagers for Stefan or Honora, but there was no sign of either of them.

Hurtling past the mills and lake into grassy fields, Agatha started to hear the sickening roar of the war: clashing metal, crushing stymph bones, and girls' and boys' screams. Soon, she could make out a few faces, lit by the burning forest—Beatrix atop her stymph, still shooting arrows; Ravan fighting a troll, fist-to-fist; Kiko being chased by a zombie witch—but most of the war was still camouflaged by trees and the blue-black sky. As she got closer to the trees, Agatha began to glimpse small holes in the air: hundreds of them, each no bigger than a grapefruit. No one had ever seen the shield from inside Gavaldon, magically diverted before they could reach it, but Agatha could see the *gaps* in the barrier now, which meant she could figure out exactly where the shield was. Racing towards these holes, she noticed that the colors outside the holes were brighter and more vibrant than the colors inside them, and for a moment, she marveled at how thin the line between stories and ordinary life really was.

Skidding up to the shield, she reached out her fingers and felt the bubbly, invisible surface between the holes. Before the war, each fairy tale that Evil had rewritten in its favor had punctured holes in the shield over the Reader World, just as it had punctured holes in Readers' faith in Good. But with Good's greatest heroes still alive, none of these holes were big enough to let the shield fall yet, nor let Evil pass into their protected realm. Which left only one question . . .

How am I supposed to get through? Agatha thought, panicking.

Through the shield, she could see snatches of heroes past the trees, trying to hold the line against the Dark Army. If the villains pushed them back any farther, they'd have them cornered against the shield—

Suddenly, Agatha glimpsed a flash of golden hair and broad shoulders.

Tedros?

He was already gone.

There was no time to think about her prince. If she wanted to help him, she had to get through the shield and find Sophie.

Agatha refocused and reached a hand through a hole, probing its edges. Breaking barriers was a personal talent. She'd gotten through the one on Halfway Bay every time she'd tried;

surely she could get through this one too. But there was no gatekeeper to fool, nor any way to get through holes this small or—

Something nipped her finger.

Agatha recoiled in surprise and saw one of Anadil's black rats planted on the Woods' side of the shield, tiny claws clasping the edges of the hole for support. *"Rat #3,"* Agatha remembered, the only one still perky enough to get this far, for the other two had yet to recover from retrieving Dovey's wand and zip-lining chocolate fog. Now, Rat #3 tittered sternly at Agatha through the hole, ordering her to pay attention, before it started crawling through the hole into Gavaldon . . .

The instant its nose crossed the plane between the Woods and the Reader World, the rat was assaulted by a fiery shock that sent it flying to the ground.

Through the shield, Agatha watched Rat #3 jerking in the dirt, still alive despite the magical shockwave.

So the shield won't let it through, she thought. She slipped her own hand through the hole again easily. *But then why does it let me?*

Agatha shook off the thought. *What does it matter? The hole's still too small for me to fit int*—

Something bit her again.

Agatha looked at Anadil's rat, who'd crawled up the shield again despite its obvious pain, and was still glowering at her. Agatha glowered right back. What did the little pest want—

She gasped.

Little.

It's showing me how to get through.

Mogrify.

It wants me to mogrify.

And there was only one animal Agatha knew how to be.

Instantly she closed her eyes and visualized the spell, feeling her fingertip glow hot gold. In a flash, she shrunk to the ground, her clothes flopping on top of her, before she crawled out from under them, a skinny black cockroach. Antennae quivering, Agatha the Roach skittered up the side of the shield, leaving her clothes behind, and scooted through one of the holes, before she followed the rat down the side of the shield and into the Woods.

The second Agatha pattered through the first trees, a green fireball scudded past her, nearly incinerating her and the rat. Petrified, she chased after Anadil's pet, zipping through the war in full flight; but as a cockroach, she was so small that all she could see were crashing feet and falling bodies and the glow of flaming arrows and magical spells shooting back and forth above her. She needed to look for Sophie, but with all the fighting around her, she'd never find her as a bug—

An arrow sheared over her tiny carapace. Spooked, Agatha accelerated behind the rat, leading her intently towards a pine bush. Agatha motored through the bush behind him, pine needles pricking her thorax, and came out the other side. She stopped cold.

Handsome, dark-skinned Nicholas was facedown in mulch, a giant gash through the back of his head. As the roar of war echoed beyond the bush, Agatha gazed at the young

Everboy, her insides crumbling. Valiant, sweet Nicholas . . . dead? Because of *her* fairy tale? Sadness and guilt rushed through her, big bug eyes filling with tears—

Anadil's rat hissed.

Agatha turned to see it glaring at her and pinching at Nicholas' uniform.

It wants me to take his clothes.

There was no part of Agatha that could do what she was about to do, and yet she had no choice.

Don't think. Don't think. Don't think.

Sick to her gut, she reverted back to human form and forced herself to change into Nicholas' uniform, while she crouched behind the pine bush. As she shoved on his big boots and pulled on his cloak, the rat nudged over Nicholas' bow and quiver of arrows, which lay by his side. Agatha leaned in and touched her shaking hand to Nicholas' black hair.

Find Sophie, she gritted.

Find her now.

From the rat, she took his weapon into hand and rose from the bush, suited in all black, her eyes darkening and jaw clamped. With a deep breath, Agatha plunged into war.

The air was so dark and foggy, filled with the smoke of flying arrows and burning zombie corpses, that at first she could only see shadows. Taking cover behind a tree, she squinted and made out Hort and Peter Pan twenty feet away, both trying to fend off Captain Hook with sticks, rocks, and whatever else they could find on the ground. Meanwhile, Tinkerbell frantically showered fairy dust over Hook, trying to fly him away, but the Captain spun and sliced into her wing with his blade, sending Tink plummeting to the ground. As Tinkerbell crawled through the grass, looking for a place to hide, Hook stabbed harder at Peter and Hort. Hort tripped backwards over Peter's feet trying to defend him and Hook bashed him aside, bolting towards Pan—

Behind a tree, Agatha knew she only had one shot to save him. With her fingerglow, she lit her arrow tip on fire and aimed it right at Hook's heart. As he launched towards Peter Pan, hook ripping towards his neck, Agatha let the arrow fly—

It missed Hook's heart but speared his cheek instead, lighting his face on fire.

As Hook staggered back in surprise, trying in vain to put out the flames, Hort and Peter didn't even look to see who'd saved their lives. Both ran for cover, as Agatha watched Hook succumb to the fire and collapse into the dirt.

One down. Even if it was by accident.

Agatha stepped out from behind the tree, another arrow drawn. She searched the trees for Sophie, but all she could find were more students and mentors trying to fight off zombie villains, who seemed to be exclusively targeting the famous heroes now: Gretel and Hester against the witch, Red Riding Hood and Dot against the wolf, Jack and Anadil against the giant. . . . With every second, the Good heroes were losing more ground against their villains, steadily being pushed out of the trees towards Gavaldon's shield. The battlefield around them was littered with fractured stymphs, dead villains, and moaning students, nursing wounds and broken limbs.

Suddenly, in the far distance, Agatha glimpsed Aric rushing at Professor Dovey with a jagged knife. The old Dean tried to shoot him with a spell, but the young Dean was coming too fast. He tackled her to the ground, knocking her out cold. Gripping Dovey by her silver hair, he kneeled over her senseless body—

Agatha bleached white. If she tried to shoot Aric from here, she'd have to be dead on-target or she'd hit Dovey instead. She'd barely even managed to hit Hook and he'd been twenty feet away. Instinctively she started dashing towards Aric, fumbling for an arrow, trying to get close enough to get a better shot. But it was too late. Aric raised his knife over Professor Dovey's throat, about to finish her. Agatha screamed—

From behind, Lady Lesso charged in and dove on top of Aric, knocking him off wounded Clarissa. Agatha choked with relief, but now Aric was on top of his mother, the two of them flailing for the dagger in the dirt. Agatha ran faster, trying to get within shooting range—

As Lady Lesso clasped the dagger, Aric punched her in the back of the neck and surged over her. His mother collapsed onto her stomach, but lurched forward, grappling Aric by the ears. Both flushed red, mother and son fighting for the knife, the gleam of metal swerving from one to the other, until Aric kicked it away. Agatha aimed her arrow from afar, trying to get a clear shot at Aric's head, but he and Lesso were both crawling madly towards the dagger now, jabbing and elbowing past each other. Lady Lesso swiped the blade first, but Aric leapt on top of her. His mother flipped over, clutching her son by the throat, their faces touching, the knife trapped between them—

Aric's eyes shot wide as he let out a stunned cry.

Standing over him, Professor Dovey stabbed a broken stymph bone deeper into his back.

Aric's big muscles went limp and he collapsed on top of his mother, blood seeping out of his mouth.

Lesso shoved her son off her, wheezing for breath. Flat on her back, the Evil Dean clutched Professor Dovey's wrist and smiled weakly at her best friend.

Agatha dropped her arrow and throttled towards Lesso and Dovey, thankful they were both safe—

Something crashed into Agatha and yanked her behind a tree.

"Where is she!" Hester barked over the chaos. "Where's Sophie!"

Agatha shook her head. "I don't know!"

Hester seized Agatha's shoulders. "Look."

Agatha followed her eyes through the trees to a fleck of light, half-buried into the horizon.

"Ten minutes. That's all we have. You have to find Sophie—" Hester commanded.

"Where's Tedros?" Agatha breathed.

"Merlin's trying to keep kids alive as long as he can," Hester said, pointing at the wizard, darting from wounded student to wounded student, treating their injuries with dust from his hat.

"*Where's Tedros?*" Agatha pressed.

They heard a high-pitched scream and whirled to see

Pinocchio chased by twenty ogres and trolls across the Woods. Just as the villains snagged him, a horde of animals burst from the forest and slammed into the zombies, dislodging Pinocchio from their grip. Princess Uma swung down from a tree and pulled the old hero up to safety in its branches, alongside Yuba and the White Rabbit, while Uma's animal army fought the zombies below.

Another yell rang out and Agatha twirled to see Lancelot battling Rafal near the first line of trees. The knight's shoulder was drenched with blood, but he was deftly deflecting the young sorcerer's spells, despite his snarls of pain.

Agatha paled.

Tedros wasn't with him.

"Agatha, listen to me," Hester hissed. "Hook's dead. Ani killed Briar Rose's fairy and I killed my zombie-mother, pretending like I was happy to see her. All that's left is Jack's giant, Riding Hood's wolf, and Cinderella's stepmother. We'll do everything we can to keep that shield from falling. But you have to find Sophie—"

"WHERE'S TEDROS!" Agatha demanded.

"HE'S FINE. PRINCE LOSER IS FINE," Hester lashed. "Lance is keeping him away from the School Master, all right?" She pointed across the forest at Tedros, brandishing Excalibur and barreling at ogres the way he once barreled at Lancelot on the moors, while Chaddick flew over the prince on a stymph, taking out wounded ogres with fiery arrows. "But you don't have time to help him or check on him or get anywhere near him, so don't even try it," Hester berated. "We need you to find

Sophie *now*. Ten minutes, Agatha."

Agatha met her eyes. "Ten minutes."

"Hurry," Hester begged before running to help Dot and Riding Hood.

On a breath, Agatha tore in the opposite direction, eyes peeled for Sophie, as she leapt over fallen students and zombies. A boom echoed behind her and she spun to see Jack's giant fall to the ground, leveled by Kiko, Beatrix, and Reena who'd fire-bombed him from the height of the trees, while Anadil, Jack, and Briar Rose distracted him from below. Behind them, the wolf was advancing on Red Riding Hood, with Dot seemingly hurt on the ground. But just as the wolf's jaws closed over Red Riding Hood's head, Dot thrust out her glowing fingertip and turned the wolf's jaws to chocolate. His chocolate teeth sunk into Red Riding Hood, crumbling down to the gums. When he recoiled in shock, Hester had a fire-tipped arrow waiting for him.

Agatha heaved relief, scanning for Sophie. The old heroes were safe for now. The shield wouldn't fall—

Her eyes bulged.

Cinderella was frozen near the shield, seeing her undead stepsisters for the first time. Agatha watched Ella's face melt to happiness, taking in the beloved sisters she'd once loved more than anyone else. It didn't matter that they were spear-wielding zombies or that they were on Evil's side. Like a moth to fire, Ella drifted towards them, hands up in peace. The closer she drew, the more her stepsisters' gnarled faces softened in turn, their grip on their spears weakening, as if they too felt the stirrings of old love for their sister, erasing all new orders to hurt her. Cinderella slowly held out her arms towards them, a beautiful glow spreading across her face . . .

She didn't hear her stepmother behind her with the axe.

"No!" Agatha cried, sprinting forwards—

Cinderella turned too late.

The axe slashed down.

As the old princess fell, Agatha's vision fogged with tears, her heartbeat dragging to a crawl.

In the fiery hell pit of the forest, a war stopped.

Even Lancelot and Rafal held their blows, watching Cinderella hit the ground only a few feet from Gavaldon's shield.

Merlin turned from nursing injured Ravan. The wizard's body went stiff, his eyes flying to Agatha.

Shell-shocked, both she and the wizard wheeled towards the shield over Gavaldon.

A young boy stood inside the protective bubble, watching them.

He was no more than seven or eight years old and held a storybook open in his hands.

Agatha recognized him immediately.

Jacob.

Honora's youngest son.

He watched Cinderella dying on the other side of the thin shield, her slumped position matching the changing painting on the last page of the fairy tale in his hands.

The rewritten book slipped out of his fingers and fell to the grass.

Behind him, Agatha glimpsed a mob of shadows, led by a tall, broad man, racing towards the young boy from Gavaldon's square. She could hear Stefan calling out Jacob's name, telling him to get away . . .

But it didn't matter now.

The holes in the shield over Gavaldon were magically expanding and bleeding into each other, growing bigger, bigger, bigger—

All at once the shield exploded with an ear-splitting crack, detonating in a blinding flash of white light that jolted the Forest like an earthquake. Heroes young and old spilled to the ground, as stymphs careened headfirst into trees, exploding on impact. Agatha spun from the sizzling glare, her body thrown to the dirt as she covered her eyes.

Then the light seemed to fade.

Little by little, she peeked up through her fingers and saw twinkles of white raining over the Reader World like stars.

The shield between the Woods and Gavaldon was gone.

In the Woods, the heroes were slow to get up . . . but the zombies were already unfurling to their feet. . . . Agatha couldn't see Tedros anywhere—or Merlin or Lancelot, for that matter—

She swiveled back to where the shield had been. Jacob had been subsumed into the throng of villagers who'd swarmed in to save him. Honora gripped him hard against her waist, his elder brother, Adam, under her other arm, as she herded them into the safety of the crowd.

Staring at the firelit battlefield, the oldest Elder quivered at the fore of the mob, too frightened to discern who was friend and who was foe. He held out his hands in surrender, backing against his people.

"Every four years you ripped our families apart. You took our children! Isn't that enough?" the Elder pleaded. "We'll do anything you want. Please don't kill us—"

"I have no intention to kill you," said a cool, hard voice.

Agatha's spine tingled.

Slowly she turned, along with the villagers, to see Rafal, standing alone inside the boundary of the Reader World.

"Well . . . except for *him*," he grinned.

The young School Master stepped aside, revealing Stefan kneeling in the grass, gagged with a stick.

Sophie stood over her father, cold-eyed and still.

"In fact, it's not me doing the killing at all. My true love will be the one to end this story." Rafal kissed Sophie's hand gently, his ring on her finger gleaming against his lips. "Sacrificing her own father's blood for *love*."

Agatha broke out in a sweat.

"The most dangerous person in a fairy tale is the one willing to do anything for love."

It was never the Readers that Rafal was after in Gavaldon. It was only one Reader. A Reader whose murder could undo the School Master's slaying of his own brother.

Merlin's words rushed back to her . . . the ones he'd spoken in the Celestium the night before the war . . . the ones that didn't make any sense . . .

What if we have the whole story wrong, Agatha?

The day Rafal had killed his own blood, he'd proven that Evil couldn't love and doomed his side to eternal defeat.

But now he had a queen who would kill her own blood to prove Evil *could* love.

An original sin erased.

The curse on Evil reversed.

An immortal School Master with no one to stop him until every last Ever was dead. Until Good was only a memory.

Just as he'd promised.

Horror-struck, Agatha looked up at Sophie standing with Rafal, his spiked white hair like icicles against the night sky. As Sophie gazed at her beautiful true love, there was nothing in her eyes but a deep green void.

Beneath her, Stefan didn't struggle. He knew he was beaten.

Agatha felt her fingertip heat up, knowing Tedros must be nearby. Lancelot and Merlin too. Surely they could help her get to Stefan in time. Somehow they'd get Sophie away from the School Master. The wizard always had a plan—

But now she saw Rafal smirking at her, his eyes on her glowing fingertip, as if she was two steps behind.

Dread rising, Agatha turned to see Rafal's zombies restraining Merlin's army, young and old, weapons to each of their necks. Zombie trolls and ogres broke heroes' bows and crushed the last stymphs with their fists, splintering their bones. Trapped at spear- and swordpoint, the young and old heroes surrendered to their knees like Stefan. First, Hort and

Peter together . . . then Jack and Briar Rose . . . Uma, Yuba, and Pinocchio . . . even Hester knew her demon was no match for a knife-wielding zombie witch and dropped to the dirt next to Anadil and Dot.

Petrified, Agatha searched for Tedros, but she couldn't see him anywhere as she scanned the grove down to the last two trolls tying prisoners to a tree—

Her heart stopped.

The prisoners were Merlin and Lancelot.

The knight had a gash in his cheek, a scorched thigh, and his shoulder looked worse than before as he drifted in and out of consciousness, trying to keep his head up. Merlin had been stripped of hat and cloak, and one of the ogres had hacked off his beard. Slumped in the dirt, in a filthy undershirt, the wizard stared at the sun through the trees, minutes from snuffing out. She could see the despair in his sad blue eyes, reflecting the last trickle of light. Together, they'd failed to destroy Sophie's ring . . . failed to hold the shield . . . failed to stop the School Master from his ending. Instead, they'd given him just enough time to seal Good's destruction forever.

Agatha waited for Merlin to look at her . . . to tell her what to do from here . . . to give Good a way out . . .

But Merlin never did.

Rafal leered at the hapless wizard and the rest of the kneeling hostages.

"Why can't some souls love?" he asked, his young, sultry tone carrying into the night. "It's a question I've wrestled a long time, watching Good win every single story, while souls like mine languished without a weapon to fight back. So many Nevers try to love in Good's way, in the hope that we might find a happy ending too. Even me: I tried to love my Good brother with just as much fervor as Evil's queen once loved a Good prince. But Evil can't love in Good's way, no matter how hard we try. Because our souls were never created with love. We are the discarded, the neglected, the beaten down. We are the hated, the castoffs, the *freaks*. Despair is our fuel; pain is our power. The love that wins Ever Afters could never be enough for us. Nothing will ever be enough to satisfy the black hole in our hearts. Unless we change what love means . . ."

A cutting smile slid across his face, his eyes lifting to Agatha. ". . . and Evil finds its *own* happy endings."

An ogre seized Agatha from behind and bound her wrists.

At the same time, muffled yells tore through the silence and Agatha swiveled to see two trolls push Tedros next to her with hands tied, the prince barechested and gagged with his balled-up shirt. He no longer had his father's sword.

Rafal leaned between them, his lips at their ears.

"I promised you an ending you'd never forget," he whispered, his breath gelid on Agatha's skin. "The Last Ever After to your fairy tale."

One troll handed Excalibur to Sophie, who instantly put it to Stefan's throat.

The second troll pulled the axe from Cinderella's corpse and handed the weapon to Rafal.

Rafal shoved Agatha and Tedros down to their knees side by side, before he pinned a black boot between each of their shoulder blades, first Agatha, then Tedros, crushing their faces over a fallen tree trunk, as two ogres kept their bodies from squirming.

The young School Master carefully lay the axe blade across Agatha's and Tedros' necks, the edge long enough to take care of both of them at once. Agatha could feel the blood dripping off the steel, along with rough speckles of rust.

"Good finds Ever After with a kiss. Evil finds Ever After with a *kill*." Rafal looked up at Sophie, smoldering red patches on his snow-white cheeks. "You've been hurt by everyone you ever trusted, my queen. But one swing and they'll be gone for good. One swing and our love is sealed forever."

There was a mad, lustful passion in his face now. "Because on this night, I take you, Sophie, as my Never After. From this day forward, in darkness and despair, for Evil and Eviler, to love and to hate, till death never do us part. This death I give to you. My one true love."

He pressed his axe into Agatha's and Tedros' necks, taking aim.

Sophie's face was still a hard, ghostly mask. She dug Excalibur deep into Stefan's windpipe.

"This death I give to you, Rafal. My one true love," she pledged.

"Sophie, no!" Agatha cried out, twisting to meet her eyes. "He's your fath—"

Rafal crunched his boot down, silencing her.

"Wait," Sophie said, sharp as a whip, stopping the young School Master cold. "I'm not finished with this one."

Rafal's boot eased up on Agatha and he smirked at his queen, surprised. "By all means, my love . . . *Unleash*."

Sophie turned to Agatha, the hardness in her face warping to something deeper, scarier. "You think this man deserves the name 'father'? A man who despises me?"

Stefan tried to speak, but Sophie jammed the sword blade against his neck.

"I tried to make him love me. I tried to show him the real me. But he hated me even more. Just like Tedros. Just like everyone Good ever did," Sophie spat at Agatha. "I am my mother. Evil to the bone. That's all anyone will ever see."

Agatha raised her head from the log. "Except me."

Her voice was surprisingly calm, as if rising from a place over which she had no control.

She could see the last slivers of sun glint in Excalibur's blade.

Merlin had warned her: she would have one chance with Sophie.

Use it wisely.

She'd tried to listen to the wizard. She'd tried to have a plan . . .

But there was no plan.

There could never be a plan for her and Sophie.

There was only the truth.

She could feel Tedros struggling against his binds like he had on a pyre, once upon a time in Gavaldon, trying to help her. But this time it was she who gently touched her foot to his leg, soothing him.

No one could help her now.

This was her and Sophie's fairy tale.

And this was The End.

Agatha looked up at her friend.

"I know what's inside you, Sophie," she said. "Beyond your mother. Beyond Evil. I know the real you."

"*This* is the real me. This has always been the real me," Sophie retorted, tightening her grip on the sword. "The one who doesn't have to pretend to be Good anymore. The one who doesn't have to feel like I'm not enough. The one who doesn't have to feel anything at all. I'm finally happy, Agatha."

"No, you're not," Agatha said quietly. "You're not happy."

Sophie bristled. "About to die with your beloved prince and still thinking about *me*. My story will go on without you, Agatha. I don't need you anymore or your pity, like one of your decrepit cats. I'm no longer your *Good Deed*."

"But I'm still yours," said Agatha. "Because without your love, I'd never have become who I really am. So even if I die, I'll always be your Good Deed, Sophie. And no Evil in the world will ever erase that."

Spots of pink seared Sophie's cheeks. Her throat bobbed. "You shouldn't have come back for me," she rasped. "You should have lived your own life and let me have mine. None of this would have ever happened."

"I would do it all over again," said Agatha.

"Because we're *sisters*?" Sophie scoffed, fighting emotion.

Stefan gurgled, confused—Sophie dug the blade deeper.

"Because we're more than sisters," said Agatha, staring

straight at her. "We chose each other, Sophie. We're best friends."

Sophie looked away. "A princess and witch can never be friends. Our story will forever prove that."

"No, our story proves a princess and a witch *have* to be friends. Because each of us has played both parts," said Agatha. "And we'll always play both parts. That's who we are. That's why we're *us*."

Sophie still couldn't look at her. "All I ever wanted was love, Aggie," she breathed, voice breaking. "All I ever wanted was a happy ending like yours."

"You already have one, Sophie. You've always had one." Agatha smiled through tears. "With me."

Sophie finally met her eyes.

For the briefest of moments, sound and space fell away, the two of them locked in a gaze so strong that they became reflections of each other. Light and Dark. Good and Evil. Hero and Villain. Only as each looked deeper, neither knew who was who. For in each other's eyes, they saw the answers to their own soul's silent questions, as if they weren't reflections at all, but two halves of the same.

A tear slipped down Sophie's cheek, her mouth falling open to the softest of gasps, as if a fire inside her had gone out.

The young School Master looked ruffled, his hands twitching on the axe, pupils darting between his prisoner and his queen—

Sophie blinked, the moment gone. She looked at Agatha as if she were a stranger, her face chilling back to its dead-numb shell. Slowly Sophie turned to Rafal.

"On three," she said.

Rafal smiled cruelly at Sophie and slammed Agatha's head back down on the tree.

"On three," said Rafal, measuring the blade against her and Tedros' necks.

Agatha went limp, her heart broken.

"One," said Sophie.

Tedros stopped thrashing as if he knew the end had come. He pressed his bare shoulder against Agatha's and she pulled even closer, wanting to feel every part of him as they died.

"Two," said Rafal, both fists on the axe.

She tasted the warmth of Tedros' breath.

"Forever," he whispered.

"Forever," she whispered.

Rafal raised the axe over their heads.

Sophie aimed her sword at her father's neck—

"Three," Sophie said.

Agatha felt the wind of the falling axe and saw Sophie swing Tedros' sword, the sun imploding to darkness in the mirror of its steel. But as Excalibur grazed Stefan's skin, about to rip into his throat, Sophie suddenly diverted her swing, looping the sword upwards. Her right hand came off the hilt, brushing across her left hand, sweeping the School Master's ring clean off her finger and high into the air, the gold circle catching the last spear of light in the sky, like a bold new sun—

The glare blinded Rafal and he froze the axe in shock, whirling back towards his queen. As the ring fell towards

Sophie, his eyes widened in horror and he thrust out his palm, a blast of black glow scorching towards her—

Clasping the sword with both fists, Sophie looked dead into the School Master's eyes and smashed Excalibur down with all her might, shattering the ring out of the air into a million shards of gold.

Gold shimmer enveloped Sophie's body like a shield as the School Master's death spell ripped into her, the black cloud breaking apart on impact and dissipating like the last mists of a storm.

Thunderstruck, Rafal watched the last embers of his ring go cold, betrayal flushing through his young, beautiful face . . .

Then he began to change. His face shriveled like rancid fruit; his thick white hair sloughed off in clumps over his mottled skull; his spine hunched with sickening crackles, jerking his body into ugly contortions. Liver spots rashed across decaying skin, his blue eyes clouding toxic gray, his muscled limbs shrinking to bony sticks. With each second, he grew older and older, thousands of years old, screams of rage tearing from inside of him as his flesh boiled with heat. His clothes burned off of him, smoke spitting through his mummifying skin, until the School Master was unmasked at last, a naked corpse of blackened, hateful flesh.

His red eyes met Sophie's. Roaring with vengeance, he staggered towards her, faster, faster, stabbing out a rotted claw for her face—

His hand crumbled to dust as he touched her.

Rafal let out a monstrous cry and burst into ashes, cascading to the ground like the sands of an hourglass.

All through the trees, his Dark Army of old villains crumbled too, their weapons dropping and clinking to earth in clouds of dust.

A last gust of wind swept trails of smoke across the Forest like a curtain.

The night was quieter than the depths of a tomb.

Stupefied, Tedros ripped out his gag and scraped to his knees first, gaping into the black sky.

"We're here," he said, spinning around. "We're still here. Agatha . . . we're alive! The storybook's closed—"

His princess hadn't moved, facedown on the log.

"Agatha?"

Slowly Agatha looked up at him. "Tedros, I think I'm going to faint."

Her prince smiled. "You catch me. I catch you."

The color drained from Agatha's face and she slackened into his waiting arms.

Across from them, petrified villagers freed Stefan, who tearfully embraced Honora and her two young sons. In the mulch of the Forest, young and old heroes pulled themselves off the ground, surveying the carnage of war. Hester cut Lancelot and Merlin loose, while Hort reunited the wizard with his hat and starry cloak. Meanwhile, Anadil and Dot hustled between old mentors, propping them up to their feet.

"We'll make you a new wing, Tink," Peter said, comforting his weeping fairy.

"Make me a new chair too," said Hansel, frowning at a

broken wheel on his wheelchair.

With his spectacles cracked, the White Rabbit depended on Yuba to guide him, while Princess Uma said a silent prayer for all the animals that had died during the war.

"Anyone seen Jack?" Pinocchio asked.

Red Riding Hood pointed to him and Briar Rose kissing behind a tree.

As Merlin tended to the wounded students, Beatrix used what few skills she'd learned leading Evil's infirmary to help Lancelot bind his bloody shoulder.

"Gwen will never let me leave the house again," he grumbled.

As Agatha stirred, she felt Tedros running his fingers through her hair.

The first thing she saw was Merlin crouched over Cinderella, wrapping her body in his cloak. The old princess looked so peaceful and light, the way she had when she saw her stepsisters one last time.

The wizard met Agatha's eyes and gave her the warmest of smiles, as if to reassure her that even though she was no longer alive, Cinderella had finally found her happy ending.

Agatha watched as Hort and Chaddick helped the wizard carry her away. Tomorrow, there would be a funeral, where she could say goodbye . . .

Tomorrow.

"The sun," she choked, peering into the dark sky. "Where's the sun?"

"Waiting to rise in the morning," said her barechested

prince, helping her up. "Thanks to you."

Agatha exhaled. "Takes two for a happy ending," she said, searching for her best friend. But Sophie was nowhere to be seen.

"You know what went through my head as the axe was coming down?" Tedros asked. "That we never had nicknames for each other, like every other couple."

"We're not like every other couple," said Agatha, looking at him.

"No, we're not," Tedros admitted. "Not every king finds a queen who's smarter, stronger, and better than him in every way."

Agatha put her hand to his golden cheek. "You are the pretty one, at least."

Tedros grinned, leaning in. "Mmm, you might have me beat there too."

He kissed her long and soft, leaving Agatha even more wobbly on her feet. Tedros steadied her with his strong arm, bringing her into his sweaty chest. After all this, he somehow smelled better than he ever did before. She kissed him again, a blush blooming on her cheeks—

Then her smile faded.

Tedros noticed and turned.

Through the trees, Sophie was kneeling beside Lady Lesso, shivering on her back, as Professor Dovey clutched her friend's hand.

The Evil Dean's dress was soaked with blood.

"Oh no," Agatha whispered.

Sophie stroked Lady Lesso's cheek, gazing into her violet eyes. The Dean was wheezing shallowly, trying in vain to say something.

"Shhh," Professor Dovey said to her, stoic and firm. "Just rest."

The Good Dean had known the moment she'd seen the wound from Aric's knife that magic would serve no use.

Sophie glanced up and saw Agatha, Tedros, and all the other young and old heroes gathered at a distance, watching solemnly.

"What . . . made you . . . do it?"

Sophie slowly looked down.

"Tell . . . me," Lady Lesso said.

Sophie smiled. "The same thing that made you turn your back on Evil too," she said. "A friend."

Lady Lesso took Sophie's hand in hers, the Dean's other hand still on Clarissa's. "The Old and the New together," she whispered. "Both in good hands."

Tears slipped down Sophie's face. "This is my fault—"

"No," said Lady Lesso, steeling willfully. "Never that. You're my child. As much as my own son. You are loved, Sophie." Her voice faltered. "Always remember. You are *loved*—"

Clarissa touched her. "Lady Lesso, please . . ."

"Leonora."

Lady Lesso looked up at her best friend. "My name . . . is Leonora."

Slowly the Dean's eyes closed. She never took another breath.

Professor Dovey finally wept, draping herself over her best friend.

Sophie quietly left the two of them alone.

Agatha was waiting for her at Gavaldon's edge.

They stood together in silence, watching Dovey hold Lesso's dead body the way Agatha once held Sophie's.

Sophie's fingers clasped Agatha's.

Agatha gently squeezed Sophie back.

"Where's Tedros?" Sophie said at last.

"Rounding up the others so we can head to the school," Agatha replied, watching Tedros and Lancelot in the Forest lifting Ravan, Professor Anemone, and the other injured atop the rumps of Princess Uma's few surviving animals. "So many hurt that we'll need the other teachers' help."

"Come on. Let's chip in," Sophie said, heading towards the trees—

"Not yet," said Agatha. "There's someone waiting for you, first."

Sophie looked over her friend's shoulder and saw Stefan, standing in the grass, the rest of the villagers gathered at a distance.

Sophie's heart caved in.

Stefan never said a word. He just hugged his daughter tight, as both of them sobbed.

"I'm sorry," she breathed. "I'm sorry, Father."

"I never hated you. Never," Stefan fought. "I tried to be a good father—you don't know how hard I tried—"

"You were," Sophie sniffled. "You were a good father."

"I love you more than anything in the world," Stefan whispered. "You're my child, Sophie."

Stefan saw Agatha crying now, watching him with Sophie.

"Though you've always made Agatha feel like one of mine too," he said, smiling tenderly at her.

Sophie wiped her cheek. "Come on, Aggie."

Agatha hugged Stefan too, nestling against him, as her tears stained his shirt. She wanted to tell him. She wanted to tell him everything. But as she caught Sophie's eyes, her friend clearly having the same thoughts, neither of them said a word. For in a single moment, they'd found everything they needed. They didn't need any more. There, in the space between worlds, two girls held their father, their bodies still and serene, as if three pieces had been made whole at last.

Agatha looked up at Stefan, smiling. With a gasp, she broke away from him—

For Stefan was shimmering, along with the rest of the villagers behind him. Within seconds, their bodies turned translucent, as Gavaldon started vanishing into a glare of white light.

Stunned, Stefan looked up and saw a shield streaking down from the sky—

Agatha felt Sophie's hand on hers, pulling her away from him.

"No. Stay with us, Sophie . . . ," Stefan begged, fading faster. "Stay with your family!"

"I love you, Father, but you have a new family now," said Sophie, eyes glistening. "The one you always deserved. The one that will make you truly happy." She held Agatha closer. "I have a new family too. One that can finally make me happy. So don't worry about me, Father. Please. Don't look back. Never look back."

"No . . . Sophie, no . . ." Stefan lunged out a hand for his daughter as the shield slashed between them—

"Wait!"

Light slipped through his fingers.

He was gone.

35

Never Ever After

Sophie rose early to watch the sun.

Wrapped in a wool blanket, she leaned over the rooftop balcony of Merlin's Menagerie, surrounded by leafy sculptures of her best friend's love story and gazed out at the brilliant fireball amidst purple shreds of sky. She'd forgotten what the sun looked like, so full and strong, brushing across her like a warm, gold kiss.

In the dawn light, she could see the glittering blue glass towers of Honor and Valor beneath her, the pink towers of Purity and Charity connected by a colored breezeway, and across the bay, the jagged black castles of Malice, Mischief, and Vice. The School Master's death had restored the School for Good and Evil

to balance, even though both the lake and moat sides of Half-way Bay continued to belch with noxious green fog. Merlin insisted the condition would resolve on its own, once Evers and Nevers resumed their classes and the magical wave responsible for sorting students began its rounds.

It had taken the wizard and Tinkerbell most of the night to fly the School Master's tower from the Blue Forest back to its rightful place between the halves of the bay. For one thing, Tink's aging fairy dust moved the structure slower than a snail would; for another, Tink was still adjusting to the new wing Merlin had made for her out of a blue butterfly he'd found in the Dean's office.

The wizard had yet to remand the Nevers to Evil's castle, preferring they all stay together for the night in the comforts of the Good dormitories. Once the Good and Evil teachers were freed, the faculty spent most of the evening treating injured students and heroes, while the rest of the Evers and Nevers had a full supper of turkey meatballs, carrot-ginger soup, green herb salad, and raspberry pie, catered by Merlin's hat. If any of the Evil teachers resented the loss of their School Master or having been sealed in their rooms during the war, none of them showed it—perhaps because they saw the extent of the wounds suffered in battle, or more likely because Lady Lesso's death meant one of them would be chosen the new Dean of Evil. With the School Master gone and Lady Lesso unable to choose a successor, it was soon widely presumed that Professor Manley would take her place. (He'd already spent the night redecorating her office.)

As the sun slipped behind a cloud, the winter chill returning,

Sophie sat down and snuggled against a topiary of Tedros proposing to Agatha at the Circus of Talents. Resting her head between them, she let her eyes close, thankful that she had nowhere to be, no one to seek, and nothing wanting in her heart.

She'd never truly loved Rafal, no matter how much she'd told herself she did. She'd used him, trying to heal the hole in her soul . . . just like he'd tried to use her. But he was gone now, the finger that once wore his ring bare and blank.

Dreams floated by and she found herself standing in front of beautiful white-and-blue spires spearing the sky, topped with vermillion flags . . .

Camelot.

She could see the white marble path leading towards the kingdom . . . the tall, silver gates wide open . . . Agatha and Tedros, hand in hand, waiting for her on the other side with big, bright smiles . . .

"Sophie?"

Her eyes fluttered open to full-blown morning.

"They're starting soon," said Hort.

He was standing at the frosted door of the roof, his muscular frame obscured by a dumpy black tunic that used to be Evil's uniform.

In his hand was a matching tunic.

"No," Sophie gasped. *"Really?"*

Hort cracked a grin. "Really."

The funerals for Cinderella and Lady Lesso took place in the Blue Forest, which was already coming back to life by the time the nymphs began laying out chairs in the Tulip Garden.

All the Nevers wore their saggy black uniforms and sat on the left side of the grass, while all the Evers sat on the right, with the girls in their usual pink pinafores and the boys in sky-blue shirts, navy jackets, and knotted slim ties. Many of the students had bruises, bandages, and casts, which they showed off to classmates with furtive whispers and the utmost pride. Indeed, there were no dirty looks across the aisle nor any of the usual rancor between the Good and Evil schools . . . but instead a silent gratitude that the other school was present at all.

The old heroes were there too, neatly fitted out in suits and dresses they'd found in the faculty closets. Only Lancelot was absent, who couldn't bear to be away from his Guinevere any longer and had absconded during the night, once the students were safely asleep.

Everyone expected Merlin to preside over the ceremony as he stepped to the dais in front of the twin coffins, but the wizard invited Professor Dovey to say a few words instead.

Dressed in her chartreuse gown, Clarissa Dovey took the lectern, her brown eyes glassy, her nose tipped red.

"So much has been written of Cinderella, a student whose fairy tale will live on forever," she began. "But there will be no stories of Lady Lesso. No tales passed down from Reader to Reader, keeping her name alive. For that, she would be thankful. Because Leonora Lesso only wanted one thing in her life. To find the true meaning of Evil. And it was in the pursuit of that meaning that she showed us why this school must endure.

For in the end, it was Evil's Dean who proved that sometimes Good isn't Evil's greatest enemy . . . but an unexpected friend."

She spoke a while longer, but it was these words that remained in the minds of young and old when the Good Dean was finished, as they each took a turn touching the coffins and saying quiet goodbyes.

After the nymphs carried the coffins out of the Blue Forest and into the Woods, where they'd be properly buried by a new Crypt Keeper, the others moved into the Blue Pumpkin Patch for tea. Reena and Millicent played their flutes and Beatrix sang an aria no one listened to, while Merlin's hat laid out a colorful spread of jam-dot cookies, coconut cake, caramel macaroons, and sugar-mint scones. Nearby, students broke into sun-drenched packs, sober faces gradually melting to smiles.

Hester, Anadil, and Dot peered at Sophie across the pumpkins, clad in Evil's saggy black robes, and idling alongside Agatha in pink and Tedros in blue.

"Strange part is I'll miss them," said Anadil, rats peeking out of her tunic. "Even the cretinous prince."

"At least with Sophie gone, Hester will finally be Class Captain," Dot said, adding chocolate chips to her scone.

"Won't mean very much without her, will it?" Hester said wistfully. "She was the greatest witch of us all."

On the other side of the patch, Sophie noticed Hester, Anadil, and Dot sharing pieces of a scone and for the briefest of moments, she wished she could take them to Camelot with her.

"You're worse than Sophie," garbled Agatha's voice.

Sophie turned to see her arguing with Tedros, Agatha's mouth full of cake.

"You keep saying you're hungry, but then you won't *eat* anything," Agatha badgered, spilling crumbs on her pink dress.

"Coronation's tomorrow, which means they paint the royal portrait, which stays up for the next thousand years. Sorry if I want to look my best," Tedros groused.

"They're painting mine too and you don't see me or Reaper acting like a ninny," said Agatha, beaming at her hideous cat, chasing squealing Kiko around the Willows.

"Reaper?" Tedros blurted. "If you think for one second I'm allowing that Satan-worshipper in my castle—"

"Your castle? I thought it was our castle."

"Which means we get a pet we *both* like."

"No Reaper, no me."

"No you, then."

"You puffed-up, lily-livered, mule-headed—"

Agatha stopped and saw Sophie goggling at the two of them.

"I really am better off, aren't I?" said Sophie.

All three of them burst into laughter.

"Tedros! Look!" Chaddick hollered.

The prince turned to see a gaggle of Evers gathered at the Blue Forest gates, ogling a white-and-blue carriage swerving up the path, pulled by two white horses, the corners of its square enclosure topped with vermillion flags.

"Is that it?" Agatha asked nervously.

Tedros smiled. "Come on, love. Camelot's waiting," he said, yanking her towards it. He glanced back. "Hurry, Sophie! There's room in the carriage for three!"

"Which means your mother and I will have to ride behind!" a deep voice hollered.

Tedros looked up to see Lancelot with Guinevere, saddled on Benedict the horse, racing alongside the carriage.

By the time Guinevere dismounted, Tedros had nearly flattened her with a hug.

"You're coming with us?" he said, tears flowing.

"Me and the ogre," said Guinevere, kissing his cheek. "A king needs his mother." She looked up at Agatha. "And so does his queen."

Agatha embraced her. "You have no idea," she breathed.

"Thank you, Mother," Tedros sniffled, putting his arms around the both of them. "Thank you—"

"You can thank her by taking that death warrant off her head," Lancelot crabbed.

"Oh Lance, must you ruin everything!" Guinevere sighed.

As Lancelot relented and joined the group hug, Sophie watched from a distance as Agatha wrapped tighter into the arms of a loving prince and new, beautiful family. Seeing the glow in her friend's face, Sophie's own heart felt light as a cloud. Lady Lesso was right. Agatha's happiness was her happiness. And that was Ever After enough.

"Sophie, come on!"

She glanced up at Tedros and Agatha, holding the carriage door open for her.

With a smile, Sophie started heading towards them—

"Dear girl, do you mind retrieving my cape from Professor Dovey's office?" said Merlin, sauntering by in his shirtsleeves. "These old bones won't make it up another flight of stairs."

Sophie frowned, pointing at her friends ahead. "But they're—"

"Don't worry," said Merlin, breezing past her. "We'll hold the carriage."

The door to Professor Dovey's office was open and Sophie hurried inside, not wanting to keep her friends waiting.

The second desk was gone and the Dean of Good's office restored the way it once was, smelling of cinnamon and cloves. But Sophie couldn't see Merlin's cloak anywhere: not on the coat hooks, nor on the chair or desk . . .

But there was something else on the desk that made Sophie stop.

Between the pumpkin paperweights and basket of fresh sour plums lay a long white box cinched with a single purple ribbon. Attached to the box was a card that read:

Sophie

"It was on my desk when we returned."

Sophie turned to see Professor Dovey at the door.

"Lady Lesso must have left it before she freed me from the

Brig," said Clarissa, stepping beside her. "There was no will, no letter . . . only this."

Sophie ran her fingers along the stiff edges of the box and her inked name on the card, nothing else on the front or back, before peeking up at the Dean.

"We won't know what it is until you look inside, dear," Dovey said.

Slowly Sophie tugged at the purple ribbon and watched it slide away. Leaning over the desk, her hand curled around the edge of the white lid and pulled the box open.

Sophie choked.

"No. . . . How—how can—"

She spun to Professor Dovey, but the Good Dean was smiling at the box through tears.

"She told us, didn't she?" Clarissa whispered hopefully. "The 'Old and the New together . . .'"

She touched Sophie's cheek. "'Both in good hands.'"

Outside the carriage, Tedros brought his mother and Lancelot cups of tea. Leaning against a wheel, Agatha picked burrs out of Reaper's warty skin while Merlin studied his beardless face in the coach's glass window.

"After every epic journey, something must be lost," he said, probing his newly visible chin.

"Merlin, I've been thinking," said Agatha. "Why could I get through the shield between Gavaldon and the Woods when no one else could?"

"The shield was made to keep Evil from breaking into the Reader World, my dear," said Merlin. "But sometimes to keep Evil from getting in, you have to let Good *out*."

Agatha watched him, her throat tightening. "Oh Merlin . . . how I'll miss you."

"Miss me?" said Merlin, swiveling. "You don't think I'll let that boy run a kingdom without my help, do you?"

"And here I thought I was too old for a tutor," Tedros grinned, sidling next to Agatha.

"Not sixteen until tomorrow, boy," piped the wizard, sizing up the young couple. "Besides, in time, you'll have a little rug rat who needs a tutor too."

Agatha and Tedros gaped at him, both hot pink.

Merlin cleared his throat. "Perhaps we should focus on making it through your coronation first."

"If only there was room in our coach, you could spend the whole ride to Camelot making Agatha and I uncomfortable," Tedros quipped. "But alas, with Sophie, our carriage is full."

Merlin looked past them, mouth curling into a smile. "Is it?"

Tedros and Agatha turned.

Sophie swept towards them, wearing Lady Lesso's majestic, sharp-shouldered purple gown.

Agatha dropped her cat.

Sophie had no makeup on, sleepless bags under her eyes, and her hair was a bit of a mess, but even so, as they faced each other in silence, Agatha had never seen her friend look so calm, so assured, so . . . beautiful.

That's when Agatha knew.

"It's what she wanted, Aggie," Sophie rasped.

Agatha's lip quivered. "You're—you're not coming with us?"

"I'll be Dean of Evil, while Professor Dovey stays on as Dean of Good. The two of us working side by side like Lesso and Dovey once did," said Sophie. "Together, we'll keep the Storian well guarded until a new School Master is named."

She could see a crowd of Evers, Nevers, teachers, and heroes, old and young, gawking as word spread. (Professor Manley broke his teacup.)

Agatha couldn't speak. "But . . . but . . ."

"You wanted me to be happy, Agatha," said Sophie. "This is where I belong. This is what I want. Teaching students like me what Evil really means."

Agatha shook her head, tears rising. "Oh, Sophie. You'll be a wonderful Dean," she gasped, throwing arms around her. "I'll . . . I'll just miss you."

"You'll be an even better queen, Aggie," Sophie promised. "You'll change their lives. Like you changed mine."

Even Tedros looked misty-eyed now. "It's only a day's ride to Camelot, Sophie. Surely you'll come visit?"

"As much as you two will have me," Sophie said.

Agatha hugged her tighter, her tear-stained cheek against her friend's. "I love you, Sophie. I love you more than you can know."

"I do know, Aggie," Sophie whispered. "Because I love you just the same."

There the two girls stayed, holding each other, until Merlin finally ushered Agatha and her prince inside. As the carriage rode off, Guinevere and Lancelot riding behind, Sophie waved one last goodbye to her friends. The coach trailed into the dappled Woods towards the shadows of spires, faint over the horizon, before the final wheel vanished into the trees.

Agatha and Tedros were gone.

Standing alone at the gates, Sophie let herself cry, shedding warm, cleansing tears.

It wasn't goodbye forever. Only goodbye for now.

And if ever the distance was too much to bear, she would just look inside her heart, for Agatha was already there.

"Hmm . . . Maybe *your* Prince Charming is just around the corner," said a voice.

Sophie looked up at Hort next to her.

She took in his playful face, well-built body, and adoring grin . . .

"I'm afraid I've already found my Ever After, Hort," said Sophie.

"What? With *who?*" Hort asked, aghast—

"On my own," she said, her voice sure and clear. "I'm happy on my own."

And for the first time, she knew it was true.

As Hort fumbled for words, the bells rang over both schools, summoning the students to their castles. Whispering Nevers gave their new Dean gobsmacked looks as they herded towards the north gates. ("What were you saying about missing her?" Dot ribbed Hester and Anadil, both deathly pale.)

Sophie took a deep breath and hustled after them. "First

things first, Evil needs a new look. Enough with black and doom and gloom, when we should be celebrating our edge, our uniqueness," she said thoughtfully. "We'll have to weed out underperforming teachers, of course, and encourage Nevers to find their Nemesis within. That's how we'll find the best talents for the Circus . . . and a Ball! Let the winning school in the Trial host the Snow Ball. . . . Oh, that'll cook Good's goose, won't it—"

"Sophie!" Hort said, chasing her.

"Mmmm?"

"You aren't jealous that Agatha gets a boy and a crown and a kingdom and everything else?" Hort pressed in disbelief. "You aren't jealous that Agatha's a *queen*?"

He saw her stop at the gates, faced away as students streamed past.

"A tiny bit, of course," she said softly. "But then I remember . . ."

Sophie looked back, smiling bright as a diamond.

"I'm *me*."